THE BOOK OF WHONIVERSAL RECORDS

BBC

DOCTOR WHO

THE BOOK OF WHONIVERSAL RECORDS

SIMON GUERRIER

An Imprint of HarperCollinsPublishers

CONTENTS

INTRODUCTION 6
CHAPTER 1: THE DOCTOR 8
CHAPTER 2: ALIEN WORLDS 44
CHAPTER 3: DESTRUCTION 66
CHAPTER 4: TARDIS 102
CHAPTER 5: EARTH AND HUMANITY 114
CHAPTER 6: DALEKS 132
CHAPTER 7: COMPANIONS 144
CHAPTER 8: TECHNOLOGY 158
CHAPTER 9: MONSTERS 170
CHAPTER 10: WORDS AND PICTURES 190
INDEX 218
ACKNOWLEDGEMENTS 223

POLICE PUBLIC CALL BOX
POLICE TELEPHONE
FREE
FOR USE OF
PUBLIC
PULL TO OPEN

INTRODUCTION

'I'VE TRAVELLED WITH A LOT OF PEOPLE, BUT YOU'RE SETTING NEW RECORDS FOR JEOPARDY FRIENDLY.'
THE NINTH DOCTOR TO ROSE TYLER, *THE DOCTOR DANCES* (2005)

He's right – Rose really does seem to love danger. Shortly before the Doctor says this, she's hanging from a barrage balloon high over London during an attack by the Luftwaffe in the Second World War, while – as if it wasn't already bad enough – sporting a prominent Union Flag T-shirt.

But has Rose really set a record for running headlong into trouble? What about Ace, who travels with the Seventh Doctor, brews her own explosives and takes on a whole squad of Cybermen with just a catapult and a bag of coins? Or there's the Fourth Doctor's companion Leela, a brave warrior who's always ready to join a fight. Or there's Jo Grant, whose eagerness to help the Third Doctor often gets her into scrapes...

Even if Rose does set a record in ***The Doctor Dances***, has it been beaten since? In ***Face the Raven*** (2015), Clara Oswald also hangs suspended high over London – she's dangling upside down from the open door of the TARDIS. But whereas Rose is scared by her experience, Clara only laughs. In fact, her fearlessness in the face of mortal danger is a key part of that story. Surely that means Clara is **the most jeopardy friendly companion**.

In the following pages, we'll hunt down more of the wildest, maddest and most exciting records in all of ***Doctor Who***, from both the universe of the Doctor and also the making of the TV series. In some cases, the record-holder isn't always clear and we need to use our judgement – which we'll discuss in each instance. We'll explore the whole history of ***Doctor Who*** – all the Doctors, all the episodes, even things beyond – and uncover plenty of surprises. Along the way, we'll chat to the companion who stars in most episodes of ***Doctor Who***, hear from the woman responsible for the series' most disgusting creature and unearth the birth certificate of the earliest born person ever to appear in an episode.

But let's start with the Doctor...

CHAPTER ONE
THE DOCTOR

'HE'S LIKE FIRE AND ICE AND RAGE. HE'S LIKE THE NIGHT AND THE STORM IN THE HEART OF THE SUN ... HE'S ANCIENT AND FOREVER. HE BURNS AT THE CENTRE OF TIME AND HE CAN SEE THE TURN OF THE UNIVERSE ... AND HE'S WONDERFUL.'

TIM LATIMER, *THE FAMILY OF BLOOD* (2007)

THE DOCTOR'S PERSONAL BEST 010
THE AGE OF THE DOCTOR 012
WAAAAAAAAH! 014
ACTION MAN 016
A LOVER NOT A FIGHTER 018
BIG AND SMALL 020
MULTIMEDIA DOCTOR 022
HIS GREATEST FRIENDS 024
OLD SCHOOL DOCTOR 026
HOWZAT! 028
THIS SPORTING LIFE 030
THE DOCTOR AND THE OLYMPICS 032
HUNTIN', SHOOTIN' AND FISHIN' 034
I'M A SCIENTIST 036
OH, THE HUMANITIES! 038
MAGIC MOMENTS 040
THE DOCTORS' DOCTOR 042

THE DOCTOR'S PERSONAL BEST

OUR FAVOURITE TIME LORD'S OWN RECORD OF ACHIEVEMENT

PRESIDENT OF THE SUPREME COUNCIL OF TIME LORDS

As seen in *The Invasion of Time* (1978), *The Five Doctors* (1983) and *Hell Bent* (2015)

The Deadly Assassin (1976) is the first *Doctor Who* story entirely set on the Doctor's home planet. The Fourth Doctor returns to **Gallifrey** after experiencing a vision of the **President of the Time Lords** being assassinated. But instead of being able to stop the assassination, the Doctor is framed for his murder.

It turns out the Doctor has been caught up in a plot by the evil **Master**, who wants to ensure another Time Lord, **Chancellor Goth**, becomes the next President. The Doctor escapes his trial for murder by *also* standing for President – **Article 17 of the Constitution of the Time Lords** says, in part, that no candidate for office shall in any way be debarred or restrained from presenting his claim, which means he has to be set free.

When the Doctor foils the Master's plan, Goth dies and the Master escapes. But that means there's no other candidate for the presidency – and the Doctor automatically becomes **President-Elect**. That's not mentioned in *The Deadly Assassin*, but in *The Invasion of Time* (1978) the Doctor returns to Gallifrey where he declares to **Chancellor Borusa**:

'I claim the inheritance of **Rassilon**. I claim the titles, honour, duty and obedience of all colleges. I claim the presidency of the council of Time Lords.'

The Doctor is confirmed and inducted a s President in a special ceremony. But it seems he claims the title just so he can stop an invasion of the planet by the **Vardans** and **Sontarans**. Once the invasion is defeated he leaves Gallifrey again.

PRESIDENT OF EARTH

As seen in *Death in Heaven* (2014)

When **Missy** turns the dead people of Earth into a vast army of Cybermen, **Kate Stewart** surprises the Twelfth Doctor by referring to him as 'President'.

'The incursion protocols have been agreed internationally,' she explains. 'In the event of full-scale invasion, an **Earth President** is inducted immediately, with complete authority over every nation state. There was only one practical candidate ... You're the commander-in-chief of every army on Earth. Every world leader is currently awaiting your instructions. You are the chief executive officer of the human race.'

It's not clear if the Doctor ***stops*** being Earth President once the Cybermen and Missy are defeated, but in *The Zygon Invasion* (2015), the Doctor refers to himself as 'President of the world', and UNIT's **Colonel Walsh** seems to acknowledge his authority.

In the very next story – *The Ribos Operation* (1978) – the Doctor's new assistant, the Time Lady **Romana**, tells him she was sent to his TARDIS by 'the President of the **Supreme Council**', suggesting someone else is now in the job. In *Arc of Infinity* and *The Five Doctors* (both 1983) Borusa is Lord President, so it's likely he took the Doctor's place after the invasion.

At the end of *The Five Doctors*, the **High Council of the Time Lords** (which may be the same thing as the Supreme Council) exercises its emergency powers to appoint the Fifth Doctor as President again, to take office immediately – but he runs away. In *The Trial of a Time Lord* (1986) we learn that in his absence the Doctor has been deposed. But he still uses the title: in *Remembrance of the Daleks* (1988), the Seventh Doctor explains to **Davros** that he is, 'President-Elect of the High Council of Time Lords, keeper of the legacy of Rassilon, defender of the Laws of Time, protector of Gallifrey'.

During the Time War, the legendary Time Lord Rassilon is again Lord President, but in *Hell Bent* (2015) he's deposed by the Twelfth Doctor who banishes him and the High Council from Gallifrey. The unnamed Time Lord general then calls the Doctor 'Lord President', suggesting he has taken supreme office for the third time.

WHAT OTHERS SAY ABOUT THE DOCTOR

In the ancient legends of the Dalek home world, Skaro, the Doctor is known as '**the Oncoming Storm**' – *The Parting of the Ways* (2005)

Dalek creator Davros names him '**Destroyer of Worlds**' – *Journey's End* (2008)

The Daleks also know him as '**the Predator**' – *Asylum of the Daleks* (2012)

When an international peace conference is threatened by strange goings on, risking a third world war, UNIT's Brigadier Lethbridge-Stewart assures a government minister that he's 'putting my **best man** on to it', meaning the Third Doctor – *Day of the Daleks* (1972)

'He's probably the **greatest scientist on this planet**,' says UNIT's Captain Mike Yates of the Third Doctor – *Invasion of the Dinosaurs* (1974)

'We recognise in you the **greatest specialist in time-space exploration**,' says Jano – leader of the Elders who can see all of time and space – to the First Doctor. 'You have taken this branch of learning far beyond our elementary calculations' – *The Savages* (1966).

THE AGE OF THE DOCTOR

BY HIS TWELFTH INCARNATION, THE DOCTOR HAS LIVED FOR MORE THAN 2,000 YEARS. BUT WHAT ABOUT THE ACTORS WHO'VE PLAYED HIM?

THE OLDEST PERSON TO PLAY THE DOCTOR

As seen in *The Day of the Doctor* (2013)

Ironically, the oldest-looking incarnation of the Doctor is also the youngest of them – the **First Doctor**.

Actor **William Hartnell** was made up and played the part to appear older than he really was. Born on **8 January 1908**, Hartnell made his debut as the Doctor in *An Unearthly Child* – the very first episode of *Doctor Who* – which was broadcast on 23 November 1963. On that day, Hartnell was **55 years, 10 months and 15 days** old.

Not including archive clips, Hartnell's last appearance as the Doctor was in episode four of *The Three Doctors* on 20 January 1973, when he was **65 years and 12 days old**. He died in 1975.

Hartnell held the record for being the oldest person to play the Doctor on screen until 50th anniversary story *The Day of the Doctor* (2013). That story features a cameo appearance by actor **Tom Baker** – best known for playing the **Fourth Doctor** between 1974 and 1981 – as the mysterious **Curator** of the National Gallery in London. It's suggested that the Curator might in fact be a future incarnation of the Doctor.

If so, that makes Baker the oldest actor ever to play the Doctor on screen. He was born on **20 January 1934** and was **79 years, 10 months and 3 days** old on the day of broadcast. Baker continues to play the Doctor to this day in new audio adventures.

THE YOUNGEST PERSON TO PLAY THE DOCTOR

As seen in *Listen* (2014)

The TARDIS lands in a **barn** that in a later episode – *Hell Bent* (2015) – we learn is on the Time Lord planet Gallifrey. In the barn, the Doctor's companion **Clara Oswald** overhears two people talking about a **crying boy**. Apparently the boy runs away all the time and doesn't want to join the army, which will jeopardise his chances of going to the Academy and of ever becoming a Time Lord.

The implication is – and Clara believes – that this crying boy is the Doctor, at the earliest point in his life we've ever seen him. But we don't see his face and the actor is not credited on the episode – adding to the mystery.

THE EARLIEST BORN PERSON TO PLAY THE DOCTOR

As seen in *The Chase* (1965)

Actor **Edmund Warwick** played Darrius in the ***Doctor Who*** story ***The Keys of Marinus*** (1964), and then doubled for First Doctor actor William Hartnell in both ***The Dalek Invasion of Earth*** (1964) and ***The Chase*** (1965). (In ***The Chase***, he also played a not altogether convincing robot duplicate of the Doctor built by the Daleks.)

Warwick was born on **15 July 1907**, so was six months older than Hartnell – and the earliest born person ever to play the Doctor.

EXCEPTIONS TO THE RULE

Generally when the Doctor regenerates, his new incarnation looks younger than the previous one. But that's not always the case:

Third Doctor actor Jon Pertwee (born 7 July 1919) was older than Second Doctor actor Patrick Troughton (born 25 March 1920).

Sixth Doctor actor Colin Baker (born 8 June 1943) is older than Fifth Doctor actor Peter Davison (born 13 April 1951).

Twelfth Doctor actor Peter Capaldi (born 14 April 1958) is older than Eleventh Doctor actor Matt Smith (born 28 October 1982).

Note that War Doctor actor John Hurt (born 22 January 1940) is older than Eighth Doctor actor Paul McGann (born 14 November 1959). However, the regeneration – seen in online mini-episode ***The Night of the Doctor*** (2013) – used footage of Hurt from the 1979 drama serial ***Crime and Punishment***, when he was younger than McGann.

WAAAAAAAAAH!

HE GETS KNOCKED DOWN BUT HE GETS UP AGAIN, YOU'RE NEVER GONNA KEEP THE DOCTOR DOWN.

THE FURTHEST FALL – THROUGH SPACE!

As seen in *The Doctor, the Widow and the Wardrobe* (2011).

One night in 1938, a **huge spaceship** passes over the Earth and is about to attack – when it suddenly starts to explode. It's been sabotaged by the clever **Eleventh Doctor**, who then not-so cleverly falls from the exploding spaceship into space.

Tumbling towards the Earth, the Doctor manages to catch up with a special **"impact suit"**, which he is wearing by the time he hits the ground. The suit means he survives, though he then tells **Madge Arwell** that the suit is "repairing him", suggesting it didn't completely protect him. Ouch.

But how far has he fallen? **Dr Marek Kukula, Public Astronomer at the Royal Observatory Greenwich**, says:

'Compare the size of the Earth as the Doctor falls towards it with images of the Earth as seen from the **International Space Station**, which orbits at 400 km above the planet's surface. The Doctor is clearly much further away. My guess is that the huge spaceship he fell from was in geostationary orbit, **37,000 km** up.

'That would explain why we don't see the Doctor and the spacesuit **glowing** as they fall – they've not yet hit the Earth's atmosphere. The impact suit will need to protect him from the impact with the ground, but a bigger challenge is probably the **extreme heat of re-entry**. And it could be a very long fall – lasting **several days!**'

The closest a real human has come to beating that? On 24 October 2014, **Alan Eustace** fell **41.4 km** to Earth in **14 minutes, 19 seconds**. Unlike the Doctor, he had a parachute.

THE FURTHEST FALL – IN SCREEN TIME

As seen in *Heaven Sent* (2015).

When the **Twelfth Doctor** is cornered by the sinister **Veil** in a room high up in a **weird castle**, he hurls a chair through a window – and then jumps out after it!

As he explains, he heard the chair fall for **seven seconds** before hitting the water below, and that's probably how long he falls in "real time". But on screen, we jump between him falling and him imagining himself inside the TARDIS as he works out his escape. As a result, from him leaping out the window to hitting the water takes **two minutes and seven seconds** of screen time.

BREAK YOUR FALL

In *Logopolis* (1981), the **Fourth Doctor** is killed and regenerates into the **Fifth Doctor** after a fall from a **radio telescope**, having just stopped the **Master**'s evil plan to blackmail the whole universe.

Although this (fictional) radio telescope is apparently based in Sussex, it looks very like the (real) **Lovell Telescope at Jodrell Bank in Cheshire** – which suggests he falls about **50 metres**.

The Doctor has clearly forgotten the technique he used to survive a fall twice as far! In *The Paradise of Death* (first broadcast on radio in 1993), the **Third Doctor** falls from the top of the **Apollo rocket**, an attraction at a new amusement park in London. This seems to be based on the **Saturn V rocket** that launched the Apollo missions to the moon – and which was **111 metres tall**.

THE FURTHEST FALL – THROUGH TIME!

As seen in *The Name of the Doctor* (2013).

We've seen various people fall through time. For example, at the end of *The Enemy of the World* (1968), the wicked **Ramon Salamander** falls out of the TARDIS into the **time vortex**, but we don't know where and when he ends up, or if he even survives.

In *Timelash* (1985), various people fall through a **Kontron time tunnel** from the planet **Karfel** to Scotland in 1179 AD (and, in once instance, to 1885 AD). But we don't know what year it is on Karfel when they leave, so don't know how long they've fallen.

In *The Name of the Doctor*, **Dr Simeon** and **Clara Oswald** both fall through the Doctor's own timeline by approximately **1,800 years**, from his death on the planet **Trenzalore** aged more than 2,000[1] to at least as far back as him **first stealing the TARDIS** aged about 209[2].

FURTHEREST MORAL FALL

According to River Song, the Battle of Demon's Run in *A Good Man Goes to War* (2011) is "the Doctor's darkest hour. He'll rise higher than ever before and then fall so much further."

1 The Doctor spends more than 1,000 years on Trenzalore in *The Time of the Doctor* (2013), and says he is more than 2,000 years-old in the next episode, *Deep Breath* (2014). Whereas *The Name of the Doctor* and other stories tell us the Doctor dies on Trenzalore, at the end of *The Time of the Doctor*, the Time Lords save the Doctor's life by giving him a new cycle of regenerations.

2 In *The Doctor's Wife* (2011), Idris claims the Doctor has travelled in the TARDIS for 700 years. Two episodes before, in *The Impossible Astronaut* (2011), the Doctor claims to be 909 years old.

FALLING, FALLING

Is the Tenth Doctor the incarnation most prone to long falls?

- He and Rose/Cassandra fall 26 floors down a liftshaft (*New Earth*, 2006)
- He lets himself fall an unknown distance to reach the Beast at the centre of the impossible planet (*The Satan Pit*, 2006)
- He drops through the layers of traffic on New Earth trying to catch up with his friend Martha (*Gridlock*, 2007)
- He dives head-first down the lift shaft to save River Song's digital memory (*Forest of the Dead*, 2008)
- He jumps out of a low-flying spaceship and crashes through the roof of Naismith's house to confront the Master – and Rassilon (*The End of Time*, 2009-2010)

ACTION MAN

THE THRILLING STUNTS PERFORMED BY THE DOCTOR HIMSELF

THE MOST DANGEROUS STUNT PERFORMED BY A DOCTOR

As seen in *The Day of the Doctor* (2013)

To open the 50th anniversary story in suitable, eye-popping style, the script called for an outrageous stunt. In the story, the TARDIS is picked up from a roadside by a **UNIT helicopter** and flown into central London – while the Eleventh Doctor and Clara Oswald are inside it. The Doctor opens the door of the TARDIS to reach for the phone to complain – and **falls out**. As the helicopter lowers the TARDIS into **Trafalgar Square**, the Doctor is hanging underneath.

The scene was shot early on Tuesday 9 April 2013. 'Obviously, we had a stunt double,' says **Crispin Layfield**, stunt coordinator on the story, who has worked on *Doctor Who* since *Father's Day* (2005). 'And he did some of the higher shots. But we also hung Matt Smith up in the air, too.' So Crispin nominates this as the most dangerous stunt in *Doctor Who* performed by the actor playing the Doctor rather than a stunt double.

'I was hoisted up **over 90 feet**,' Matt said at the time, '**double Nelson's Column**, hanging on a wire under the TARDIS. They used the biggest crane I think they had ever brought to Trafalgar Square. I really had to persuade them to let me go up, but I had the most wonderful view of London. It was raining and really windy, but I loved it and would do it again. It was one of the rare brilliant opportunities that you only get with *Who*.'

The fact the stunt was performed in such a prominent location meant there was soon a crowd watching. 'Yeah, and there were logistics with that,' says Crispin. 'We did it very early in the morning, but we still had an awful lot of people around and had to cordon off the area.'

Isn't it risky letting the star of the show do such a potentially dangerous stunt? After all, if something went wrong, Matt might not have been able to continue filming, which would have scuppered the anniversary special. 'We do think about that sort of thing,' says Crispin. 'But Matt was in a harness, we had professional wire people running the stunt and I was there to supervise it. And Matt was happy, so all the boxes were ticked and we were good to do it. And it looked great, him doing it, didn't it?'

THE MOST DANGEROUS STUNT ON *DOCTOR WHO*

As seen in *Closing Time* (2011)

'Every stunt has its own risks,' says Crispin. 'Of course, we plan every stunt but the bigger ones – the high falls, fire and stuff like that – tend to be meticulously worked out so are generally, overall, safer. It's the smaller, little stunts where you just think, 'Yeah, that's fine, you've just got to trip up over there...' that are usually the ones where you end up getting injuries.'

So while there have been plenty of impressive big stunts in the series – the Doctor hanging from the TARDIS 90 feet in the air or running through a corridor as it explodes – Crispin chooses a much smaller stunt as the most dangerous ever performed.

'In *Closing Time*, we had **Gordon Seed** doubling for Matt's Doctor as he flies through some French windows made of **toughened glass**. That was particularly dangerous because even though the special effects team break the glass at just the right moment, he's still diving through it and you can cut yourself very badly. That takes a lot of preparation, but you always get cut at least a bit – as Gordon was, but he was fine.'

THE DOCTOR WHO DOES MOST STUNTS HIMSELF

Sixth Doctor actor Colin Baker says he **never** had a stunt double in his time on *Doctor Who* (1984–1986).

A LOVER NOT A FIGHTER

OH, IT'S *ALL* THE FEELINGS WHEN YOU'VE GOT TWO HEARTS

THE DOCTOR'S GREATEST WEAKNESS

As seen in *The Magician's Apprentice* and *The Witch's Familiar* (2015)

In *Genesis of the Daleks* (1975), the Time Lords send the Fourth Doctor back in time to stop the Daleks ever being created. He's never flinched from battling Daleks before and takes great satisfaction in seeing them destroyed. But changing history so that they never even existed seems a step too far.

'Just touch these two strands together and the Daleks are finished,' he says to his companions Sarah Jane Smith and Harry Sullivan in the final episode of the story – but then he can't continue. 'Have I that right?' he asks, and seems to conclude that he doesn't.

'Compassion, Doctor,' jeers **Davros, creator of the Daleks**, years later in *The Magician's Apprentice*. 'It has always been your greatest indulgence.'

There are plenty of stories where the Doctor's compassion works against him. In *Earthshock* (1982), the **Cyberleader** argues that the Fifth Doctor's emotional attachments to other people 'restrict and curtail the intellect and logic of the mind'. To demonstrate this, the Cyberleader orders the death of the Doctor's friend Tegan Jovanka – to which the Doctor protests.

'Such a reaction is not a disadvantage?' taunts the Cyberleader – if Cybermen went in for emotional things like taunting. 'I now have control over you, Doctor. All I need do is threaten the woman's death for you to obey me.'

Davros also uses the Doctor's emotions against him. In *The Witch's Familiar*, Davros is sick and dying, and wants to see one last sunset – but he can't open his eyes. Feeling compassion for even this dreaded enemy, the Doctor offers Davros some of his own regeneration energy, which is exactly what Davros was planning.

'The ancient magic of the Time Lords,' he crows, suddenly no longer sick or dying. 'I thought I would have to tear you apart to take it from you but, as always, your compassion is your downfall.' Except it isn't – because the Doctor has foreseen Davros's double-dealing, and the regeneration energy destroys rather than aids the Daleks.

But there's another twist in the tale to come. As the Doctor escapes, he is confronted by a Dalek which he's told by the devious **Missy** has just killed his friend Clara Oswald.

It's yet another trick: Missy placed Clara inside this Dalek, and the Dalek systems change what she says to make it sound more aggressive. When she tries to tell the Doctor who she really is, it comes out as 'I am a Dalek.' When she tries to say, 'I'm your friend,' it comes out as 'I am your enemy.'

Missy hands a Dalek gun to the Doctor so he can take revenge on this Dalek who killed his friend. But the Doctor once again hesitates – and the Dalek asks for mercy. The Doctor is dumbfounded that a Dalek could even know the word.

It turns out that, long ago – long before the Fourth Doctor held those two all-important wires in his hands – the Twelfth Doctor visited Skaro and taught the young Davros the value of mercy. That was then programmed into the Daleks so they now understand the concept. And it's that program which means the Doctor doesn't shoot the Dalek in front of him. So the Doctor's mercy saves Clara.

We see it again and again in story and after story. His compassion isn't a weakness: it's the Doctor's greatest strength.

THE DOCTOR WHO KISSES THE MOST PEOPLE

The Eighth Doctor is the first Doctor to go in for snogging – kissing Dr Grace Holloway on two occasions in the TV movie **Doctor Who** (1996). The Ninth Doctor is kissed by Captain Jack Harkness and kisses Rose Tyler in **The Parting of the Ways** (2005). Then things get a bit wild.

The Tenth Doctor kisses or is kissed by **12 people**: Lady Cassandra O'Brien. Δ17 when she has possessed the body of Rose; Jeanne Antoinette Poisson (also known as 'Reinette' or 'Madame de Pompadour'); Rose Tyler (now not possessed by Cassandra); Rose's mum Jackie Tyler; Martha Jones; Joan Redfern; Astrid Peth; Donna Noble; Lady Christine de Souza; Queen Elizabeth I; a Zygon; and Clara Oswald (on the hand).

The Eleventh Doctor kisses or is kissed by **10 people**: Amy Pond; River Song; Marilyn Monroe (not seen on screen but he has tell-tale lipstick on his face); Idris (the TARDIS); Rory Williams; Kate Stewart; Clara Oswald (the barmaid/governess from 1892); Jenny Flint; Ada Gillyflower and Clara (the 21st-century one). He also kisses a doll in **Cold War** (2013).

The Twelfth Doctor has, to date, been kissed by only Missy, Clara and River and isn't a great fan of hugging, either. But perhaps he'll catch up...

BIG AND SMALL

THE SCALE OF THE DOCTOR

THE LONGEST-LIVED DOCTOR

As seen in *The Time of the Doctor* (2013)

The Doctor's age is a little tricky to puzzle out, especially as he sometimes seems to age backwards.

In *The Tomb of the Cybermen* (1967), the Second Doctor says he must be about **450** years old. Although not stated on screen, the people making *Doctor Who* at the time worked out this age by subtracting 200 from **650** – the age of the First Doctor as given on paperwork in the *Doctor Who* production office – to account for the **rejuvenating effect** of his regeneration.

The Third Doctor seems to suggest in both *Doctor Who and the Silurians* (1970) and *The Mind of Evil* (1971) that he is **thousands** of years old. He might be exaggerating, or perhaps he means that, as a time traveller, he has thousands of years of experience.

The Fourth Doctor claims to be **756** in *The Ribos Operation* (1978) – though his companion Romana thinks he's lost count somewhere and is really **759**. In *Revelation of the Daleks* (1985) the Sixth Doctor describes himself as **900** years old, and in *Time and the Rani* (1987), the Seventh Doctor says he is **953**.

Yet the Ninth Doctor says in *Aliens of London* (2005) that he is **900** – suggesting that somewhere along the line he's again lost some years. It's not just that he's rounding down: the Tenth Doctor claims to be **902** in *Voyage of the Damned* (2007) and **906** in *The End of Time* (2009–2010) – the story in which he regenerates into the Eleventh Doctor.

That regeneration doesn't seem to knock any years off the Doctor's age as the Eleventh Doctor claims to be **909** in *The Impossible Astronaut* (2011) – in which we also see an Eleventh Doctor from the future, when he is **1103**. In *The Day of the Doctor* (2013), the Eleventh Doctor says he is now **1200**.

In *The Time of the Doctor* (2013), the Eleventh Doctor spends the last years of his life on the planet Trenzalore. We're not told on screen how many years that is, but it's at least 300. A 2014 book, *Tales of Trenzalore: The Eleventh Doctor's Last Stand*, says he's there for 900 years, meaning the Eleventh Doctor is at least **2,100** when he regenerates at the end of the TV episode. That matches what the Twelfth Doctor says in the next story, *Deep Breath* (2014), when he claims to be **more than 2,000**.

That means the Eleventh Doctor lives for more than 1,000 years – roughly **half** the total time the Doctor has been alive.

In *Heaven Sent* (2015), the Twelfth Doctor arrives by teleport inside a confession dial where he dies over and over for **4.5 billion years**. However, each time he dies, a 'new' version of him is teleported into the dial, exactly the same age as the last time – so he's not 4.5 billion years old at the end.

THE TALLEST DOCTORS

The tallest incarnations of the Doctor – the **Third Doctor** and the **Fourth Doctor** – are both **1.91 metres** or **six feet three inches** tall.

THE SMALLEST DOCTOR

As seen in *The Invisible Enemy* (1977)

In about the year 5000, the Fourth Doctor is infected by a **sentient virus** that threatens the entire Solar System. Using the **relative dimensional stabiliser** from the TARDIS, clones of the Fourth Doctor and his companion Leela are miniaturised to **'micro-dimensions'** so that they can be injected into a vein behind the real Fourth Doctor's ear and then voyage through his **brain** to battle the virus.

We're not told exactly how tiny they are, but they're too small to break the surface tension of water. 'Micro dimensions' suggests they're larger than the quantum scale, so bigger than 100 nanometres. But can we be any more precise?

'Watching the episode, it looks like the mini-Doctor and Leela are about the same height as a **neuronal cell body**,' says Dr Niall Boyce, editor of the medical journal *The Lancet Psychiatry*. 'Neurones vary considerably in size; the ones shown on screen look rather like pyramidal cells which, assuming Time Lord neurones are about the same size as human brain cells, might make them about **10–20 micrometres** in size.' A micrometre is one millionth of a metre. 'We also see the mini-Doctor and Leela attacked by the big Doctor's phagocytes – a type of white blood cell. In a human those would again be about **10 – 20 micrometres**.

'Having said that, the medical details given in *The Invisible Enemy* are a little… whimsical,' adds Niall, tactfully.

The Twelfth Doctor, Clara and a team of soldiers are miniaturised in *Into the Dalek* (2014), this time using a **moleculon nanoscaler**, so that they can voyage through the brain and other parts of a **malfunctioning Dalek**. Such nanoscalers are apparently commonly used to shrink surgeons so that they can climb inside their patients – suggesting this story takes place long after AD 5000, when people react with surprise to the idea.

That it's a nanoscaler suggests the size it can reduce people to: 'nano' means one billionth. So it seems to have the **ability** to make the Twelfth Doctor about **100 times smaller** than the clone Fourth Doctor. But compared to the size of the Dalek's eye, into which the Doctor and his friends crawl, it looks like they've been shrunk to about **1.5 centimetres** – about **10,000 times larger** than the clone Fourth Doctor. It's roughly the same size as the miniaturised First Doctor and his friends in *Planet of Giants* (1964) and the miniaturised Third Doctor and his companion Jo Grant in *Carnival of Monsters* (1973) – small, but not microscopic.

MULTIMEDIA DOCTOR

DOCTOR WHO IS MUCH MORE THAN JUST A TV TIME LORD...

THE DOCTOR IN MOST TV *DOCTOR WHO*

The **Fourth Doctor**, as played by Tom Baker, was first seen in the closing moments of Part 6 of ***Planet of the Spiders*** (1974) and regenerated into the Fifth Doctor at the end of Part 4 of ***Logopolis*** (1981), after a total of **42 stories** comprising **173 episodes**.

He appears again in ***The Five Doctors*** (1983), in material filmed for the unfinished and not broadcast story ***Shada***. Since that's effectively 'new' material, we'll include ***The Five Doctors*** – bringing the total to **174 episodes**.

Tom also appeared in ***The Day of the Doctor*** (2013), but playing the **Curator**. Even if, as suggested, the Curator is a future incarnation of the Doctor, he's not the *Fourth* Doctor, so we can't include it for this record.

But it counts for another one: at a total 175 episodes playing two separate incarnations, Tom is **the person who has appeared in the most episodes of *Doctor Who***.

Tom Baker also appeared as the Fourth Doctor in the two-part ***Dimensions in Time*** (1993), a special, short ***Doctor Who / EastEnders*** crossover, shown as part of the ***Children in Need*** charity night. He also appeared in character in a number of programmes such as ***Disney Time*** (1975), and in TV advertisements in New Zealand.

THE DOCTOR IN MOST *DOCTOR WHO* COMICS

The Eleventh Doctor appears in **260 comic strip stories** published between 2010 and December 2016. That total counts a story with multiple instalments once, and includes two **full-length graphic novels** – *The Only Good Dalek* (2010) and *The Dalek Project* (2011) – but not his appearances in back-up comedy strips.

THE DOCTOR IN MOST *DOCTOR WHO* COMPUTER GAMES

The Eleventh Doctor appears in **seven separate official *Doctor Who* computer games** released between 2010 and 2013 – the first of them, *Doctor Who: The Adventure Games* (2010–2011) comprising five distinct episodes, arguably separate games in their own right.

THE DOCTOR IN MOST *DOCTOR WHO* BOOKS

Not including novelisations of TV episodes, the Seventh Doctor appears in **78** original, licensed ***Doctor Who*** novels published between 1991 and 2005. But that includes four very brief appearances in what are otherwise Eighth Doctor novels, so really the total should be 74 novels.

Which means the Eighth Doctor just beats him, appearing in **75 original novels** published between 1997 and 2005.

THE DOCTOR IN MOST *DOCTOR WHO* AUDIO RELEASES

Released on vinyl LP and cassette in July 1976, ***Doctor Who and the Pescatons*** was the first original **Doctor Who** story on audio ever released, and saw the Fourth Doctor and Sarah Jane Smith battle an invasion of London by **shark-like** aliens.

Three months later, in October 1976, an episode of BBC Radio 4 educational series ***Exploration Earth*** included an episode called 'The Time Machine', in which the Fourth Doctor and Sarah battled **Megron, High Lord of Chaos**, as our planet is forming. ***Slipback***, featuring the Sixth Doctor, was broadcast on Radio 4 in 1985, and two Third Doctor stories – ***The Paradise of Death*** and ***The Ghosts of N-Space*** – were broadcast in the 1990s.

Since then, hundreds of audio **Doctor Who** stories featuring different Doctors have been released commercially, from full-cast dramas to narrated books and short stories. Many of these stories have been broadcast or webcast. In fact, there's such a wide range of audio ***Doctor Who***, we need to agree some qualifying criteria. For this record we are:

Including new fictional adventures – not documentaries, music soundtracks, soundtracks of TV episodes or narrated novelisations of TV episodes

Counting individual releases – not the number of individual episodes or stories included in a release (so we count a box-set of four stories as one release)

Counting each appearance of each incarnation of the Doctor – so if more than one Doctor appears in an audio, both have it added to their score

By these criteria, between the release of ***Doctor Who and the Pescatons*** and the end of December 2016, there were ***614 Doctor Who* audio releases**. The **Sixth Doctor** appears in **114** of them – narrowly beating the Fifth Doctor (102) and the Fourth and Seventh Doctors (both 101).

HIS GREATEST FRIENDS

THE DOCTOR IS A MAN OF MYSTERY, BUT WITH WHOM DOES HE SHARE HIS SECRETS?

THE PERSON WHO KNOWS THE DOCTOR BEST (IN THE SERIES)

As seen *in The Name of the Doctor* and *The Day of the Doctor* (2013), and *Deep Breath* (2014)

River Song is the Doctor's wife and apparently knows his real name – which is more than we've ever been told. But she doesn't know him well enough to spot him by sight if he's in an incarnation she's not met before. Instead, she carries with her pictures of all the Doctors up to the Eleventh Doctor. However, that means in *The Husbands of River Song* (2015) she fails to recognise the Twelfth Doctor when she meets him, because his picture isn't included. Other people know the Doctor much better than that.

The **Daleks** can generally recognise the Doctor whatever body he's in, as can most other **Time Lords**. The **TARDIS** and the Doctor have a very close relationship – in *The Power of the Daleks* (1966), he even says that his ability to change his physical appearance is part of the TARDIS and 'Without it, I wouldn't survive.' When the TARDIS becomes human, briefly, in *The Doctor's Wife* (2011), she explains that if she didn't always take him where he wanted, she always took him where he needed to go – the suggestion being that she knows him better than he does himself.

But according to the Doctor's great friend **Madame Vastra** in *Deep Breath*, **Clara Oswald** is the person who 'knows him best in all the universe'. It doesn't seem to be conscious on Clara's part: Vastra says this because Clara has changed into suitable clothes as if knowing the TARDIS is about to arrive to spirit her away – which it then does.

But this is at the end of an episode in which Clara questions whether she does in fact know the Doctor, struggling to come to terms with his latest regeneration, even though, in *The Name of the Doctor* and *The Day of the Doctor* she meets all his previous incarnations.

Even when she's made her peace with the new Doctor, she still doesn't know he's lying to her in *Death in Heaven* (2014) when he says he's tracked down his lost home planet, Gallifrey. But, like the TARDIS, she also seems to know the Doctor better than he does himself – like when she intercedes at the end of the **Time War** to stop him from using the **Moment** to destroy his own people.

'THE BEST DAY OF YOUR LIFE'

In the mini-episode *He Said, She Said* (2013), Clara says that meeting the Doctor is 'the best day of your life ... because he's brilliant and he's funny and mad and, best of all, he really needs you.'

'WHOSE SIDE ARE YOU ON?'

Even those who know the Doctor very well can still find themselves surprised by him, and not always in a nice way. In ***The Evil of the Daleks*** (1967), the Second Doctor's friend Jamie McCrimmon – who has by then travelled with him for several adventures, is appalled by his friend's ploys and calls him 'callous'. When the Doctor counters that he cares about life and human beings, Jamie still isn't sure and asks, 'Just whose side are you on?'

In ***The Invasion of Time*** (1978), we're not sure if the Fourth Doctor has betrayed his own people and his friend Leela to the alien Vardans – at least not for several episodes. In ***The Curse of Fenric*** (1989), the Seventh Doctor is mean to his friend Ace so that she loses all faith in him. Even though he does it to stop a monster, and he and Ace are friends again afterwards, it's still a side of the Doctor we're not used to seeing. (The Eleventh Doctor does something similar to Amy Pond in ***The God Complex*** (2011).)

In ***Into the Dalek*** (2014), the Doctor asks Clara to be a pal and tell him if he's a good man. She's not sure, but she thinks he tries to be. But the fact that it's even a question suggests that after more than 53 years and 827 episodes we still don't fully know the Doctor...

THE PERSON WHO KNOWS THE DOCTOR BEST (IN REAL LIFE)

Who is the ultimate authority on the Doctor and ***Doctor Who***?

Today, the series is made by **BBC Wales** and the team there also watch carefully over the books and toys and other ***Doctor Who*** merchandise being produced to ensure it matches the character and style of the programme on TV. They'll spot if a proposed story has been done before or contradicts established ***Doctor Who*** history. So we might assume that the people in charge of ***Doctor Who*** know it best.

Except that on 22 November 2015, the Doctor Who Festival in Australia held a quiz about the series. One of the teams taking part comprised Twelfth Doctor actor **Peter Capaldi**, head writer and executive producer **Steven Moffat** and writer **Mark Gatiss**. Surely they were unbeatable...

They came third.

That's not to suggest they ***don't*** know the intricate history ***Doctor Who*** extremely well – it's just that there are plenty of fans with even more detailed knowledge. Some fans dedicate their lives to uncovering yet more facts about the programme, their findings detailed in publications such as the official ***Doctor Who Magazine***.

So who does ***DWM*** editor Tom Spilsbury think is the ultimate authority on the Doctor and ***Doctor Who***? 'Me, probably,' he grins.

'THE ULTIMATE GUIDE TO THE DOCTOR'

Flemming says that River's diary is of great value because it is 'the ultimate guide to the Time Lord known as the Doctor' – ***The Husbands of River Song***.

OLD SCHOOL DOCTOR

HE'S KNOWN AS THE DOCTOR, BUT IS HE QUALIFIED AS ONE?

THE DOCTOR'S SCHOOL RECORD

In *The Ribos Operation* (1978), the Fourth Doctor is sent a new companion, a Time Lady called **Romanadvoratrelundar** – or Romana, for short. He worries that she's too young and inexperienced for travelling in time and space, but Romana counters that she graduated from the Time Lord Academy with a triple first. When the Doctor isn't impressed, she reminds him that he only scraped through with **51% – at the second attempt**.

In *Terror of the Autons* (1971), the Third Doctor refers to renegade Time Lord the **Master** as 'an unimaginative plodder', but another Time Lord reminds him that, 'His **degree in cosmic science** was of a higher class than yours.' Flustered, the Doctor admits he was a 'late developer', but even if he didn't achieve the same grades as the Master, he still apparently got his degree.

The suggestion is that the Doctor was never the most gifted student. In *The Deadly Assassin* (1976), we meet his former teacher, **Borusa**, who clearly likes the Doctor but chides him for his attitude: 'As I believe I told you long ago, Doctor, you will never amount to anything in the galaxy while you retain your propensity for vulgar facetiousness.'

But when Borusa says this, the Doctor has just stopped the Master from destroying the Time Lord planet, Gallifrey, and Borusa is grateful. As the Doctor heads back to his TARDIS, Borusa offers a last assessment. 'Oh, Doctor? ... **Nine out of ten**.'

The Second Doctor says in *The Moonbase* (1967) that in 1888 he also took a **medical degree** under Joseph Lister in Glasgow – but the famous professor of surgery left Glasgow in 1869 for the University of Edinburgh, so the Doctor's memory is clearly a bit off. A medical degree also takes years to complete, and the Doctor only mentions one year so perhaps he never finished his studies. Is he a qualified doctor?

In *The Ark in Space* (1975), the Fourth Doctor admits that his 'doctorate is **purely honorary**', but in *The Armageddon Factor* (1979), Drax – a non-Time Lord from Gallifrey, who studied a **technical course** with the Doctor some 450 years previously – congratulates him on 'getting your doctorate'. When asked what he's actually a doctor of, he is often vague – '**everything**', says the Fifth Doctor in *Four to Doomsday* (1982).

But perhaps that's beside the point: the Doctor doesn't need to study for a doctorate because, as River Song explains in *A Good Man Goes to War* (2011), the word 'doctor', meaning '**healer**' and '**wise man**' throughout the universe, is derived from him and his adventures anyway.

Or, as the Fourth Doctor explains to UNIT's Dr Harry Sullivan in ***Robot*** (1974–1975), 'You may be ***a*** doctor, but I'm ***the*** Doctor. The **definite article**, you might say.'

CHILDHOOD OF THE DOCTOR

As well as not being the most able student, we know the Doctor wasn't always the happiest child. In ***Listen*** (2014), we glimpse a **boy** who it seems is the Doctor at an early age, crying at night in a barn we later learn is on Gallifrey. We're told that this boy runs away all the time, doesn't want to join the **army** and is unlikely to go to the Academy or ever become a Time Lord.

In ***The Time Monster*** (1972), the Third Doctor recalls what he claims was 'the **blackest day** of my life ... I was too unhappy even for tears.' On that day, he went to see the **hermit** who sat under a tree behind the Doctor's house, halfway up a mountain in south Gallifrey. In ***State of Decay*** (1980), the Fourth Doctor says this hermit would tell him **ghost stories**, but on the black day he listened to the young Doctor pour out his troubles, then simply pointed to a wild flower, like a daisy, and made the Doctor realise the wonder in nature. It made him laugh.

There were other simple pleasures, too. In ***The End of Time*** (2009–2010), we're told the young Doctor would run across the fields and pastures of **red grass** on the estates owned by the Master's father, calling up at the sky. In the TV movie ***Doctor Who*** (1996), the Eighth Doctor remembers lying in the grass with his **father** on a warm Gallifreyan night, watching a brightly coloured meteor storm.

We also know a little about what inspired the young Doctor. In ***The Three Doctors*** (1972–1973), the Third Doctor says he always thought of **Omega** – the grumpy solar engineer who first gave the Time Lords the power to travel in time – as a hero. In ***Black Orchid*** (1982), the Fifth Doctor admits that as a boy he wanted to drive a **steam engine**.

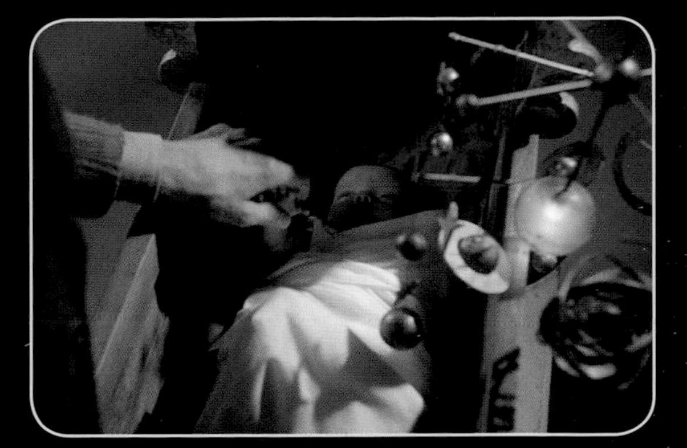

Perhaps because of the hermit's pep talk, or because **Clara Oswald** comforts the crying boy in ***Listen***, the Doctor did go to the Time Lord Academy. He took a technical course with Drax, referred to in ***The Armageddon Factor***, and studied alongside the Master and possibly the **Rani**, so maybe his poor academic record was because he fell in with the wrong crowd.

Or it could be something else. According to the Tenth Doctor in ***The Sound of Drums*** (2007), the children of Gallifrey were taken from their families to enter the Academy at the age of eight. As novices, and as part of their initiation, they were made to look into the **Untempered Schism**, a gap in the fabric of reality through which they'd see the whole vortex of time and space. The raw power of it seems to have sent the Master mad, while the Doctor ran away.

But he didn't run ***from*** the vortex but towards it, his travels in the TARDIS embracing all the strange wonder of the universe.

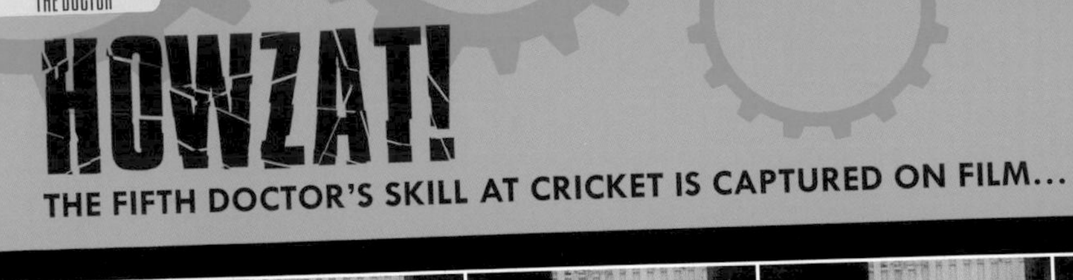

HOWZAT!

THE FIFTH DOCTOR'S SKILL AT CRICKET IS CAPTURED ON FILM...

THE DOCTOR'S BEST SPORTING MOMENT

As seen *in Black Orchid (1982)*

When actor **Peter Davison** was cast as the Fifth Doctor, he wasn't sure how he'd play the part or shape the character. As he later recalled, he discussed ideas with producer **John Nathan-Turner** and they agreed on a '**certain British eccentricity, and a sporty tone to emphasise youth**.'

Davison suggested a **cricketing outfit**, which costume designer **Colin Lavers** used as the basis for the Fifth Doctor's distinctive look. The natural next step was to then work into the series the Doctor playing cricket.

In *Four to Doomsday* (1982) – the first Fifth Doctor story to be recorded, but not the first to be broadcast – the Doctor makes ingenious use of a **cricket ball** to manoeuvre himself back to the TARDIS when both are stuck floating in space. But in *Black Orchid*, he plays in a proper cricket match.

The match was filmed at **Withyam Cricket Club** in East Sussex on **9 October 1981**. As written in the script, the sequence is pretty straightforward. Lord Cranleigh's side are being thrashed 56 for 9 when the Doctor comes into bat. He quickly shows his prowess, scoring at least 88 runs before it's his turn to bowl.

Davison is clearly still proud of what happens next. 'This is where **I bowl the guy out – in shot**,' he enthuses in the commentary on the DVD of the story. 'No trick photography involved here. Look at this.'

All in one shot, we see him throw the cricket ball, which arcs smoothly through the air, bounces on the ground, neatly dodges the batsman and smacks the wicket with enough force to knock the bails from the stumps.

'That was a **mistake,**' Davison then admits, gleefully. 'The cameraman was just meant to be framing up on me running in and inadvertently framed the whole lot in. [But] look at that action.'

It's a glorious mistake – and the delight of Davison and the rest of the players is clearly evident on screen.

THIS SPORTING LIFE

IT'S NOT EASY KEEPING UP WITH THE DOCTOR'S SPORTING PROWESS...

THE MOST GOALS SCORED

As seen in *The Lodger* (2010)

'Football's the one with the sticks, isn't it?' asks the Eleventh Doctor just before he joins his friend **Craig Owens** and the rest of the side from the King's Arms for a match in the pub league against the Rising Sun. It turns out that this incarnation of the Doctor has natural talent and we see him score at least **three goals**.

But for all the Eleventh Doctor is a gifted player, he's not a very generous one – he hogs the glory for himself, doesn't pass to other players and even runs in when Craig is about to take a penalty to kick the ball himself.

Except that this ill-mannered behaviour is all part of an ingenious plan. While the rest of the team don't notice that the Doctor's actions make Craig feel miserable, it's spotted by Craig's friend **Sophie**. It's another step towards the Doctor's ultimate goal: to make Craig and Sophie realise they're in love.

Long before he became the Eleventh Doctor and while still at school, **Matt Smith** played football for the youth teams of Northampton Town, Nottingham Forest and Leicester City. A back injury meant he had to give up on his plans to become a professional footballer, and he started acting instead. So football's loss was ***Doctor Who***'s gain.

THE BEST WRESTLER ON PELADON

As seen in *The Curse of Peladon* (1972)

The Third Doctor and Jo Grant arrive on the planet Peladon and pose as delegates from Earth, there to discuss whether Peladon can join the **Galactic Federation**. To the Doctor's horror, the delegates from other worlds include his old enemies, the **Ice Warriors** – and someone is keen to sabotage the talks, even resorting to murder.

Keen to uncover what's happening, the Doctor responds to a request from **Grun**, the strong but silent champion to the young **King Peladon of Peladon**. Grun leads the Doctor through some secret tunnels and then leaves him to find his way into an ornate room.

But the Doctor is in the inner sanctum of the temple of **Aggedor**, the mythical royal beast. It's a crime for anyone but the high priest to enter the sanctum – a crime punishable by death.

Jo appeals to King Peladon (who fancies her), and the king decides that because the Doctor is an Earth delegate he is also an honorary nobleman of Peladon. That means he has a right to trial by combat: he must fight Grun to the death.

The Doctor wins the contest – showing mercy rather than killing the king's champion. Grateful, Grun helps the Doctor uncover the villains plotting against peace. They also reveal that Aggedor is more than merely a myth.

THE BEST HORSEMANSHIP

As seen in *The Girl in the Fireplace* (2006)

It's the 51st century and in the Diagmar Cluster, some two and half galaxies from Earth, a spaceship called the SS ***Madame de Pompadour*** drifts quietly through space. When the Tenth Doctor, Rose Tyler and Mickey Smith arrive, they think the ship has been abandoned – but the truth is something more horrible.

An ion storm about a year before caused 82% systems failure, but **clockwork robots** are programmed to repair the ship using any resources to hand. Unfortunately, the only resources to hand were the more than 50 members of the crew – so they were used for spare parts. The ship hasn't finished its repairs, so looks further afield for resources...

It opens '**time windows**' to France in the 18th century, allowing its clockwork robots to look in on the life of **Jeanne-Antoinette Poisson**, known to her friends as Reinette ('little queen') and to history as Madame de Pompadour.

The ship thinks that because it shares a name with this woman they must be compatible. It just needs to wait until 1758 when she turns 37 – the same age as the ship – and she'll be able to provide exactly the spare part it needs to complete its repairs. It wants to take her brain.

To save Reinette from the clockwork robots, the Doctor must sever the connection between the spaceship and France. To do that, he says, he needs to smash the glass of what on the ship-side of the link is a '**hyperplex**' but on the France-side just looks like a mirror. Ideally, he'd drive a truck through it – but he doesn't have a truck.

So instead he climbs on a horse he's decided to call **Arthur**, who wandered through one of the time windows from France onto the ship. Together, they leap through the mirror – smashing the time windows and saving Reinette in the very nick of time.

Which means the Doctor rides a horse **through a mirror**, and in doing so rides back in time **at least 3,243 years** and some **56 trillion kilometres** (about 37 trillion miles).[1] As a single bit of horsemanship, that will take some beating.

1 Andromeda, the nearest galaxy to Earth, is approximately 22.5 trillion kilometres (15 trillion miles) away, so we've multiplied that by 2.5.

THE DOCTOR ON A HORSE

- The Fourth Doctor rides a horse in *The Masque of Mandragora* (1976)
- The Seventh Doctor rides a horse in ***Survival*** (1989)
- The Tenth Doctor rides horses in ***The Girl in the Fireplace*** and ***The Day of the Doctor*** (2013) – though the latter turns out to be a disguised Zygon
- The Eleventh Doctor rides horses in ***The Pandorica Opens*** (2010) and ***A Town Called Mercy*** (2012) – in the latter, the horse is called Susan
- The Twelfth Doctor rides a horse in ***Deep Breath*** (2014)

The Doctor is also skilled in fencing and sword-fighting – see p. 84.

THE DOCTOR AND THE OLYMPICS

EVERY FOUR YEARS, THE WORLD'S GREATEST ATHLETES COMPETE AT THE OLYMPIC GAMES TO SET NEW WORLD RECORDS – SOMETIMES WITH HELP FROM THE DOCTOR.

776 BC – Olympia, Greece
The very **first Olympic Games**. According to legend, the cook **Coroebus of Elis**, was the first champion of the 'stadion' running race (from which we get the word 'stadium'). The Tenth Doctor implies in *Fear Her* (2006) that he might have been there.

AD 67 – Olympia, Greece
Three years after meeting the First Doctor in *The Romans* (1964), the **Emperor Nero** competed in a 10-horse chariot race and an acting competition at the Games. He won both contests, but perhaps that's because the judges were scared of the man in command of the Roman army.

393 – Olympia, Greece
Generally thought to be the date of the **last ancient Games**. Various contests calling themselves 'Olympic Games' took place in the 1600s, 1700s and 1800s.

1896 – Athens, Greece
The **first modern Olympic Games** – that is, on Earth – as we know them today.

1948 – London, UK
The **Games of the XIV Olympiad**, to give them their formal title, were so good that the Tenth Doctor says in *Fear Her* he went twice.

1968 – Mexico City, Mexico
A **souvenir** from these Games helps the Second Doctor, Polly, Ben Jackson and Jamie McCrimmon work out they've landed on Earth in about the year 1970 in *The Underwater Menace* (1967).

1972 – Munich, West Germany
In *Invasion of the Dinosaurs* (1974), Sarah Jane Smith says that at 'the last Olympics' Great Britain's **John Crichton** jumped 2.362 metres, before changing his name to 'Mark' and joining what he thinks is a spaceship heading to another world.

1984 – Sarajevo, Yugoslavia
In February 1984, the BBC's coverage of the 1984 Winter Olympics meant *Doctor Who* couldn't be shown in its usual timeslot. As a result, ***Resurrection of the Daleks*** was broadcast on a different day of the week, and as two episodes of 45 minutes instead of the usual four episodes of 25 minutes.

SACRED FLAME, SACRED FIRE

When the bearer of the Olympic Torch stumbles in *Fear Her*, the Tenth Doctor quickly steps in and, in front of the more than 80,000 spectators and 13,000 athletes in the Olympic Stadium and many millions more watching on TV, he lights the Olympic Flame. The *Doctor Who* story was made and broadcast six years before the real London 2012 Olympic Games – where the Olympic Flame in the stadium was lit by a specially nominated group of up and coming young athletes.

Except that *Doctor Who* was still involved. On 24 May 2012, the Eleventh Doctor and Amy Pond starred in *Good as Gold*, a special mini-episode of *Doctor Who* in which they save a Torch Bearer from a Weeping Angel – and the Doctor is given a gold medal as a reward.

Two days later, Eleventh Doctor actor Matt Smith was one of the Torch Bearers when the Olympic Torch passed through Cardiff. The sound of the TARDIS materialising was also included in the Games' opening ceremony on 29 July.

2012 – London, UK
In *Fear Her*, the Tenth Doctor and Rose use the goodwill of the London Games to stop the alien **Isolus** from making everyone on Earth disappear.

2044 – Havana, Cuba
Fifteen years before he met the Tenth Doctor in *The Waters of Mars* (2009), **Dr Tarak Ital** represented Pakistan in athletics at the Games and won gold.

2048 – Paris, France
According to a web page seen in *The Waters of Mars*.

2074 – Unknown
The Eleventh Doctor says in *The Bells of St John* (2013) that he rode an anti-gravity motorbike at the Anti-Grav Olympics – and came last.

45th century - space
In *Resurrection of the Daleks* (1984), the Daleks rescue their imprisoned creator, **Davros**, who has been cryogenically frozen for 90 years. At the time, he's on one of two spaceships linked by a time corridor to London in the present day. Although not confirmed in the story as broadcast, the script says the spaceships are in the year 4590.

A little before Davros was frozen – so in about 4500 – the Fourth Doctor told him that the star system Arcturus recently won the **Galactic Olympic Games**, with the star system of Betelgeuse coming second (*Destiny of the Daleks* (1979) – so some time in the 45th century (4400–4499).

HUNTIN', SHOOTIN' AND FISHIN'

HE'S A LORD OF TIME, BUT HOW DOES THE DOCTOR FARE AT THE TRADITIONAL SPORTS OF THE GENTRY?

THE DOCTOR'S BEST HUNTIN'

As seen in *Survival* (1989)

The **Cheetah people** have the ability to leap across space and time to other worlds in the hunt for food, which they bring back to their own, unnamed planet. The food they like best seems to be intelligent, on two legs and ready to run – in short, they like to chase humans.

When the evil Master finds himself their prisoner, and begins to **turn into** a Cheetah person, he hunts down the Seventh Doctor. Surely this especially wily incarnation of the Doctor will puzzle out a way for them both to escape.

The Doctor does: he, his companion Ace and the other humans on the planet must simply wait for one of their number to start to change, just as the Master has. As long as that person doesn't escape – or kill them – their new powers can be harnessed.

One of Ace's old friends from Earth, **Midge**, is the first to turn, and the Master quickly captures him. 'Go hunting,' the Master tells him. 'Go home.' He and Midge promptly dash across space and time back to Earth.

Ace is the next to change, but before the Doctor can stop her she runs off with another of the Cheetah people, **Karra**. The Doctor must hunt for her, then persuade her not to give in to her wild side. Ace gets the Doctor and the remaining humans home. Then the Doctor uses Ace's powers to hunt down Midge and the Master... But he's becoming a Cheetah person himself.

THE DOCTOR'S BEST SHOOTIN'

As seen in *The Time of Angels* and *Flesh and Stone* (2010)

The Doctor is not generally a fan of guns. Indeed, the First Doctor despairs in *The Gunfighters* (1966) that, 'People keep giving me guns and do I wish they wouldn't.'

The Doctor certainly has skill as a marksman: he shoots an **Ogron** during *Day of the Daleks* (1972) and expertly shoots out the **lock** of a door in *The Visitation* (1982), despite the lock mechanism not being quite where we'd expect.

But surely his most skilful bit of shooting is on **Alfava Metraxis**. The Eleventh Doctor, Amy Pond, River Song and a squad of military clerics are picking their way through the underground **Maze of the Dead** towards the crashed spaceship, ***Byzantium***. They find it, positioned far above their heads. But they're also found by the deadly **Weeping Angels**, who start to close in.

At first it's not clear what the Doctor is going to do when he asks **Father Octavian** for his gun. The Doctor says it's going to be 'something incredibly stupid and dangerous', and that as soon as he shoots they're all to jump as high as they can. But how will that possibly help them? As the Doctor teases Octavian, it's a leap of faith.

The next thing they know, everyone is standing – upside down – on the hull of the *Byzantium*. Its power is still clearly still on, which the Doctor realised would include its artificial gravity. With perfect aim, he shot a hovering gravity globe to create an updraft, and when everybody jumped they all fell up towards the ship.

There's not much time to celebrate this achievement, though – as the Weeping Angels are still in pursuit...

THE DOCTOR'S BEST FISHIN'

As seen in *A Christmas Carol* (2010)

The Fourth Doctor is a keen angler. In *The Talons of Weng-Chiang* (1977), he boasts that around the start of the 8th century he and Saint Bede (c.672–735) caught a **salmon** in the River Fleet so large it would have hung over the sides of a table. That's an extraordinary achievement – but he does better yet.

In *A Christmas Carol*, the Eleventh Doctor is intrigued by the **flying fish** in the icy fog of the planet controlled by the miserly **Kazran Sardick**. If the Doctor can understand the fish and the fog a bit better, he'll be able to stop a spaceship from crashing – a spaceship whose passengers include his companions Amy Pond and Rory Williams. The Doctor pops back in time to when Kazran was a not-miserly boy, and they attempt to catch one of these fish, using the **sonic screwdriver** as bait.

The bait works a little too well. They catch a fish that is then promptly swallowed by an enormous **flying shark**, which also chomps down the sonic. This is a bit of a problem because the sonic contains all the readings taken from the fog that the Doctor desperately needs. So the shark wants to eat the Doctor, and he wants to get into the shark's mouth to retrieve the sonic and its readings. Perhaps they can come to some arrangement...

Later in the story, the Doctor catches the shark again and tethers it to a **rickshaw** so that he, Kazran and Kazran's friend Abigail can take a Christmassy ride through the sky. At the end of the story Kazran and Abigail take one last flying shark ride – did the Doctor help them catch a shark for a third time?

I'M A SCIENTIST

HE HAS THE ADVANTAGE OF – USUALLY – BEING AHEAD OF US SCIENTIFICALLY, BUT WHAT CONTRIBUTION HAS THE DOCTOR MADE TO THE SUM TOTAL OF KNOWLEDGE?

THE DOCTOR'S GREATEST ACHIEVEMENT IN PHYSICS

As seen in *The Day of the Doctor* (2013)

In *Remembrance of the Daleks* (1988), the Seventh Doctor lays a trap for the Daleks, letting them steal '**the Hand of Omega**', the rather pretentious name of a device for customising stars. Long ago, it created the **supernova** that was the initial power source for the time travel experiments of the Doctor's people and led to the establishment of the **Time Lords**.

'And didn't we have trouble with the prototype,' says the Doctor of this awesome device – suggesting he was involved in originally testing it. But when his friend Ace picks him up on the word 'we', he sheepishly corrects himself and says 'they'. He might have been involved, but we can't be sure.

If we don't know that the Doctor helped create Time Lord society, we know he saved it at a critical moment. On the last day of the **Time War**, he stopped the Daleks from destroying Gallifrey by moving the entire planet into another universe, frozen in a single moment.

It's an extraordinary feat of physics – just the calculations involved took **hundreds and hundreds of years**. That's why it takes **all the incarnations of the Doctor** working together. Having worked out the mathematics, they must then all fly their TARDISes into Gallifrey's lower atmosphere at equal distances from one another to do the actual moving. So it takes some fiendishly clever physics and some fancy flying, too.

THE DOCTOR'S GREATEST CONTRIBUTION TO ETHICS IN SCIENCE

As seen in *Carnival of Monsters* (1973)

The Third Doctor and Jo arrive on the SS *Bernice*, a ship apparently in the Indian Ocean in 1926 – but events keep repeating and they're attacked by a **plesiosaur**. Escaping through a hatch, the Doctor and Jo find themselves in the workings of some kind of machine. The plesiosaur isn't the only monstrous creature in it, either – soon the Doctor and Jo are chased by gigantic **Drashigs.**

Eventually, they discover they're inside a **Miniscope** on the planet **Inter Minor**. A Miniscope collects and miniaturises specimens from all through time and space, which can then be viewed by paying customers for fun – like goldfish in a bowl. Jo is horrified that real, intelligent beings are trapped in this sort of artificial zoo, and the Doctor agrees with her. He explains that he once persuaded the High Council of the Time Lords that such machines are an offence against the dignity of sentient life forms, and made such a nuisance of himself that the things were called in and destroyed.

This Miniscope somehow escaped the ban, but the Doctor is determined to shut it down. However, the Drashigs are still in pursuit of the Doctor and Jo, and they, too, escape the machine...

THE DOCTOR'S GREATEST CONTRUBUTION TO SCIENCE ON EARTH

In *The Pirate Planet* (1978), the Fourth Doctor says that he had to give **Isaac Newton** a bit of a prod before he worked out his laws of planetary motion and universal gravitation, as published in *Philosophiæ Naturalis Principia Mathematica* (1687). The Doctor apparently climbed a tree and dropped apples on Newton's head – but rather than inspire him, it only annoyed Newton who told him to clear off. Later the Doctor explained the scientific principles to Newton over dinner.

OH, THE HUMANITIES!

HE'S A DOCTOR OF SCIENCE BUT A MASTER OF THE ARTS...

THE DOCTOR'S GREATEST CONTRIBUTION TO LITERATURE

As seen in *The Shakespeare Code* (2007)

We've watched the Doctor meet many famous authors – including **Agatha Christie**, **Winston Churchill** (who won the Nobel Prize for Literature in 1953) and **Charles Dickens**.

In *The Romans* (1965), the First Doctor claims to have given the idea for the story 'The Emperor's New Clothes' to **Hans Christian Andersen**. In *Timelash* (1985), **HG Wells** travels with the Sixth Doctor to the planet Karfel, and his adventures there seem to at least partly inspire the novels *The Time Machine* (1895), *The Invisible Man* and *The War of the Worlds* (both 1897) – and perhaps much more of Wells's writing.

But surely the Doctor's greatest influence on literature is his friendship with **William Shakespeare**. When the Tenth Doctor and Martha Jones meet Shakespeare in 1599, their encounter with the wicked **Carrionites** is the likely inspiration for *Macbeth* (first performed in 1606). The Carrionite Lilith even threatens to turn the world into a '**blasted heath**' – a phrase Shakespeare then reuses in Macbeth's first meeting with witches.

Shakespeare's conversation with the Doctor and Martha about the recent death of his son, Hamnet, also prompts perhaps the most famous scene he ever wrote. 'It made me question everything,' he tells them. 'The futility of this fleeting existence, **to be or not to be**. Oh, that's quite good.' The Doctor also provides him with another line used in *Hamlet*: 'The play's the thing.'

The Doctor says, '**All the world's a stage**', a line Shakespeare will include in *As You Like It*, and mentions the alien **Sycorax** (seen in *The Christmas Invasion* (2005)) – thus providing Shakespeare with the name of Caliban's mother in *The Tempest* (1611). He and Martha also help Shakespeare compose the last lines of the lost play, *Love's Labour's Won* – with some help from *Harry Potter* author JK Rowling.

Meanwhile, Martha seems to be the '**Dark Lady**', to whom Shakespeare would address a series of 14-line poems called sonnets. His most famous sonnet is apparently composed on the spot, and again for Martha, when he asks, '**Shall I compare thee to a summer's day? Thou art more lovely and more temperate...**'

Martha also affects the way that Shakespeare – and writers more generally – are acknowledged, prompting the audience to call for the '**Author!**' at the end of a performance of *Love's Labour's Lost*. The Doctor even makes Shakespeare wear a frilly **ruff** round his neck, making him look more like his future portraits.

In *Planet of Evil* (1975), the Fourth Doctor says he met Shakespeare 'once' and that he was a 'charming fellow' but a 'dreadful actor'. It's possible he's exaggerating something we saw in an earlier episode: using a **space-time visualiser**, the First Doctor watched a conversation between Shakespeare and Elizabeth I in *The Chase* (1965).

In *City of Death* (1979), the Fourth Doctor also claims to have known Shakespeare as a taciturn boy who never said a word. 'I said to him, "There's no point in talking if you've got nothing to say."' In the same story, the Doctor says that the grown-up Shakespeare dictated *Hamlet* to him, and that the Doctor warned him about mixing metaphors in the 'To be or not to be' speech. Again, the suggestion is that the Doctor influenced and honed Shakespeare's writing.

THE DOCTOR WITH THE MOST MUSICAL ABILITY

As seen in *The Magician's Apprentice, Before the Flood, The Woman Who Lived, The Zygon Invasion* and *Hell Bent* (all 2015)

The First Doctor doesn't seem able to play a **lyre.** The Second Doctor can play the **recorder** reasonably well. The Fourth Doctor plays a **reed pipe** and claims to be able to play the **trumpet**. The Fifth Doctor plays the **harp**. The Sixth and Tenth Doctors both play the **organ**, and the Seventh Doctor plays the **spoons**. In *Music of the Spheres* (2008), a special mini-episode shown as part of the BBC Proms concert series, the Tenth Doctor claims to have played the tuba at the first Prom in 1895 – 'I was brilliant'. Several Doctors sing and whistle. But surely the Twelfth Doctor's skill with an **electric guitar** – seen in five episodes in 2015 – beats them all.

THE DOCTOR WHO KNOWS THE MOST LANGUAGES

The Doctor shares a Time Lord gift with his companions: the **telepathic field** of the TARDIS gets into their brains so that whatever language they might encounter in time and space, they – and we – almost always hear or see it in English.

The Doctor also knows a number of languages we don't hear or see in English – for example the Eleventh Doctor speaks 'baby' and 'horse' – which suggests he's not using the TARDIS and can really converse in them. The Ninth Doctor claims to speak 'five billion languages', but from what we see on screen, the Third Doctor speaks the most languages of any Doctor.

Languages understood by the Third Doctor:

- English (all stories)
- Delphon (in *Spearhead from Space* (1970), he says the people of the planet Delphon communicate with their eyebrows)
- Chinese – Hokkian dialect (in *The Mind of Evil* (1971))
- Venusian (he first sings in Venusian in *The Daemons* (1971), then provides an English translation)
- Tibetan (in *Planet of the Spiders* (1974), he apologises to his old teacher for not bringing him a cotton scarf, showing he also knows Tibetan customs)
- Old High Gallifreyan (in *The Five Doctors* (1983))

MAGIC MOMENTS

THE DOCTOR IS WELL SCHOOLED IN WITCHCRAFT AND WIZARDRY

THE DOCTOR'S GREATEST FEAT OF REAL MAGIC

As seen in *The Ambassadors of Death* (1970)
'You're right, Jo,' says the Third Doctor at the end of *The Dæmons* (1971), 'there is magic in the world after all.'

We might find that surprising coming from the Doctor, a **scientific hero**. In *The Three Doctors* (1972–1973), he performs simple tricks – vanishing a pencil and then producing a bunch of flowers – to explain that the strange things happening in the story are 'a scientific conjuring trick of a very high order'. The point is that such tricks are not real magic.

The Fourth Doctor performs conjuring tricks in *The Talons of Weng-Chiang* (1977) but, as he tells Leela in *The Robots of Death* (1977), 'To the rational mind nothing is inexplicable, only **unexplained**.' Many of the Doctor's adventures involve finding rational, scientific explanations for things that otherwise seem magical. In *The Dæmons* he seems able to command his car, Bessie, to do whatever he says – and then reveals he's also holding a **remote control**.

In stories set in history or in more primitive civilisations, his scientific brilliance is often seen as magical. In *The Time Warrior* (1973–1974), the Third Doctor ends a Sontaran-led attack on a castle in the 13th century by throwing **stink bombs** to scare off the human attackers. They complain about him being a 'wizard'.

But elsewhere, the Doctor's actions are harder to explain rationally. In *Battlefield* (1989), the Seventh Doctor draws a **chalk circle** on the ground that, while his friends Ace and Shou-Yuing are inside it, keeps them safe from the enchantress Morgaine. This Doctor also speaks of magic as if it's a real thing. In *Silver Nemesis* (1988), he explains how Lady Peinforte travelled 350 years into the future from 1638: she used an arrow made from a special Time Lord metal called validium and had some basic knowledge of time travel. '**Black magic,** mostly,' he says.

THE MOST USEFUL MAGICIAN

UNIT is meant to be a top-secret organisation, and to prevent mass panic it tries to keep alien invasions and other strange phenomena secret, too. In *The Day of the Doctor* (2013), we learn that UNIT's **cover story** for the arrival of the TARDIS in Trafalgar Square, watched by a large crowd, is that it's a stunt by well-known illusionist **Derren Brown**. This is apparently not the first time UNIT has used Brown as cover, either – and they send him **flowers** as an acknowledgement. That suggests he's in on the secret.

THE DOCTOR'S GREATEST FEAT OF MAGIC TO COME

It seems the Doctor will become an even more powerful magician in some future incarnation. In ***Battlefield***, the Seventh Doctor learns that

he will one day be the wizard **Merlin** – in another dimension, where **King Arthur** is real. The knight Ancelyn even speaks of his prowess at the battle of Badon, where he 'cast down' the enchantress Morgaine 'with his **mighty arts**'. It must have been – or rather, it *will be* – quite a moment. Other knights confirm the story and as a result are very wary of the Doctor.

Of course, people from the 17th century did not see a distinction between science and magic as we do. Isaac Newton's interest in magic, and his hope of being able to exert force over a distance, led him to formulate his law of universal gravitation, still used in astrophysics today to explain the movements of the planets – though see also p. 37. So perhaps when the Doctor speaks of 'black magic' it's not that he necessarily believes in it; he means that's how Lady Peinforte would understand what she's done.

That seems to match what the Tenth Doctor says in *The Shakespeare Code* (2007) to explain the magic of the **Carrionites**. 'It's just a different sort of science. You lot, you chose mathematics. Given the right string of numbers, the right equation, you can split the atom. Carrionites use words instead.' Or, as the famous science-fiction writer Arthur C Clarke put it, 'Any sufficiently advanced technology is indistinguishable from magic.'

Even so, the Doctor can still perform tricks that seem difficult to explain. Vanishing a pencil is one thing, but in *The Ambassadors of Death* (1970), the Doctor vanishes a whole **spool of magnetic tape,** the size of a hardback book, right in front of the villainous Taltalian. The Doctor's friend Liz Shaw – a highly accomplished scientist – wonders if he sent it into the future. 'No, that was simply transmigration of object,' he tells her. 'There's a great deal of difference between that and pure science, you know.'

If it's not science, surely it's magic...

THE DOCTOR'S MOST USEFUL MAGIC TRICK

As seen in *Planet of the Spiders* (1974)

The Doctor knows a number of tricks that we might expect to see in the act of a stage magician. He can vanish pencils and produce pieces of chalk apparently from the air, and in ***The Greatest Show in the Galaxy*** (1988) he even performs a whole magic show for the angry **Gods of Ragnarok**.

But given the sorts of scrapes he gets into, perhaps the greatest trick the Doctor knows is how to **compress his muscles**, which requires a lot of concentration but allows him to escape tight bonds. The trick was taught to him, he says in *Planet of the Spiders*, by the great illusionist **Harry Houdini**. The Second Doctor's companion Ben Jackson also knows the trick in *The Highlanders* (1966), so perhaps he met Houdini, too.

THE DOCTORS' DOCTOR

WE ALL HAVE OUR FAVOURITE DOCTOR, BUT WHICH INCARNATION DO THE MAJORITY OF OTHER DOCTORS RATE MOST HIGHLY?

CHRISTOPHER ECCLESTON

THE NINTH DOCTIOR

'The first one I remember is Patrick Troughton. For some reason when people say ***Doctor Who***, I have this black and white image of his fantastic face.'

SYLVESTER McCOY

THE SEVENTH DOCTOR

'Patrick Troughton is the first Doctor I saw [so] my distant memory when I arrived in the TARDIS was Patrick Troughton as well.'

WILLIAM HARTNELL

THE FIRST DOCTOR

'There's only one man in England who can take over [the role of the Doctor], and that's Patrick Troughton.'

PETER DAVISON

THE FIFTH DOCTOR

'I grew up watching ***Doctor Who*** and my Doctor was Patrick Troughton … Of all my influences [in playing the Doctor], the most dominant was drawn from him … I wanted to bring a certain recklessness back to the character, a certain vulnerability that I liked in his character.'

COLIN BAKER

THE SIXTH DOCTOR

'For me, he was **the Guv'nor**. He did the hard job: the first regeneration. If it hadn't been as classy and successful as it was, there would never have been all us other Doctors. His wonderful, sly, oblique, louche performance as the Second Doctor changed the mould of ***Doctor Who***. It was a very compelling performance. So I was a bit in awe of him but within minutes of rehearsing ***The Two Doctors*** (1985), I realised that I was working with not only a gentleman and a very fine actor, but a very nice man as well. We had great fun – enormous fun. I have perfectly good relationships with all the Doctors but, for me, the daddy of them all is Patrick. Let's hear it for Patrick Troughton. '

MATT SMITH

THE ELEVENTH DOCTOR

'My favourite Doctor is Patrick Troughton. What I think is wonderful about him is that he's weird and peculiar without ever asking you to find him weird or peculiar, and that's quite a feat when you're playing the Doctor.'

CHAPTER TWO
ALIEN WORLDS

'YOU'RE NOT AS DOUBTFUL AS YOUR FRIEND, I HOPE? ... IF YOU COULD TOUCH THE ALIEN SAND AND HEAR THE CRIES OF STRANGE BIRDS AND WATCH THEM WHEEL IN ANOTHER SKY, WOULD THAT SATISFY YOU?'

THE FIRST DOCTOR, *AN UNEARTHLY CHILD* (1963)

THE WORST PLACES IN THE UNIVERSE............... 046
A HOLIDAY FOR THE DOCTOR............... 048
THE MOST IMPROBABLE WORLDS............... 050
THIS IS GALLIFREY............... 052
THE MOST USEFUL WORLDS............... 056
NATURAL RESOURCES............... 058
ORE-SOME POWER............... 060
HAZARD WARNINGS............... 062
WORLDS' RECORDS............... 064

POLICE PUBLIC CALL BOX
POLICE PUBLIC CALL BOX
POLICE TELEPHONE
FREE
FOR USE OF
PUBLIC
ADVICE & ASSISTANCE
OBTAINABLE IMMEDIATELY
OFFICERS & CARS
RESPOND TO ALL CALLS
PULL TO OPEN

THE WORST PLACES IN THE UNIVERSE

THE TARDIS CAN TAKE YOU ANYWHERE IN TIME AND SPACE – BUT TRY TO AVOID ALL OF THESE...

THE WORST WEATHER

As seen in *The Robots of Death* (1977)

In *The Doctor, the Widow and the Wardrobe* (2012), the Eleventh Doctor takes **Madge Arwell** and her family to an unnamed planet in the year **5345**. It's supposed to be a safe place to spend Christmas – but then the people of **Androzani Major** use **acid rain** to melt down the forests of **sentient trees** for battery fluid. However, this burning and deadly acid rain isn't a natural phenomenon: it's caused by satellites that must be moved into position.

In *The Robots of Death*, the Fourth Doctor takes Leela to a different unnamed planet where, almost as soon as they arrive, they're nearly cut to pieces by a **sandstorm** measuring scale 3.4 and building, and travelling at perhaps 1,000 miles per hour.

Having been saved from this danger, they learn that huge vehicles called **sandminers** actively pursue these storms. The mobile mines pass over the planet's surface searching for useful ores but heavier elements tend to sink into the substrata. A good sandstorm is a bonus because it stirs things up.

With huge profits to be made, there's an obvious motive when one of the crew of the sandminer is found murdered. But as the Doctor and Leela investigate, they head into a storm of **scale 16**.

THE WORST EDUCATIONAL SYSTEM

As seen in *The Krotons* (1968)

The **Gonds** live on a bleak-looking planet with two suns, the atmosphere a mix of ozone and sulphur that makes it smell of **bad eggs**.

Since a war thousands of years ago, the Gonds have lived under the rule of the alien **Krotons**, who provide their laws, science and culture through teaching machines in the Learning Hall.

Every now and then, tests on these machines identify the two brightest young Gonds, who are then granted the huge honour of joining the alien Krotons. It's a chance to escape the monotony – isn't it?

Except, as the Second Doctor and Zoe Heriot discover, having passed the tests, the selected students are drained of their **mental power**, which is converted into energy to revitalise the Krotons. The drained students are then entirely **dissolved**. It seems the stinky atmosphere is the Krotons' fault, too.

THE WORST RACIAL POLITICS

As seen in *The Mutants* (1972)

By the 30th century, the **Earth Empire** has colonised the planet **Solos** for 500 years, in which time it has mined out almost all its **thaesium**, one of the richest fuel sources in the galaxy. The native **Solonians** are oppressed by the **Overlords** from Earth – they must even use separate transmat booths.

'Once,' says young Solonian **Ky**, 'the land [of Solos] was green, the rivers ran clear, the air was sweet to breathe. And then the Overlords came, bringing Earth's poisons with them, calling it progress. We toiled in their mines, we became slaves. Worse than slaves.'

The Overlords also kill any Solonians if they mutate into '**Mutts**' – which the Third Doctor and Jo Grant help to show is a natural part of Solonian development.

THE MOST DECEPTIVE NAME

As seen in *Nightmare of Eden* (1979)

The name makes planet **Eden** sound like a nice place and from what little we see of it, it is – all dense, alien jungle. But it also has a terrible secret.

Eden is home to the **Mandrels**, fierce if lumbering creatures who attack and kill human beings. Worse still, the Fourth Doctor and Romana discover by chance that when Mandrels die they reduce down to powder. The powder is the dangerous and addictive **vraxoin**, the biggest killer drug in existence.

'I've seen whole communities, whole planets destroyed by this,' says the Doctor in horror.

THE WORST GENDER POLITICS

As seen in *Galaxy 4* (1965)

The **Drahvins** from Drahva in Galaxy 4 have three classes of humanoid people. There are the superior elite females, such as the callous **Maaga**. Then there are women Maaga doesn't even class as human beings, 'cultivated in test tubes [and] grown for a purpose and capable of nothing more.'

The First Doctor and Steven Taylor ask if the Drahvins are all women. Maaga replies, 'Oh, we have a small number of men, as many as we need. The rest we **kill**. They consume valuable food and fulfil no particular function.'

A HOLIDAY FOR THE DOCTOR

THE GREATEST PLACES TO ESCAPE TO IN ALL OF TIME AND SPACE

THE MOST TRANQUIL PLACE IN THE UNIVERSE

As seen in *The Five Doctors* (1983)

The Eye of Orion looks a bit like both northern Wales (on Earth) and the not exactly nice-sounding Death Zone (on Gallifrey). It has the feel of Earth after a **thunderstorm** because of the high bombardment of **positive ions**. Yet for some, says the Fifth Doctor, it's the most tranquil place in the universe and a good place for a rest. His companion Turlough, who has been before, agrees.

That makes it the ideal place for the Doctor to recuperate after his next regeneration, but in his post-regenerative confusion in ***The Twin Dilemma*** (1984) the coordinates elude the Sixth Doctor so he tries for **Vesta 95** instead – which is, he tells Peri Brown, 'a marvellous place for a holiday'.

The Sixth Doctor clearly mentions the Eye of Orion to Peri again. In ***Timelash*** (1985), she wearily reminds him that she's 'heard all about this elusive place', and doesn't think much of what he's told her. '**No one lives there**,' she says, 'and few visit – apart from you.'

Perhaps the appeal is not in the Eye of Orion itself but what can be seen from it. The Doctor has apparently told

Peri more than once of the '**Astral starbursts** creating a myriad celestial bodies against a timeless royal blue backdrop.' She still isn't very impressed and wants to go somewhere more interesting.

The Eleventh Doctor seems to agree with her when, in ***The Doctor's Wife*** (2011) he considers another visit. 'The Eye of Orion's restful, if you like restful. I can never really get the hang of restful.' It's up the TARDIS, though, whether he actually gets there…

THE BEST BEACH IN THE UNIVERSE

As mentioned in *Death to the Daleks* (1974) and *The Big Bang* (2010)

In *The Big Bang*, the Eleventh Doctor tells Amy Pond that **Lyle beach**, apparently in Space Florida, is the best of beaches because its **automatic sand** cleans up lolly sticks by itself.

A close second is the sand of the planet **Florana** which, the Third Doctor tells Sarah Jane Smith in *Invasion of the Dinosaurs* (1974), is as soft as swan's down. Florana is one of the most beautiful places in the universe, always carpeted with perfumed flowers, the seas like warm milk and the streams flowing with water clearer than crystal.

In the next story, *Death to the Daleks*, the Doctor tells Sarah that it's impossible to sink in the water on Florana because it is **effervescent** and the bubbles support you. He also says the air is like a magic potion and that he always comes back from Florana feeling 100 years young

So if Lyle beach has the best sand, surely Florana has the best beaches overall. It's a shame Sarah never gets to see it, because the TARDIS is drawn off course to the icy, foggy planet Exxilon instead. What rotten luck.

THE BIGGEST AND BEST AMUSEMENT PARK IN THE UNIVERSE

As seen in *Nightmare in Silver* (2013)

The Eleventh Doctor takes Clara Oswald and the children she nannies, Angie and Artie Maitland, to **Hedgewick's World**. The Doctor has a golden ticket that means they'll be able to ride the **Space Zoomer** and get free ice cream.

Hedgewick apparently bought the planet cheap after it had been trashed in the wars with the Cybermen. It seems to have flourished during that conflict, but from Hedgewick's World you can see the awful way those wars ended. A patch of blackness in space was once the Tiberion spiral galaxy until **Emperor Ludens Nimrod Kendrick Cord Longstaff XLI** gave the order for it to be destroyed to stop the Cybermen once and for all. A million star systems, a hundred million worlds and a billion trillion people war were all lost in the implosion.

Perhaps they were the customers that Hedgewick's World depended on. Or perhaps the sight of the missing galaxy in the sky is what put off the punters. Either way, it's rather quiet when the Doctor visits. To begin with, that's good – there are no queues and Angie and Artie enjoy being weightless in the Space Zoomer. But in another attraction, **Webley's World of Wonders**, the Doctor discovers that the Cybermen have not been entirely defeated. And to stop them again, the Emperor must destroy the planet – while the Doctor and his friends are still on it.

THE MOST BEAUTIFUL PLACE IN THE UNIVERSE

As seen in *The Girl Who Waited* (2011)

Two billion light years from Earth is the paradise planet **Apalapucia**, voted second in the top 10 greatest destinations for the discerning intergalactic traveller. But as a result everyone now goes to the place voted number one and it has become hideous – 'planet of the coffee shops', mutters the Eleventh Doctor. So Apalapucia is, by default, the best.

However, we don't see much of it – or the 'sunsets, spires [and] soaring silver colonnades' that the Doctor promises – because there's a planet-wide **quarantine** owing to an outbreak of the horrible one-day plague, **Chen7**.

Even so, there's still plenty of fun to be had. The Twostreams facility hospital offers a range of entertainment zones: a mountain zone including Apalapucia's **Glasmir Peaks** for those wanting a taste of adventure, and a roller-coaster zone authentically modelled on the famous **Warp-speed Death Ride at Disneyland Clom**. There's also a cinema, aquarium and a garden that is a perfect replica of the **Shill Governor's Mansion on Shallanna**.

As Amy Pond says, there's so much on offer you could spend a lifetime in the facility. Unfortunately, she does.

THE MOST IMPROBABLE WORLDS

THE STRANGEST PLACES WE'VE EVER WITNESSED

THE IMPOSSIBLE PLANET

As seen in *The Impossible Planet* (2006)

The weirdest world we've ever seen the Doctor visit is surely the one he himself calls impossible. 'A black hole's a **dead star**,' the Tenth Doctor tells Rose Tyler. 'It collapses in on itself, in and in and in until the matter's so dense and tight it starts to pull everything else in, too. Nothing in the universe can escape it – light, gravity, time. Everything just gets pulled inside and crushed.'

So it's against all the known laws of physics for him to be saying this while standing on **Krop Tor**, a planet in perpetual orbit round a black hole. In the scriptures of the Veltino, 'Krop Tor' means a '**bitter pill**' that couldn't be swallowed.

From their vantage point on this impossible world, the Doctor and Rose watch the Scarlet System, home to the Pallushi civilisation for a billion years, being ripped apart while they remain perfectly safe.

That is, until the impossibly old **Beast** imprisoned deep inside the planet is awake...

On the planet Barcelona, the Ninth Doctor tells us in *The Parting of the Ways* (2005), they have dogs with no noses.

THE HIDDEN PLANET

As seen in *The Magician's Apprentice* (2014)

The Twelfth Doctor, Clara Oswald and Missy are captured by the Daleks and taken to what appears to be a space station hanging in silent space. But in that case the gravity should be artificial and, as Missy says, '**coppery smelling** round the edges [and] a tiny bit sexy'. Instead, it feels real.

To test her theory, she boldly opens the airlock and steps out into the vacuum. Instead of dying of exposure, she reveals the Daleks' secret. Their planet **Skaro** was destroyed by the Seventh Doctor in ***Remembrance of the Daleks*** (1988). But the Daleks reconstructed it, in secret, and have kept it hidden from view.

THE PLANET IN THE WRONG PLACE

As seen in *The Trial of a Time Lord* (1986)

The Sixth Doctor takes Peri Brown to the planet Ravalox, which she doesn't like very much. It's drizzly and grey, reminding her of a wet November on Earth.

But that's exactly why the Doctor brought her: Ravalox has the same mass, angle of tilt and period of rotation as Earth. It's quite a phenomenon to find two planets so similar.

The fact that both planets rotate on a tilted axis – and at the same angle – explains the November feeling as it's what causes seasonal changes. When part of the planet is angled towards the star it orbits, it receives a greater density of starlight and for a longer period each day, so experiences summer. When the same part of the planet is angled away, it is winter.

But the similarities between the planets are not just a happy coincidence. The Doctor and Peri discover a tunnel signposted 'Marble Arch' – like the Underground

Station in the London of Peri's time. Perhaps, says the Doctor, the people of Ravalox collect railway stations. Peri says that's ridiculous – but he says it's no more ridiculous than the other explanation: that Earth and its entire 'constellation'[1] has moved a couple of light years across space and become known by a different name without anyone even noticing.

Except, as the wicked Master takes great relish in explaining later in the story, that's exactly what happened. The Earth was moved – and by the Doctor's own people, the Time Lords…

	EARTH	RAVALOX
MASS	5,973,600,000,000,000,000,000,000 kg	5,973,600,000,000,000,000,000,000 kg
OBLIQUITY (AXIAL ANGLE OF TILT)	23.4371°	23.4371°
PERIOD OF ROTATION (LENGTH OF DAY)	23 hours, 56 minutes and 4 seconds – relative to the stars other than the one it is orbiting (the Sun)	23 hours, 56 minutes and 4 seconds – relative to the stars other than the one it is orbiting

1 The Sixth Doctor and the Master in *The Trial of the Time Lord* both use the word 'constellation', apparently to mean 'star system'. But astronomers on Earth use the word to mean a pattern of stars as they appear to us from Earth. It's a bit of a parochial definition, so perhaps that's why the Time Lords use the word to mean something else.

THE UPSIDE-DOWN PLANET

As seen in *The Tenth Planet* (1966)

To the astonishment of Earth's **International Space Command** and the world media, in 1986 a planet is spotted between the orbits of Venus and Mars – a new planet now racing towards Earth.

The planet is closely observed by **Snowcap Base in Antarctica**, where the technicians are joined by the First Doctor, Ben Jackson and Polly. They're just in time to see the first good images of this new planet – and it looks rather familiar. In fact, it looks just like Earth but upside down.

The Doctor is the only one not to seem surprised and tells the others that soon they will receive visitors from this other world. He's right: Snowcap Base is invaded by **Cybermen**.

The upside-down planet is **Mondas**, which millions of years ago was Earth's twin planet but then drifted away to '**the edge of space**'. Perhaps that's what caused the people of Mondas to weaken, their lives getting ever shorter. Then their cybernetic scientists constructed **spare parts** for their bodies to help them survive. But in this process of mechanisation, the Cybermen **lost their emotions** and became creatures of cold, emotionless **logic**.

Their plan is to drain the power of Earth for themselves – except that Mondas reaches saturation point and disintegrates. But then, as the Second Doctor observes in a later Cyberman story, 'Logic … merely enables one to be wrong with authority.'

THIS IS GALLIFREY

THROUGH THE MILLENNIA, THE TIME LORDS OF GALLIFREY LED A LIFE OF PEACE AND ORDERED CALM, PROTECTED FROM ALL THREATS FROM LESSER CIVILISATIONS BY THEIR GREAT POWER. BUT THIS WAS TO CHANGE...

THE RECORDS OF GALLIFREY

We first visit the then-unnamed planet of the Time Lords in ***The War Games*** (1969), when the Second Doctor is forced to stand trial for interfering in the affairs of other worlds.

We glimpse Time Lords apparently on their home planet in ***Colony in Space*** (1971) and ***The Three Doctors*** (1972–1973). The Third Doctor finally tells us its name – Gallifrey – in ***The Time Warrior*** (1973–1974). After that, the stories at least partially set on Gallifrey are:

The Deadly Assassin (1976)
The Invasion of Time (1978)
Arc of Infinity (1983)
The Five Doctors (1983)
The Sound of Drums (2007)
The End of Time (2009–2010)
The Name of the Doctor (2013)
The Day of the Doctor (2013)
Listen (2014)
Heaven Sent (2015)
Hell Bent (2015)

We also meet Time Lords and other people from Gallifrey, and learn details about its history and culture, in various other stories.

The Fourth Doctor says he 'can't' take Sarah Jane Smith with him to Gallifrey, so she rather abruptly has to leave the TARDIS at the end of *The Hand of Fear* (1976).

THE MOST DANGEROUS CRISIS IN GALLIFREY'S HISTORY

As seen in *Hell Bent* (2015)

At the beginning of *The Deadly Assassin*, the Fourth Doctor tells us that the events in this story are the most dangerous crisis that the Time Lords ever face in their long history. It is quite a crisis: the evil Master attempting to open a **black hole** at the heart of the planet. But is that worse than the events of *The Three Doctors*, where energy being drained through a black hole by **Omega** threatens the power of the Time Lords and to tear the universe apart?

Gallifrey has also suffered a number of crises since the events of *The Deadly Assassin*: the **occupation** in *The Invasion of Time*, the attempted **coup** by President Borusa so that he can rule for ever, and the **Time War**, to name but a few.

But perhaps the greatest crisis comes about in facing a threat yet to come. The Time Lords' extraordinary living computer, the Matrix, predicts that one day a creature known only as the **Hybrid**, cross-bred from two warrior races, will stand in the ruins of Gallifrey, unravel the web of time and 'destroy a billion billion hearts to heal its own'.

The Time Lords are obviously keen to know who the Hybrid might be, and subject the Twelfth Doctor to an interrogation lasting **4.5 billion years** inside a **confession dial** in the hope of gleaning what he knows. That action – that desperation – is surely their greatest moral crisis.

There are various theories about who the Hybrid might be. In *The Witch's Familiar* (2015), Davros assumes it will be a cross between the two most powerful species in the universe – half-Dalek and half-Time Lord. In *Hell Bent*, Ashildr thinks it might be the Doctor – and we're told in the TV movie *Doctor Who* (1996) that he's **half-human** on his mother's side. The Doctor counters that the hybrid might be the immortal Ashildr, who is half-human and half-Mire since the events of *The Girl Who Died* (2015).

Yet it seems the Hybrid is not one person but **two** – the Doctor and his companion, Clara Oswald. Their meeting was never a coincidence: it turns out that they were thrown together by Missy, aware of the prophecy and eager to cause chaos. The Doctor will do anything to save Clara: holding out against the rigours of the confession dial and later breaking all the Laws of Time to bring her back to life. He even shoots a Time Lord general, forcing him to regenerate.

But the Doctor is still wary of fulfilling the awful prophecy. In the end, this greatest of all crises is averted when the Doctor makes himself forget Clara entirely.

THE GREATEST POTENTIAL THREAT TO GALLIFREY

In the Time War, the Time Lords seem pretty evenly matched against the **Daleks** – in fact, we learn in *The Day of the Doctor* that were it not for the Doctor's intervention, the Daleks would obliterate Gallifrey.

But that's not the first time the planet has been conquered – we see the **Vardans and Sontarans** take over in *The Invasion of Time*. However, in that story they're aided by the Fourth Doctor – at least to begin with.

The fact is that often the greatest threats to Gallifrey are individual Time Lords. In *The Three Doctors* the planet is threatened by **Omega** and in *The Deadly Assassin* by the **Master** and the political ambitions of **Chancellor Goth**. In *The Invasion of Time* the invaders have help from the oleaginous **Castellan Kelner**. In *Arc of Infinity*, Omega is helped by **Councillor Hedin** and in *The Five Doctors* **President Borusa** is behind all the sinister goings on.

The **High Council** are the culprits in *The Trial of a Time Lord*, and it's **President Rassilon** and the High Council that are at fault at the end of the Time War. Then there is the **Hybrid**...

But there's a difference between a potential threat to Gallifrey and the crises it actually faces.

THIS IS GALLIFREY

THE GREATEST HERO ON GALLIFREY

As seen in *Hell Bent* (2013)

The Third Doctor says in ***The Three Doctors*** that he has always honoured the stellar engineer Omega who long ago created the black hole that gave the Time Lords their power as '**our greatest hero**'. But the implication is that other Time Lords don't share this view and Omega has generally been overlooked – in favour of one of his contemporaries.

In ***The Five Doctors*** (1983), the Second Doctor says that Rassilon – who stabilised Omega's black hole and then founded Time Lord society – is the '**greatest single figure**' in his people's official history. But he also warns of rumours that other Time Lords rebelled against his **cruelty** and locked him up in the Dark Tower at the heart of the Death Zone on Gallifrey, in **eternal sleep**.

Later in that story, Rassilon awakes – and in ***The End of Time (2009–2010)*** we see him back as President, leading Gallifrey's forces in the Time War.

When the Twelfth Doctor returns to Gallifrey in *Hell Bent*, Rassilon orders his men to shoot the Doctor. But they can't do it – they know the Doctor to be a **war hero**, the man who won the Time War. We're told many of them served under him directly. And that gives the Doctor authority to depose the President and the whole of the High Council, and send them into exile.

If the Doctor trumps Gallifrey's greatest single figure, he must surely be its greatest hero.

THE GREATEST POWER ON GALLIFREY

As seen in *The Deadly Assassin* (1976)

All the power of the Time Lords devolves from the '**Eye of Harmony**', a black hole set in an eternally dynamic equation by Rassilon, and apparently contained inside Gallifrey itself (see p. 162).

THE GREATEST HONOUR ON GALLIFREY

As seen in *The Invasion of Time* (1978)

According to Andred, commander of the Chancellery Guard, the greatest honour the planet can bestow is the ceremony in which a candidate is invested as President of the Supreme Council of the Time Lords of Gallifrey.

THE TIME LORDS' GREATEST SECRET

As seen in *The Trial of a Time Lord* (1986)

There are plenty of skeletons in the cupboards of Gallifrey. In *The Deadly Assassin*, the Time Lords have even forgotten that they're sitting on a black hole – the Fourth Doctor must deduce the fact from their half-remembered legends.

In *The Five Doctors*, the Master calls the Death Zone 'the **black secret** at the heart of your Time Lord paradise' – as if there's only one such secret. Information about the Death Zone, such as the **Black Scrolls of Rassilon**, is forbidden and quickly destroyed.

But since those ancient times, the Time Lords have become much more civilised – haven't they?

Well, not really.

In *The Trial of a Time Lord* (1986), the Sixth Doctor discovers that three people from the galaxy of **Andromeda** broke into the Matrix and stole advanced technological information. These people operated from Earth so, when the Time Lords discovered the leak, the High Council ordered the use of a device called the **Magnotron** to move Earth and its star system light years across space, causing a fireball that nearly destroyed the planet.

With the Earth in a different location, a robot recovery mission from Andromeda failed to find it and the three Andromedans died while in suspended animation waiting for rescue. So the Time Lords' secrets were safe – that is, until the Sixth Doctor stumbled upon them.

We learn in *Underworld* (1978) that the Time Lords' policy of non-interference in the affairs of other worlds followed them sharing medical and scientific information with the planet Minyos – whose population then went to war and ended up destroying the planet.

consciously echoes the real-life situation facing ***Doctor Who*** at the time. The BBC were unsure whether to continue making the series and criticised its depiction of violence. In the story, the Doctor is on trial for his life, facing tough questions about the nature and tone of his adventures.

As evidence in the trial, we watch what are effectively ***Doctor Who*** stories, his travels having been recorded by the Matrix. The tapes stolen from the Matrix by the Andromedans look very like AGFA film cases – perhaps because the production team making ***Doctor Who*** took them from the BBC film library. The suggestion is that the stolen tapes contain not data or blueprints but recordings of events just like those used in the Doctor's trial.

At this point in his life, the Doctor is in his sixth incarnation and we're told the stolen tapes come from records covering six phases. We're not told what they are phases of, but the **Valeyard** dismisses the first two phases as primitive – and the adventures of the First and Second Doctor were made in black and white rather than colour. Perhaps the fact the Valeyard doesn't have these first two phases is a reference to the fact that many of those old episodes of ***Doctor Who*** are missing from the BBC archive. The Valeyard also turns out to be an evil, future version of the Doctor, trying to gain control of his past life – so stealing recordings of his old adventures makes a kind of sense.

So it's not said explicitly, but there's circumstantial evidence to suggest that the greatest secret of the Time Lords – which they're prepared to move heaven and Earth to protect – is a complete run of ***Doctor Who*** stories.

THE MOST USEFUL WORLDS

WHATEVER YOU NEED, SOMEWHERE IN THE UNIVERSE CAN PROVIDE...

THE GREATEST BANK IN THE GALAXY

As seen in *Time Heist* (2014)

The **Bank of Karabraxos** is the most secure bank in the galaxy. All movement is monitored, all air consumption regulated and DNA is authenticated at every stage. Any intruders are incinerated, while a creature called the **Teller** scans visitors' thoughts for criminal intent and eats the minds of the guilty. Each vault, buried deep in the earth, is accessed by a drop-slot at the planet's surface that is atomically sealed with an unbreakable lock – the atoms have been scrambled. No wonder the bank contains, as the Twelfth Doctor says, the **greatest treasures in the universe**. It is, in short, completely impossible to break into this bank. Which is exactly what the Doctor then does...

THE BIGGEST MUSEUM EVER

As seen in *The Time of Angels* (2010)

In the 12,051st century, the **Delirium Archive** on an unnamed asteroid is the final resting place of the **Headless Monks** and the biggest museum ever. The Eleventh Doctor doesn't seem impressed by the exhibits – they are 'Wrong, wrong [and a] bit right, mostly wrong'. Then he sees what he's after – a 12,000 year-old **Home Box**, the spaceship equivalent of a black box on a plane, collecting data securely that can then be analysed in the event of an accident.

Burnt into this particular Home Box are words in a language that, the Doctor tells Amy Pond, could themselves once burn stars. It's **Old High Gallifreyan**, the ancient language of the Time Lords. Here, it gives coordinates in time and space, and says '**Hello Sweetie**'.

THE BIGGEST LIBRARY IN THE UNIVERSE

As seen in *Silence in the Library* and *Forest of the Dead* (2008)

In the 51st century, the **Library** is a whole planet devoted to books. The planet's core is the index computer – and the **biggest hard drive ever**. It contains copies of every book ever written, with brand new and specially printed editions. Unfortunately, the forests of the **Vashta Nerada** were pulped to make the paper these books are printed on – and the deadly Vashta Nerada hatch from spores in those trees, so now hatch from the books. So enjoy the books – biographies are stacked near the planet's equator – but don't touch the shadows or they'll eat you.

Based on three connected asteroids, the **Shadow Proclamation** is a form of outer space police, employing the Judoon as gruff, rather narrow-minded enforcers of the law.

THE GREATEST HOSPITAL IN THE UNIVERSE

As seen in *Let's Kill Hitler* (2011)

Having poisoned the Eleventh Doctor with a kiss, the brainwashed River Song then thinks better of what's she done and uses all her **remaining regenerations** to heal him. Afterwards, she needs rest so the Doctor leaves her in the care of the **Sisters of the Infinite Schism** – despite the name, the greatest hospital in the universe. We're not told exactly when this takes place, but we then see River enrol at the **Luna University in 5123** to study archaeology.

THE PLANET SAVING THE WHOLE UNIVERSE

As seen in *Logopolis* (1981)

The essence of the **second law of thermodynamics**, explains the Fourth Doctor, is that the more you put things together, the more they keep falling apart. Unfortunately, what's true of his battered old TARDIS also holds for all of time and space.

'The universe long ago passed the point of **total collapse**,' admits the **Monitor**, leader of the mathematicians on the planet Logopolis. But his brilliant people have been able to postpone the end of the universe, at least in the short-term, by creating voids called **charged vacuum emboitments** into other universes. Their **advanced research unit** is busy working on more permanent solutions, but for the meantime the universe is held from collapsing by some very clever maths running on the Logopolitans' reproductions of some rather clunky Earth computers.

So, with the fate of the universe hanging in the balance, the Master turns those computers off...

NATURAL RESOURCES

THE UNIVERSE IS FULL OF WONDERS – AND THEY CAN EXPLOITED

ANDROZANI MINOR has a native population of space bats which leave deposits of **Spectrox**. Although raw Spectrox is deadly – it contains a chemical similar to mustard nitrogen – refined Spectrox is a powerful restorative. Taking regular small doses can extend a normal lifespan by more than twice, making Spectrox **the most valuable substance in the universe**. – *The Caves of Androzani* (1984)

The people of **Andozani Major** also melt down the sentient trees of an unnamed planet for battery acid. It's apparently the '**greatest fuel source ever**'. – *The Doctor, the Widow and the Wardrobe* (2012)

BANDRAGINUS 5 is rich in the rare mineral **oolion**, or it was until the planet and its billion inhabitants were destroyed. – *The Pirate Planet* (1978)

CATRIGAN NOVA has whirlpools of **gold**. – *Last of the Time Lords* (2007)

EXXILON is a rich source of parrinium, a mineral found in trace amounts on Earth and elsewhere but that cures and gives immunity to a virulent space disease. – *Death to the Daleks* (1974)

KARN is a planet in the vicinity of Gallifrey. Chemicals in its rocks can be oxidised with fire, resulting in a chemical reaction with rising superheated gases that produces the Elixir of Life. – *The Brain of Morbius* (1976)

SOLOS was exploited by the Earth Empire for 500 years for its **thaesium**, one of the richest fuel sources in the galaxy. – *The Mutants* (1972)

URANUS in our Solar System is the only known source of **taranium**, essential in building a Time Destructor. – *The Daleks' Master Plan* (1965–1966)

METEBELIS 3 is known as the 'blue planet' because its moonlight is blue. It also boasts blue crystals with a powerful psychic effect.
– *The Green Death* (1973) and *Planet of the Spiders* (1974)

MIDNIGHT is a planet made of **diamond**. – *Midnight* (2008)

SARN boasts natural resources of blue-burning **numismaton** gas, an immensely rare catalytic reagent which is one of the greatest energy sources in the universe. – *Planet of Fire* (1984)

ZETA MINOR... see over page.

ORE-SOME POWER

JUST HOW GREAT IS THE GREATEST DISCOVERY IN SCIENTIFIC HISTORY?

THE GREATEST EVER FUEL SOURCE

As seen in *Planet of Evil* (1975)

When the Fourth Doctor and Sarah Jane Smith arrive on the planet **Zeta Minor** – the last planet of the known universe – in the year 37,166, they meet a rather excited Professor Sorenson who claims to have made '**the greatest discovery in scientific history**'. The discovery is an ore, in abundant supply on this planet. Sorenson says that just 6 lbs (a little over 2.5 kg) of it will produce heat equivalent to the output of a dying sun over three years..

How much heat is that? Dr Marek Kukula, Public Astronomer at the Royal Observatory Greenwich, explains:

'We can compare it to our Sun, which generates energy in the form of electromagnetic radiation via a process called **nuclear fusion**. Deep in the Sun's core, under immense temperatures and pressures, the nuclei of hydrogen atoms are fused together to form the nuclei of helium atoms. In the process about 0.7% of the mass of the hydrogen is converted into energy in accordance with Einstein's equation $E=mc^2$, where E is the energy generated (in Joules), m is the mass converted (in kilograms) and c is the speed of light, or 299,792,458 metres per second.

'About **4.26 billion kilograms** of matter is converted in this way by the Sun every second, so the amount of energy generated is **3.846×10^{26} Joules of energy per second**. Over three years – or 94,608,000 seconds – this adds up to a total energy output of 3.639×10^{34} Joules or roughly **36 billion trillion trillion Joules**.

'This energy emerges as electromagnetic radiation, including visible light and ultraviolet radiation, with around 50% of it in the form of infrared radiation – which is what we experience as 'heat'. So the Sun's heat output over three years amounts to around **18 billion trillion trillion Joules of energy**.

'In ***Planet of Evil***, Sorenson's miraculous ore is supposedly made of antimatter. Antimatter is composed of particles that have equal but opposite electric charges to the particles that make up normal matter – instead of positively charged protons it contains negatively charged antiprotons and instead of negatively charged electrons it has positively charged antielectrons (also known as positrons).

'When a particle of antimatter comes into contact with an equivalent particle of normal matter they destroy each other in a process known as "annihilation", and the mass of both particles is entirely converted into a burst of electromagnetic energy in the form of gamma rays – a much more efficient energy-generating process than nuclear fusion which, as we've seen, only converts 0.7% of the available mass into energy.

'If Sorenson intends to use matter-antimatter annihilation as the bases of his scheme then we can work out the energy yield of 2.5 kilograms of antimatter ore, again using Einstein's equation $E=mc^2$. Adding in 2.5 kilograms of normal matter to react with the antimatter, and assuming 100% conversion of mass into energy, yields a total of 4.55×10^{17} or **455 thousand trillion Joules**.

'Although this is a great deal of energy, it is still a lot less than the heat output of the Sun over three years, so it seems Sorenson is wildly exaggerating the potential of his discovery. By comparison, the International Energy Agency estimates that the energy consumption of human civilisation here on Earth was 3.89×10^{20} Joules in 2013 – almost a thousand times greater than Sorenson's yield.

'However, possibly this isn't the whole story. It may be that Sorenson intends to use the energy released by the antimatter to trigger the release of significantly more energy from another source (a bit like the way a hydrogen bomb uses a nuclear fission process to trigger a more powerful nuclear fusion process, greatly enhancing the total energy of the resulting explosion).

'Or perhaps we can call on science fiction to save Sorenson's reputation. In the story, the Zeta Minor ore has some very unusual properties. Unlike antimatter in our world, it doesn't spontaneously explode on contact with normal matter, and the implication is that it has somehow "leaked" out of a different, antimatter-based universe in a weirdly stable, crystalline form. Perhaps the ore retains a link to its universe of origin, allowing Sorenson's conversion process to access significantly greater quantities of antimatter by some mysterious transdimensional connection?

'In science fiction (almost) anything is possible...'

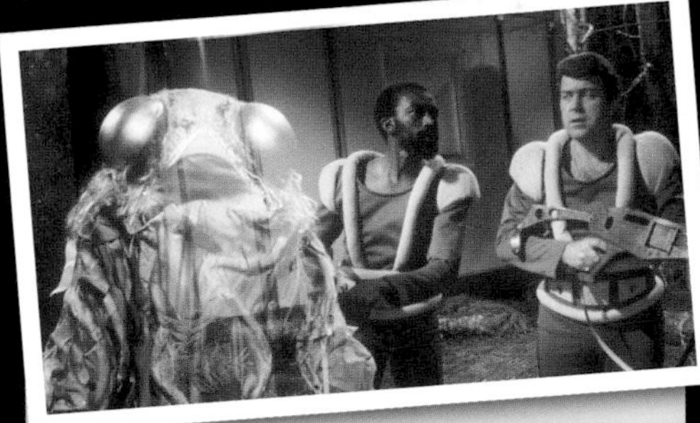

WARNING

Removing the ore from Zeta Minor can be dangerous: it turns Sorenson into what the Doctor calls '**Antiman**' – half-antimatter, half-man. Other antimatter beings attack the Doctor and Sorenson's crew, and don't relent until all the ore is returned to the planet.

For more planetary hazards, see over the page...

HAZARD WARNINGS

THE PRINCIPAL DANGERS ON OTHER WORLDS

The **THIRD MOON OF DELTA MAGNA** is so rich in methane it could provide the protein requirements of one-fifth of the planet. However, the methane is produced by a huge creature called Kroll, who is not best pleased at being disturbed by the mining. – *The Power of Kroll* (1978–1979)

EARTH is home to an extremely aggressive, dangerous species. The Tenth Doctor says he should have warned the **Sycorax** to 'run and hide' from these monsters, called the **human race**. – *The Christmas Invasion* (2005)

GRUNDLE is home to the ravenous **Drashigs** – *Carnival of Monsters*. (1973)

MANUSSA, planet G139901KB in the Scrampus system, is the home of a powerful snake creature, the Mara, that infects its victims' dreams. – *Snakedance* (1983)

KARASS DON SLAVA has candle meadows that are home to **psychic pollen**, a mind parasite that feeds on the darkness inside you and turns it against you. – *Amy's Choice* (2010)

MOGAR, a planet of the Perseus arm of the Milky Way galaxy, is where a human-run experiment in hydroponics produces a species of intelligent plant life intended for use as slave labour. But the **Vervoids** have other ideas, and start killing and composting humans. – *The Trial of a Time Lord* (1986)

MARS has water. In our efforts to find life on other worlds, we're looking for signs of water. But on Mars it's in the form of a monstrous life form called the Flood which takes over people's bodies. Let's leave that stuff alone. – *The Waters of Mars* (2009)

METEBELIS 3 boasts a number of giant and aggressive creatures – we glimpse a flying one and a tentacled one in *The Green Death* (1973) – and its blue crystals mutate Earth **spiders** to monstrous size and intelligence. – *Planet of Spiders* (1974)

SKARO is home planet of the **Daleks**, one of the deadliest species in the universe. It's also the domain of other gruesome mutations produced in its centuries-long war, including carnivorous **clams** and **hand mines**. The local vegetation is also deadly: a person infected by a thorn from a **Varga** plant becomes homicidal before transforming into a Varga plant themselves. – *The Daleks* (1963–1964), *Mission to the Unknown* (1965), *Genesis of the Daleks* (1975), *The Magician's Apprentice* (2015)

THOROS BETA is home to the cruel and tyrannical **Mentors** such as Sil, who delights in inflicting pain and conducting experiments on living subjects. – *The Trial of a Time Lord*

WORLDS' RECORDS

THESE PLANETS ARE ALL SOMETHING SPECIAL

THE LAST PLANET IN THE UNIVERSE

As seen in *Listen* (2014)

The Twelfth Doctor takes Clara Oswald to what he says is the last planet in the universe, which is where time-travel pioneer Colonel Orson Pink ends up for six months. (The Twelfth Doctor and Clara meet Ashildr / Me at the very end of time in ***Hell Bent*** (2015), but that's in a special reality bubble, so isn't the same thing as a planet on its own.)

THE ODDEST-NAMED PLANET

As seen in *The Chase* (1965)

The TARDIS lands in the Segaro desert of the planet **Aridius**. That seems a good name for such an arid world, but we soon learn that the desert was once a vast ocean and the native Aridians lived in a city beneath the water. Perhaps it was called something else back then.

THE OLDEST PLANET IN THE UNIVERSE

As seen in *The Big Bang* (2010)

Planet One is, says the Eleventh Doctor when he takes Amy Pond there, the oldest planet in the universe. It has lush vegetation and cliffs of diamond.

Tivoli is the **most invaded planet in the galaxy**. – *The God Complex* (2011)

THE COLDEST PLACE IN THE GALAXY

As seen in the animated story *The Infinite Quest* (2007)

The Tenth Doctor and Martha Jones are searching time and space for data chips that, together, will lead them to the ancient starship ***Infinite***, which can grant a heart's desire. One data chip is hidden on the icy prison planet **Volag-Noc**, which holds records on the Doctor – for 3,005 convictions and 6,000 more offences to be taken into consideration. He is sentenced to two billion years in prison.

THE MOST VALUABLE PLANET IN THE UNIVERSE

As seen in *The Pirate Planet* (1978)

The planet **Calufrax** is really one of the six pieces of the Key to Time, a cube that maintains the equilibrium of time itself. – see p. 163

THE FIRST OF THE LEISURE PLANETS

As seen in *The Leisure Hive* (1980)

After a hideous war with the Foamasi wiped out most of the planet **Argolis**, the surviving Argolins built a recreation centre with cells of different environments designed to produce physical, psychic and intellectual regeneration.

THE EMPTIEST PLANET

As seen in *The Pirate Planet* (1978)

The planet **Zanak** is hollow.
– see pp. 163.

We never see the Ninth Doctor on an alien world.

UNSEEN WORLDS OF WONDER

The people making ***Doctor Who*** often show us the strangest, most extraordinary worlds, but also have the Doctor mention planets that are even more peculiar. It's an inexpensive way of adding richness and colour to the universe of the series.

While working on ***Survival***, the final story in the 1989 series of ***Doctor Who***, the production team discovered that there was unlikely to be a 1990 series – or any more ***Doctor Who*** for the foreseeable future. Script editor Andrew Cartmel added a closing speech by the Seventh Doctor, suggesting that he and his companion Ace would be off to the most amazing places, even if we couldn't see them…

'There are worlds out there where the sky is burning, where the sea's asleep and the rivers dream. People made of smoke and cities made of song. Somewhere there's danger, somewhere there's injustice, and somewhere else the tea's getting cold. Come on, Ace, we've got work to do.'

It's surely **the most defiant mention of unseen worlds in the series**: the BBC weren't going to make any more of the Doctor's adventures, but he was jolly well going to have them anyway.

CHAPTER THREE
DESTRUCTION

'YOU TWO ARE ESPECIALLY PRIVILEGED. YOU ARE ABOUT TO DIE IN THE BIGGEST EXPLOSION EVER WITNESSED IN THIS SOLAR SYSTEM. IT WILL BE A MAGNIFICENT SPECTACLE. UNHAPPILY, YOU WILL BE UNABLE TO APPRECIATE IT.'

CYBER LEADER, *REVENGE OF THE CYBERMEN* (1975)

FIRST BLOOD 066
THE PLANET KILLERS 068
STAR WARS 070
BIG BANGS! 074
BEST EFFECTS 076
TOTAL DESTRUCTION 078
THE MOST UNEXPECTED WEAPONS 080
SOLDIER, SOLDIER 082
FIIIIIIIGHT! 084
WAR! 086
YOU AND WHO'S ARMY? 088
THE WAR DOCTOR 090
TIME LORD WEAPONS 092
KILL YOUR SPEED 094
CENSORED VIOLENCE 096
GET HER OUT OF THERE! 098
WE WILL SURVIVE 100

VWORP
VWORP
POLICE PUBLIC CALL BOX
FREE
PUBLIC
PULL TO OPEN

FIRST BLOOD

A BRIEF HISTORY OF KILLINGS IN DOCTOR WHO

Eileen Way also played Old Woman in the film ***Daleks Invasion Earth 2150AD*** (1966), and was Karela in ***The Creature from the Pit*** (1979). In both, her characters survive.

THE FIRST PERSON TO DIE IN *DOCTOR WHO*

As seen in *An Unearthly Child* (1963)

In the very first ***Doctor Who*** story, schoolteachers Barbara Wright and Ian Chesterton follow their strange pupil, Susan Foreman, back to her home. As a result, they stumble into what looks like a police box but is really a vast, futuristic ship for travelling through space and time, in which Susan lives with her grandfather. Horrified that their secret has been discovered, the First Doctor kidnaps the teachers, operating the controls of what he calls the TARDIS – but without setting a destination…

In the second episode of the series, they find that the TARDIS has landed them in **prehistoric times**, where they are soon captured by a tribe of primitive humans who have lost the secret of making fire. Desperately cold and hungry, these people threaten the Doctor and his friends – if they can't make fire, they'll be killed. So, in just the second episode of ***Doctor Who***, we're facing matters of **life and death**. The Doctor and his friends are even imprisoned in a cave of skulls.

Having failed to reason with the primitive, surly tribe, the Doctor and his friends manage to escape. But as they race through a forest to get back to the TARDIS, Barbara trips over something – a boar that's been recently killed by a larger animal. Barbara's cry of horror is heard by **Za**, one of the tribe who has

discovered their escape. But as he charges after them, whatever killed the boar attacks him – we don't see the large creature.

The Doctor wants to use this distraction to escape back to the TARDIS, but Barbara is determined to help the badly wounded Za. As she says, whatever he and his people have done to them, they can't just let him die. Ian and then Susan join her – the Doctor thinks they're out of their minds. By showing kindness, Barbara and the others make a connection with Za and his friend **Hur** – but, just as the Doctor feared, they are also recaptured. So there's a conflict running through the story: how our heroes respond to the threat of death, even to their adversaries.

Meanwhile, another member of the tribe, **Kal**, discovers how the Doctor and his friends escaped in the first place – they were helped by the wily **Old Mother**. She is then found murdered. Old Mother – played by **Eileen Way** – is the first person killed in the series.

THE FIRST PERSON WE SEE DIE IN *DOCTOR WHO*

As seen in *An Unearthly Child*

Now the Doctor and his friends have a problem: their lone ally among these people is Za, because they helped him when he was wounded. But Kal says Za murdered Old Mother – and the tribe believes him. The Doctor cleverly works out who really killed Old Mother – it was Kal – and is able to explain his reasoning so that these primitive people understand. Kal is driven out of the tribe.

In the fourth ever episode of ***Doctor Who***, Kal seeks revenge on the Doctor and his friends, who are again held prisoner in the cave of skulls and guarded by an unnamed man. Kal kills the guard – the first person we see die in ***Doctor Who***. We don't know the name of the actor who played the non-speaking guard, but Kal – the first person to kill someone in ***Doctor Who*** – is played by **Jeremy Young**.

THE FIRST PERSON KILLED BY THE DOCTOR

As seen in *The Daleks* (1963–1964)

In *An Unearthly Child*, when Za is wounded, it looks for a moment as if the Doctor considers killing him with a rock – though he denies it when challenged. Later, when he reveals that Kal killed Old Mother, he must surely expect repercussions but not necessarily that Za will kill Kal.

In the next story, the TARDIS lands on a planet we'll soon learn is Skaro, home of the Daleks. It's a strange, desolate world – but the Doctor spies an advanced-looking city. He's keen to investigate, but then Susan is scared by something moving nearby, and Ian and Barbara are keen to leave. However, the Doctor pretends there's a problem with the '**fluid link**' – a vital component of the TARDIS – so they must stay and explore.

In the city, the Daleks capture the Doctor and take the fluid link from him, stranding him and his companions on Skaro. To get it back, he encourages the peaceful people called **Thals** to fight the Daleks. The Thals are reluctant: the desolate state of the planet is the result of their last war with the Daleks, more than 500 years previously. But the Doctor is still keen to convince them.

'Why should they help us?' asks Ian. 'Some of them are bound to get killed.'

That's the point: the Doctor and his friends know what this will lead to. Despite Ian's misgivings, the Thals are persuaded that their own survival depends on fighting the Daleks. Ian, Barbara and a group of Thals head off to find a back way into the Dalek city. A young Thal called **Elyon** suggests it would be quicker if they crossed a lake, but is told it's too dangerous – the lake is full of mutations. Elyon goes to fill the water bags anyway – and ***something*** in the water grabs him.

Jeremy Young returned to ***Doctor Who*** to play Gordon Lowery in ***Mission to the Unknown*** (1965). Infected by a Varga plant, he tries to kill his friend Marc Cory – who kills him first.

More Thals die in the journey to the city and in the battle with the Daleks when they get there. At the end of the story, it seems all the Daleks have been killed, too. Now, the Doctor doesn't kill Elyon directly and it's Ian who ultimately convinces the Thals to act against the Daleks. Without the intervention of the Doctor and his friends, the Thals would all have been killed in a Dalek ambush. And if the Thals didn't stand up against the Daleks, the Daleks seem to have been ready to wipe them all out. But the chain of events is set in motion by the Doctor's selfish act of deceit, pretending there's a fault with the fluid link. So Elyon – played by **Gerald Curtis** – is the first person to die as the result of the Doctor's actions.

THE PLANET KILLERS

HOW MANY PEOPLE DOES IT TAKE TO DESTROY A WHOLE WORLD?

THE PLANET DESTROYED BY THE LEAST NUMBER OF ITS OWN PEOPLE

As seen in *The Hand of Fear* (1976)

Kastria was a cold, inhospitable planet ravaged by solar winds. That was until **Eldrad** built the spatial barriers to keep them out. It seems that the harsh space weather also prevented life from flourishing, because Eldrad also devised a crystalline silicone form for the Kastrians' physical needs. Eldrad built machines to replenish the planet's surface and the atmosphere, bringing Kastria to life.

But the young and strong Eldrad had further ambitions, wanting to usurp the weak and old Kastrian leader, **Rokon**, and then lead Kastrians to become masters of the galaxy. When Rokon ordered the obliteration of Eldrad, Eldrad destroyed the spatial barriers and the winds came again to dehydrate the planet.

Eldrad's **hand** survived obliteration and, discovered by the Fourth Doctor and Sarah Jane Smith on Earth 150 million years later, uses nuclear radiation to regenerate a whole body – in female form, modelled on Sarah. Taken back to Kastria by TARDIS, Eldrad takes male form, and then reveals his plan to again lead Kastrians in the conquest of other worlds.

But the long-dead Rokon has left a message for Eldrad: without the spatial barriers and facing a miserable subterranean existence, the Kastrians killed themselves.

Eldrad decides that in that case he'll rule Earth – but in a struggle with the Doctor he falls to his death. So the Kastrians are gone and the planet is once more cold and inhospitable, all down to one individual.

THE MOST PLANETS DESTROYED BY AN INDIVIDUAL

As seen in *Logopolis* (1981)

The mathematicians on the planet **Logopolis** are holding back the forces of **entropy** from ravaging the universe – at least they are until the Master gets in the way.

The scale of the damage that follows is extraordinary. Inside the TARDIS and beyond space and time, the Doctor's companions Adric and Nyssa can look out on the whole universe. As they watch in horror, a dark cloud obscures about a third of the screen.

Adric checks the systems and confirms that Earth and its galaxy have a few hours left before the shadow passes over them. But Nyssa is not so lucky. Her home planet **Traken** and its star **Metulla Orionsis** – and all the other worlds of the Traken Union – have already been lost. Logopolis, too, is destroyed.

Now, almost all of the universe is destroyed in *The Pandorica Opens* (2010) – a greater act of destruction – but the Eleventh Doctor and Amy Pond are able to undo the damage in the next episode. In ***Logopolis***, approximately one-third of the universe is lost forever, and all the fault of the Master.

THE PLANET EATERS

As seen in *Planet of the Dead* (2009)

The Tenth Doctor rides a number 200 bus through a wormhole from London to the planet **San Helios**. It's a barren, desert world – but the Doctor and **Lady Christina de Souza** learn that a year before there was a city, oceans, mountains, wildlife and 100 billion people there.

In less than a year, San Helios has been utterly devoured by the **Swarm** of metallic, stingray-like creatures. There are billions of them, flying in formation around the planet. The speed, numbers and size are the subject, rupture time and space to create a wormhole to the next planet they can feed on. Which in this case is Earth…

The fifth ever episode of ***Doctor Who*** is called ***The Dead Planet***, but it becomes clear at the end of the episode that it's not a lifeless world: **Skaro** is home to the Daleks, the Thals and a number of mutated creatures.

STAR WARS

STAGGERING DESTRUCTION ON THE STELLAR SCALE

The Time War between the Daleks and the Time Lords destroyed the home worlds of the Nestene Consciousness and the Zygons, and reduced the Gelth to gaseous forms.

THE MOST DESTRUCTIVE WEAPONS TEST

As seen in *Colony in Space* (1971)

Jo Grant isn't best pleased to be spirited away in the TARDIS for her first trip to another planet. The Third Doctor tries to impress her with the prospect of an alien world, but **Uxarieus** in the year **2472** is a bleak place, with a few scant flowers growing in the pale mud. It also looks pretty cold.

While the planet's human colonists – who've escaped the over-polluted Earth – and the **Interplanetary Mining Corporation** argue about their respective rights to exploit the planet's resources, the Doctor discovers that the indigenous, apparently primitive Uxariens were once a very advanced civilisation.

When an **Adjudicator** arrives to settle the dispute between the colonists and miners, the Doctor and Jo are horrified to see it is really the Master. In fact, he's on Uxarieus to look for the '**Doomsday Weapon**', which he learnt about in a report he stole from the Time Lords.

The Master says that just testing the weapon created what we now call the **Crab Nebula** – the exploded remains of a star. We're not told whether the star had planets or, if so, whether they were populated, but it's still an enormous act of destruction.

The Doctor and the Master explore underground caverns, where they find the remains of a city – and the Doomsday Weapon, which is still operational. The Master is keen to find and use it to dominate the galaxy, making Uxarieus the centre of the greatest empire ever known. But confronted by a wise and ancient Uxarien called the **Guardian**, the Doctor asks if the weapon ever brought any good to the planet.

'Once the weapon was built,' replies the Guardian sadly, 'our race began to decay. The radiation from the weapon's power source poisoned the soil of our planet.' The Guardian agrees to destroy the weapon – and the city – rather than let it be used again.

His plans thwarted, the Master escapes. But without the weapon's poisonous radiation, says the Doctor, the planet's soil will recover so the human colony can flourish. The miners agree to help the colonists.

THE DOCTOR'S GREATEST ACT OF DESTRUCTION

As seen in *Remembrance of the Daleks* (1988)

The Seventh Doctor tricks **Davros**, now the emperor of the Daleks, into stealing and using a special Time Lord device. This remote stellar manipulator, known as the '**Hand of Omega**', can be used to customise stars, providing the enormous levels of power needed for the Time Lords' mastery of time travel.

Davros sends the Hand of Omega to impact the with the star around which orbits the Dalek home world, **Skaro** – and, from what we see on screen, at least another five planets. (In *The Daleks* (1963–1964), we're told Skaro is the 12th planet in its system). But the Hand of Omega doesn't give Davros power over the star – instead it destroys it. Skaro and presumably the other planets in the system are vaporised. The Hand of Omega then returns to the Dalek spaceship from which Davros launched it and destroys that, too.

THE EXPLODING STAR

On **4 July 1054**, Chinese astronomers recorded a new star in the sky – one so bright it could be seen during the day. It could still be seen with the naked eye almost two years later. But what was it and why did it then fade away?

A bit more than 700 years later, the French astronomer **Charles Messier**, observing the night sky through a telescope, spotted an object he thought was a comet. He thought it was significant, listing it as '**M1**' in his catalogue of 110 comet-like astronomical objects – but he was wrong; it was something else.

Since even through a telescope M1 looked indistinct and blurry, it and other objects like it became known as '**nebulae**' – meaning 'clouds'. We now know nebulae are vast clouds of gas and dust. In 1844, the English astronomer **William Parsons**, 3rd Earl of Rosse, made a drawing of this particular example, which he thought looked like a crab. It's been known as the **Crab Nebula** ever since.

Then in 1913, American astronomer **Vesto Slipher** compared photographs of the Crab Nebula taken many years apart and spotted that it had grown. In 1928, another American astronomer, **Edwin Hubble**, worked out that this was the same object seen in 1054 – and what the Chinese astronomers had observed was a supernova, the explosion of a whole star. It's the first time a supernova has been linked to a historical observation.

BIG BANGS!

HE'S LIT THE BLUE TOUCHPAPER AND FOUND THERE'S NOWHERE TO RETIRE TO...

In the radio story *Slipback* (1985), the Sixth Doctor learns that the Big Bang was caused (or *also* caused) by the explosion of a time-travelling spaceship, the *Vipod Mor*.

THE BIGGEST EXPLOSION OF ALL TIME!

As seen in *Terminus (1983)*.

According to the **Fifth Doctor**, the biggest explosion of all time is **"Event One"**, otherwise known as the **Big Bang**, when the universe was created.

Today's scientists on Earth say that the Big Bang wasn't really an explosion as such – more a sudden increase in **energy density** followed by the universe **expanding** very quickly. But let's assume the Doctor knows more about this stuff than our scientists.

What the Doctor didn't know until he visited the **time-travelling space station Terminus** was *why* the Big Bang exploded. He discovers that Terminus had been carrying **unstable fuel**, which the pilot decided to **jettison** while in flight though time. Most of that fuel was dumped into a **void**, where it caused a **chain reaction** and exploded, creating the whole universe.

Terminus was propelled by the blast billions of years into the future, where the Doctor discovered it at the **exact centre** of the known universe. (Today's scientists on Earth don't think the universe actually has a centre, but again let's assume the Doctor knows best here.)

However, the Doctor discovered that not all the unstable fuel had been jettisoned, and the station's computers were preparing to dump the rest of it. The Doctor and a big dog-like creature, the Garm, were able to stop that happening before it *destroyed* the universe in a second colossal explosion.

THE BIGGEST FIRE ON EARTH!

As seen in *The Poison Sky* (2008). The Tenth Doctor stopped the Sontarans converting our atmosphere so that it was deadly to humans by burning off the poisonous gas. Flames swept across the whole of the sky!

***And as seen in In the Forest of the Night* (2014).** A massive flare of high-energy radiation ejected from the Sun threatened all life on Earth, but the planet's trees created a protective shield of oxygen that acted like a highly inflammable airbag.

LONDON'S BURNING!

On 23 April 1988, fire crews rushed to the scene of an explosion near Waterloo East Station in central London – and were amazed to discover warring factions of Daleks! The blast had been a special effect set off during recording of *Remembrance of the Daleks*.

YOU BLEW IT!

On 26 June 2010, the Kovarian Chapter of the Church of the Papal Mainframe blew up the TARDIS to stop the Eleventh Doctor doing what they had foreseen: restarting the Time War and putting the universe at risk. Unfortunately, destroying the TARDIS almost destroyed the universe anyway. Oops. – see *The Pandorica Opens* and *The Big Bang* (both 2010) and *The Time of the Doctor* (2013)

THE FIRST EXPLOSION SEEN IN *DOCTOR WHO*

As seen in *The Rescue* – episode seven of *The Daleks* (1964)

The First Doctor works the controls of the TARDIS as it departs from Dalek planet Skaro. Suddenly, there's a crash, a flash of light and the Doctor and his friends are thrown to the floor! We later learn – after two episodes of speculation – that this explosion was caused by a broken spring.

THE MOST EXPLOSIVE SEQUENCE

As seen in *The Day of the Doctor* (2013)

SFX supervisor Danny Hargreaves has worked on ***Doctor Who*** since ***Rose*** (2005), and is justly proud of the explosive work on the 50th anniversary special, ***The Day of the Doctor***.

'There's that sequence early on, the fall of Gallifrey, where we had all those explosions and Daleks blowing up. And running in between them, we had children. That was super, super hard to achieve, what with the [story being made in] 3D. We had ash, we had explosions, we had fire, we had smoke, we had Daleks, we had all sorts. And we only had two nights to do it. I'm immensely proud to get that sequence. And [director] Nick Hurran bought me a bottle of Champagne afterwards, he was so happy with the way it looked.'

It's no surprise that the episode won Best Special Effects at the 2014 British Academy Television Awards, the award shared between Real SFX (Danny's company), Milk VFX and the Model Unit.

BEST EFFECTS

WE ASKED THESE EXPERTS TO NOMINATE THE BEST SPECIAL EFFECTS EVER SEEN IN *DOCTOR WHO*

Note: we asked our judges not to nominate their own work.

MIKE TUCKER

Visual effects designer who has worked on *Doctor Who* – especially in miniatures and model work – since *The Trial of a Time Lord* (1986)

'An almost impossible task. My personal choice would be either **Richard Conway's shot of the helicopter approaching the Arctic base** in part one of *The Seeds of Doom* (1976) because it's ambitious, technically excellent and essential for the scene setting of that story, or the work done by **Colin Mapson and Dave Chapman on the bubble traps** for *Time and the Rani* (1987) because it was a perfect indicator of the way that effects would evolve during the following decade, marrying practical and digital effects. Yes, I worked on that one but Colin was the supervisor.'

LUKE SPILLANE

Presenter of *Doctor Who – The Fan Show*

TARDIS motorway chase in *The Runaway Bride* (2006)

'I love this effect because you really believe it, the Tenth Doctor interacting with Donna Noble from within the TARDIS, her jumping from a moving taxi into the ship. Again, it's something which you only really expect to see in big films.'

The Time War in *The Day of the Doctor* (2013)

'*Doctor Who* does an action film sequence. We flick between computer-generated flying Daleks blowing up Arcadia and the physical miniatures of the TARDIS smashing through that wall. It really puts *Doctor Who* visually on par with action films of its times.'

Entering the TARDIS in *Into The Dalek* (2014)

'A small effect, but Clara enters a school cupboard to the find the Doctor, then follows him straight into the TARDIS – all in one shot. It's a small effect but visionary director **Ben Wheatley** went to the extent of having the cupboard set built round the TARDIS doors.'

CHRISTEL DEE

Presenter of *Doctor Who – The Fan Show*

Spaceship crashing into Big Ben in *Aliens of London* (2005)

'*Doctor Who* is often very rooted in the everyday and the most chilling and exciting of stories for me bring the alien threat to your doorstep. Strong, realistic visuals are needed to make this believable and this is an excellent example, achieved using a model. CGI can date badly and I don't think it would be possible to achieve such a level of detail using CGI without huge amounts of time and money. This episode is over 10 years old and still looks fantastic today. Model work truly stands the test of time.'

PAUL FRANKLIN

Visual effects supervisor at Double Negative, Paul won Academy awards for his work on *Inception* (2010) and *Interstellar* (2014) – but has not worked on *Doctor Who*

'Watching old *Doctor Who* again with my kids, I'm amazed by what they achieved. I mean, there's the **title sequence**. [Designer] **Bernard Lodge** told me all about creating the titles for Tom Baker [used 1974–1980], reverse-engineering the slit-scan photography process that Douglas Trumbull created for the film *2001*. He'd had no information about how it had originally been done, and no digital motion control systems or any of the things you'd need to be create that today. It was a real feat of engineering and creativity – and those titles are beautiful.

'I love the **Kaled dome in the fog and murk** in *Genesis of the Daleks*, and that amazing **alien jungle** in *Planet of Evil* (both 1975). There's the weird juxtapositions that *Doctor Who* is so good at – the **spaceship over the stone circle** in *The Stones of Blood* (1978) or the **sailing ships racing through space** in *Enlightenment* (1983). But there's simple stuff, too – the way they used coloured filters to sell the **volcanic disaster** in *Inferno* (1970), or the original **Dalek death-ray effect** where the picture turns to negative. That's so cool and terrifying. And then there's the make-up: the **Ogrons** look fantastic with sideburns growing out of their mouths. There's a lot of good stuff.

'The series today doesn't have the budget we have on movies but the prosthetic work is easily the equal of any American TV shows – which have a lot more money spent on them. Creatures like the **Ood** and the **redesigned Silurians** look fantastic. They don't have our budgets for visual effects but they make good choices – just enough shots of **Gallifrey** or the **traffic jam** in *Gridlock* (2007) to convey the scale and wonder.

'Some big movies could learn from *Doctor Who* about using effects more effectively. On *Interstellar*, we used bits of the *Doctor Who* title sequence – Bernard Lodge's one for Tom Baker, and the Mill's one for David Tennant – as a placeholder. It gave the right feel – and it looked really good – as we edited the film's key scenes. We then had to replace that, spending millions of dollars to create our own thing. But inspired by *Doctor Who*.'

TOTAL DESTRUCTION

YOU CAN CHECK THEM ON OUT, THEY'RE THE WEAPONS OF CHOICE

THE MOST DANGEROUS WEAPON IN THE UNIVERSE

As seen in *The Day of the Doctor* (2013)

A weapon of ultimate mass destruction, the **Moment** was apparently the final work of the ancients on the Time Lord planet Gallifrey. Also known as the **Galaxy Eater**, the Moment is so powerful that its operating system has become **sentient** – and developed a conscience.

But how can you use such a weapon, and cause such devastation as it unleashes, when it stands in judgement over you? Did it judge the ancients who created it? Is that why it was their last creation?

The **War Doctor** tries to use the Moment to end the **Time War** between the Time Lords and the Daleks – saving the rest of time by destroying both races and himself.

Appearing to him as a figure from his future – the Bad Wolf, in the form of Rose Tyler – the Moment shows him the consequence of ending the war in such a way. She lets him meet his future selves, the **Tenth Doctor** and the **Eleventh Doctor**, both haunted by what he's about to do.

Despite their horror, these two Doctors agree it had to be done – and decide to stand by the War Doctor's side as he activates the Moment so he doesn't have to do it alone. They're all set to destroy billions of lives.

At the last minute, **Clara Oswald** intervenes, convincing the Doctors to find another way to end the Time War, one that will not destroy the Time Lords. It is not known what happens to the Moment after this. Is it still in the Doctor's possession?

IS IT USED? NO

IS IT USED? NO

THE MOST DANGEROUS WEAPON ON EARTH

As seen in *Journey's End* (2008)

When the Daleks transport the Earth through space to become part of Davros's Reality Bomb, Earth's forces retaliate. The Doctor's friend **Martha Jones** threatens to activate the **Osterhagen Key**.

As she explains, a chain of **25 nuclear warheads** has been placed at strategic points under the Earth's crust. If Martha uses the key, these warheads will detonate and the Earth will be ripped apart.

But Davros only laughs at this threat. And he delights in pointing out what are really the most dangerous creations on Earth – not the Osterhagen Key and the nuclear warheads, but the **Doctor's friends**. Ordinary people the Doctor has fashioned into weapons.

THE MOST POWERFUL WEAPON IN TIME

IS IT USED?
YES

As seen in *The Daleks' Master Plan* (1965–1966)
The **Time Destructor** is, says the **First Doctor**, one of the most evil weapons ever devised. It seems to have a relatively short range, but those caught within its power suffer appalling effects – as we see in the harrowing conclusion to an epic *Doctor Who* story that lasted a whole 12 weeks.

Constructed by the Daleks and their alien allies, the Time Destructor is not an easy weapon to come by. It works by burning **taranium**, apparently the rarest mineral in the universe. To work at all, the Time Destructor needs a full measure of it, which takes 50 years to mine.

Once the taranium is supplied and the Time Destructor activated, the weapon makes time itself rush forward. The effects are hardly noticeable at first, but soon it's like a wind whips up – and anyone nearby is aged to death. The Doctor's friend **Sara Kingdom** is one unfortunate victim, and the Doctor only barely survives.

That's because the Time Destructor is thrown into reverse. This makes time race backwards. The Doctor escapes, but Daleks are split apart, the creatures inside them turning to dust as millions of years of evolutionary progress is turned round. The destructor continues its merciless work until the taranium is all burnt up.

THE BIGGEST WEAPON IN THE UNIVERSE

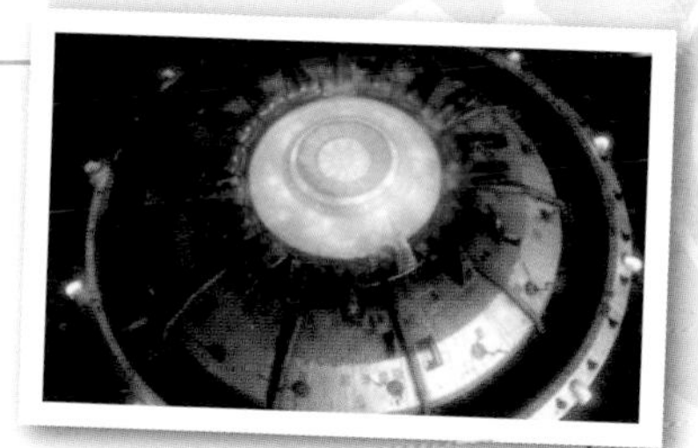

As seen in *Journey's End*
The **Reality Bomb** is a huge and appalling weapon constructed by **Davros**, creator of the Daleks.

As Davros explains, every atom in existence is bound by an **electrical field**, which the reality bomb simply **cancels out** so that all structures collapse. It will kill people, stars – all matter in the universe, including every dimension and parallel. Nowhere will escape.

The size of the Reality Bomb machine is boggling. It's housed on a Dalek spacecraft called the **Crucible**, but Davros needs a vast transmitter to blast the signal out across space. To do this, he steals **27 planets** – including the Earth – as well as the lost moon of Poosh, and transports them to the **Medusa Cascade**, the centre of a rift in time and space. Together, the planets (and moon) naturally realign themselves into the optimum pattern, in perfect balance, like the pieces of an engine.

That's an extremely big operation, and likely to be noticed by people who might want to stop Davros. So he cunningly hides all the planets in a pocket of time **one second in the future**. It's the biggest weapon in the universe – and impossible to see.

IS IT USED?
It is tested, killing a group of human prisoners.

THE MOST UNEXPECTED WEAPONS

THERE ARE GUNS, BOMBS AND INGENIOUS TECHNOLOGICAL DEVICES, BUT OTHER THINGS CAN BE JUST AS USEFUL FOR BATTLING MONSTERS

The Master's tissue compression eliminator reduces the people it kills to the size of dolls – deadly but also tidy.

KNOWING STUFF

'The Doctor is not weaponless. He has the greatest weapon of all: knowledge.' – Camilla, ***State of Decay*** (1980)

SHOUTING

'A **heroic war cry** to apparently peaceful ends is one of the greatest weapons a politician has.' – Mavic Chen, ***The Daleks' Master Plan*** (1965).

LOOKING STUFF UP

'You want weapons? We're in a library. Books! Best weapons in the world. This room's the greatest arsenal we could have.' – The Tenth Doctor, ***Tooth and Claw*** (2006)

SACRIFICE AND ACTING AND SMELL

In several ***Doctor Who*** stories, the ultimate weapon against an otherwise implacable monster is some brave person prepared to sacrifice themselves.

In ***The Family of Blood*** (2007), the titular family bombard the village of Farringham on Earth and say they won't stop until a human schoolteacher, **John Smith**, hands over a pocket watch.

The pocket watch contains everything the Doctor is, stored when the Tenth Doctor used a Chameleon Arch to rewrite his biology and become human. The Doctor is now John Smith. But what can one, ordinary human do against the powerful, alien family? It's not like he has any weapons…

So John walks, unarmed, into the family's spaceship, so scared he stumbles into the controls. But in fact, he's acting – he's not John Smith at all. Realising what was at stake, John sacrificed himself to become the Doctor once more.

The Doctor **pretends** to still be John and, when he stumbles into the controls of the spaceship, without the family seeing he presses buttons that cause energy feedback all the way through the retrostabilisers, feeding back into the primary heat converters. It destroys the ship. The family can't understand how they didn't sniff out that it was the Doctor all along. He explains that they were 'fooled by a simple olfactory misdirection, [a] little bit like **ventriloquism of the nose**.'

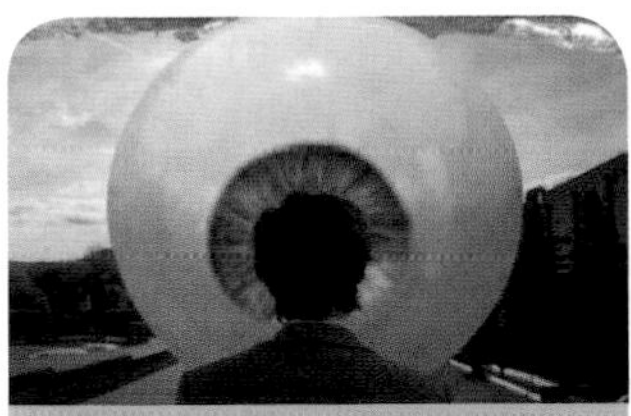

TRACK RECORD

'Is this world protected? Because you're not the first lot to come here. Oh, there have been so many. And what you've got to ask is, what happened to them? Hello. I'm the Doctor. Basically, run.' – The Eleventh Doctor, ***The Eleventh Hour*** (2010)

SCREAMING

The Second Doctor faces monstrous seaweed creatures in ***Fury from the Deep*** (1968), and it seems nothing can stop the onslaught, until his companion **Victoria Waterfield** screams. 'Noise!' proclaims the Doctor. 'Sound vibrations … It's [Victoria's] scream, her particular pattern of sound that does the trick.'

Fury from the Deep – a story about the practical power of sound – is also the story that features the Doctor's **sonic screwdriver** for the first time.

SOLDIER, SOLDIER

THE DOCTOR IS OFTEN WARY OF SOLDIERS – YET THEY'RE AMONG HIS BEST FRIENDS

The Doctor's finest bit of archery is in ***Robot of Sherwood*** (2014) when he, Clara Oswald and Robin Hood together loose an arrow that propels a spaceship out of Earth's atmosphere.

THE BEST ARCHER THERE'S EVEN BEEN

As seen in *The Woman Who Lived* (2015)

On 25 October 1315, England's young **King Henry V**, leading some 1,500 men-at-arms and 7,000 archers, battled with a much larger French army – estimates of its size vary between 15,000 and 50,000 soldiers. This was just the latest skirmish between the English and French in a much longer conflict that would come to be called the Hundred Years War.

The armies met not far from Calais in northern France, and the battle was named after a nearby castle, Azincourt – or **Agincourt**. Despite being so heavily outnumbered, it's generally thought that the range of the English longbows and the huge volume of arrows loosed gave the decisive advantage. The English victory that day entered into national myth.

The battle is the centrepiece of **Shakespeare**'s play, *Henry V* (c.1599–1600). And that play was made into a famous film in 1944, at the request – if indirectly – of the British Government, who sought to 'enhance the British cause' during the Second World War. The film premiered shortly before the start of the D-Day landings – also in northern France, so there were explicit parallels drawn between the modern conflict and this 630 year-old, mythic victory. So it's a day in history that survives into the present.

The Fourth Doctor once says that his warrior friend Leela would 'have loved Agincourt', but we can't be sure the Doctor witnessed or took part in events there. However, he knows someone who did.

'No one will ever know that a mere woman helped win the Hundred Years War,' the immortal **Ashildr** tells the Twelfth Doctor in *The Woman Who Lived*. She says that Agincourt was her 'first stint' at disguising herself as a man, but more importantly she tells us who was the greatest of the bowmen who provided that extraordinary victory.

She was.

'Ten thousand hours is all it takes to master any skill,' she explains – and being immortal, she could spare the time. 'Over 100,000 hours and you're the **best there's ever been**. I don't need to be indestructible, I'm superb. You should have seen me. I could shoot six arrows a minute. I got so close to the enemy, I penetrated armour.'

THE GREATEST SOLDIER ON EARTH

On 17 February 1968, in Episode 3 of ***The Web of Fear***, viewers were introduced to a character who would play a major role in ***Doctor Who***. But for much of that story we're unsure whether to trust the army's **Colonel Lethbridge-Stewart** – played by Nicholas Courtney – who might be under the thrall of the **Great Intelligence**. That might explain why, in the next episode, he's the only one of a squad of soldiers to survive an encounter with the **Yeti**.

In fact, his survival is down to Lethbridge-Stewart being an especially capable soldier. By the end of the story, we know we can trust him, and in his next appearance – ***The Invasion*** (1968) – he's been promoted to Brigadier and become head of **UNIT**, a group that investigates alien happenings on Earth. In *Spearhead from Space* (1970), the Third Doctor ends up working for him as **scientific adviser**.

The Brigadier is a brave man of action, often leading his men from the front. In a thrilling shootout in *The Ambassadors of Death* (1970), he stands in the middle of the action and coolly shoots three villains.

But what also makes him a great leader – and such a popular character – is the **wry humour** with which he meets so many strange phenomena.

When he finally steps inside the TARDIS in *The Three Doctors* (1972–1973), his response his typically unflappable: 'So this is what you've been doing with UNIT funds and equipment all this time. How's it done? Some sort of **optical illusion**?'

Even once retired from UNIT, Alistair Gordon Lethbridge-Stewart is a good man in a fight: he knocks out the Master with a well-aimed punch in *The Five Doctors* (1983) and in his final appearance in *Doctor Who* – *Battlefield* (1989) – he takes on a demon called the **Destroyer** with just a loaded pistol.

'Pitiful,' says the Destroyer on seeing him. 'Can this world do no better than you as their champion?'

'Probably,' says the Brig, with his usual modesty. 'I just do the best I can.'

He fires the pistol – containing silver bullets – and so saves the world.

The last appearance of Lethbridge-Stewart is in *The Sarah Janes Adventures: Enemy of the Bane*. '**Sir Alistair**', remains UNIT's **special envoy**.

We learn of his death in *The Wedding of River Song* (2011), but his daughter – **Kate Stewart** – has been in charge of UNIT since *The Power of Three* (2012).

FIIIIIIIGHT!

FOR A MAN WHO ABHORS VIOLENCE, THE DOCTOR'S PRETTY GOOD IN A SCRAP

THE MOST MENTAL FIGHT

As seen in *The Three Doctors* (1972–1973)

In *The Brain of Morbius* (1976), the Fourth Doctor challenges the renegade Time Lord **Morbius** to a 'mind-bending contest', using a device that allows them to pit their brain power against one another. This Time Lord form of wrestling is usually a game but can end in death lock. Just a short contest almost kills the Doctor.

A similar battle takes place in *The Three Doctors*, when the Third Doctor battles the 'dark side' of the mind of renegade Time Lord, **Omega**. Rather than using a special device, this contest seems to take place purely by effort of will – surely making it a more powerful demonstration of mental prowess. The Doctor loses.

The Eleventh Doctor fights a mental contest against the **Cyberplanner** in *Nightmare in Silver* (2013). They battle over a chess problem but, before there's a clear winner, the Doctor uses his sonic to get the Cyberplanner out of his brain.

THE FINEST SWORDSMAN THE DOCTOR EVER MET

As mentioned in *The Masque of Mandragora* (1976)

'The finest swordsman I ever saw,' the Fourth Doctor tells Duke Giuliano in late 15th-century Italy, 'was a captain in **Cleopatra**'s bodyguard. He showed me a few points.'

The Doctor is clearly a gifted swordsman: in *The Masque of Mandragora*, he saves Giuliano from Count Federico's guards, and in *The Androids of Tara* (1978) he wins a duel with **Count Grendel** – who until then claimed to be the best swordsman on that planet, so that title must now be the Doctor's.

The Third Doctor is also adept with a sword – in a duel with the Master in *The Sea Devils* (1972), he even manages to wolf down a **sandwich** mid-fight. The Tenth Doctor bests the leader of the Sycorax in a duel in *The Christmas Invasion* (2005), even after losing one hand. Because the fight takes place within 15 hours of the Doctor's regeneration cycle, he has enough residual cellular energy to grow a new one – and it's a **fighting hand**.

THE MOST CIVILISED FIGHTING STYLE

First seen in *Inferno* (1970)

'I'm quite spry for my age,' says the Third Doctor when surrounded by armed and mean-looking guards in ***The Green Death*** (1973). When the guards attack him, he fends them off with a neat display of martial arts.

'**Venusian aikido**, gentlemen,' he tells them afterwards. 'I do hope I haven't hurt you.'

Up to this point, the Third Doctor had referred to his fighting skills as **Venusian karate**. But *Doctor Who*'s producer, Barry Letts, was concerned about the Doctor's use of violence, so it was changed to 'aikido' as the Japanese martial art of that name – which means 'the way of the harmonious spirit' – is entirely defensive.

The Twelfth Doctor seems to use Venusian aikido – just like the Third Doctor, he calls out 'Hai!' as he acts – to knock a sword out of Robin Hood's hand in ***Robot of Sherwood*** (2014).

THE MOST POETIC CONTEST

As seen in *The Curse of Fenric* (1989)

The Seventh Doctor plays chess against the ancient evil known as **Fenric**, setting up the pieces in a puzzle for Fenric to solve in one move.

In fact, the puzzle can't be solved within the strict rules of the game. Instead, the puzzle has a philosophical solution. As the Doctor's friend Ace explains, it requires, 'A brilliant move. The black and white pawns don't fight each other, they join forces.'

Unfortunately, she's just explained this to Fenric…

THE MOST LOGICAL WAR

As seen in *Destiny of the Daleks* (1979)

The Daleks have been at war for centuries with a race of robots, the **Movellans** – but both sides depend on battle computers that run entirely on logic, which means they're perfectly matched. Each computer can predict the move of the other and counter it.

The Fourth Doctor argues that the first side to ignore their computers and do something irrational will win. 'Yes,' he says. 'Make **mistakes** and confuse the enemy.'

'Is that why you always win?' responds his friend Romana, archly. 'Because you always make mistakes.'

WAR!

WE SING IN PRAISE OF TOTAL WAR...

THE LONGEST-RUNNING WAR

First seen in *The Daleks* (1963–1964)

It's difficult to know how long the Time War lasts because it's fought between two time-travelling races – the Time Lords and the Daleks.

Anyway, when did it start? The first we hear mention of a '**war**' is from the Ninth Doctor in ***Rose*** (2005), but it's been suggested that we should include the Seventh Doctor destroying the Dalek home planet Skaro in ***Remembrance of the Daleks*** (1988) or the Fourth Doctor being sent back in time by his people to stop the Daleks ever being created in ***Genesis of the Daleks*** (1975).

In fact, the first time we know of the Time Lords acting against the Daleks is ***Planet of the Daleks*** (1973), when they help the Third Doctor get to the planet Spiridon to deal with a secret Dalek army. Or we could trace the origins of the conflict to the Second Doctor in ***The War Games*** (1969) alerting his people to the Daleks as '**the worst of all**' evils he's fought, 'a pitiless race of conquerors exterminating all who came up against them'.

We could even say the trouble starts when the First Doctor first arrives on Skaro in the story that introduced these deadly foes, ***The Daleks***. Given that's the second ever story in ***Doctor Who***, his battles with the Daleks are the longest-running conflict in the series.

Malpha seems to think the Daleks are from Earth's Solar System – or he could just mean that the Daleks are already based there, on the edges, waiting to invade.

THE GREATEST EVER WAR FORCE

As seen in *Mission to the Unknown* (1965)

On the planet Kembel around the year 4000, alien delegates meet in deadly secret. One them, **Malpha**, addresses the others:

'This is indeed an historic moment in the history of the universe. We six from the outer galaxies, joining with the power from the Solar System, the Daleks. The seven of us represent the **greatest war force ever assembled**. Conquest is assured. Mars. Venus. Jupiter. The Moon colonies.'

'They will all fall before our might,' agrees the Black Dalek. 'But the first of them will be Earth.'

This might be the 'greatest' war force, but what about the largest? See over the page...

THE LONGEST-RUNNING WAR WITHOUT TIME TRAVEL

First seen in *The Time Warrior* (1973–1974)

Some time in the 13th century, a star falls near the castle occupied by the bullish Captain Irongron. In fact, the 'star' is the spaceship of **Commander Linx**, officer of the Sontaran Army Space Corps – who promptly claims Earth, its moons and satellites for the greater glory of the Sontaran Empire.

'So,' says the Third Doctor when he catches up with Linx, 'the perpetual war between the Sontarans and the Rutans has spread to this tiny planet, has it?'

Lynx has limited ability to time travel – he can kidnap a few scientists from the present day, but that's it. This suggests the war with the Rutans is also waged in linear time. That war is still going when the Fourth Doctor meets **Field Major Styre** of the Sontaran G3 Military Assessment Survey in *The Sontaran Experiment* (1975), a story set at least **11,700 years later**. There, the Doctor refers to the war against the Rutans as 'endless'.

In *The Poison Sky* (2008), the Tenth Doctor says the war with the Rutans has 'been raging, far out in the stars, for **50,000 years**.' But he says that while on Earth in the present day – suggesting, given his experience with Styre, that the war has at least another 11,000 years to run.

YOU AND WHO'S ARMY?

THE FEARSOMEST FORCES FENDING OFF ALL FOES.

THE LARGEST ARMY EVER

As seen in *The Pandorica Opens* (2010)

The Eleventh Doctor, Amy Pond and River Song visit Stonehenge in AD 102. Having found a secret entrance, they head down into the **Underhenge**, in which waits the legendary **Pandorica** – a large box containing... Well, no one seems to know.

The Doctor is fascinated by the mystery – but he's not the only one. River suddenly picks up readings that around the Earth are at least **10,000 starships**, perhaps even a million – there are simply too many readings.

Among them is a **Dalek fleet** that the Doctor says will comprise a minimum 12,000 battleships. There are **Cyberships** brimming with Cyberman and four battle fleets of **Sontarans**. We're told there are also Terileptil, Slitheen, Chelonian, Nestene, Drahvin, Sycorax, Haemogoth, Zygon, Atraxi and Draconian participants, and we see Judoon, Uvodni, Hoix and a Blowfish.

'You lot, working together,' says the Doctor in amazement. 'An **alliance**. How is that possible?'

It turns out the monsters have seen **cracks** in the skin of the universe, and know all reality is threatened. But they've not come to help the Doctor solve whatever's happening – they think it's his fault and want to save the universe from him...

THE GREATEST MILITARY MACHINE IN THE HISTORY OF THE UNIVERSE

As seen in *The Pandorica Opens* (2010)

Are the Romans really the greatest military machine in the universe, as the Eleventh Doctor claims? We asked Dr Andrew Gardner, Senior Lecturer in the Archaeology of the Roman Empire at UCL Institute of Archaeology.

'We only know about a tiny proportion of the history of the universe, but certainly among military institutions in Earth antiquity, Roman forces were effective, and over a long period, spanning hundreds of years. This came about less through being like a "machine", though, and more through being quite adaptable in terms of making use of different technologies and harnessing the variety of people and fighting styles across and beyond the empire. However, like other more modern armies that enjoyed some advantages in technology or organisation over their rivals, they could be outmatched by more creative opponents, and particularly had problems in difficult terrain when faced with more guerrilla-style tactics. It should also be noted that, as another sci-fi icon, Yoda, said, "wars not make one great".'

Amy Pond's favourite subject at school was the Roman invasion of Britain, and her favourite book at school ***The Legend of Pandora's Box***.

THE MONSTER ALLIANCE (AND THEIR SPECIES' FIRST APPEARANCE)

Atraxi	*The Eleventh Hour* (2010)
Blowfish	*Torchwood: Kiss Kiss, Bang Bang* (2008)
Chelonians	*The Highest Science* (1993, a novel)
Cybermen	*The Tenth Planet* (1966)
Daleks	*The Daleks* (1963–1964)
Draconians	*Frontier in Space* (1973)
Drahvins	*Galaxy 4* (1965)
Haemogoths	*The Forgotten Army* (2010, a novel)
Hoix	*Love & Monsters* (2006)
Judoon	*Smith and Jones* (2007)
Nestene	*Spearhead from Space* (1970)
Slitheen	*Aliens of London* (2005)
Sontarans	*The Time Warrior* (1973–1974)
Sycorax	*The Christmas Invasion* (2005)
Terileptils	*The Visitation* (1982)
Uvodni	*The Sarah Jane Adventures: Warriors of the Kulak* (2007)
Zygons	*Terror of the Zygons* (1975)

THE WAR DOCTOR

NIGHT WILL FALL AND DROWN THE SUN WHEN A GOOD MAN GOES TO WAR...

THE MOST MILITARY DOCTOR

In the special mini-episode ***The Night of the Doctor*** (2013), the dying Eighth Doctor realises he can't put off getting involved in the Time War any longer. So he asks the **Sisterhood of Karn** to prepare their **Elixir of Life** so that it will not only make him regenerate but also shape the sort of man he becomes. 'Make me a warrior,' he tells them.

Once the blast of regeneration energy fades, a new man stands in his place. 'Doctor no more,' says the young-looking man often referred to as the **War Doctor**.

When we next see the War Doctor, in ***The Day of the Doctor*** (2013), he's very much older – and we know little of the presumably many intervening years he's spent fighting. We're told in ***Hell Bent*** (2015) that many Time Lords served under him. And in ***The Day of the Doctor*** we see him on the last day of the Time War during the fall of Arcadia, Gallifrey's second city. From a soldier, he takes a large gun and blasts a message into a wall. He then flies his TARDIS so that it smashes through some Daleks about to exterminate a group of Gallifreyan grown-ups and children.

Books, comics and audio adventures have told us more about the War Doctor's activities during the Time War, but if we work only from what's seen in the TV episodes, perhaps a different picture emerges of the most military of Doctors. He uses the TARDIS as a weapon and he kills three Daleks – but the whole point of the story is that, at the crucial point, he ***doesn't*** destroy his own people to end the war. He is not the black-hearted soldier we've been led to believe.

Third Doctor actor Jon Pertwee served in the Royal Navy during the Second World War, and then in Naval Intelligence, where he reported to Winston Churchill.

In *The Zygon Inversion* (2015), the Twelfth Doctor is still so haunted by the decision he almost made – but, importantly, didn't – to destroy his own people that it helps him broker peace between humans and aliens.

'When you fire that first shot,' he says, 'no matter how right you feel, you have no idea who's going to die. You don't know whose children are going to scream and burn. How many hearts will be broken. How many lives shattered. How much blood will spill until everybody does what they were always going to have to do from the very beginning. ***Sit down and talk.***'

Though the Twelfth Doctor refers to having done 'worse things than you could ever imagine' in what was presumably the Time War, from what we see on screen in ***The Day of the Doctor***, the War Doctor is not nearly so destructive as the Seventh Doctor, who we watch destroy the Dalek home planet in ***Remembrance of the Daleks*** (1988). Likewise, the Third Doctor sets off an icecano to kill an army of 10,000 Daleks in ***Planet of the Daleks*** (1973).

In fact, while exiled to Earth, the Third Doctor is an employee of the military organisation, UNIT. He's skilled in hand-to-hand combat and a master of Venusian aikido. We see him fight with great skill, using swords, poles and other weapons. There's his attitude, too. In ***The Dæmons*** (1971), he reminds Jo Grant that she should show respect to the Brigadier because he's her superior officer. When a man called Galloway blows himself up to destroy the Daleks, too, in ***Death to the Daleks*** (1974), this incarnation of the Doctor coolly responds that he 'did his duty'.

In ***Day of the Daleks*** (1972), he says he advised Napoleon on managing his forces ('Boney, I said, always remember an army marches on its stomach...') and later in the story, during a siege, he grabs a futuristic gun and coolly shoots an Ogron.

The Third Doctor is often a diplomat, a peacemaker. But that doesn't mean he's not ***also*** a soldier. At the end of ***Planet of the Daleks*** he counsels the victorious Thals that when they return to Skaro having defeated the Daleks, their own people will treat them as heroes. 'Everybody will want to hear about your adventures,' he says. 'So be careful how you tell that story, will you? Don't glamorise it. Don't make war sound like an exciting and thrilling game. Tell them about the members of your mission that will not be returning ... Tell them about the fear.'

Like the speech in ***The Zygon Inversion***, those are the words of not merely a peacemaker but a veteran with experience of the grim reality of conflict. But of all his incarnations, at least from what we see, the Third Doctor is the most adept at war.

THE LARGEST ARMY LED BY THE DOCTOR

As seen in *A Good Man Goes to War* (2011)

The sinister **Madame Kovarian** kidnaps the pregnant Amy Pond, so the Eleventh Doctor calls in old favours to help get her back safely. At the **Battle of Demon's Run** – the asteroid home of the Headless Monks – the Doctor turns up with an army that includes **Madame Vastra** and a squad of Silurians, Vastra's human wife **Jenny Flint**, **Strax** and a squad of Sontarans, the pirate **Captain Henry Avery** and his son **Toby** in their spaceship, and **Spitfires** apparently on loan from **Winston Churchill** in the Second World War.

TIME LORD WEAPONS

THE DEADLIEST ARSENAL IN THE UNIVERSE

PARTICLE DISSEMINATOR

As seen in *The Trial of a Time Lord* (1986)

Inside the Matrix – the Time Lord's living computer – the evil Valeyard has set up a device that the Sixth Doctor identifies as a particle disseminator. 'The ultimate weapon,' the Valeyard crows. 'Every subatomic particle – gravitons, quarks, tau mesons – all completely disseminated.'

PLANETARY DESTRUCTION

As seen in *Image of the Fendahl* (1977)

107 million miles and 12 million years back in time, the Fourth Doctor and Leela discover a 'fifth planet' in the Solar System – so between Mars and Jupiter. All memory of this planet has been erased by a circle of time, making data and its records invisible. 'Only a Time Lord could do that,' says the Doctor.

It turns out this lost planet was home to the **Fendahl**, creatures that prospered by absorbing the energy wavelengths of life itself, so threatened all other living beings. The Time Lords decided to destroy the planet – we don't know how they did it – and hid the records. 'They're not supposed to do that sort thing,' broods the Doctor.

BOW SHIPS

As seen in *State of Decay* (1980)

In the ancient account *The Record of Rassilon* there are details of the Time Lords long ago war with giant vampires.

Energy weapons were useless because the monsters absorbed and transmuted the energy using it to become stronger. Therefore **RASSILON** ordered the construction of **BOWSHIPS**, swift vessels that fired a mighty bolt of steel that transfixed the monsters through the heart. For only if his heart be utterly destroyed will a vampire die.

DEMAT GUN

As seen in *The Invasion of Time* (1978)

The Fourth Doctor explains in ***The Invasion of Time*** that the sum total of Time Lord power is provided by three ceremonial items that contain awesome properties – the **Rod of Rassilon**, the **Sash of Rassilon** and the **Great Key of Rassilon** – linked to the living computer, the **Matrix**.

We know from *The Deadly Assassin* (1976) that the Rod and the Sash give a person access to and protect them from the black hole called the **Eye of Harmony** at the heart of Gallifrey. But what about the Great Key?

When Gallifrey is invaded by Sontarans, the Doctor gets K-9 and a Time Lady called **Rodan** to construct a **Demat Gun**. This seems to be something from the dark past of the Doctor's people. He calls it the 'ultimate weapon', but his old teacher, Chancellor Borusa, worries that it will throw Gallifrey back into the darkest age. And the gun is armed using the Great Key. When Sontaran **Commander Stor** threatens to destroy Gallifrey and the entire galaxy with it, the Doctor has no other choice than to fire the Demat Gun...

We don't see what happens next, but the Sontarans are suddenly no longer on Gallifrey. The invasion is over, but the Demat Gun has also vanished and the Doctor has no memory of what happened. It is, says Borusa, the wisdom of Rassilon.

DEMATERIALISATION

As seen in *The War Games* (1969)

The first time we visit the Doctor's home planet and learn his people are called Time Lords, they stand in judgement on the evil **War Lord**, who forced different armies from human history to fight in phoney wars.

The Time Lords place a force field round the War Lord's home planet so that his warlike people will remain prisoners for ever. But as for the War Lord and immediate cronies, the Time Lords are without mercy.

'You have been found guilty of all charges,' they declare. 'You and your murderous associates will be **dematerialised**. It will be as though you had never existed.'

THE MOMENT
As seen in *The Day of the Doctor* (2013)
See p. 78.

KILL YOUR SPEED

RECORD-BREAKING CRASHES AND COLLISIONS

THE MOST CRASHES IN THE SAME CAR

As seen in Father's Day (2005)

In *The Claws of Axos* (1971), the Third Doctor deals with an invading alien force by putting it into a '**time loop**', doomed to circle round and pass through the same point in time for eternity. The Doctor – and the Master – are almost caught in it, too.

This is the first of many time loops in the series. For example, in *Meglos* (1980), the Fourth Doctor and Romana get stuck repeating the same conversation, and in the TV movie *Doctor Who* (1996) the TARDIS is flying in a **temporal orbit** which apparently means that people killed while on board can come back to life.

In *Father's Day*, Rose Tyler gets the Ninth Doctor to take her back in time to **7 November 1987** – the day, when Rose was still a baby, that her dad **Pete** was hit by a car and killed. But the grown-up Rose can't just watch her dad die, and before the Doctor can stop her she rushes in and saves his life.

This change to established history causes a wound in time and soon huge, winged creatures come to sterilise the area – by consuming everyone on Earth. Even the Doctor is eaten, but not before he's worked out the solution. As has Pete.

'The car that should have killed me, love,' he tells Rose. 'It's here. The Doctor worked it out way back, but he tried to protect me.'

It's true. The same beige **Vauxhall Chevette hatchback**, registration **NEH 793W**, keeps suddenly appearing on Waterley Street, the unnamed young driver sees something in front of him and raises an arm across his face – and then the car vanishes once more. To save the world, Pete runs out to meet it, head on…

Technically, Pete can only die once, but since Rose changes history after the first time, he is hit by the car twice. But the driver clearly seems to think he's hitting *something* in the road another six times on screen, bringing the total to **eight crashes**. (The same car also almost hits Pete's car when he drives Rose to Waterley Street – but Pete swerves out of the way so we won't count it in this total.)

THE BEST AVOIDANCE OF A CRASH

As seen in *Voyage of the Damned* (2007)

A **Sycorax spaceship** sits in the sky above London on Christmas Day, and ordinary Londoners are compelled to stand on their roofs, waiting the order to jump. A year later, a **Christmas star** electrocutes larges numbers in the capital and the River Thames drains away...

So the following Christmas, it seems Londoners think better of staying in the capital and scarpers off elsewhere. That is, we're told, everyone except **Wilf Mott**, defiantly manning his newsstand, and **Queen Elizabeth II**. Her Majesty will stay in Buckingham Palace throughout the festive season to show the people of London, and the world, that there's nothing to fear.

Which means that on Christmas Day she must peg it – still in her dressing gown and slippers – out of the palace as a vast spaceship hares down towards it.

Originally, writer and executive producer **Russell T Davies** intended to have the Tenth Doctor just manage to regain control of the starship ***Titanic*** at the last minute before hitting Earth – but not before smashing through Buckingham Palace. The Queen would not be amused.

However, the ambitious story already required a wealth of complex special effects, so it was agreed by the production team to simplify this sequence. In the episode as broadcast, the Doctor steers the spaceship so that it just *misses* the palace.

'Thank you, Doctor!' the Queen calls up to him, from the road outside. 'Thank you! Happy Christmas!'

It's not very likely he'd hear.

Queen Elizabeth II also appears in ***Silver Nemesis*** (1988) and ***The Idiot's Lantern*** (2006). She shares the record for the monarch in most ***Doctor Who*** stories with Elizabeth I, who can be seen in ***The Chase*** (1965), ***The Shakespeare Code*** (2007) and ***The Day of the Doctor*** (2013).

THE WORST EVER CRASH

As seen in *Earthshock* (1982)

In **2526**, the heads of many powerful planets meet on Earth to sign a pact uniting their military forces against the **Cybermen**. To stop this, the Cybermen lock the controls of a **space freighter** on a collision course with Earth. The freighter is powered by **antimatter**, which annihilates matter on contact – so the crash will be devastating.

The Fifth Doctor's companion Adric solves two of the three **logic codes** the Cybermen placed on the ship's computer. That means the freighter is locked on the same spatial coordinates but spirals back in time.

It seems the freighter hit Earth some **65 million years** ago, long before humans were on the planet. We know from the fossil record that vast numbers of living creatures were wiped out – many whole species, including the **dinosaurs**, became extinct. It's also thought we can identify where the massive object responsible crashed: in the rocks of the **Yucatán Peninsula** in Mexico, there are traces of a crater **180 kilometres** or 112 miles wide – more than the distance between London and Cardiff.

CENSORED VIOLENCE

WHEN *DOCTOR WHO* IS EVEN TOO HORRIFYING FOR THE PEOPLE WHO MAKE IT

THE MOST VIOLENT MOMENT IN *DOCTOR WHO*?

As seen in *The Deadly Assassin* (1976)

In February 1985, as *The Two Doctors* was being broadcast, news emerged that the BBC would postpone production of the next series of *Doctor Who* by a year.

Several reasons were given for this decision: the numbers of people watching the series had fallen; the BBC needed to save money after some other, expensive projects; and the executives in charge didn't like science fiction in general or *Doctor Who* specifically. But another reason given at the time was that the series had become **too violent**.

There's certainly some evidence of this in the 1985 stories. The Cybermen **crush the hands** of a man called Lytton in *Attack of the Cybermen*, while the Sixth Doctor **guns down** the Cyber-Leader. In *Vengeance on Varos*, the TARDIS lands on a planet devoted to **televised torture**, and the Doctor makes a joke as two guards fall into an **acid bath**. In *The Two Doctors*, the Doctor uses a kit for catching butterflies to **kill the man-eating chef**, Shockeye, who has only recently **stabbed to death** the nice owner of a restaurant.

But *Vengeance on Varos* is itself a **satire on violence on TV**, and the Doctor has battled and killed adversaries before, so was the 1985 series any more violent than other eras of *Doctor Who*?

In fact, this concern goes back a long way. On 23 September 1967, Episode 4 of *The Tomb of the Cybermen* included a scene of **white goo foaming from a dead Cyberman's chest**. This led to complaints, and on 26 September co-writer Kit Pedler appeared on a new BBC programme, *Talkback*, to discuss whether the series was suitable for children. Afterwards, presenter David Coleman joked, **'perhaps it's too scary for grown-ups...'**

The production team on *Doctor Who* seemed to take that to heart. Soon afterwards they recorded a special trailer for forthcoming story *The Web of Fear* (1968), in which the Second Doctor addresses young viewers directly to warn that he'll soon meet a monster he's fought before – **the Yeti**. 'Only

In six *Doctor Who* stories – ***The Rescue*** (1965), ***Pyramids of Mars*** (1975), ***Horror of Fang Rock*** (1977), ***Attack of the Cybermen*** (1985), ***The Parting of the Ways*** (2005) and ***The Doctor's Wife*** (2011) – all seen, speaking characters die except the Doctor and companions.

this time, they're just a little bit more frightening than last time. So I want to warn you that **if your mummy and daddy are scared**, you just get them to hold your hand...' The production team weren't making their stories any **less** violent and scary; they were saying it was a reason to watch.

Those making *Doctor Who* must always use their judgement to ensure the series isn't *too* frightening. There have been debates about what **time of day** the series should be broadcast and the kind of violence shown – whether it's presented **realistically**, or in ways the viewer might **copy**. There are guidelines and conventions, but it's also a matter of personal preference – and can depend on context. For example, both the TV movie *Doctor Who* (1996) and the episode *Robot of Sherwood* (2014) had violent scenes **cut shortly before broadcast** because of events in the (real) news.

How can we quantify what counts as the most violent moment in *Doctor Who* if it largely comes down to a matter of personal taste? A single episode had a violent moment cut from the master tape ***after it was broadcast***.

At the end of Part 3 of *The Deadly Assassin*, the Fourth Doctor battles a Time Lord called **Goth** in a swamp. Goth holds the Doctor down in the water, and the last shot of the episode is the **Doctor apparently drowning**. Following complaints, **Charles Curran**, the then Director-General of the BBC, formally apologised and the last shot cut was from the master tape of the episode – so it wasn't included when the story was repeated the following year. (Copies of the story as originally broadcast were used to restore the ending when *The Deadly Assassin* was released on video in 1991 and on DVD in 2009.)

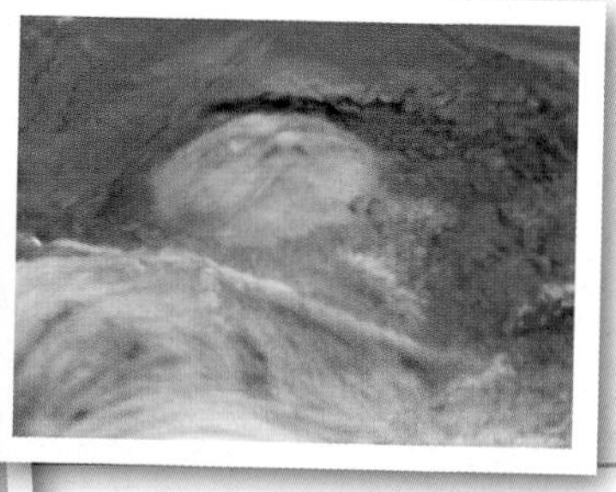

GET HER OUT OF THERE!

THE DOCTOR GETS TO BE A HERO IN REAL LIFE

THE WORST EVER ACCIDENT ON THE SET OF *DOCTOR WHO*

As seen in *Battlefield* (1989)

'**DR WHO GIRL CHEATS DEATH**' reported the *News of the World* newspaper on 18 June 1989. And it wasn't just her – the story quoted an unnamed member of the production team on *Doctor Who* claiming, 'We could **all** have been killed.' This was surely the worst accident ever to occur in making the programme – but what exactly happened?

Thursday 1 June marked the final day of studio recording on the Seventh Doctor story, ***Battlefield***. The last scene to be recorded was the cliffhanger of Part 2: a glass panel sliding down to trap the Doctor's companion Ace in the narrow confines of an airlock, which then starts to fill with water.

Playing Ace, actress Sophie Aldred was lowered into the **glass-fronted watertank** from above by the visual effects crew. Sophie later said that she 'hadn't realised what the weight of the water would be as it poured out of the pipe onto my head, and the incredible noise it would make'.

That made it impossible to hear what else was happening on set. On the other side of the glass, Sylvester McCoy – playing the Doctor – shouted to ask if she was OK. Sophie could only give him a smile and thumbs up.

DR WHO GIRL CHEATS DEATH

Sophie is sucked into tank

By CHARLES CATCHPOLE

DR Who's assistant was almost killed and dozens of others had to jump for their lives when a studio stunt went wrong.

The accident happened when actress Sophie Aldred, who plays Ace, was thrown into a glass-lined cylinder full of water.

The glass shattered, sucking Sophie to the bottom of the tank, and sending hundreds of gallons of water flooding on to electrical cables at the BBC Television Centre in West London.

A member of the production team said: "We could all have been killed, as the floor was covered with live cables.

"We jumped on to chairs or hung on to camera gantries—anything to keep our feet off the ground."

A BBC spokesman said: "Quick thinking prevented a serious disaster.

"Sophie swallowed some water and was shaken, but not hurt."

An inquiry has been launched, but the new series will be ready for the autumn.

SOPHIE: Dice with death

'The camera seemed to be running, so I shouted my lines,' she recalled later. She had to shout 'Doctor, look out!' – because while he is trying to save Ace, he's also being attacked. 'There was now a lot of water in the tank,' Sophie said, 'and I was **bobbing** slightly, my jacket filling with air and acting as a buoyancy aid. I spread my hands on the glass in front of me to steady myself, and a few seconds later heard a **loud cracking sound**, and felt the glass give way beneath my fingers.'

It seems the thickness of the glass had been calculated on the basis of only the volume of water it would contain – and had not taken into account the actress, in her costume and carrying a sword, thrashing around in it for the dramatic scene.

Recalling the moment years later, Sylvester said he saw the glass bulge before it cracked and realised that once the water broke through Sophie would 'be pushed out [with it] with great force, maybe drowned, maybe cut to pieces [by the broken glass], maybe electrocuted because we were in the studio [and] there's plugs all over the place. So I thought, "I must shout a command that everybody must obey. They mustn't think I'm acting."'

Before anyone else realised what was happening, he yelled a rude word – which got people's attention – and then, '**Get her out of there!**'

Instinctively, Sophie pulled her hands back from the broken glass and raised her arms, and the crew – alerted by Sylvester's cry of alarm – pulled her up to safety. As they pulled her up, she remembered, 'I could see the front of this tank [and] the glass gradually billowed out and cracked, and this water and broken glass cascaded into the studio. For a second or two, no one moved, and then suddenly there was a mad dash for the studio doors, as the front of the tank buckled and bowed, and gallons of water gushed forth, spilling onto the studio floor and sending cameramen, actors and crew running for safety – water and electric cables are not a good mix.'

The power was shut off in time, and Sophie escaped with nothing more serious than glass splinters in her hands – but it could have been a lot worse. The incident, including the recorded footage, were made part of a **BBC safety training video**. In fact, you can see the broken glass and the water draining away in Part 3 of the story.

'Having been shown the clip, I realised that it was **the heroic Mr McCoy who probably saved my life**,' says Sophie. 'His reactions were amazingly quick, and his shouts which alerted the studio to prompt action undoubtedly averted major disaster. I owe you one, Mr McCoy.'

WE WILL SURVIVE

HOW MUCH OF *DOCTOR WHO* IS MISSING – AND HOW MUCH HAS BEEN FOUND?

WHY IS THERE MISSING *DOCTOR WHO* ANYWAY?

It seems incredible, doesn't it? Today, if we can't watch a new episode of ***Doctor Who*** as it is first broadcast, there's no reason to think that we'll ***never*** see it.

But in the early days of ***Doctor Who*** things were very different. There was no iPlayer, no DVD, Blu-ray or download, and home video recorders only started to become affordable in the late 1970s. There were strict limits on the BBC as to how many programmes – at all, not just ***Doctor Who*** – could be repeated in a year. Also, the two-inch videotapes on which programmes were recorded were very expensive, and it was also costly to store large quantities of tapes.

Given that there didn't seem much chance of showing most episodes again or sharing them with the public, it didn't seem such a bad idea to save money by wiping old videotapes and reusing them to record new programmes. As a result, all the original videotapes of First Doctor and Second Doctor episodes – a total of 253 episodes – were wiped in the late 1960s and early 1970s. Copies of most if not all of them had been made on 16mm film for selling to broadcasters in other countries. But these, too, were being routinely destroyed in the early 1970s, once there seemed to be no further interest from overseas buyers.

And then suddenly things changed…

Using soundtracks recorded at the time of broadcast, animations have been made of 3 missing First Doctor episodes and 12 missing Second Doctor episodes.

THE PERSON WHO SAVED MOST *DOCTOR WHO*

In the mid-1970s the BBC finally acknowledged the value of old programmes and in 1978 **Sue Malden** was made the first ever **Television Archive Selector**, responsible for overseeing the collection of programmes to retain on a permanent basis.

To begin with, Sue needed to understand the reasons why programmes were lost and how the BBC might fill the gaps in its collection. To do this, she decided to investigate the history of one programme in particular. She chose *Doctor Who* because it was a 'seminal, classic, television series that clearly had run a long time, and was still running, and had influenced a lot of people.' To her surprise, the BBC Film Library had only a very meagre collection, with:

117 missing of 134 First Doctor episodes

89 missing of 119 Second Doctor episodes

69 missing of 128 Third Doctor episodes

That meant a total of **275 missing episodes**. But Sue quickly made contact with BBC TV Enterprises – which sold *Doctor Who* abroad – and with the British Film Institute, both of which held collections of programmes. They donated their episodes of *Doctor Who* or allowed copies to be made, so that by the end of 1978 there were **147 missing episodes** – just two of them from the Third Doctor's era.

Now, Sue wasn't working alone. As well as her colleagues at the BBC, a number of *Doctor Who* fans – notably record producer **Ian Levine** – doggedly worked to turn up missing episodes from all over the world (and they continue to do so). But, as Ian says, Sue's official position gave authority to the search. For example, 'She put in a holding order,' he says, to stop BBC TV Enterprises destroying its collection before it could be checked.

By the time Sue moved on from her role as Television Archive Selector in 1983, there were **134 missing episodes**: 59 from the First Doctor, 74 from the Second Doctor and 1 from the Third Doctor. An amazing 141 episodes had been returned to the archive since she started.

Just imagine if she'd chosen some other series as her example.

~~DEATH~~ SURVIVAL BY 1,000 CUTS

Clips from several otherwise missing episodes have also turned up over the years. When *Doctor Who* was sold for broadcast in New Zealand and Australia, especially **violent or scary** moments were cut – literally, the offending film was snipped from the reel. In many cases, these snippets of film were filed away – and then rediscovered many years later. As a result, the BBC has short, dramatic clips from **14** otherwise missing episodes.

THE CURRENT RECORD OF LOSS

Today, there are **97 missing episodes** of *Doctor Who*, of a total of 827 (up to and including 2016 Christmas special *The Return of Doctor Mysterio*).

There are 26 incomplete *Doctor Who* stories. There are 44 missing First Doctor episodes from 12 stories, and 53 missing Second Doctor episodes from 14 stories.

CHAPTER FOUR
TARDIS

'MY TARDIS. THE BEST SHIP IN THE UNIVERSE.'

THE NINTH DOCTOR, *BOOM TOWN* (2005)

PIONEERS OF TIME TRAVEL 104
SHORT TRIPS 106
BACK AND FORTH 108
WITHOUT THE TARDIS 110
BIGGER ON THE INSIDE 112

POLICE PUBLIC CALL BOX

PIONEERS OF TIME TRAVEL

IT'S HARD TO KNOW WHO FIRST TRAVELLED IN TIME AS WHOEVER WAS SECOND COULD TRAVEL BACK FURTHER AND BEAT THEM TO IT.

THE INVENTION OF TIME TRAVEL

We don't know who first invented time travel or who first travelled in time, but the Doctor's own people – the **Time Lords of the planet Gallifrey** – seem to have been among the first.

The **Seventh Doctor** tells us in *Remembrance of the Daleks* (1988) that, 'It was **Omega** who created the **supernova** that was the initial power source for Gallifreyan time-travel experiments. He left behind him the basis on which **Rassilon** founded Time Lord society.'

In the very first episode of *Doctor Who* (*An Unearthly Child*, 1963), the **Doctor's granddaughter Susan** says she is responsible for the name we now use for Gallifreyan capsules that can travel in time: 'I made up the name **TARDIS** from the initials: Time And Relative Dimension In Space.'

In *The Time Meddler* (1965), we meet another member of the Doctor's people, the **Monk**, who does not use the word TARDIS to describe his own, very similar time machine. But when we visit the Doctor's planet for the first time – in *The War Games* (1969) – the Time Lords refer to the Doctor's ship as a TARDIS. Time Lords have used the word TARDIS to refer to such capsules – not just the Doctor's one – ever since.

If the name Susan coined is used by Time Lords generally, does that mean Susan was some kind of pioneer or expert in time travel before she left home? Or have the Time Lords adopted the word from the Doctor *since* he and Susan ran away? Alternatively, we know the TARDIS translates other languages, so is 'TARDIS' what it chooses to be known as? We just don't know.

Earliest known humans to travel in time (Doctor's own timeline)
Ian Chesterton and Barbara Wright, AD 1963 – *An Unearthly Child*.

Earliest known people to be able to travel in time	The Time Lords of Gallifrey 
Earliest known Earthling to travel in time	Unnamed dinosaur, at least 65 million years ago[1]
Earliest known human to travel in time (chronologically)	 Queen Nefertiti of Egypt, 1334 BC – *Dinosaurs on a Spaceship* (2012)
Earliest known humans to travel in time by their own means	Lady Peinforte and Richard Maynarde, who travel from AD 1638 to 1988 using rudimentary knowledge of time travel (black magic, mostly) – *Silver Nemesis* (1988)
Earliest known human-built time machine	Professor Whitaker's machine built c. AD 1974 transports dinosaurs to the present and people to the past – Invasion of the Dinosaurs (1974)[2]
Earliest known person to be killed by time travel	Professor Fyodor Nikolai Kerensky, AD 1979 – *City of Death* (1979)
First 'official' human to travel in time by human-built time machine	Colonel Orson Pink, c. AD 2114 – *Listen* (2014) 
Earliest date in the past to which anyone has travelled	 Pilot of space station Terminus, the Big Bang – *Terminus* (1983)
Furthest date into the future to which anyone has travelled	Clara Oswald and the Twelfth Doctor, the last hours of the universe – *Hell Bent* (2015)

1. But which of the dinosaurs is it, from the ones seen in *Invasion of the Dinosaurs* (1974), *The Mark of the Rani* (1985) and *Deep Breath* (2014)?

2. In *The Evil of the Daleks* (1967), Professor Theodore Maxtible and Edward Waterfield build a machine in 1866 that attracts the attention of the Daleks, but it's not stated explicitly that this machine can be used for travelling in time.

WHO ELSE CAN TIME TRAVEL?

Apart from the Doctor and his people, the first species we saw capable of time travel were the **Daleks** in *The Chase* (1965). Other species able to travel in time include the **Cybermen** and **Sontarans**.

Some powerful individuals can even travel in time and space without using a time machine, just through their own mental power. These include the **giant spiders** of the planet **Metebelis 3** and the Doctor's old teacher **K'Anpo Rinpoche** (both in *Planet of the Spiders*, 1974).

THE TIME TRAVEL OF ANGELS

In *Blink* (2007), the **Weeping Angels** live off **potential energy**. With one touch, they zap you into the past and let you live to death. Meanwhile in the present, the Angels feast on the energy of all the days you might have had.

SHORT TRIPS

THE TARDIS CAN TRAVEL VAST DISTANCES THROUGH SPACE AND TIME, BUT SOMETIMES SMALL IS BEAUTIFUL

THE SHORTEST DISTANCE TRAVELLED BY TARDIS

As seen in *Fear Her* (2005)

The **Tenth Doctor** lands the TARDIS in London in the year **AD 2012**, in a narrow gap between two **shipping containers**. However, the TARDIS has materialised with its doors facing and right up against the side of one of the containers – which means the Doctor can't get out. 'Ah,' he says, and quickly dematerialises and rematerialises the TARDIS, rotating it round by **90 degrees**.

We can't be sure that between dematerialising and rematerialising he's not gone off somewhere else for another, unseen adventure (it's the sort of the thing the Doctor does). But if not this must be the **shortest trip** he's ever made in the TARDIS. The TARDIS moves forward in time by about **2 seconds** to avoid materialising on itself, but lands in exactly the same spot on Earth.

Except, of course, that the Earth is moving. In *Rose* (2005), the **Ninth Doctor** – while also in London – says the Earth is spinning at **1,000 miles an hour** and the entire planet is hurtling round the Sun at **67,000 miles an hour**. The Sun and its system of planets (including Earth) is also moving, part of a spiralling galaxy.

Somehow, the TARDIS must **compensate** for all this movement to land exactly in the 'same' spot. No wonder short hops are tricky.

THE LEAST TRAVELLED COMPANION

In ***Death of the Doctor*** – a 2010 episode of *The Sarah Jane Adventures* – we learn that the Doctor's companion **Liz Shaw** is on 'the **Moonbase**'. Yet when she was the Doctor's companion in the 1970s, she never left the Earth. At the time, the **Third Doctor** was stranded on Earth, the secrets of the TARDIS taken from him by the Time Lords. Liz travels in time just once – and then by not very much. In *The Ambassadors of Death* (1970), the Doctor attempts to get the TARDIS working. He and Liz are both caught in the **time warp field** of the TARDIS console and projected some **15 seconds** into the future.

The longest single *Doctor Who* story is the 14-episode ***The Trial of a Time Lord*** (1986).

THE SHORTEST EPISODE OF *DOCTOR WHO*

The shortest full episode of *Doctor Who* is **Episode 1 of *The Mind Robber*** (1968), which is just **18 minutes**' long – less than half the length of a modern episode of the series. It features only the **Second Doctor** and his companions **Jamie and Zoe**, plus some non-speaking robots. (The cast had complained to the series' producer that this meant a lot of work for them to learn lines and so on, so the episode was cut down.)

The shortest broadcast 'mini' episode of *Doctor Who* is ***Good as Gold*** (2012), in which the **Eleventh Doctor** and his companion **Amy** stop a **Weeping Angel** from stealing t he Olympic Flame. Written by the children of Ashdene School – who won a special writing competition – it ran for **2 minutes and 57 seconds**.

THE LEAST SEEN INCARNATIONS OF THE DOCTOR

The **Eighth Doctor** appears in one full story, the television movie *Doctor Who* (1996), and then isn't seen in person again until the online mini-episode *The Night of the Doctor* (2013). The **War Doctor** appears briefly at the end of the episode *The Name of the Doctor* and then in one full story, *The Day of the Doctor* (both 2013).

But in *The Brain of Morbius* (1976) we glimpse seven faces intended to be **incarnations prior to the First Doctor**. Each face – in fact, members of the production team at the time – is seen for between **2 and 3 seconds** each.

The shortest single ***Doctor Who*** story is the 1-episode ***Mission to the Unknown*** (1965) – the only ***Doctor Who*** story not to feature the Doctor or his companions.

BACK AND FORTH

TRULY TREMENDOUS TREKS IN THE WELL-TRAVELLED TARDIS

THE FURTHEST DISTANCE BACK IN TIME TRAVELLED BY THE TARDIS

As seen in *Castrovalva* (1982)

In ***Logopolis*** (1981), the mysterious Watcher takes the TARDIS right out of time and space. In ***Inferno*** (1970), ***Full Circle*** (1980), ***Rise of the Cybermen*** (2006), ***Journey's End*** (2008) and ***The Doctor's Wife*** (2011), the TARDIS travels into other universes of one sort or another. But what is its single furthest journey inside the regular universe?

In ***Logopolis*** (1981), air hostess **Tegan Jovanka** is on her way to catch a flight from Heathrow Airport when circumstance leads her into the TARDIS, where she meets the Fourth Doctor and helps him stop the universe coming apart. On what seems to be the same day on Earth that Tegan was due to catch her flight, the Doctor falls from the **Pharos radio telescope** and then regenerates.

In the very next story, ***Castrovalva*** (1982), the newly regenerated Fifth Doctor and his companions escape back to the TARDIS, which the Master then forces back in time towards **Event One**. The Doctor's companion Nyssa explains that this is, 'The **creation of the galaxy** out of a huge in-rush of hydrogen'.

In the next story, ***Four to Doomsday***, we're told Tegan's flight was due to depart at 17:30 on **28 February 1981**. So the TARDIS seems to leave Earth with the newly regenerated Doctor on that day and then head back to the formation of the galaxy – presumably the same one in which Earth resides. Our galaxy, known as the **Milky Way**, is thought to be **13.2 billion years old** – a little younger than the universe, which is estimated to be 13.8 billion years old.

In ***The Doctor's Wife*** (2011), Idris – the TARDIS inside a person – says that if she's not always taken the Doctor where he wanted, "I always took you where you ***needed*** to go."

THE FURTHEST DISTANCE FORWARDS IN TIME TRAVELLED BY THE TARDIS

As seen in *Listen* (2014)

In what seems to be the present day, school teacher **Clara Oswald** is in a restaurant, not having the best first date with her colleague **Danny Pink**. It doesn't help that she's distracted by the incongruous sight of an astronaut. Danny leaves, and the exasperated Clara follows the astronaut into the restaurant's kitchen, where the TARDIS is waiting. Inside, the astronaut removes his helmet – revealing not the face of the Twelfth Doctor as Clara expected but someone who looks just like Danny.

This is **Colonel Orson Pink**, who is apparently from about 100 years in Clara's future – but the Doctor found him somewhere much further in time than that, because the colonel is a pioneer time traveller. The Doctor pilots the TARDIS back to the colonel's time ship, which for six months has been stranded on the unnamed **last planet in the universe**, at the end of time. 'The TARDIS isn't supposed to come this far,' says the Doctor, 'but some idiot turned the safeguards off.'

If this is the last planet in existence, the TARDIS has arrived further forward in time than it does in *Utopia* (2007), when it arrives on **Malcassairo** some **100 trillion years** in the future. There, the last of humanity is eager to get back out into space and look for a new home – suggesting there are still more worlds out there.

THE BIGGEST CROSSING OF THE DOCTOR'S OWN TIME STREAM

As seen in *The Name of the Doctor* (2013)

In *The Three Doctors* (1972–1973), the unnamed Chancellor of the Time Lords is horrified by the prospect of teaming up different incarnations of the Doctor. 'You can't allow him to cross his own time stream,' he says. 'Apart from the enormous energy it would need, the **First Law of Time** expressly forbids him to meet his other selves.'

Even after the Time War, when the Time Lords are no longer around to enforce such laws, the Doctor rarely meets his previous incarnations. But in *The Name of the Doctor*, the Eleventh Doctor goes even further – as he explains while struggling with the controls of the TARDIS. 'She's just figured out where we're going,' he says – referring to his ship. 'She's against it [because] I'm about to cross my own timeline in the biggest way possible.'

Why is this trip worse than other times he's met himself? Because here he's not off to visit a previous incarnation, he's heading forward in his own time stream to the planet **Trenzalore**, site of his future grave.

In *The Time Monster* (1972), the Doctor's TARDIS lands inside the Master's TARDIS, which is inside the Doctor's TARDIS, which is inside the Master's TARDIS...

WITHOUT THE TARDIS

HOW DOES THE DOCTOR GET ABOUT WHEN HE DOESN'T HAVE HIS SHIP?

THE LARGEST NUMBER OF CONSECUTIVE TRAVELS BY THE DOCTOR NOT USING THE TARDIS

As seen in Frontier in Space (1973)

The TARDIS avoids crashing into Earth **cargo ship C982** while it is in **hyperspace** by materialising on board. The Third Doctor and Jo Grant find themselves sometime in the **26th century** when Earth is on the brink of war with **Draconia**.

The Doctor is just explaining who he and Jo are to the crew of the cargo ship when **Ogrons** attack – but the crew see them as Draconians. The Ogrons steal the TARDIS.

A distress call sent out by the cargo ship gives its position at the time of attack as 'coordinate **8972/6483**', apparently a long way from Earth as it's not easy to send help. Plus the cargo ship travels through hyperspace, suggesting it covers long distances. But before the Doctor can recover his TARDIS, he:

Flies from coordinate 8972/6483 in space to spaceport 10 on Earth

Is moved variously between the office of the President of Earth, a prison cell and the office of the Draconian Ambassador

Travels by **shuttle** to a penal colony on the Moon

Flies on Earth **police spaceship 2390** in the direction of the unnamed planet of the Ogrons – but his journey is interrupted

Flies on a **Draconian spaceship** to the planet Draconia

Flies on Earth police spaceship 2390 (again) in the direction of Earth – but his journey is (again) interrupted

Arrives on Earth, either in the police spaceship or as prisoner on board an **Earth battlecruiser** (we don't see which)

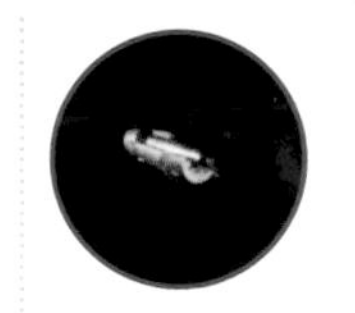

Flies from Earth on **General Williams's personal scoutship** to the unnamed planet of the Ogrons, located at galactic coordinates 2349/6784, which is in 'a completely uninhabited sector of the galaxy'.

On the planet of the Ogrons, the Doctor is finally reunited with the TARDIS, which he asks the Time Lords to direct in pursuit of an army of Daleks.

THE LARGEST NUMBER OF CONSECUTIVE EPISODES WITHOUT US SEEING INSIDE THE TARDIS

In the first episode of ***Death to the Daleks*** – broadcast on 23 February 1974 – the Third Doctor attempts to take Sarah Jane Smith swimming on the planet Florana, but they step from the TARDIS control room out onto the eerie wastes of the planet Exxilon.

We don't see the inside of the TARDIS in the remaining three episodes of the story, or again for that series of ***Doctor Who***, at the end of which the Doctor regenerates.

We don't see inside the TARDIS for the next 20 episodes, either – the whole of the Fourth Doctor's first series of adventures. In fact, in ***The Sontaran Experiment*** and ***Genesis of the Daleks*** (both 1975), the Doctor is separated from the TARDIS altogether, travelling first by **matter transmitter** and then via a **Time Ring** given to him by the Time Lords. Nor do we see inside in the TARDIS in the first story of the following series.

Finally, after **39 consecutive episodes** in which we don't see inside the TARDIS, the first episode of ***Planet of Evil*** [broadcast on 27 September 1975] shows the Doctor and Sarah Jane at the controls of the ship – and again they don't arrive where they should.

THE FURTHEST THE DOCTOR TRAVELS NOT USING A TARDIS

As seen in *The Sound of Drums* (2007)

The Tenth Doctor, Martha Jones and Captain Jack Harkness use Jack's wrist mounted vortex manipulator to travel from the planet Malcassairo some 100 trillion years in the future back to Earth in the present day.

THE FURTHEST THE DOCTOR TRAVELS NOT USING HIS TARDIS

As seen in *Hell Bent* (2015)

The Twelfth Doctor travels from the end of time itself to Nevada, USA, apparently in the present day. He doesn't make this journey in ***his*** TARDIS, but in another TARDIS stolen from Gallifrey.

BIGGER ON THE INSIDE

HOW TRANSCENDENTAL IS TRANSCENDENTAL?

THE LARGEST THE TARDIS EVER GETS WHILE STILL A POLICE BOX

As seen in *The Name of the Doctor* (2013)

On the planet **Trenzalore**, the Eleventh Doctor, Clara Oswald and River Song discover a vast graveyard commemorating the future battle in which the Doctor will die once and for all. The graves are for soldiers who fought in this final conflict. 'The bigger the gravestone, the higher the rank,' explains the Doctor And then they see an enormous memorial in the shape of a police box but ragged and worn – and the size of an office block.

But this is not a TARDIS-shaped monument; it's the Doctor's TARDIS from the future, which has been used as his future self's **tomb**. 'When a TARDIS is dying,' the (still alive) Doctor explains, 'sometimes the dimension dams start breaking down. They used to call it a "size leak": all the bigger on the inside starts leaking to the outside.'

THE TARDIS'S LEAST EFFECTIVE DISGUISE

As seen in *An Unearthly Child* (1963)

The TARDIS should be able to change its shape to completely blend in with its surroundings, but the **chameleon circuit** isn't working. Even so, why, of all things, is it a police box?

In the second ever episode of *Doctor Who, The Cave of Skulls*, the Doctor's granddaughter Susan Foreman is surprised that, on arriving in prehistoric times, the TARDIS is still a police box – so this is the first time the chameleon circuit has gone wrong.

Surely that means the TARDIS took the form of a police box to blend into the London of the 1960s, where Susan has been going to school for five months. At the time, police boxes were a common sight across the country.

But in this form the TARDIS *doesn't* blend into the **junk yard** at **76 Totters Lane**, the address the school secretary has for Susan. 'It's a police box!' exclaims Ian Chesterton when he and Barbara Wright visit. 'What on earth's it doing here? These things are usually on the street.'

He and Barbara stumble into the TARDIS and end up travelling in time because the police box is such a poor disguise.

THE LARGEST THE TARDIS EVER GETS

As seen in *The Big Bang* (2010)

When the TARDIS explodes at the end of *The Pandorica Opens* (2010), it causes **cracks in time** and a **total event collapse**. Every star at every moment in history explodes in supernovae, so the whole universe has never existed.

Except in the next episode there's still a planet Earth, albeit one with no stars in its night sky and where **penguins** live on the Nile. But without its local star, the Sun, how is this Earth kept warm enough for the penguins – and humans, and all the other life forms – to survive? The Eleventh Doctor points up to what looks like the blazing Sun but is really his TARDIS burning up.

Does that mean the exploding TARDIS is the same size of the Sun? They look a similar size as seen from Earth, and clearly the TARDIS radiates a similar level of heat if penguins and other life forms on Earth survive without freezing or being cooked. (See pp. 60–1 for more about exactly how much heat the Sun generates.)

The radius of the Sun is **695,000 kilometres**, but the TARDIS would only be exactly the same size if it occupies the same position the Sun did, and so is the same **150 million kilometres** from Earth. If it's further away but appears the same size from Earth, it must be larger than the Sun – and vice versa. Are there any clues as to the distance of the TARDIS?

Well, it takes light eight minutes to reach us from the Sun. It takes **42 seconds** of screen time for the Doctor, flying the Pandorica, to get from Earth to the exploded TARDIS – so either he's travelling several times faster than the speed of light or the TARDIS is much closer than the Sun, and so not as big.

THE SMALLEST THE TARDIS EVER GETS

As seen in *Flatline* (2014)

The **Boneless** are life forms from a universe of just two dimensions, leeching off the third dimension on Earth. They're naturally drawn to the TARDIS, which is so much bigger than three dimensions ought to allow, and as they feed, the TARDIS starts to shrink, at least as seen from outside. The normal-sized Twelfth Doctor finds himself trapped inside when the exterior door is no longer large enough to pass through, and still the TARDIS is shrinking.

When the miniature TARDIS is about to be hit by a speeding train, the Doctor manages to turn on '**siege mode**', leaving the exterior of the TARDIS a sealed cube, each side **75 millimetres**.

CHAPTER FIVE
EARTH AND HUMANITY

'IT MAY BE IRRATIONAL OF ME, BUT HUMAN BEINGS ARE QUITE MY FAVOURITE SPECIES.'

THE FOURTH DOCTOR, *THE ARK IN SPACE* (1975)

THE HUMAN FACTOR 116
SEVEN AGES OF MEN AND WOMEN 118
HELLO, OLD GIRL 120
FOOD AND DRINK 122
THEY WOULD SAY THAT 124
I'M ONLY SLEEPING 126
DISASTER! 128
THE RIGHT STUFF 130

PRIVATE
PROPERTY
ER'S LANE

THE HUMAN FACTOR

WHAT MAKES US AND OUR PLANET SO GREAT? CAN THE DOCTOR GIVE US AN OBJECTIVE VIEW AS A NEUTRAL, OUTSIDE OBSERVER?

THE DOCTOR'S FAVOURITE SPECIES

More than half of all *Doctor Who* episodes – **482** of 827 – are at least partially set on Earth, and many of those that aren't, such as *The Ark in Space (1975)*, feature human beings in space.

What makes Earth so special? Well, a lot of the other planets we see in time and space don't look especially inviting. While Earth is abundant with life and colour and interest, many other worlds are little more than dreary rock and mud – they resemble **quarries** on a grey day on Earth.

The Doctor also seems taken by the culture, history and potential of humanity, and often delights in meeting major figures in Earth history. We might be '**stupid apes** blundering on top of this planet', as the Ninth Doctor says in *Rose* (2005), and our lives might be very brief compared to his, but perhaps that's why our achievements and successes – when we have them – seem all the more impressive to him.

Perhaps there's a more personal reason, too. In the TV movie *Doctor Who* (1996), the Eighth Doctor claims, 'I'm **half-human** – on my mother's side'. That seems to be more than a joke because the Doctor having the same **retinal structure** as a human – rather than Time Lord – eye is a factor in the plot.

THE BEST BIT OF EARTH HISTORY

As seen in *Day of the Moon* (2011)

The Reign of Terror that swept through post-revolutionary France at the end of the 18th century is, says the Doctor's granddaughter Susan Foreman, his '**favourite period in the history of Earth**'.

In the very first episode of *Doctor Who*, we see evidence of this when Susan eagerly borrows a book on the French Revolution from her teacher, Barbara Wright. But in *The Reign of Terror* (1964), the TARDIS actually lands Susan, Barbara, the First Doctor and Ian Chesterton in France on 24 July 1794, and they're soon swept up in the violent political storm. At the end of the story, Barbara and Ian spy the young **Napoleon Bonaparte** and seem keen to talk to him. 'Don't stand around, it's too dangerous,' the Doctor chides, keen to get away. After all the horrors they've faced in the story, it seems that this moment in history is no longer his favourite.

Has the Doctor found another favourite moment in history since then? When the Third Doctor is **exiled** to Earth without the use of his TARDIS in what's apparently the near future, he resents being stuck here and makes a number of disparaging comments about Earth and its level of sophistication. But having regained his freedom to travel in time and space, he keeps returning to contemporary Earth at the end of the 20th and then into the early 21st centuries.

We can narrow it down even further. In *Blink* (2007), Martha Jones says she and the Tenth Doctor have been to see the **first Moon landing** – on **20 July 1969** – four times. She says it's 'brilliant'. We don't know of any other point in Earth history the Doctor has been back to so many times.

THE BEST OF HUMANITY

As seen in *The Evil of the Daleks* (1967)

The Daleks are bothered that human beings, though clearly so inferior, keep defeating them. To find out what's going on, they steal the TARDIS and force the Second Doctor to conduct a secret experiment to work out humanity's secret.

The Doctor closely watches his companion Jamie Macrimmon as he undertakes a difficult quest to rescue Victoria Waterfield, avoiding traps set by the Daleks. From this, the Doctor distils all the elements that make Jamie successful into a 'human factor'.

According to the Doctor's experiment, the best of humanity is made up of **courage**, **pity**, **chivalry**, **friendship** and **compassion**. These he programmes into a positronic brain and inputs into three Daleks. But the Daleks that receive the human factor then display other qualities: **playfulness** (they play a game of trains with the delighted Doctor) and **insatiable curiosity** – which makes them question their orders and leads to Dalek civil war.

SEVEN AGES OF MEN AND WOMEN

ALL *DOCTOR WHO* IS A STAGE, THE MEN AND WOMEN IN IT MERELY PLAYERS...

THE FIRST PERSON IN *DOCTOR WHO*

As seen in *An Unearthly Child* (1963)

As the opening titles faded for the first time, viewers watched a policeman explore a mysterious scrapyard, in which an ordinary-looking police box emits a strange, machine-like hum. The policeman was played by Reg Cranfield. [illegible] Cranfield played non-speaking roles in further stories, alongside the First Doctor, Second Doctor, Third Doctor and Fourth Doctor. His final appearance was as a Time Lord in *The Deadly Assassin* (1976).

[illegible] The 50th-anniversary special, *The Day of the Doctor* (2013) also begins with us following a policeman in a deliberate echo of that first ever sequence.

THE YOUNGEST PERSON TO WRITE *DOCTOR WHO*

On 25 February 1979, **Andrew Smith** was commissioned to write what became Fourth Doctor adventure *Full Circle*. At the time, he was **17 years old**, and 18 when the story was broadcast the following year.

Andrew is the youngest person ever to write a full episode of *Doctor Who*. But the Eleventh Doctor appeared in two mini-episodes written by **10 and 11 year-old** schoolchildren as part of BBC competitions. *Death is the Only Answer* (2011) was written by **Daniel Heaton**, **Katie Hossick**, **Adam Shephard** and **Ben Weston** from Oakley Junior School in Basingstoke, while *Good as Gold* (2012) was written by **Emily Gaskin**, **Rebecca Howitt** and **Libby Pratt** from Ashdene Primary School in Wilmslow.

THE EARLIEST-BORN PERSON IN *DOCTOR WHO*

As seen in *The Smugglers* (1966)

Gaptooth, seen in the final episode of *The Smugglers* (1966), is a greedy, argumentative, violent and drunken pirate in the crew of the villainous Captain Pike. He was played by actor **Jack Hodges Bligh**, who was born on **31 December 1889** at 1 Beaufort Villas, Ramsgate.

THE LATEST-BORN PERSON IN *DOCTOR WHO*

As seen in *The Return of Doctor Mysterio* (2016)

While Grant Gordon and Lucy Fletcher fly off to dump a spaceship in the Sun, the Twelfth Doctor is left to change the nappy of baby **Jennifer Fletcher**.

THE LONGEST-LIVED PERSON IN DOCTOR WHO

As seen in *Marco Polo* (1964) and *The Crusade* (1965)

Actress **Zohra Segal** first appeared in *Doctor Who* in three episodes of *Marco Polo* (1964), playing an unnamed attendant to Lady Ping-Cho. A year later, she appeared in an episode of *The Crusade* as **Sheyrah**, a servant employed by the great sultan Saladin. Born on 27 April 1912, Segal was in her 50s when she appeared in *Doctor Who*. She died on 10 July 2014, aged **102 years, two months and 13 days**.

THE YOUNGEST PERSON TO DIRECT *DOCTOR WHO*

Waris Hussein, born 9 December 1938, was 24 years old when he directed *An Unearthly Child* (1963) – the first ever *Doctor Who* story.

THE YOUNGEST PERSON IN CHARGE OF *DOCTOR WHO*

Today, *Doctor Who* has a **'showrunner'**, a head writer in charge of the fictional universe of the series, who oversees the scripts. From 2005 to 2010, that showrunner was Russell T Davies. From 2010 until the end of the 2017 series, the showrunner is Steven Moffat. From 2018, the showrunner will be Chris Chibnall.

Before 2005, *Doctor Who* didn't have showrunners, and the person in charge of the fictional universe of the series was the **script or story editor**. The youngest ever script editor in this sense on *Doctor Who* was **Andrew Cartmel**, who oversaw the Seventh Doctor's adventures. Andrew was **28 years old** when he started in the role.

Doctor Who continues to have story editors, but the job title doesn't mean the same thing as it used to. Even in the old days, the script or story editor was always answerable to the producer, who was ultimately responsible for all aspects of the programme. Born on 27 November 1935, **Verity Lambert** was **27 years old** when she became the first producer of *Doctor Who*. At the time, she was also the youngest and the only female drama producer at the BBC.

HELLO, OLD GIRL

THE LONGEST-LIVED HUMAN IN THE UNIVERSE

'IMMORTALITY ISN'T LIVING FOREVER. THAT'S NOT WHAT IT FEELS LIKE. IMMORTALITY IS EVERYBODY ELSE DYING.'

The Twelfth Doctor, *The Girl Who Died* (2015)

c.851

Ashildr lives with her father, **Einarr**, in a **Viking village** that is attacked by the alien **Mire**. She helps the Twelfth Doctor fend of the Mire – but it kills her. The Doctor uses a **Mire repair kit** to restore her to life – but it makes her **immortal**. The Doctor gives her a second repair kit so she can make someone else immortal to share her life with.

Over time, Einarr and everyone else in the village died and Ashildr moved on.

Date unknown

Ashildr cures an entire village of **scarlet fever** and is almost drowned as a witch for her troubles

1348 –

Ashildr gets sick from the ***Yersinia pestis bacterium*** that sweeps the world – but recovers. Her children do not, and, grief-stricken, she vows not to have any more.

1415 – Battle of Agincourt

Ashildr ties up a bowman and takes his place in this famous battle – see p. 82.

Date unknown

Ashildr is a **medieval queen**, but it's a life mostly of paperwork and backgammon so she fakes her own death and escapes.

1651

Ashildr no longer uses her old name and instead calls herself '**Me**'. She is barely able to remember the Viking village or much else of her life and her memories fill enough books to fill a library. She is now a highwayman called '**the Knightmare**', and plots with the leonine alien **Leandro** to escape from Earth – but Leandro is really planning an invasion. Me helps the Doctor and uses her spare Mire repair kit – which she has not previously used on anyone – to save the life of fellow highwayman, **Sam Swift**.

It's not clear if Sam Swift also becomes immortal, or how much time Me spends in his company.

1815 – The Battle of Waterloo

It seems Me might have been at this famous battle, before hiding in the secret **trap street** in London – which is why the Doctor, who has been keeping tabs on her life, loses track of her.

c.1915

The last act of violence in the trap street, under Me's stewardship, for 100 years.

c.2015

Me keeps watch on the Doctor and Clara Oswald, appearing at **Coal Hill School** where Clara works.

When the Doctor and Clara find Me in the trap street, Me doesn't remember that she and Clara have already met. An error leads to Clara's death, but Me – though regretting this – has also made a deal to deliver the Doctor to someone...

100,000,000,000,000

At the end of the universe, Me waits in a reality bubble for the Doctor. She had made her deal with the **Time Lords**. Now, Me has outlived 'the other immortals' – whoever they might be. She and Clara take charge of a **stolen TARDIS** and head off to new adventures.

FOOD AND DRINK

INVADING THE EARTH CAN WORK UP AN APPETITE, SO WHERE CAN HUNGRY ALIENS GRAB A BIT TO EAT?

In *Death in Heaven* (2014), we learn that the ad in the *Times* was placed by **Missy**, who's keen to keep the Doctor and Clara together.

THE BEST DINNER IN LONDON

As seen in *Deep Breath* (2014)

The newly regenerated Twelfth Doctor is somewhere in late Victorian London, investigating cases of people – and a **dinosaur** – apparently exploding. Then it seems he's ready to share what he's discovered with Clara Oswald, because she spots an advertisement in the personal column of the ***Times*** newspaper addressed to his nickname for her.

'Impossible girl,' it says. 'Lunch on the other side?'

It takes a moment to understand – but on the other side of the page in the newspaper is an advertisement for '**Mancini's Family Restaurant, the Best Dinner in London**'.

Clara meets the Doctor at Mancini's – but he thinks *she* placed the ad in the paper. They have both been manoeuvred into a trap. The other diners are **clockwork robots**, and it's the Doctor and Clara who are now on the menu. Liver, spleen, brain stem, eyes, lungs and skin – anything can be used.

It might not sound the most appetising meal, but it's surely the best dinner in London if you're a clockwork robot.

THE BIGGEST APPETITE ON EARTH

As seen in *Battlefield* (1989)

The demon called the **Destroyer** wants to devour our whole planet.

THE GREATEST FEAST ON EARTH

As seen in *Love & Monsters* (2006)

Perhaps there's a theme emerging here, but in London in the present day the **Abzorbaloff** describes the prospect of absorbing the Tenth Doctor as 'the greatest feast of all' because of all his experience and knowledge.

THE GREATEST CHEFS IN EARTH HISTORY

As cited in *The Two Doctors* (1985)

The Second Doctor is turned into an **Androgum** – a race of ravenous gourmets. He and another Androgum called **Shockeye** then wander into **Seville** in southern Spain in search of a suitably enormous meal.

On the way, they argue culinary customs. Shockeye can see no point in serving **hors d'oeuvres** as 'eight or nine dishes are quite enough in my opinion.'

But the Doctor, with his wide knowledge of history and culture, responds that, 'On this planet, it is the custom. All the greatest chefs agree, **Carême**, **Brillat-Savarin**, the noble **Escoffier** ... that one should begin with a light dish, something to bring relish to the appetite.'

Marie Antoine Carême (1784–1833) was an early pioneer of 'grande cuisine' cooking; Jean Anthelme Brillat-Savarin (1755–1826) wrote *The Physiology of Taste* (1825), which has never been out of print; and George Auguste Escoffier (1846–1935) was a restaurateur and writer keen on traditional French cooking methods. So the Doctor's tastes – at least as an Androgum – favour the French in the late 18th and 19 century. Which isn't a surprise given what his granddaughter says is his favourite part of Earth history (see pp. 116–17).

THE DOCTOR'S BIGGEST MEAL

As seen in *The Two Doctors*

Shockeye and the Second Doctor (still turned into an Androgum) dine at the **Las Cadenas** restaurant in the picturesque **Barrio de Santa Cruz**, Seville. There they eat:

- Lobsters
- Clams
- Squid
- Brains in white sauce
- A whole suckling pig each
- A ham with figs (between them)
- Four steaks each
- A family paella – 12 servings between the two of them

Six bottles of wine each

They then order a dozen breasts of pigeons to share and are still happily eating. That's even more astonishing given that before he's turned into an Androgum, this Doctor is rather abstemious: at the start of the story, he tells his friend Jamie Macrimmon that 'one meal a day is quite sufficient.'

THEY WOULD SAY THAT...

ENTIRELY RELIABLE, OBJECTIVE RECORDS GIVEN IN *DOCTOR WHO* BY COMPLETELY UNBIASED SOURCES

THE BEST BEER IN THE UNITED KINGDOM

'Arthur's Ale' brewed by Pat Rawlinson at the Gore Crow Hotel near Lake Vortigern, according to Pat Rawlinson of the Gore Crow Hotel near Lake Vortigern – ***Battlefield*** (1989)

THE BEST KNIGHT IN THE WORLD

Ancelyn from an alternative Earth, according to Ancelyn from an alternative Earth – ***Battlefield***

"Your leader will be angry if you kill me," the Second Doctor tells the Ice Warriors in *The Seeds of Death* (1969), modestly. "I'm a genius."

THE GREATEST MAN INTELLIGENCE EVER ASSEMBLED ON EARTH

The Brotherhood of Logicians, according to Eric Klieg, member of the Brotherhood of Logicians – ***The Tomb of the Cybermen*** (1967)

THE BEST AND BRAVEST PILOT

Reg Arwell, pilot of a Lancaster bomber during World War II, according to his wife Madge Arwell – ***The Doctor, the Widow and the Wardrobe*** (2012)

THE BEST GUNS

Arturo Villar's guns, according to Arturo Villar – *The War Games* (1969)

THE MIGHTIEST WARRIOR

Achilles, according to Achilles – ***The Myth Makers*** (1965)

THE GREATEST IN BATTLE

Achilles, according to Achilles – ***The Myth Makers***

THE HUMBLEST OF ZEUS'S SERVANTS

Achilles, according to Achilles – ***The Myth Makers***

I'M ONLY SLEEPING

TRY TO GET SOME REST

Rogin says that instead of sleeping on the Ark, some Earth people thought they'd survive the solar flares by going into 'thermic shelters'. We don't know if they survived.

THE LONGEST HUMAN SLEEP IN HISTORY

As seen in *The Ark in Space* (1975)

The TARDIS arrives on **Space Station Nerva** which was built, the Fourth Doctor deduces by spotting a **macro-slave drive** and a modified version of a **Bennett oscillator**, in the late 29th or early 30th centuries. But that's not the date now – the Doctor, Sarah Jane Smith and Harry Sullivan have arrived at some point well beyond that.

The space station contains hundreds of what Harry thinks are dead bodies, but the Doctor shows are people in **suspended animation**. Solar flares were about to destroy all life on Earth, and scientists calculated it would be 5,000 years before the biosphere was habitable again. So hundreds of citizen volunteers made what Earth's High Minister calls the 'supreme sacrifice', and were irradiated and biocryonically preserved to sleep through the catastrophe.

Unfortunately, an alien **Wirrn** burrows into Nerva's systems and affects the alarm clocks, so the sleepers don't wake for 10,000 years. The Wirrn also starts to feed on the bodies...

THE MOST VIVID SHARED DREAM

As seen in *Amy's Choice* (2010)

Years after their travels with the Eleventh Doctor, Amy Pond and Rory Williams are living in a nice cottage in the sweet little village of **Upper Leadworth** – which is more upmarket than ordinary Leadworth. When the Doctor pops into visit, Amy is pregnant and life seems pretty good, apart from Rory growing a **ponytail**.

Except then the Doctor, Amy and Rory **wake up** and find themselves in the TARDIS – Upper Leadworth was merely a dream they all shared. Except then they wake up ***again*** back in Upper Leadworth. Which is the real place and which one are they dreaming?

The Fourth Doctor says 'sleep is for tortoises' and the Doctor doesn't seem to need much rest – but when injured he can put himself in a self-induced coma.

THE MOST PEOPLE ASLEEP

As seen in *The Invasion* (1968)

International Electromatics is the world's biggest electronics manufacturer – its technicians are, boasts smooth managing director **Tobias Vaughn**, the best in the world and you can hardly buy a piece of electronic equipment that doesn't come from the company.

But everything IE produces contains a **micro-monolithic circuit** that's an artificial nervous system. Once Vaughn activates these circuits, almost every electronic device produces a hypnotic force that controls human beings, sending them to sleep while the **Cybermen** invade.

UNIT's **Captain Jimmy Turner** says there must be 'hundreds, thousands of these circuits in IE equipment all over the world' – but surely that's an understatement. From what we see, only the Second Doctor and his friends – and UNIT's soldiers – wear the '**depolarisers**' that resist the effects of the Cyber-control waves. Which surely means the Cybermen have put millions to sleep.

Then, from the sewers of London, hundreds of Cybermen emerge…

DISASTER!

POOR OLD EARTH DOESN'T HALF TAKE A BEATING SOMETIMES

THE WORST NATURAL DISASTER IN EARTH HISTORY

As seen in *Kill the Moon* (2014)

In *Doctor Who and the Silurians* (1970), we learn that millions of years ago Earth's ancient population of intelligent reptiles spotted a small planet approaching through space. They calculated that this would draw off Earth's atmosphere and so destroy all life. That's the reason the **Silurians** hibernated in shelters deep underground – only to emerge years later to find 'their' planet over-run by primitive apes called humans.

The Third Doctor assumes that the 'small planet' the Silurians saw was captured by Earth's gravity and is now the **Moon**; whether or not he's right, it's clear that it didn't destroy all life and so wasn't the disaster predicted.

In *The Sontaran Experiment* (1975), the Fourth Doctor arrives on Earth 10,000 years after **solar flares** apparently killed all life on the planet – but though the only humans there are space travellers from an Earth colony, the planet is clearly alive: we see grass and trees. Besides, the colonists are proof that humans escaped the disaster, and in the previous story, *The Ark in Space*, we learn that animal and botanic specimens have been saved, too, as well as a complete record of human thought and achievement. So it's a disaster, but one we cope with pretty well.

But in *Kill the Moon*, set in 2049, very few humans can get into space to escape a global calamity. The Twelfth Doctor and Clara Oswald join what seems to be the only people able to get away: the Doctor describes them as 'third-hand astronauts' on a 'second-hand space shuttle' pinched from a museum. These people are on a mission to destroy the Moon.

It seems the Moon has put on weight, and this increase in mass is causing chaos on Earth – as the Doctor says, the **tides** must be so high that whole cities are drowned. The astronaut Lundvik calls it the greatest natural disaster in history. 'It is killing people. It is destroying the Earth.'

It turns out the Moon is an **egg**, and the changes in weight are because the huge **baby** inside is ready to hatch. Lundvik realises that will mean huge chunks of the Moon are soon raining down on Earth – which would have a far more devastating effect than the Cyber-controlled space freighter that wiped out the dinosaurs (see pp. 94–95). So there's only one choice, isn't there? They must destroy the giant baby...

THE WORST UNNATURAL DISASTER IN EARTH HISTORY

As seen in *Inferno* (1970)

Professor Stahlman is leading a project to mine 20 miles down through the Earth's crust to exploit 'a vast new storehouse of energy' even more powerful than North Sea gas. He's modestly named this new resource 'Stahlman's gas'.

But the mining operation also pulls up some icky **green slime** – and anyone who touches this **primordial** stuff is transformed into a slavering, hairy monster.

The Third Doctor is, at least to begin with, more interested in using the energy generated by the mine to get his TARDIS working. However, his experiments don't send him forwards or backwards in time, but **sideways** to another Earth populated by crueller versions of his friends. There, a version of Stahlman is even further with his mine operations – but as well as unleashing more slavering monsters, he also destroys the world.

The Doctor is the only one on that whole other Earth to escape, arriving back in his own version in time to stop the original Stahlman make the same mistake.

THE WORST MISTAKE ON EARTH

As seen in *The Pandorica Opens* (2010)

'This may qualify as the worst miscalculation since life crawled out of the seas on this sad planet,' says the Seventh Doctor in *Silver Nemesis* (1988), about a comet containing the living metal **validium**, which he launched into space from Windsor in 1638, but in a decaying orbit that will land it back where it started exactly 250 years later.

But the Doctor hasn't made a mistake: it's all a devious plan to get the validium into the midst of a thousands-strong **Cyber war fleet** and destroy it.

So what is the worst miscalculation in history? Surely it's the alliance of the Doctor's enemies – including the Cybermen – who think that trapping the Doctor in the **Pandorica** under Stonehenge will prevent the end of the universe, but actually he's the only one who can stop it – so everything explodes!

THE GREATEST PERIL IN HUMAN HISTORY

As seen in *Pyramids of Mars* (1975)

In 1911, the Fourth Doctor says that in **Sutekh the Osiran** – an alien that the ancient Egyptians saw as a god – he and Sarah Jane Smith face 'greatest peril in human history'. To prove it, he returns Sarah to her own time in 1980 to see the desolate Earth Sutekh will leave unless they go back and stop him. Which they do, so it's OK.

THE RIGHT STUFF

WHY DO WE THINK WE HUMANS ARE SO SPECIAL?

THE GREATEST RESOURCE ON EARTH

As seen in *Evolution of the Daleks* (2007)

In many stories, we see human beings in the depths of space searching for planets that are rich in useful minerals and other natural resources (see pp. 58–59). But what about what's here on Earth?

Plenty of aliens want to invade Earth for different reasons: it's a temperate, stable world that supports life, though many aliens would need to modify it to suit their needs. It offers other potential, too. In *World War Three* (2005), the **Slitheen** want to start a nuclear holocaust and then sell irradiated chunks of the planet for scrap. In *The Dalek Invasion of Earth* (1964), the **Daleks** want to replace the Earth's core with a motor and turn the whole planet into a vast spaceship.

But in *Evolution of the Daleks*, the Daleks' experiments lead them to recognise the planet's greatest resource: humanity itself. They're not alone, as many alien beings – from the **Cybermen** to the **Gelth**, from **clockwork robots** to the **Chameleons** – want to harvest our bodies.

THE DOCTOR'S VERDICT

'Homo sapiens. What an inventive, invincible species… It's only a few million years since they crawled up out of the mud and learned to walk. Puny, defenceless bipeds, they've survived flood and famine and plague. They survived cosmic wars and holocausts. And now here they are, out among the stars, waiting to begin a new life… ready to out-sit eternity. They're indomitable. **Indomitable**.'
The Fourth Doctor, *The Ark in Space* (1975)

In an early draft of the script for *Aliens of London*, one of the experts is General Muriel Frost, strategic adviser to UNIT, who the Doctor describes as a 'good woman'. Frost was a character from the *Doctor Who Magazine* comic strip, who first appeared in 1991 helping the Seventh Doctor.

THE GREATEST EXPERTS IN EXTRA-TERRESTRIAL EVENTS

In *Aliens of London* (2005), a spaceship piloted by a **pig in a spacesuit** crashes into the Thames and is soon global news. Alien experts – including the Ninth Doctor – are summoned to 10 Downing Street – but not to discuss what's happened. 'This is all about us,' realises the Doctor. 'The only people with knowledge how to fight them gathered together in one room.' They've walked into a Slitheen trap and all but the Doctor are killed.

There are plenty of other experts in dealing with aliens: **Torchwood**, established by **Queen Victoria** in 1879, has by 2006 developed a defensive system capable of destroying a **Sycorax** spaceship as it leaves the Earth. **UNIT**, established after the **Yeti** take over the London Underground apparently in the mid-1970s, is constantly defending the Earth – and takes pride in doing so without the Doctor's help.

Some of the Doctor's companions work for UNIT and/or Torchwood. In the case of **Brigadier Lethbridge-Stewart**, **Liz Shaw**, **Jo Grant** and **Harry Sullivan**, that's how the Doctor meets them. But for **Rose Tyler**, **Captain Jack** and **Martha Jones**, it's their experience in travelling with the Doctor that qualifies them for the job after they leave the TARDIS.

Martha doesn't stay with UNIT long: the last time we see her, in *The End of Time, Part Two* (2010), she and her husband, **Mickey Smith**, have gone freelance and are on the trail of a Sontaran. **Sarah Jane Smith** is still out investigating strange phenomena by herself, decades after leaving the TARDIS.

In *Death of the Doctor* (2010), a story from the spin-off series *The Sarah Jane Adventures*, Jo Grant (now Jones) is still off adventuring round the world, battling for good causes. Sarah has also searched out some of the Doctor's other former companions: **Tegan Jovanka** is in Australia fighting for Aboriginal rights; **Ben Jackson** and **Polly** run an orphanage in India; Harry Sullivan – a doctor – did good work with vaccines and saved thousands of lives; **Ace** has raised billions through a charity; **Ian and Barbara Chesterton** are professors at Cambridge.

'Echoes of the Doctor, all over the world,' Sarah concludes. Experts in not just aliens and strange goings on, but also the best way to live.

CHAPTER SIX
DALEKS

'IMAGINE THE WORST POSSIBLE THING IN THE UNIVERSE, THEN DON'T BOTHER, BECAUSE YOU'RE LOOKING AT IT RIGHT NOW.'

THE TWELFTH DOCTOR, *INTO THE DALEK* (2014)

DALEK NO.1 134

MORE DALEK FIRSTS 136

EXTERMINATE! 138

DALEK ARMY! 140

FRIEND OR FOE 142

DALEK NO.1

THE DALEKS WERE THE FIRST LIVING ALIEN CREATURES SEEN IN *DOCTOR WHO*

THE FIRST EVER DALEK

As seen in *The Daleks* (1963–1964)

The very first ***Doctor Who*** story, ***An Unearthly Child*** (1963), took the TARDIS back to prehistoric times where primitive humans had lost the secret of making fire. At the end of the story, and the fourth episode of the series, the Doctor and his friends escaped back to their ship and journeyed to another planet – which we'd soon learn was **Skaro**, planet of the Daleks.

For this first Dalek story, four full-size Dalek props were constructed by **Shawcraft Models** from designs by **Raymond Cusick**. They were meant to look identical, which led to confusion

during rehearsals so labels were stuck to the Daleks' domes, identifying them as '1', '2', '3' and '4'. These labels can be seen in some photographs taken on set – but the labels were removed for the actual recording of the episodes.

However, the Dalek labelled '1' in any particular episode or story wasn't necessarily the first Dalek that Shawcraft Models constructed. Is it possible to tell which Dalek came first?

In fact, Shawcraft Models also numbered the four Daleks – but in a much subtler way. On the back of each Dalek, between its silver collars, is a **horizontal tally mark**, with one, two, three of four strokes.

'So what I call "**Dalek One**" has a single notch,' says Dalek expert Gavin Rymill. 'But we can't be sure that Shawcraft numbered them as each one was finished.'

Even so, Gavin argues, 'Dalek One has a narrower collar at the front than all the others and it's a bit wonky. It also hasn't had its rods chamfered to stop them catching on the dome which may have been something they realised was worth doing after the first one was finished. In the story, a Dalek needed to have its top swing open for Ian to peep out from, so this one has an extra latch that the others don't. And it seems logical that any extra modifications needed would be done to the first Dalek that was finished…'

So is Dalek One the first ever Dalek? Gavin phrases his answer with care. 'There's no irrefutable proof to say yes, but some circumstantial evidence suggests it.'

WHERE'S ONE NOW?

Dalek One appeared in the first five TV Dalek stories. After *The Power of the Daleks* (1966), the top and bottom half were separated. The bottom half – or "skirt" – matched with the top of what Gavin Rymill calls Dalek Two appeared in *The Evil of the Daleks* (1967) and then made a number of publicity appearances. After the Schoolboys and Girls Exhibition at London Olympia Hall in early 1968, it seems to have been junked during a clear-out of the BBC prop stores. The top half continued to appear in *Doctor Who* until 1988 and then appeared in exhibitions. It's been owned by collector Chris Balcombe since 2011.

MORE DALEK FIRSTS

EXTERMINATING THEIR WAY INTO THE RECORDS

THE FIRST ALIEN SEEN IN *DOCTOR WHO*

As seen in *The Daleks* (1963–1964)
The first alien seen in *Doctor Who* is **Susan Foreman**, who appears four minutes and 38 seconds into the very first episode of the series. The **First Doctor** – also an alien – makes his first appearance 11 minutes and 38 seconds into the same episode.

What about aliens other than the Doctor and his companions? At the end of that first episode the TARDIS leaves Earth in the 1960s and seems to go back to prehistoric times. We're not told explicitly that we're still on Earth, so it's *possible* the tribe of primitive people we meet there are aliens – but we can't be certain.

In the fifth episode of the series, *The Dead Planet* (1963), the Doctor and his friends explore what is definitely another planet and discover a dead animal – but not one composed of flesh and blood. 'I should say originally it was some pliable metal held together by ... an inner magnetic field,' surmises the Doctor. 'It may have had the ability to attract its victims towards it, if they were metal, too.'

In fact, it's this discovery of so alien a creature that confirms they're no longer on Earth. A little while later, a human-looking hand reaches out to touch Susan, the first *living* alien we can be sure of in the series. In reality, the hand belonged to the production assistant on the story, **Michael Ferguson** – who would later go on to direct four *Doctor Who* stories. But in terms of the story, we learn two episodes later that the hand belongs to a Thal called **Alydon**, played – when we finally see him in full – by actor John Lee. The Thals are natives of the planet Skaro but, like many aliens we've encountered over the years, their species has evolved to look very like Earth's human beings.

Before we meet Alydon in person, the Doctor and his friends encounter the first ever living, non-humanoid aliens in *Doctor Who* – the **Daleks**.

THE FIRST SPECIES CAPABLE OF TRAVELLING IN TIME

As seen in *The Chase* (1965)

We don't know of anyone with the power to travel in time before the **Time Lords** – though that doesn't necessarily mean that they were the first.

In *The Time Meddler* (1965), we meet the **Monk**, the first of the Doctor's own people other than the Doctor and Susan to appear in the series. The Monk has his own time machine just like the TARDIS – though he doesn't use that name for it. Until then, we might have believed that only the Doctor had such a vehicle.

But in the story before this, we see the first alien creatures other than the Doctor (and his people) with the ability to travel in time. In *The Chase* (1965), the Daleks complete a time machine of their own and use it to pursue the Doctor and his companions through time and space to exact revenge because they 'delayed our conquest of Earth'.

Dalek casings are made of a special metal called **Dalekanium**. First described in *The Dalek Book* published in September 1964 – but spelt 'Dalekenium' – it's the very first idea from a spin-off book or other media to then appear in TV *Doctor Who*.

THE ULTIMATE SURVIVOR

As seen in *Genesis of the Daleks* (1975)

In the ancient history of Skaro, a war has raged for centuries between the **Kaleds** and the Thals. Kaled scientists had originally worked on devising ever more devastating chemical weapons that might end this war, before realising that was futile and instead researching ways that their people might survive. Unfortunately, the chemical weapons they'd devised were already causing widespread genetic mutations. One Kaled scientist, the brilliant **Davros**, believes this trend could not be reversed, so carries out experiments to find the ultimate mutational form – and then how to ensure its survival.

He proudly demonstrates his progress to his astonished colleagues: a living, thinking, self-supporting creature housed inside a **Mark III travel machine**.

Or, as the Fourth Doctor knows it, a Dalek.

EXTERMINATE!

DALEKS CONQUER AND DESTROY

THE BIGGEST ACT OF DESTRUCTION COMMITTED BY DALEKS

As seen in *The Parting of the Ways* (2005)

The desolate state of the planet **Skaro** in *The Daleks* (1963–1964) is the result of a nuclear war that raged for centuries between the **Kaleds** and the **Thals**. In *Genesis of the Daleks* (1975) we learn that the Daleks were born out of this conflict – so they can't be blamed entirely for the damage done.

The **Time War** between the Daleks and the Time Lords wreaks havoc on much of the universe – whole planets and higher civilisations are lost, and reality itself is endangered. But we don't have many details about specific acts of destruction, and don't know which side committed them. So it's difficult to claim this as a record.

What's the worst destruction for which we do have verifiable details? In *The Parting of the Ways*, the **Dalek fleet of 200 ships** bombs Earth in the year **200,100**. 'They're bombing whole continents', **Lynda** – with a Y – tells the Ninth Doctor. 'Europa, Pacifica, the New American Alliance… Australasia's just gone.'

THE MOST DEATHS ON SCREEN IN A SINGLE STORY

As seen in *Resurrection of the Daleks* (1984)

Within two minutes of the opening titles of *Resurrection of the Daleks*, **nine humans** have been gunned down in the street by two men in police uniform. Three minutes later, a man called **Galloway** is shot off screen – we hear him cry out, and then see his dead body.

It's just the start of the story with the highest on-screen body count of any *Doctor Who*. In the first episode, **29 humans die on screen**: 10 exterminated by Daleks; 15 shot by other humans; and four by other means. In addition, five humans die off-screen but we see their bodies afterwards. Two Daleks are also blown up, so there are **36 verifiable deaths** in an episode lasting 46 minutes and 24 seconds – a death every 1 minute 17 seconds.

We also hear that the captain of the prison ship and half the crew have been killed before the Daleks even dock, but since we never see these deaths or the bodies afterwards (we never see the captain, even when he's alive.) we won't include them in our total.

In the second episode, we must wait almost 20 minutes for another death – when the men in police

uniform shoot a man with a metal detector. By the end of the end of the episode, 14 humans have been shot and killed on screen and 10 have been exterminated – including four duplicates of human soldiers. Six Daleks die on screen and we see four more that have been killed by a plague (but not the moment they die). That's a total of **34 verifiable deaths**.

In addition, when two spaceships are destroyed at the end of the story, it seems at least three Daleks, the Dalek Supreme and Dalek-built duplicates of the Fifth Doctor and his companions Tegan and Turlough are on board – and so destroyed in the explosion. But since we know from *Revelation of the Daleks* (1985) that **Davros** escaped at the last minute, we can't be sure who else might have got away.

So *Resurrection of the Daleks* has a total of **70 verifiable deaths**, 61 of them on screen.

THE QUICKEST A STORY KILLS SOMEONE ON SCREEN

As seen in *Death to the Daleks* (1974)

How do you best ensnare the audience at the start of a *Doctor Who* story? Since 2005, almost every episode has begun with a thrilling **'teaser'** sequence before the opening titles – we glimpse something weird and intriguing, and often a bit scary, that's sure to get us hooked. The titles themselves – with that brilliant, eerie music, help get us in the mood.

But *Doctor Who* stories from before 2005 often begin with a scene that sets up a thrilling mystery. In *Death to the Daleks*, after 30 seconds of the opening titles – the name of the story itself a brilliant lure – we cut to a man in some mud.

The man, played by stuntman **Terry Walsh**, glances quickly about him as fog curls softly by, and then he sets off in a run. Almost immediately, he stumbles over in exhaustion before carrying wearily on. Without a word being said, we can see he's tired and scared of *something* in the fog, wherever this might be. He's also wearing a blue uniform with a futuristic insignia. Given we're watching *Doctor Who*, we've probably already worked out that he's a space traveller on a hostile alien world.

We cut to a new angle and the man hurries towards us, providing a close-up of the cuts and bruises on his face. Just what has he been through – and what is he so afraid of? Then an arrow shunks into his side, he lets out a sigh and tumbles down a hill, dead.

From the end of the opening titles, it takes just **28 seconds** for us to see this man, absorb who and where he is, and that's it's very dangerous, and then watch him die.

We abruptly cut to the Third Doctor inside the TARDIS, twirling a multi-coloured sunshade and singing 'I Do Like To Be Beside The Seaside', oblivious to the threat that awaits him. But **we** know, because we've just seen it, that there's something horrid coming. We can't look away…

'A LOT OF GOOD PEOPLE HAVE DIED TODAY. I THINK I'M SICK OF IT.'

Tegan Jovanka, *Resurrection of the Daleks*

DALEK ARMY!

DALEKS CONQUER AND DESTROY – AND IN ASTONISHING NUMBERS!

THE MOST DALEKS IN ONE PLACE

As seen in *The Day of the Doctor* (2013)

On the last day of the massive **Time War** between the Daleks and the Time Lords, **Arcadia** – second city of the Time Planet planet **Gallifrey** – falls to the Daleks, who then close in for the kill. Dalek fleets surround the planet, ready to obliterate it.

As the **War Doctor** says, there are a **billion billion** Daleks up there, attacking Gallifrey all at once. A billion billion is a **quintillion**, or 1,000,000,000,000,000,000 – a 1 with 18 zeroes. It's the largest number of Daleks we know of ever assembled in one place.

That's more than 100,000,000 times the number of people living on Earth today – an estimated 7.4 billion. The Tenth Doctor says there are 2.47 billion children on Gallifrey at the time. If, like on Earth, there's an average 1.25 children per adult on Gallifrey, we're looking at a total population of about 5 billion people. So the Daleks *massively* outnumber them.

But numbers this big are difficult for us to get our heads around, so here's one way to think about the size of this Dalek army.

There are about **800 million** – 800,000,000 – blades of grass in a football field. (Of course, the exact number depends on the size of the particular football field and how densely packed the grass is, but we'll use 800 million as an example.)

So, imagine a football field. For **every one** of the 800 million blades of grass on it, add another football field of 800 million blades of grass. You end up with 800 million times 800 million blades of grass – or 640,000,000,000,000,000. And that's a bit more than **half** the number of Daleks attacking Gallifrey!

THE MOST DALEKS DESTROYED IN ONE PLACE

As seen in the *The Day of the Doctor*

On the last day of the Time War, the vast Dalek army surrounds the planet Gallifrey, firing on it constantly. But at the last moment, the **Doctor's 13 incarnations** team up to freeze Gallifrey in an instant of time. It's as if the whole planet just disappeared...

That means the vast Dalek army is firing on itself, and all but one Dalek is destroyed in the crossfire. So, we take a billion billion Daleks and subtract one that fell back through Time: **999,999,999,999,999,999** Daleks.

DALEKS, DALEKS, DALEKS

With limited budgets and resources, it's not always been easy for the people making ***Doctor Who*** to present vast armies of Daleks.

In the very first Dalek story, ***The Daleks*** (1963-4), the First Doctor visits a city on the Dalek home planet, Skaro. To populate the city, just four full-sized Dalek props were built. A fifth, more roughly assembled prop with collapsible elements was provided for scenes of Dalek destruction, and nine full-size photographs helped bulk out the numbers. So in the first Dalek story we see a total of 14 different Daleks.

Two more full-size Dalek props were built for their next story, ***The Dalek Invasion of Earth*** (1964), bringing the total to six. A small model Dalek was also used in the final episode of the story, ***Flashpoint***, looking on as a capsule of explosive (also a model) is lowered towards the Earth's core.

A seventh full-scale Dalek was built for ***The Chase*** (1965) – an uncompleted version, again used for effects work. No new props were built for the Daleks' next few stories, but ***The Power of the Daleks*** (1966) showed an army of Daleks by having the few full-size props move out of shot on the left-hand edge of the screen, circle round behind the set and come back in on the right-hand side. Full-size photographs and model Daleks – in fact, commercially available toys – also helped swell the ranks.

Toys, models and new props helped increase numbers over the years, but only into double figures. Since 2005, we've seen huge numbers of computer-generated Daleks. In ***Asylum of the Daleks*** (2012) and ***The Witch's Familiar*** (2015), the production team also borrowed full-sized props built by fans of the series to increase the numbers on screen.

But the cheapest way to present a huge army of Daleks is just to ***tell us*** there are lots of them. "Somewhere on this planet there are 10,000 Daleks!" declares the Third Doctor in ***Planet of the Daleks*** (1973) – though we never see nearly that many.

Even with CGI Daleks, we're now often told of many more than we actually see. The Ninth Doctor calculates he's facing an army of "just about half a million of them" in ***The Parting of the Ways*** (2005), there are "millions, certainly" in the ***Asylum of the Daleks*** and "a billion billion Daleks up there, attacking [Gallifrey]" in ***The Day of the Doctor***.

THE MOST PEOPLE KILLED BY A SINGLE DALEK ON SCREEN

As seen in *Dalek* (2005)

The sole Dalek to survive the end of the Time War landed on Earth, on the **Ascension Islands**, sometime before AD 1962. By **2012**, it was in the secret collection of **Henry van Statten**, 53 floors or about half a mile below the ground in Utah, USA.

Despite the **Ninth Doctor**'s warnings, the Dalek escapes. We see it kill at least 18 people on screen and are told at the end of the story that 200 of van Statten's personnel are dead. The Dalek then self-destructs, bringing the total number individuals we know of killed by this single Dalek to **201**.

FRIEND OR FOE

YOU CAN JUDGE THE DOCTOR BY THE QUALITY OF HIS ENEMIES

THE MOST FULL-SIZE DALEK PROPS IN ONE STORY

As seen in *Asylum of the Daleks* (2012)

Computer-generated and model (or toy) Daleks are one thing, but for the legions seen in ***Asylum of the Daleks*** the production team of ***Doctor Who*** asked for help from the Daleks' greatest **fans**.

The Asylum of the title is a planet into which the Daleks dump the millions of their race that have gone wrong: the battle-scarred, the insane, the ones they can't control. It wouldn't be right to kill them, the **Prime Minister of the Daleks** explains to the Eleventh Doctor, because the hatred inside them is – to other Daleks – divine. All in all, the Asylum isn't the sort of place anyone would ever want to drop into.

But that's exactly what the Doctor, Amy Pond and Rory Williams do, having heard a rather unusual transmission coming deep within this world of fuming Daleks. It's '**L'amour est un oiseau rebelle**' (Love is a rebellious bird), an aria by George Bizet from his opera *Carmen* (1875). The Doctor soon traces the transmission to a young woman called **Oswin Oswald**, whose ship crash-landed in the Asylum. While she's been waiting for rescue, the plucky Oswin has been listening to opera and baking soufflés. So, the Doctor and his friends attempt a rescue, and head into the Asylum. That means facing Daleks of all shapes and styles from Dalek history.

To make the story, the production team hunted down surviving props from previous Dalek stories, such as the original **Special Weapons Dalek** from ***Remembrance of the Daleks*** (1988), the surviving exhibition models built for BBC Worldwide (all then on display at the Doctor Who Experience), and a number of replicas built and owned by dedicated fans.

These props weren't all on set on the same day, but the story as a whole features **28 full-size Dalek props**, plus a number of specially built damaged or partially disassembled ones – and some CGI Daleks to fill out the numbers.

DALEK RUSTLING

When the Doctor leaves the intensive care chamber on the Asylum, a grey Dalek blocks his path. This was a replica lent to the production team by **Russell T Davies** – writer and executive producer of the series from 2005 to 2010.

'I knew Russell has a replica Dalek in his house in Manchester,' explained **Caroline Skinner**, executive producer of ***Asylum of the Daleks***, at the time the story was broadcast. 'I asked him whether he'd like to lend it to us because, you know, the more Daleks the merrier. So we shipped it down. And it's there on screen, in some of the final, climactic moments of the episode ... And having "acted" on the show, it's now no longer a replica. It is an official "canonised" Dalek. And Russell's thrilled.'

Davros, creator of the Daleks, is the Kaled people's 'greatest scientist', according to his loyal second-in-command, Nyder – *Genesis of the Daleks* (1975). Generations after the First Doctor's visit to Skaro and battle with the Daleks, it has entered into the legends of the Thal people as the 'greatest peril' they ever faced – *Planet of the Daleks* (1973)

THE DALEKS' GREATEST ENEMY

As seen in *The Chase* (1965)

'I will be the destroyer of our greatest enemy,' says a Dalek in ***Evolution of the Daleks*** (2007) – and it means the Tenth Doctor. He in turn accepts the title – the Eleventh Doctor refers to himself as the Dalek's greatest enemy in ***Victory of the Daleks*** (2010). But when was he first recognised as such?

In the Doctor's first every encounter with them, in *The Daleks* (1963–1964), they don't know who he is and aren't especially impressed by his claim to travel in time. At the end of the story, the Daleks are apparently all killed – but even moments before this they fail to see the First Doctor as a particular threat.

When he meets them again in ***The Dalek Invasion of Earth*** (1964), they don't know who he is – and the Doctor speculates that, for them, this must be a time ***before*** that previous encounter.

But by their third meeting – *The Chase* (1965) – the Daleks recognise the threat the Doctor presents, and build a time machine solely to pursue the TARDIS. Launching this mission, they speak of the Doctor and his three companions as 'our greatest enemies'.

CHAPTER SEVEN
COMPANIONS

'MY FRIENDS HAVE ALWAYS BEEN THE BEST OF ME.'

THE ELEVENTH DOCTOR, *THE WEDDING OF RIVER SONG* (2011)

A MATTER OF LIVES AND DEATHS........ 146
THE AGE OF HEROES........ 148
BAD GIRLS........ 150
MOST FAITHFUL FRIENDS........ 152
MORE MOST FAITHFUL FRIENDS........ 154
THE SARAH JANE ADVENTURES........ 156

A MATTER OF LIVES AND DEATHS

TOTALLING UP THE LIVES – AND ENDS OF THEM – OF THE DOCTOR'S BEST FRIENDS

THE COMPANION WHO ENCOUNTERS MOST INCARNATIONS OF THE DOCTOR

As seen in *The Name of the Doctor, The Day of the Doctor* and *The Time of the Doctor* (all 2013)

In ***The Name of the Doctor***, companion **Clara Oswald** bravely steps into the **Eleventh Doctor**'s time stream to save him from the sinister Dr Simeon. She is torn apart by the time winds and a million pieces – a million **echoes** of Clara – are scattered through the Doctor's past.

We 'd already seen two of these echoes meet the Eleventh Doctor. In ***Asylum of the Daleks*** (2012), Oswin Oswald, a junior entertainment officer on Starship *Alaska*, is turned into a Dalek. Then in ***The Snowmen*** (also 2012), Clara Oswin Oswald dies in 1892 battling the Great Intelligence.

But in *The Name of the Doctor* we see echoes of Clara running to save the Doctor again and again – even if he hardly hears her. We see her not quite reaching the Sixth Doctor, the Fourth Doctor, the Seventh Doctor, the Third Doctor, the Second Doctor and the Fifth Doctor. She even advises the First Doctor on which time capsule to steal from his own planet, introducing him to his TARDIS!

With a million echoes of Clara in the Doctor's past, it's likely there are more meetings with his various incarnations that we don't see. Later, when the Eleventh Doctor comes to rescue Clara, she tells him: "I saw all of you. Eleven faces – all of them you. You're the eleventh Doctor."

In the next story – ***The Day of the Doctor*** – she meets and briefly travels with the War Doctor, who wasn't one of the eleven she saw before. In the story after that – ***The Time of the Doctor*** – she's with the Eleventh Doctor when he regenerates into the Twelfth Doctor, who she continues to travel with afterwards. So Clara has encountered a total of **13 Doctors**.

THE COMPANION WHO DIES THE MOST TIMES

As seen in *The Name of the Doctor*

In ***Hell Bent*** (2015), Clara Oswald is **extracted** from the end of her time stream, moments before her death at the end of ***Face the Raven*** (also 2015). In this extracted state, she doesn't even have a heartbeat as her physical processes have been **time looped**. The Time Lords plan to send her back to her death just as soon as she's helped them.

Clara **escapes**, and is last seen at the controls of **her own TARDIS**, hurtling through time and space. She has dodged death, at least for the time being...

But what about the **million** echoes of Clara, all through space and time? We see two die young in other episodes, but even if the other **999,998** echoes live to enjoy their old age, they must surely die sometime...

The trouble is, we don't know what happens to these echoes of Clara. So which companion dies the most times with evidence on screen for those deaths?

THE COMPANION WHO DIES THE MOST TIMES – VERIFIABLE

As seen in *The Parting of the Ways* (2005), *Gridlock* (2007), *Utopia* (2007), *The Sound of Drums* (2007), *Last of the Time Lords* (2007) and *Journey's End* (2008)

Captain Jack Harness is killed by the Daleks in *The Parting of the Ways*. Then the powerful Bad Wolf brings him back to life.

Jack dies again in ***Utopia***, clinging to the outside of the TARDIS as it travels through the Vortex to the year 100 trillion. Then he suddenly sits up, alive.

As Jack tells the Doctor, he's died and recovered many times: he was shot through the heart in a fight on Ellis Island in 1892; he fell off a cliff; he was trampled by horses; he died in the First and Second World Wars; he's been killed by poison, starvation and even a stray javelin. He's then killed by stet radiation.

In ***The Sound of Drums***, he's killed by the **Master** who apparently then kills him again and again, but we don't know how many times. In ***Last of the Time Lords***, Jack dies at least once to get past the **Toclafane** guarding the TARDIS. In *Journey's End*, he's exterminated by a Dalek.

In *Last of the Time Lords*, Jack tells us that he was once known as 'the Face of Boe', which is also the name of a very long-lived creature the Doctor saw die on the planet New Earth in the year 5,000,000,053 in *Gridlock*. It seems the creature is Jack in the future.

This means we see Jack die on screen six times, we know he dies off-screen at least once (getting past the Toclafane) and we're told of another eight deaths, bringing the total to **15 deaths** we can be certain about. In the spin-off series ***Torchwood***, we see or are told about a great many more times Jack has died and come back to life.

THE AGE OF HEROES

THE DOCTOR'S YOUNG FRIENDS ARE HOW OLD, EXACTLY?

THE EARLIEST-BORN COMPANION

As seen in *The Myth Makers* (1965)

In *The Myth Makers*, the TARDIS lands outside the ancient city of **Troy** in the last days of the legendary siege by the Greeks. Soon the First Doctor and his companions **Steven Taylor** and **Vicki** are mixing with mythic figures such as Odysseus, Achilles and the clairvoyant Cassandra.

No date is given on screen, but those classicists who think the story of the siege of Troy is based on a real, historical event have argued that that event took place sometime between about **1260 and 1180 BC**.

In the final episode of the story, *Horse of Destruction*, we're introduced to Trojan handmaiden **Katarina**, played by actress **Adrienne Hill**. When Steven is wounded, she helps him back to the TARDIS – and joins the Doctor on his travels. Sadly, those travels do not last long and Katarina dies just four episodes later.

That decision seems to have been made by the series' then script editor **Donald Tosh**. "I realised the character we had created wasn't going to work," he explained to the Doctor Who Appreciation Society in 2011, "when I started reading Paul Erickson's early scripts for [subsequent story] *The Ark* and it was very clear what the problem was. Everything had to be explained to this girl – and I mean absolutely everything – because she came from a primitive and distant past and was being transported to a far distant future. And I said, 'We can't do this! Every story will be dragged down again and again to make room for explanations!'"

Those in charge of *Doctor Who* since Tosh's day seem to agree. The next earliest-born companion in all of *Doctor Who* is **Jamie McCrimmon**, born in the early 1720s – nearly 3,000 years after Katarina!

Most *Doctor Who* companions are either from the present day, so that they reflect the audience watching, or from the future – where they better understand the technology and science they encounter on their travels, saving time in explanations.

THE EARLIEST-BORN PERSON TO PLAY A COMPANION

As seen in *The Daleks' Master Plan* (1965–1966)

In ***The Destruction of Time***, the twelfth and final episode of the epic *The Daleks' Master Plan*, the First Doctor and his companion **Sara Kingdom** are caught in the terrible effects of a Dalek super-weapon, the **Time Destructor.**

The Doctor survives – barely – but Sara is aged to death. To accomplish this on screen, the 31 year-old actress playing Sara, **Jean Marsh**, was doubled by 74 year-old **May Warden**. An actress and comedian, Warden was born on **9 May 1891**.

THE LATEST-BORN COMPANION

As seen in *The Face of Evil* and *The Invisible Enemy* (both 1977)

We don't know what century let alone year several companions are from.

For example, space pilot **Steven Taylor**, companion of the First Doctor, is from sometime in our future but before the year 4000 (where the technology is "hundreds of years" of advance of his own time, when he visits in *The Daleks' Master Plan*). **Adric**, companion of the Fourth Doctor and Fifth Doctor, is the descendant of human colonists 1,000 years after they settled on the planet **Alzarius** – but we don't know what year they arrived.

Captain Jack Harkness, who travelled with the Ninth Doctor and Tenth Doctor, claims to be from the **51st century**. Although we know he doesn't always tell the truth (even about his real name), without evidence to dispute that – or another contender – he seems to be the latest born companion.

(At the time of her death in *Silence in the Library* (2008), **River Song** is also living in the 51st century – the same century that Captain Jack is from. But earlier in her life River applies to study archaeology at the **Luna University in 5123** – the 52nd century – and we know she often travels in time. However, we're not told the date of the **Battle of Demon's Run**, the day that River is born, so we don't know if it's before or after the birth of Captain Jack.)

But in *The Invisible Enemy* (1977), the Fourth Doctor tells **Leela** – a warrior descended from a human space expedition – that the year 5000 is "the time of your ancestors". That suggests she's from much later than the 51st century.

THE MOST RECENTLY BORN PEOPLE TO PLAY A COMPANION

As seen in *A Good Man Goes to War* (2011)

It comes as quite a shock to the Eleventh Doctor's companion **Amy Pond** to discover that she's not, in fact, travelling in the TARDIS with the Doctor but is really the prisoner of the devious **Madame Kovarian** – and pregnant, and about to give birth.

In *A Good Man Goes to War* we learn that the new-born baby, who Amy names **Melody**, will grow up to be **River Song**. We know that the grown-up River travels with the Doctor in the TARDIS on many more adventures than those we see on screen, so surely she counts as a companion. For most of the recording of *A Good Man Goes to War*, baby Melody was played by an animatronic doll, but for close-ups she was played by twins **Harrison** and **Melody Mortimer**.

BAD GIRLS

WANTON DESTRUCTION OF PUBLIC PROPERTY? CERTAINLY...

THE MOST DESTUCTIVE COMPANION

As seen in *The Parting of the Ways* (2005)

The Seventh Doctor's companion **Ace** frequently carries round her homemade explosive, **Nitro 9**, which is used to destroy doors, walls, Daleks and even a Cyberman spaceship. Ace blows up and shoots various robots, battles – and defeats – Cybermen with a **catapult**, and destroys the underwater spaceship that is the final resting place of the legendary **King Arthur**. We learn that before she even met the Doctor she blew up the school art room and burnt down a haunted house.

Compared to this trail of mayhem, most other companions look pretty tame. But one companion commits a single act of destruction that would surely even shock Ace.

When **Rose Tyler** looks into the TARDIS and the Time Vortex in *The Parting of the Ways*, it turns her into the **Bad Wolf**. This lets her see the whole of time and space, all that is and was and ever could be. It also gives her the power to divide every single atom of the entire Dalek fleet poised over Earth in the year 200,100. **Half a million Daleks** – including the Dalek Emperor – on some 2,000 ships are simply turned to dust.

THE BEST JAIL BREAK

As seen in *The Daleks* (1963–1964)

When the First Doctor first **meets the Daleks**, in their city on the planet Skaro, they take him prisoner and place him in a **cell** with his companions. It's the first of many cells in *Doctor Who*, and the first of many the Doctor escapes from.

When a Dalek arrives to deliver the Doctor and his friends some food, they grab the Dalek and manoeuvre it onto a cape they've put down on the floor. The cape is made of something that's neither plastic nor nylon.

The moment it's on top of the cloak, the Dalek stops struggling and calling for help – it's been cut off from the metal floor from which it draws its power. This is exactly what the Doctor and his friends had hoped for, having worked out the power source through a series of logical deductions after the Doctor notes that the Daleks have an **acrid smell**, like the dodgem cars at a fairground which also draw their power from the floor (or ceiling).

Yes, the Doctor escapes a prison cell using his nose.

THE MOST CRIMINAL COMPANION

As seen in *Let's Kill Hitler* (2011)

In *Survival* (1989), we learn that the police let **Ace** off with a warning after some incident before she met the Doctor. Perhaps that was when she blew up her school art room and Class 1C's prizewinning pottery pig collection (referred to in *Battlefield* (1989), or burned down the old house, **Gabriel Chase** (referred to in *Ghost Light* (1989)).

Captain Jack Harkness and **Martha Jones** are made enemies of the state when **Harold Saxon** (really, the Master) becomes Prime Minister in *The Sound of Drums* (2007). Jack was also some kind of criminal before he met the Ninth Doctor – but we don't know the details.

In *Planet of the Dead* (2009), the Tenth Doctor refuses to let **Lady Christina de Souza** join him in the TARDIS, even though she's surrounded by police at the time and likely to go to prison. Christina thinks this is because she's a thief – just before she met the Doctor, she broke into the International Gallery and stole the Cup of Athelstan, given to the king of Britain in AD 924 as a coronation gift from Hywel, king of the Welsh. It seems she has form, too – Detective Inspector Macmillan has been trying to arrest her for a long time. But the Doctor doesn't seem to mind her stealing, and says he's worried about losing anyone else who travels with him.

In 1969 in America, **Amy Pond** and **Rory Williams** are hunted down as criminals by the FBI – but it's all a trick to fool the sinister Silence (*Day of the Moon* (2011)).

But the Doctor's most criminal companion is identified by justice department vehicle 6018 – the **Teselecta** – which travels through history tracking down major criminals who were not punished in their own lifetimes and then executes them near the end of their established timelines. The Teselecta is hunting down Nazis in Berlin in 1938, but spots a better prize: the biggest war criminal ever.

The target is **River Song** – and it seems her crime is that she killed the Doctor. In other stories, we see her imprisoned for this crime for several years in the **Stormcage Containment Facility** in the 52nd century. But we also learn in *The Wedding of River Song* (2011) that the Doctor used the Teselecta to fake his own death – so River didn't kill him.

So she's imprisoned for years and has this terrible reputation – all for a crime she didn't actually commit. Now *that* is criminal.

MOST FAITHFUL FRIENDS

TRAVELLING WITH THE DOCTOR TO ANYWHERE IN TIME AND SPACE... WHY WOULD YOU EVER WANT TO STOP?

THE COMPANION IN MOST EPISODES

On 14 November 1966, the *Doctor Who* production team were at Frensham Common in Surrey, the heathland doubling for 18th-century Scotland. In *The Highlanders*, the **Second Doctor** and his companions Ben Jackson and Polly are caught up in the bloody aftermath of the **Battle of Culloden**.

That location filming was the first day's work on *Doctor Who* for actor Frazer Hines, playing young Scots piper **Jamie McCrimmon**. Filming at Frensham continued the next day, and among the scenes recorded there was the end of the story, in which Jamie helps the Doctor and his friends back to the TARDIS – but doesn't leave with them.

However, the production team already thought Jamie might make a good companion. Story editor **Gerry Davis** – who largely wrote the story – and producer **Innes Lloyd** discussed this possibility with **Shaun Sutton**, the BBC's Head of Serials, who suggested Frazer for the part having worked with him before. Frazer's contract for the four episodes of the story, issued on 2 November, included an option for the BBC to retain him for three more four-part stories – a total of **16 episodes**.

Having seen Frazer in the role on those two days recording at Frensham, and apparently after discussing it with the series' lead actor **Patrick Troughton**, the production team offered Frazer the chance to join the TARDIS, and a new scene was recorded at Frensham on 21 November, this time with Jamie leaving in the TARDIS. Jamie made his on-screen debut on 17 December when the first episode of *The Highlanders* was broadcast.

Frazer and Patrick Troughton clearly had great on-screen chemistry, and were good friends off screen. The producers decided to keep Jamie in the series for longer than his initial 16 episodes.

That's a bit of an understatement. Frazer appeared in an incredible **112 episodes** of *Doctor Who* over the next three years – missing only one, the fourth episode of *The Enemy of the World* (1968), when he took a week's holiday. He finally left at the end of Patrick Troughton's own last story as the Doctor, *The War Games* (1969).

But that wasn't the end. Frazer returned to the role in *The Five Doctors* (1983) and *The Two Doctors* (1985), bringing the total to **116** on screen appearances as Jamie. That's more episodes of *Doctor Who* than any other actor except those who played the first four incarnations of the Doctor. Frazer continues to play Jamie in new audio adventures.

THE BEST OF TIMES

'Innes took me aside and said, "How do you fancy being in the old TARDIS crew for a year?"' remembers Frazer Hines today.

At the time, Frazer had recorded the location scenes for ***The Highlanders*** – which he thought would be his one and only ***Doctor Who*** story. He didn't know that the production team had always had the character of Jamie in mind as a potential new companion – even though his contract gave the BBC an option for him to appear in more episodes.

'Oh no,' says Frazer. 'We were filming and Innes just said, "Frazer, I'll give you a lift home…" He had a Volkswagen Beetle, I remember. And that's when he asked me. Which was great – and a total surprise.'

So Frazer quickly said yes? He laughs. 'I went, "Oh, I can't do it. I've already filmed my goodbyes." And Innes said, "Oh, to hell with that. We'll go back to Frensham Ponds and have you going into the TARDIS." Which we did. It was wonderful.'

But Frazer admits that this late decision to have him join the TARDIS caused some headaches for the production team. 'Yes, because the next stories – ***The Underwater Menace*** and ***The Moonbase*** – had all been written, without me.' The scripts were hastily reworked, with Jamie unconscious for much of ***The Moonbase***, and otherwise taking lines of dialogue originally written for the Doctor's other companion, Ben Jackson.

'I did feel, understandably, that Mike Craze [who played Ben] and Anneke Wills [who played companion Polly] were watching me going, "Why have we got this new guy?" They didn't say anything – and Anneke denies it now. But if after I'd been in the series a year, Innes had brought in another new companion, I know I'd have thought, "Hey, why do we need another one?"'

And it wasn't long after that it was decided to write Ben and Polly out of the series. 'Yeah, so that was a bit awkward. But not with Patrick – never with Patrick. We'd worked together on a series called ***Smuggler's Bay***. He was such a great actor, such a kind, funny man.'

So that explains how Frazer got the part, but why did he stay for so many more episodes than any other companion?

'We had a fun show. You never felt anxiety going into work: "Oh, I hope Patrick's in a good mood." There was nothing like that. The scripts were good, we had good actors coming in and we knew we were making something people liked.'

Even so, it was hard work. 'We'd rehearse Tuesday to Friday and then go into the studio to record on Saturday. And we'd have the odd Sunday or Monday filming on location. The thing is, I know people have said they felt under pressure, but I never did. I'd be going out to nightclubs. Or I'd be opening fêtes or judging a beauty contest, or all the stuff like that. There were 39 or 40 episodes a series back then, but we did them one a week so that meant 12 weeks off a year.' He laughs. 'It was a good life.'

MORE MOST FAITHFUL FRIENDS

TO A MORE THAN 2,000-YEAR-OLD TIME LORD, WE HUMANS HAVE SUCH TINY, BRIEF LIVES – BUT SOME COMPANIONS STAY WITH HIM FOR A VERY LONG TIME...

THE COMPANIONS IN EPISODES OVER THE LONGEST SPAN OF TIME

In the first episode of *The Time Warrior*, broadcast on 15 December 1973, the Third Doctor meets plucky young journalist Sarah Jane Smith.

Played by **Elisabeth Sladen**, Sarah was with the Doctor when he regenerated into the Fourth Doctor and continued to travel with him until *The Hand of Fear* (1976), appearing in 80 episodes. She returned in *The Five Doctors* (1983), *School Reunion* (2006), *The Stolen Earth* and *Journey's End* (2008) and, her 85th episode, *The End of Time, Part Two*, broadcast on 1 January 2010 – **36 years and 17 days** after her first.

But she continued to appear in her own spin-off series, *The Sarah Jane Adventures*. The last time we saw her alongside the Doctor was in the second episode of *Death of the Doctor*, first broadcast on 26 October 2010 – **36 years, 10 months and**

THE COMPANION WHO SPENDS MOST TIME TRAVELLING WITH THE DOCTOR

As seen in *The Power of Three* (2012)

Amy Pond first enters the TARDIS at the end of *The Eleventh Hour* (2010), on the night before her wedding day on **26 June 2010**. After several adventures with Amy, the Eleventh Doctor decides that her fiancé **Rory Williams** should join them, and in *The Vampires of Venice* (2010) he collects Rory from his own stag night.

This event must be held on the night before the wedding – any earlier and surely Amy would mention in *The Eleventh Hour* that Rory had gone missing. So Rory and Amy both join the TARDIS on the same night, but Amy is aboard for at least three more adventures than Rory.

Amy and Rory both leave the TARDIS for the last time in *The Angels Take Manhattan* (2012), stepping from the police box into a graveyard which we'll discover contains their shared grave. The Doctor tells us that the year is 2012 – so it's been about two years since they first entered the TARDIS.

But again, for them it's been longer. 'We think it's been **10 years**,' Amy tells the Doctor in the preceding story, *The Power of Three*). 'Not for you or Earth but for us.' In the same episode, they leave a party to travel in the TARDIS for seven weeks before returning to the same party just at the moment they left.

We don't know how accurate Amy's estimate of 10 years is, or how much more time passes for her between sharing that estimate with the Doctor and leaving the TARDIS for good in the next episode. But no other companion seems to spend **more than 10 years** of their life travelling with the Doctor.

(The Eleventh Doctor also sees Amy in the TARDIS in *The Time of the Doctor* (2013), but that seems to be in his imagination, just before he regenerates.)

11 days after her debut. Elisabeth Sladen sadly died in April 2011, but the last new episode of *The Sarah Jane Adventures* was broadcast on 18 October 2011, **37 years, 10 months and 3 days** after we saw her first meet the Doctor.

However, if we're including *The Sarah Jane Adventures*, then we must count the appearance of Jo Grant, played by Katy Manning, in the same second episode of *Death of the Doctor* – **39 years, 9 months and 24 days** after her debut in the first episode of *Terror of the Autons* on 2 January 1971.

THE COMPANION IN EPISODES OVER THE LONGEST SPAN OF TIME – ANY MEDIA

Though not on TV, former Doctors and their companions continue to enjoy new adventures in other forms. *The Age of Endurance* is a new audio adventure for the First Doctor, released on 14 September 2016. **Carole Ann Ford** and **William Russell** reprise their roles as companions **Susan Foreman** and **Ian Chesterton**, both of whom first appeared on 23 November 1963 in *Doctor Who*'s very first episode.

William then starred in another new adventure, *The Fifth Traveller*, released on 13 October 2016 – **52 years, 10 months and 20 days** after Ian Chesterton's first appearance.

THE SARAH JANE ADVENTURES

THE PLUCKY REPORTER WHO WON THE HEARTS OF US ALL

THE COMPANION IN MOST EPISODES OF *DOCTOR WHO* AND ITS SPIN-OFFS

Elisabeth Sladen appeared as **Sarah Jane Smith** in 85 episodes of *Doctor Who*, but she also played the character in the spin-off *K-9 & Company* (1981) and 53 episodes of *The Sarah Jane Adventures* (2007–2011), making a total of **139 episodes** of *Doctor Who* and its spin-offs – second only to one other actor (see p. 22). She also appeared in *From Raxacoricofallapatorius with Love* (2009), a special mini-episode for the Comic Relief charity evening.

THE LONGEST-RUNNING DOCTOR WHO SPIN-OFF SERIES

The very first TV spin-off from *Doctor Who* was *K-9 & Company*, in which the Doctor sent his robot dog as a gift to former companion Sarah. Sadly, this pilot episode did not lead to a series, at least not straight away.

Sarah and K-9 returned to *Doctor Who* for the special 20th-anniversary story *The Five Doctors* (1983) and then again for *School Reunion* (2006). While this latter story was in production, the channel **CBBC** approached *Doctor Who*'s then executive producer **Russell T Davies** about a potential spin-off series – perhaps about the Doctor in his youth. Russell instead suggested a series about Sarah and K-9, but this time with the focus on Sarah.

The first episode of *The Sarah Jane Adventures* – called *Invasion of the Bane* – was broadcast on 1 January 2007, and a full series followed later that year. It proved hugely popular with critics and the public alike: 'This is **what the BBC does best**,' said Abi Grant, reviewing the series for the *Daily Telegraph*.

After five seasons, the series was only brought to an untimely end in 2011 by the sad death of its star – which made front-page news and led to an outpouring of public grief. 'Tributes to the **best Dr Who girl ever**,' reported *The Sun*.

SARAH'S GREATEST CHALLENGE

As seen in *The Sarah Jane Adventures* story *The Wedding of Sarah Jane Smith* (2009)

She battles Daleks and Cybermen. She braves the freezing cold of Antarctica. She's carried off by a giant robot. She's blinded by the Sisterhood of Karn. She's hypnotised, knocked out, teleported, poisoned by radiation, replaced by an android and possessed by a rock. But the Tenth Doctor recognises Sarah's greatest challenge when he turns up at her wedding.

In fact, the Doctor reveals that ceremony itself is all the diabolical invention of the **Trickster**, a creature from beyond the universe who wants to break into our reality and manifest himself – and then wreak havoc. The Trickster traps the Doctor, Sarah and her friends in single seconds of time. And the only way to escape the trap will unleash the Trickster on the world.

Except that Sarah has met the Trickster before and knows how he operates. She knows he must have made a deal with her fiancé, **Peter Dalton** – and must have done so at the moment of Peter's death. The horrible truth is that Peter died in an accident before ever meeting Sarah. Despite being brought back to life by the Trickster to be part of this trap, Peter really has fallen in love.

'It all rests with you, Sarah,' says the Doctor. 'Your greatest challenge. The hardest thing you'll ever face in your life.'

But can she do it? She and Peter are the perfect match. And that's why they both understand what must be done...

SARAH'S GREATEST SUCCESS

As seen in *The Sarah Jane Adventures* story *The Man Who Wasn't There* (2011)

She's defeated countless monsters and saved the Earth at least a dozen times, but Sarah seems proudest of her adopted children, **Luke** (rescued from the evil Bane who created him) and **Sky** (rescued from the Fleshkind who created her).

Sarah insists that her children lead as normal lives as possible – sending them to the local school and encouraging them to make friends with other kids. In the final story of ***The Sarah Jane Adventures***, Luke's friend Clyde Langer is keen to take credit for what this achieves.

'Sky, behold my greatest success,' he says of teenage Luke. 'Frankenbane's monster, now a normal human student living off Pot Noodles, rising at 12 sharp to watch ***Loose Women***.' What mother wouldn't be proud of that?

CHAPTER EIGHT
TECHNOLOGY

'OH, THERE'S NOTHING I HATE MORE THAN A COCKY COMPUTER.'

THE SIXTH DOCTOR, *SLIPBACK* (1985)

MUST KEEP CONTROL.......... 160

WE'RE GOING TO NEED A BIGGER BOAT.......... 162

GREAT INTELLIGENCE.......... 164

BURST YOUR BRAIN WITH NOISE.......... 166

TECHNOLOGICAL FIRSTS.......... 168

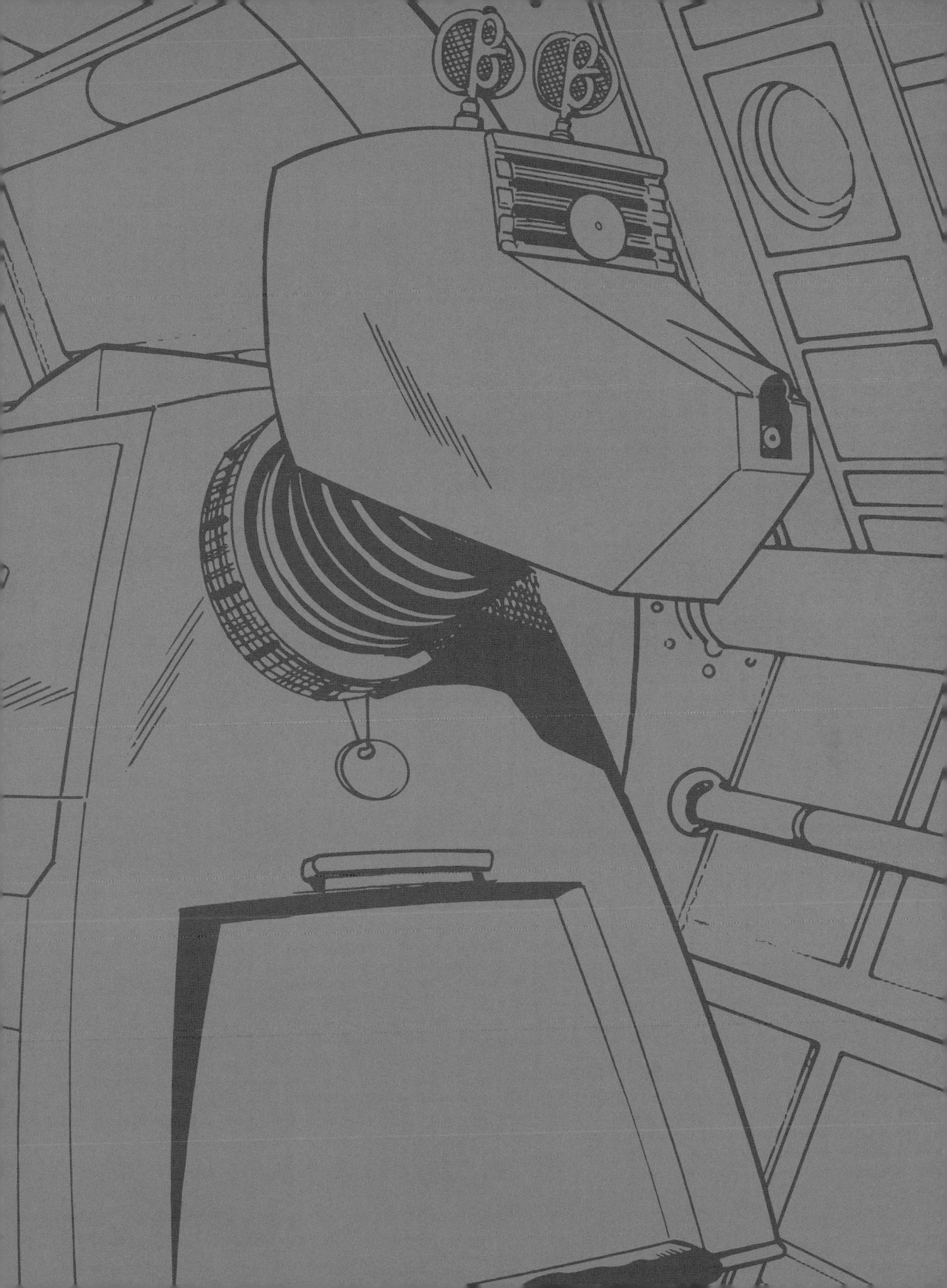

MUST KEEP CONTROL

PIONEERING TECHNOLOGY COULD PRODUCE JAW-DROPPING RESULTS – AT A COST

THE MOST EXPENSIVE SPECIAL EFFECT

As seen in *The Trial of a Time Lord* (1986)

The 1986 season of *Doctor Who* begins with a spectacular model shot as we zoom down towards a sinister, gothic-looking **space station**, swooping over and round its minutely detailed surface before it unleashes a blinding white light – into which the TARDIS is drawn.

The sequence was the work of visual effects designer **Mike Kelt** and his team at the BBC. The model space station was six feet in diameter and the central spire six feet tall, but built in separate pieces so that it could be transported from the effects department in west London to Peerless Studios in Elstree, where it would be filmed using the company's new **motion control** system.

The motion control technique had been pioneered in films in the 1960s such as *2001: A Space Odyssey* (1968) and was used on a large scale in *Star Wars* (1977), but Peerless was among the first companies to have such equipment in London.

The technique uses a computer to track the movement of a camera so that exactly the same movement can be repeated many times. For the space station sequence:

The sequence was shot with the space station lit perfectly, in what's called the 'beauty pass'. This was shot at a slow rate of between 2 and 4 frames per second to allow long exposure times to get a good depth of field. As a result, the beauty pass alone took more than an hour.

A second pass had the camera make an identical journey over and round the space station, now with just its

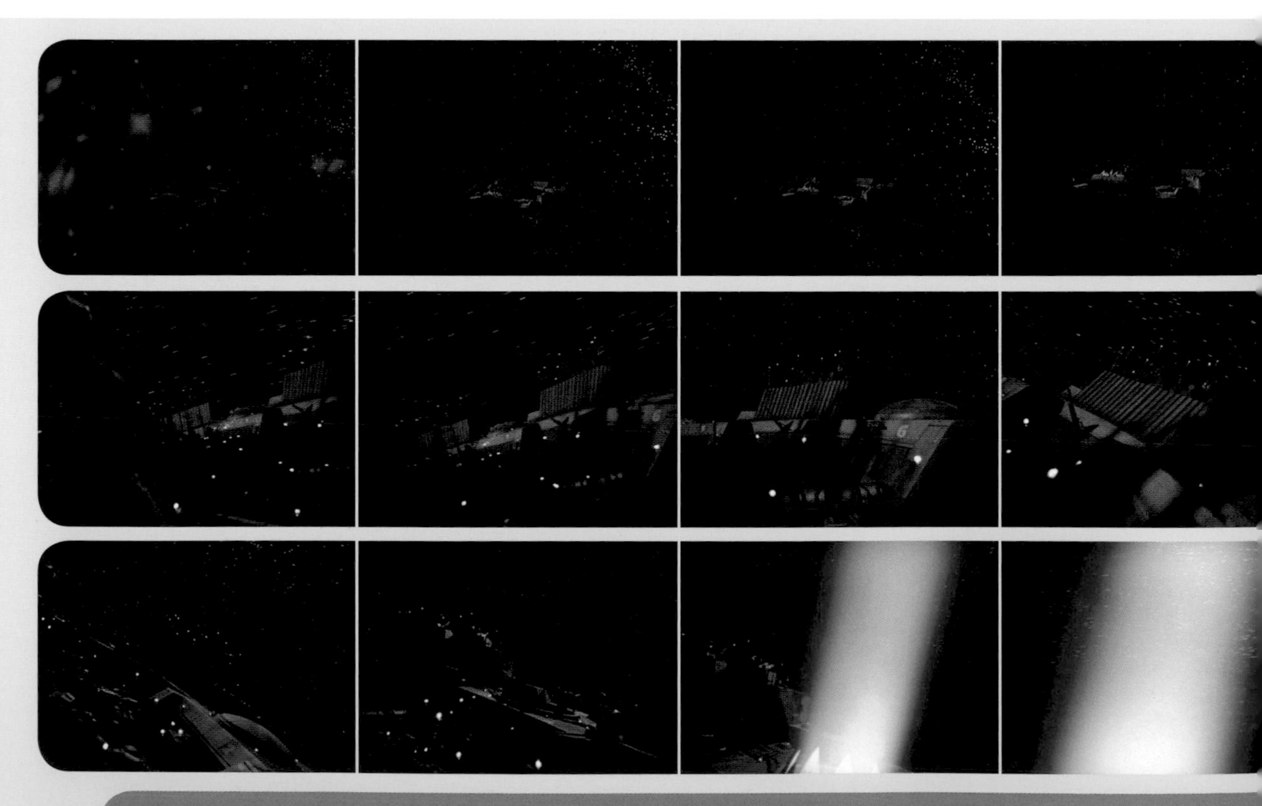

lights on (and no other lighting). Put together with the 'beauty pass', the perfectly lit spaceship would now have perfectly bright lights.

For the 'matte' pass, the space station was lit in black silhouette against boards of white polystyrene – but on negative film. This produced a clean, black background for the previous passes.

Finally, a starfield was shot using the same camera motion, so that as we swoop over the space station the distant stars wheel by.

Because exactly the same motion had to be recorded in each pass, an error on one pass meant the whole sequence had to be started from scratch. As a result, shooting this 40-second sequence took about a week.

With the cutting edge technology involved, that meant the shoot was extremely expensive, judged relative to the overall cost of making the programme. Mike Kelt's budget for the visual effects on four episodes of ***Doctor Who*** was £2,550 – or £637.50 per 25-minute episode. For the 40-second opening sequence, he was granted an additional £5,000.

cc: John Nathan-Turner 304 UN.H

Tina,

Further to John Nathan-Turner's preliminary discussion with Peter Pegrum, and our conversation yesterday, Mike Kelt's agreed budget for the above programme is as follows:

CASH

Special allocation for the opening model shot	£5,000
Normal cash allocation	£2,550
TOTAL cash allocation	£7,550

RESOURCES

Designer days	55
Extra Hrs.	156
Assistant Hrs.	1,200

WE'RE GOING TO NEED A BIGGER BOAT

THE BIGGEST SHIPS IN ALL OF TIME AND SPACE

THE BIGGEST SPACESHIP IN THE UNIVERSE

As seen in *Journey to the Centre of the TARDIS* (2013)

In *The Deadly Assassin* (1976) we're told that the Time Lords get their power to travel in time from something called the **Eye of Harmony**, which the Doctor realises is a stabilised **black hole**. In the TV movie *Doctor Who* (1996), we learn there's another (or perhaps the same) Eye of Harmony inside the Doctor's TARDIS. And in *Journey to the Centre of the TARDIS* (2013), the Eleventh Doctor finally confirms what we might have inferred – that it's the engine of his ship:

'The Eye of Harmony [is an] exploding star in the act of becoming a black hole. Time Lord engineering. You rip the star from its orbit, suspend it in a permanent state of decay.'

One way astronomers think a black hole can form is during the death of a very massive star; one that contains at least 10 times as much material as our own Sun. Stars like this end their lives in a devastating explosion known as a **supernova**, in which the star's outer layers are blasted violently into space. But the core of the dying star meets a very different fate: it collapses under its own gravity until it reaches a state of zero size and infinite density – a **singularity**. This incredible concentration of matter produces an extremely powerful gravitational field and, as the Tenth Doctor explains in *The Impossible Planet* (2006), anything that comes too close will never escape its pull.

At a boundary called the **event horizon**, the escape velocity an object would need to resist that field is faster than the speed of light – so not even light can escape from the region inside the event horizon. This means that these 'black holes' are very hard to see directly. However, we can detect them indirectly by their gravitational effect on neighbouring bodies, and we can also observe the intense radiation emitted by matter falling towards a black hole, before it disappears forever inside the event horizon. In 2016, astronomers announced that they'd detected gravitational waves, ripples in space and time, created by two colliding black holes.

In theory black holes can come in a range of sizes – from event horizons with a radius of 0.1 millimetres (called **micro black holes**) to 60,000,000,000 kilometres (**supermassive black holes**). The circumference of the event horizon, and hence the size of the black hole, depends on the amount of matter that it contains – which increases as the black hole devours nearby material.

Normally, we can calculate the volume contained inside a sphere by measuring its external dimensions and using the formula $\frac{4}{3}\pi r^3$ but black holes don't work like that. The incredible concentration of matter at the centre of a black hole warps and stretches the time and space around it. This means that, like the TARDIS, black holes are bigger on the inside.

If we were in a spacecraft caught in the gravitational field of a black hole, we'd notice some other extraordinary effects as we were drawn towards the singularity. To observers watching from a safe distance time for us would appear to slow as we approached the black hole, and our fall would appear to take an infinite amount of time even though we ourselves would experience time passing at a normal rate. Inside the event horizon the distortion of space and time would become so extreme that our ordinary ideas about distance, direction and the passage of time cease to apply. The space direction that we would normally think of as 'down', towards the centre of the black hole, would become the time direction 'into the future' and, in effect, the singularity would become our future as all possible paths through space would lead inevitably towards it.

So time inside a black hole passes at a different rate from the rest of the universe and a black hole also contains far more space than its external dimensions would suggest. Sounds familiar? As the Eleventh Doctor confirms in the same episode, the TARDIS is effectively infinite. Perhaps having a black hole at its centre can explain this, along with many of its other most striking characteristics.

THE FASTEST, FURTHEST AND BEST

As seen in *Boom Town* (2005)

In *Voyage of the Damned* (2007), Max Capricorn says that his cruiseliners – such as the starship ***Titanic*** – are 'the fastest, the furthest, the best'. But then he would say that, wouldn't he? And anyway, we later learn that his company has gone bust.

But in *Boom Town*, the Ninth Doctor calls his TARDIS 'the best ship in the universe' – and it's hard to disagree. We've seen the TARDIS tow the Earth back into place from the **Medusa Cascade**, save Gallifrey from the Daleks, and play an essential role in the Doctor surviving his first regeneration. It can arrive at a destination before it even sets off, we've seen it journey back to the birth of the galaxy and to the year **100 trillion**... It's a record no other ship can beat.

THE BIGGEST PIRATE SHIP

As seen in *The Pirate Planet* (1978)

'The greatest raiding cruiser ever built,' claims the **Captain** of Zanak, the hollow pirate planet. Vast **transmat engines** hidden underground enable the whole planet to drop out of the space dimension and flip halfway across the galaxy to materialise round other, smaller planets. These are then smothered, crushed and mined for their mineral wealth – whether they're populated or not.

'And I built it,' says the Captain. 'I built it with technology so far advanced you would not be able to distinguish it from magic.'

GREAT INTELLIGENCE

THE HIGHEST OF THE HIGH BRAINS IN *DOCTOR WHO*

THE GREATEST PHYSICISTS ON EARTH

As seen in *The Evil of the Daleks* (1967)

In *Time and the Rani* (1987), the Rani kidnaps geniuses to exploit in her latest wicked scheme. Among them are Earth scientists **Hypatia**, **Louis Pasteur** and **Albert Einstein**, who the Doctor refers to as among 'the greatest minds ... in the universe'.

But as well as the famous names in history, we've met lots of unrecognised geniuses in *Doctor Who*. In *City of Death* (1979), there's **Professor Fyodor Nikolai Kerensky** who – under the direction of **Scaroth**, last of the alien **Jagaroth** – builds a working time machine in a Paris basement in 1979. Other humans exploit alien technology to make scientific advances – such as Henry Van Statten in *Dalek* (2005) and the staff of Torchwood seen in *Army of Ghosts* (2006)

In *Invasion of the Dinosaurs* (1974), **Professor Whitaker** develops a workable theory of time travel and builds a machine capable of reaching back more than 65 million years. Whitaker's colleagues at Oxford – presumably the university – tell Sarah Jane Smith that he's a brilliant scientist, as do the science correspondent of *The Times* and the editor of *Nature*. But given that Whitaker is working with colleagues in UNIT and the government, there's a good chance he's able to draw on technology recovered from alien encounters, perhaps even reports on the Doctor and his ship. (Can we really believe UNIT wouldn't have them?)

THE MOST IMPORTANT LESSON IN CYBERNETICS

As seen in *Destiny of the Daleks* (1979)
While trying to repair his robot dog **K-9**, the Fourth Doctor shares with his companion Romana the most important thing his cybernetics tutor ever taught him: 'When **replacing a brain**, always make sure the arrow A is pointing to the front.'

In *Pyramids of Mars* (1975), **Laurence Scarman** has, in 1911, built a working radio telescope 21 years before **Karl Guthe Janksy's** dipole array in New Jersey, USA – which is generally regarded as the first of its kind. It's a remarkable achievement given that Scarman apparently knocked it up on his own. But there's a more impressive feat of science ahead of its time.

In *The Evil of the Daleks*, eminent Victorians **Professor Theodore Maxtible** and **Edward Waterfield** build a cabinet of mirrors into which they project static electricity, and apparently make some link across space-time to attract the attention of the Daleks. Maxtible says that he has the money to support their investigations, while Waterfield is 'an expert in certain technical matters' – but that doesn't mean Waterfield does all the practical work. Maxtible has a good knowledge of the technically complex scientific papers written by Michael Faraday (1791–1867) and James Clerk Maxwell (1831–79), and it's these, rather than alien technology, that inspire his joint project with Waterfield.

Given this, their reaching the Daleks on the planet Skaro via a cabinet in a house outside Canterbury in 1866 is surely the greatest achievement in physics by humans.

See also the Doctor's contributions to science (36–37) and the most qualified companion (192–195).

The Third Doctor mentions 'the Chinese scientist called **Chun Sen**' – apparently an authority on the science of time travel – then remembers that 'he hasn't been born yet.' – *Invasion of the Dinosaurs*

THE GREATEST INVENTORS IN THE UNIVERSE

'[The **Daleks** are] brilliant technicians. It was their **inventive genius** that made them one of the greatest powers in the universe, remember that.' The Third Doctor, *Death to the Daleks* (1974)

BURST YOUR BRAIN WITH NOISE

MAKING MONSTROUS HORRORS SOUND GOOD

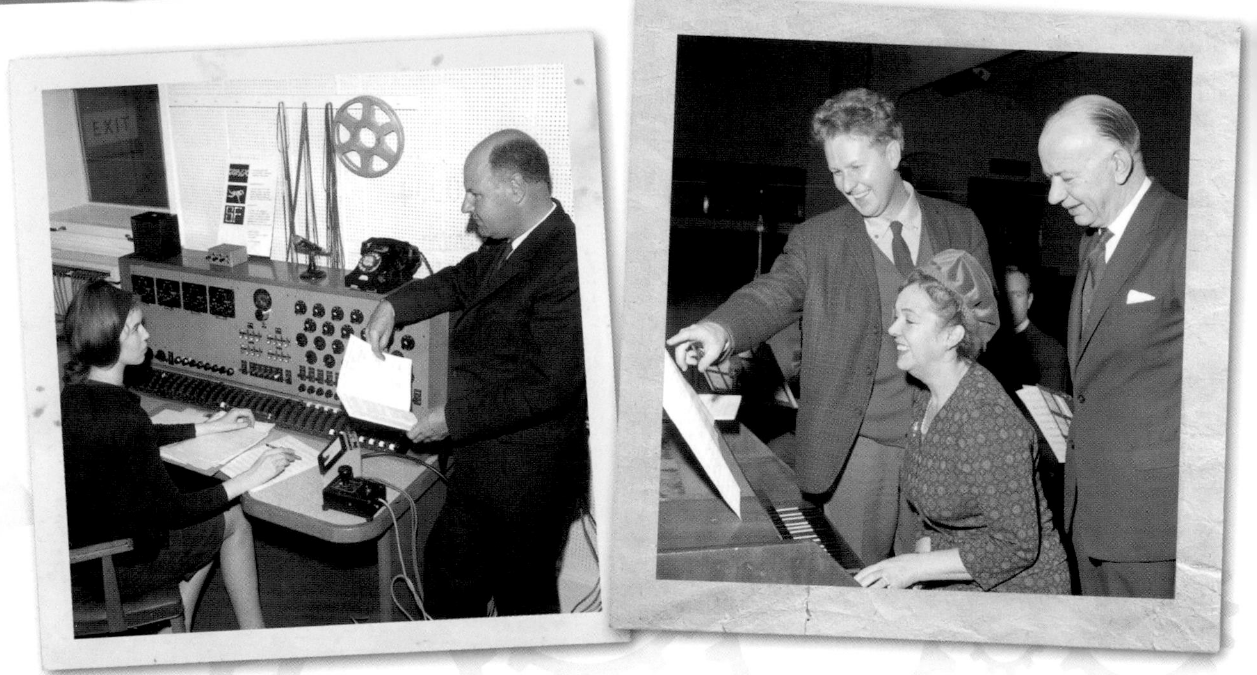

THE PERSON WITH MOST ON-SCREEN CREDITS IN *DOCTOR WHO*

'Did I write that?' According to the story, this was the amazed response of **Ronald Erle 'Ron' Grainer** when he first heard the theme tune to ***Doctor Who*** in August 1963 – three months before it was first broadcast to the nation. But he did write it, by hand, on a single sheet of A4.

It was his only work on the series, but he deserves full recognition for it. In fact, Ron receives an on-screen credit for composing the theme on every one of the first 102 episodes of the series – up to the end of ***The Daleks' Master Plan*** (1965–1966), and most but not all episodes since. In total, his name appears at the end of 636 of the 826 episodes – or **77%** – of ***Doctor Who*** up to and including ***The Return of Doctor Mysterio*** (2016). That's substantially more than anyone else in the cast or crew.

So why would Grainer have questioned whether it was his work? At the time he worked on ***Doctor Who***, he'd already made a name for himself as a composer of theme tunes. His work on the detective series ***Maigret*** (1959–1963) won him an Ivor Novello award which in turn led to him composing theme tunes for many popular series, such as the sitcom ***Steptoe and Son*** (1962–1974).

His commission for ***Doctor Who*** was a bit different because it wouldn't be played on conventional musical instruments. The job came about on the recommendation of Desmond Briscoe, co-founder and manager of the BBC's **Radiophonic Workshop** which specialised in electronic sounds. The Workshop had been approached by ***Doctor Who***'s first producer, Verity Lambert, about a suitably spacey-sounding theme and sound effects for the series. Ron had recently collaborated with the workshop on a documentary, ***Giants of Steam*** (1963), and the music for that had proved so popular that it was released on an EP. On 30 July 1963, Ron was formally contracted to compose the theme for ***Doctor Who***, which would then be realised electronically by the Workshop.

The page he wrote gave plenty of steer on what the

theme should sound like: a baseline with a swooping melody, full of effects suggesting 'clouds' and 'wind bubbles'. This was handed to **Delia Derbyshire**, a young composer with a degree in mathematics and music from Girton College, Cambridge, who'd joined the Workshop just the year before.

In November 2016, it was announced that Delia Derbyshire's pioneering work in electronic music – including on *Doctor Who* – would be recognised by her home town of **Coventry** by the naming of a street after her: **Derbyshire Way**.

At the time, there were no synthesizers or any of the modern equipment so commonplace in music production today. Instead, electronic music was a slow, laborious and technically challenging process. Delia used a bank of **12 test-tone generators**, some **equalisers**, a **white noise generator** and a **low frequency oscillator** (called a '**wobbulator**') to produce individual sound elements, recording them on **quarter-inch magnetic audio tape**. This she then cut up and stuck together in **tape loops** – so that when she played them, the sounds constantly repeated. She had to **adjust the speed** and **correct the pitch** of these loops before recording them onto yet more tape, which she then cut up to give her the separate elements from which she would stitch together the theme. There was then a **final mix** using outputs from three machines.

The outcome was extraordinary – Delia's original version of the *Doctor Who* theme tune is widely recognised as ground-breaking and influential. Ron, on hearing it, was thrilled. But when he asked – in delight – if he'd really written it, she was modest about all that hard work she'd put in. 'Most of it,' she said.

Unlike Ron, Delia worked on *Doctor Who* again. For *The Macra Terror* (1967), she produced a slightly revised version of the theme tune which was used in the series until 1980 (including modifications she made in the early 1970s), and also realised some incidental music composed by **Dudley Simpson** for use in the market scene of the story. But she didn't receive an on-screen credit for her work. In fact, her name appears in the credits of just a **single** episode of *Doctor Who* – for 50th-anniversary story *The Day of the Doctor* (2013), where some of the original version of the theme tune is used in the opening sequence.

THE COMPOSER WHO HAS WRITTEN MUSIC FOR THE LARGEST NUMBER OF EPISODES

Dudley Simpson composed the music for 62 *Doctor Who* stories, from *Planet of Giants* (1964) to *The Horns of Nimon* (1980) – covering **284 episodes**.

THE COMPOSER WHO HAS WRITTEN MUSIC FOR THE LARGEST NUMBER OF CONSECUTIVE EPISODES

Murray Gold composed the music for every one of the **131 episodes** between *Rose* (2005) and *The Return of Doctor Mysterio*.

TECHNOLOGICAL FIRSTS

THE PERPETUALLY PIONEERING PRODUCTION OF THE PROGRAMME

YEAR ONE

August 1963
Delia Derbyshire electronically constructs Ron Grainer's theme tune for *Doctor Who* (see p. 166.)

20 August 1963
The first ever filming on *Doctor Who*. Supervised by graphics designer Bernard Lodge, working with executive producer Mervyn Pinfield, filming took place on Stage 3A of Ealing Film Studios, elements of the opening titles were shot on 35 millimetre film.

31 August 1963
The first recording for *Doctor Who* in an electronic studio – onto videotape rather than film. This session, in Studio 5 of BBC Television Centre, was again for the opening titles.

13 September 1963
A test recording in Studio D of Lime Grove – soon to be the regular home of the series – to experiment with methods of making the TARDIS materialise and dematerialise.

19 September 1963
The first filming of material to be used in an episode of *Doctor Who* (not including the titles), with inserts and test effects shot on 35 millimetre film to be played in during studio recordings of the first four-episode story. It included the first footage of the TARDIS dematerialising seen from outside – i.e. the police box fading away – used in the fourth episode.

27 September 1963
Studio recording on the first ever episode of *Doctor Who* – a pilot that would not be broadcast until 1991.

18 October 1963
Studio recording of *An Unearthly Child* – the first broadcast episode of *Doctor Who*, transmitted on 23 November. It was recorded in black-and-white onto 405-line videotape.

24 October 1963
Actor Peter Hawkins attends an experimental session to try different voice treatments for the Daleks.

13 November 1963
Peter Hawkins and David Graham record the first Dalek dialogue to be used in *Doctor Who*.

22 November 1963
Studio recording of *The Survivors*

– the first episode in which we see the Daleks, and the first episode in which we see them shoot someone. To achieve the effect, the camera was over-exposed, turning the picture to negative.

YEARS AFTER

8 October 1966
A malfunctioning mixing desk which caused TV images to flare is used to record the Doctor's first regeneration.

2 December 1967
Studio recording of episode 1 of *The Enemy of the World* (1968) in Studio D of Lime Grove – the first episode of *Doctor Who* to be recorded on 625 rather than 405-line videotape, offering a better quality picture.

6 August 1969
Tests conducted for using colour separation overlay (CSO or 'green screen') in *Doctor Who* – a technique that could be used on studio-recorded material in colour.

13 September 1969
Filming begins on *Spearhead from Space* (1970) – the first *Doctor Who* story in colour.

21 December 1969
The first use of CSO for recording cave scenes in *Doctor Who and the Silurians* (1970).

28 April 1974
Shooting begins on *Robot*, the first *Doctor Who* story with location footage recorded on videotape rather than film, to allow more use of CSO.

2 April 1980
The first use of Quantel image processing allowed more complex visual effects in *The Leisure Hive* – including the TARDIS materialising while the camera pans.

March 1986
The first use of motion control technology on model filming (see p. 160).

Early 1987
BBC graphic designer Oliver Elmes and CAL Video collaborate on the first entirely computer-generated sequence in *Doctor Who* – with the TARDIS in space, being hit by some kind of energy and then tumbling out of control. This would be used to open *Time and the Rani* (1987), together with new, wholly computer-generated opening titles and logo. The work took three months to complete.

26 January 1996
Recording of the regeneration of the Seventh Doctor into the Eighth uses a computer-generated morphing effect in *Doctor Who* for the first time.

19 January 2009
Recording begins on *Planet of the Dead*, the first episode of *Doctor Who* to be shot in high definition.

28 March 2013
Recording begins on *The Day of the Doctor*, the first – and, so far, only – episode of *Doctor Who* to be shot in 3-D. (A 3-D release of 2014 episodes *Dark Water* and *Death in Heaven* had the effect applied afterwards.)

CHAPTER NINE
MONSTERS

'THERE ARE SOME CORNERS OF THE UNIVERSE WHICH HAVE BRED THE MOST TERRIBLE THINGS. THINGS WHICH ACT AGAINST EVERYTHING THAT WE BELIEVE IN. THEY MUST BE FOUGHT.'

THE SECOND DOCTOR, *THE MOONBASE* (1967)

DEADLIEST ENEMIES 172
ALL CREATURES GREAT AND SMALL 174
THEY'RE ALIVE 176
MOST EFFECTIVE MONSTERS 180
VOICES OF TERROR 182
BAD INFLUENCES 184
MIXED MONSTERS 186
BIG BADS 188

DEADLIEST ENEMIES

ACCORDING TO THE DOCTOR HIMSELF, WHICH MONSTERS ARE THE VERY WORST IN SPACE AND TIME?

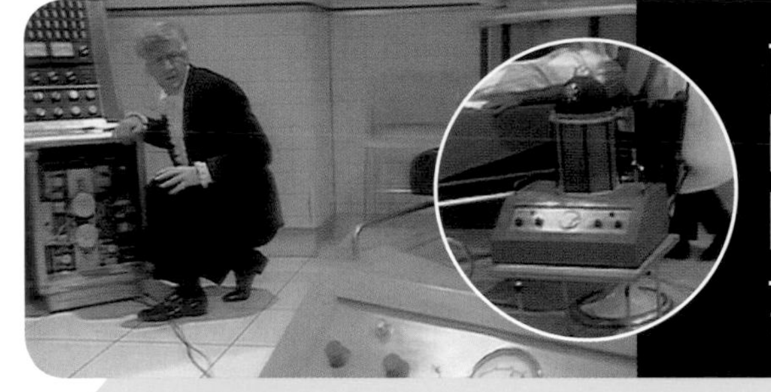

THE MIND PARASITE INSIDE THE KELLER MACHINE IS "THE DEADLIEST THREAT TO MANKIND SINCE THE BEGINNING OF TIME."

– The Third Doctor, *The Mind of Evil* (1971)

THE MASTER IS "THE MOST EVIL GENIUS IN THE UNIVERSE."

– The Fourth Doctor, *Logopolis* (1981)

THE MASTER "IS THE MOST EVIL FORCE IN THE UNIVERSE."

– The Fifth Doctor, *Castrovalva* (1982)

"THE DALEKS HAVE NO CONSCIENCE, NO MERCY, NO PITY. THEY ARE MY OLDEST AND DEADLIEST ENEMY."

– The Eleventh Doctor, *Victory of the Daleks* (2010)

THE TIME LORD OMEGA IS "ONE OF THE MOST POWERFUL BLOKES IN THE COSMOS."

– The Second Doctor, *The Three Doctors* (1972–1973)

"A WEEPING ANGEL, AMY, IS THE DEADLIEST, MOST POWERFUL, MOST MALEVOLENT LIFE FORM EVOLUTION HAS EVER PRODUCED"

– The Eleventh Doctor, *The Time of Angels* (2010)

"A RASTON WARRIOR ROBOT [IS] THE MOST PERFECT KILLING MACHINE EVER DEVISED."

– The Third Doctor, *The Five Doctors* (1983)

THE MOMENT IS "THE MOST DANGEROUS WEAPON IN THE UNIVERSE."

– The War Doctor, *The Day of the Doctor* (2013)

WHAT OTHERS ARE SAYING

We know the Doctor lies, or at least exaggerates. So who do other people think are the worst creatures in the universe?

"The Drashigs . . . are, without doubt, the most evil, the most vicious and undoubtedly the most frightening form of life in the whole of the universe!"

– Vorg, *Carnival of Monsters* (1973)

"We're talking about the Daleks, the most evil creatures ever invented."

– Sarah Jane Smith, *Genesis of the Daleks* (1975)

To the Master: "You are one of the most evil and corrupt beings this Time Lord race has ever produced. Your crimes are without number and your villainy without end."

– Borusa, Lord President of the Time Lords, *The Five Doctors* (1983)

The Daleks are "the dead-liest race in all of history"

– Missy, *The Witch's Familiar* (2015)

RUNNERS UP

Not everyone can be the very worst – but this lot are bad enough...

The Master is now "**one of** my oldest and deadliest of enemies"

– **The Seventh Doctor, *Survival* (1989).**

"A Skovox Blitzer [is] one of the deadliest killing machines ever created."

– The Twelfth Doctor, *The Caretaker* (2014)

The Mire "are one of the deadliest warrior races in the entire galaxy."

– The Twelfth Doctor, *The Girl Who Died* (2015)

The Zygons are "some of the most dangerous creatures imaginable."

– Twelfth Doctor, *The Zygon Invasion* (2015)

ALL CREATURES GREAT AND SMALL

IT TAKES A LOT OF DIFFERENT LIFE FORMS TO MAKE A UNIVERSE...

THE LARGEST LIFE FORM SEEN IN *DOCTOR WHO*

As seen in *42* (2007)

The Tenth Doctor and Martha Jones arrive on the SS ***Pentallian***, a spaceship plunging towards the star of the **Torajii** system, half a universe from Earth. We're not told the name of the star, but the usual method is to name the surrounding system after it – so our 'Solar System' is named after our star, Sol (better known as the 'Sun'). That would make this the star Torajii.

Torajii is a **living sun**, and it's not best pleased about the crew of the *Pentallian* using **fusion scoops** to strip its surface for fuel. 'Burn with me,' it pronounces as it takes control of members of the crew – and even the Doctor.

THE SMALLEST LIFE FORM SEEN IN *DOCTOR WHO*

As seen in *Flatline* (2014)

There are plenty of very little creatures in ***Doctor Who***, such as the Isolus in ***Fear Her*** (2006), the psychic pollen in ***Amy's Choice*** (2010) and the microscope nucleus of the swarm in ***The Invisible Enemy*** (1977). We learn in ***The Unquiet Dead*** (2005) that the Time War devastated higher forms such as the Gelth so that their physical bodies wasted away, leaving gaseous forms – but it's not clear how much volume they take up.

But if we're measuring by volume, there's clearly a winner. The **Boneless** in ***Flatline*** (2014) exist in only two dimensions, so if we multiply their length and width and height, we end up with **zero**.

Torajii must be the largest living creature ever seen in the series. We know our own Sun has a radius of about 695,700 kilometres but we're not told how big Torajii is in comparison. But can Dr Marek Kukula, Public Astronomer at the Royal Observatory Greenwich, work out the size from what we're shown in the story?

'It's hard to say from the episode how big the star is because there's no real indication of how far away it is from the foreground spaceship. However, the star has a distinctly orange-red appearance, characteristic of stars of spectral class M, with surface temperatures less than 4,000 degrees Celsius (our yellow-white G-class Sun has a surface temperature of 5,000 degrees or so).

'That could suggest either of two possibilities:

a **red dwarf star,** less than half the mass and half the radius of the Sun (so **less than 347,850 km**)

a **red giant star,** with a mass similar to or greater than that of the Sun and a radius more than 100 times larger (so **at least 6,957,000 km**)

'The appearance of the star in ***42*** shows it to be much more active than the Sun, with large bright areas covering much of the surface and numerous prominences of ionised gas rising off it into space. This could be consistent with either a red dwarf or a red giant, both of which are known to show more extensive surface activity than the Sun.

'However, red giants are stars at the end of their lives – most stars like the Sun will cool and swell up into red giants as they exhaust their nuclear fuel, but this phase only lasts for a billion years or so before the star fades and dies. Could this explain why the living star in ***42*** is so bad tempered?

'Alternatively, red dwarf stars are stable and long lasting – they can live for trillions of years, and many red dwarfs around today are much older than the Sun. Perhaps the star in ***42*** has been around for a very long time, giving it a chance to develop its strange life-like characteristics?'

THEY'RE ALIVE

MAKING MONSTERS IS ALL IN A DAY'S WORK FOR THE TEAM AT MILLENNIUM FX. BUT WHAT DO THEY THINK ARE THEIR RECORD-BREAKING CREATURES?

THE MOST DIFFERENT SPECIES IN ONE EPISODE

As seen in *The Rings of Akhaten* (2013)

For her first trip away from the Earth, the Eleventh Doctor takes Clara Oswald to the Rings of Akhaten, populated by a myriad different species. First, there are the prominent characters in the story: the Time Lord Doctor, the human Clara Oswald, the Doctor's old friend Dor'een, **Akhaten** himself and the Vigils.

There are various human-looking species, such as **Merry Gejelh** and her people. Of the non-human creatures, the Doctor gleefully points out Panbabylonians, a Lugal-Irra-Kush, some Lucanians, a Hooloovoo, a Terraberserker of the Kodion Belt and an Ultramancer. We can also spot a Hoix from *Love & Monsters* (2006). In fact, at the Festival of Offerings, we can see 146 individual creatures, though it's not clear how many of these are of separate species.

'Budgets being what they are,' says **Kate Walshe**, SFX producer at animatronics and prosthetics company **Millennium FX**, 'we knew that it wasn't going to be possible to populate an entire planet or big town' – as the script required. 'At the end of the day, it's TV not a massive Hollywood production, so it had to be a smallish group of aliens that we could swap around and make look larger. The deal was that we'd provide the aliens but we could reuse them afterwards – which means they pop up again in other episodes of *Doctor Who*, and some other things, too.

'So we assembled a team of great sculptors, fabricators and painters and just let them sculpt away and build suits. We re-purposed some costumes from other productions. And it was great fun. We had a lot of new sculpts but we also cast from our moulds and stuck things together. Yeah, it was make and do. In fact, we produced far more creatures than ended up on screen. We had more than 30 in the truck that went down to the studio in Cardiff, and they used, I think, **18** of them, and also doubled things up with make-up and wigs.'

THE MOST PEOPLE TO REALISE A CREATURE

As seen in *Nightmare in Silver* (2013)

How many people are employed on a *Doctor Who* special effect? 'It varies hugely,' says Kate. 'For example, on the Foretold' – the titular ***Mummy on the Orient Express*** (2014) – 'I think in total we had three sculptors, one fabricator and one mould maker. Five people working on one monster is quite small. But when we brought in the **new Cybermen** [in *Nightmare in Silver*] we had close to **40 people** working on them.'

THE MOST DISGUSTING CREATURE

As seen in *Hide* and *The Crimson Horror* (both 2013)

'There's been a few creations where we hear back from [the production team] saying, "God, that's disgusting!"' beams Kate. 'When we did the **Crooked Man** [in *Hide*], that freaked everyone out. There was the nicest guy in the costume – Aidan Cook. He was all "Oh, hello," to everyone. But people couldn't bear it. They found it so creepy and they kept away. So we must have done a good job there.'

'The idea in the original script was that he'd be a Time Lord who'd spent too long in the vortex and been warped out of shape. So you had this melted, dislocated thing going on. And though that changed in the story, they liked the designs we'd come up with. But it's weird – because he's not fierce or scary, he's unsettling – he looks like he's in pain.'

But Kate also nominates another creature – one that didn't have an actor inside it – seen in *The Crimson Horror*. '**Mr Sweet** is this blob with teeth, clinging to Diana Rigg [playing Mrs Gillyflower]. And basically, yuck.'

THE MOST COMPLICATED CREATURE

As seen in *The Caretaker* (2013)

'The **Skovox Blitzer** was part costume, part puppet, part rig,' says Kate. 'That was quite taxing. We had a couple of different ways of making it move. There was a version where a connection comes out the back with a gimbal weighted so that it could be pushed from a distance so there's nothing underneath and you just see him running along on his legs, nothing underneath. Then there was a version on wheels. We needed to get an actor in there. We needed it to scuttle. There was a whole lot of stuff it had to do.

'The schedules for making ***Doctor Who*** are really intense and the Skovox needed set-up time and it could only be shot in certain ways to make it look right. So, at the same time as he was shooting other parts of the episode, director Paul Murphy held sessions with us in the workshop over Skype, so he could see it all working and what angles he had. Then, obviously, we had the wonderful post-production team at BBC Visual Effects and Mill VFX who help remove things like the connections at the back. That's why it works for the audience – everyone pulling together.'

THE CREATURE THAT TOOK LONGEST TO PREPARE

As seen in *The Name of the Doctor* (2013)

'For a simple-looking creature,' says Kate, 'the Whispermen in ***The Name of the Doctor*** were actually really tricky. They wear these tights over their heads – a particular type and make of tights, which we obviously bought all the stocks of from all across the country. And you'd think it was just going to be "Put this on over your head" – but there's a lot of getting it to look just right. And then the actors move and the tights wrinkle – or tear. So we were spending four hours to get them ready, and then constantly dashing back in to correct things.'

MOST EFFECTIVE MONSTERS

OUR EXPERTS CHOOSE THE BEST BEASTS...

JON PERTWEE

The Third Doctor

'I liked the **Draconians** and **Ogrons** [in *Frontier in Space* (1973)] better than any other monsters. Because [the actors playing these creatures wore] half masks, you can see the human eye and you can see the mouth. Therefore, you get real, true expression. Unlike the Ice Warriors, in my opinion, or the Cybermen, that just had a slit [for the mouth] and you just heard the voice ... this makes a tremendous difference.'

KATE WALSH

SFX producer at Millennium FX, who has worked on *Doctor Who* since *Silence in the Library* (2008).

'I don't know all of *Doctor Who* as well as I should do, but I'll tell you one that sticks in my mind from when I saw it at the [exhibition of props and costumes] Doctor Who Experience. The **Vervoids** [from *The Trial of a Time Lord (1986)*] are these extraordinary plant creatures. They're beautifully crafted, it's just a really good design, and there's something really strange about them.'

MATT SMITH

The Eleventh Doctor

'I think you've got to be scared of the **Weeping Angels**. I'm very scared of them, but they're also my favourite of the *Doctor Who* monsters.'

PETER DAVISON

The Fifth Doctor

'The **Cybermen** have always been my favourites: I loved them right from the early days when they had cloth faces and what looked like car headlights on their heads [in ***The Tenth Planet*** (1966)]. I thought my incarnation of the Cybermen [seen in ***Earthshock*** (1982) and ***The Five Doctors*** (1983)] were pretty good – they still hold up today. You could see just see a hint of their shrivelled faces behind their face masks.'

DANNY HARGREAVES

Special effects supervisor who has worked on *Doctor Who* since *Rose* (2005).

'I remember Sylvester McCoy being chased round some vat of something by the **Kandyman** [in *The Happiness Patrol* (1988)], who just freaked me out. As with episodes now, you take something in everyday life – an object, a person or even a sweet – and turn them into a monster that people can relate to, and it's really scary. *Doctor Who* does that really well.' But it's was more than just the costume and effects that made the Kandyman scary. 'Totally. There's the way he's played, the movement, all of that. Yeah, it's really weird. To be honest, if they ever bring him back, someone else can do it. I'm not going to be on set.'

VOICES OF TERROR

WHO SPEAKS FOR *DOCTOR WHO*'S MYRIAD MONSTERS?

In *An Adventure in Space and Time* (2013), the drama about the earliest days of *Doctor Who*, Nicholas Briggs can be seen playing Peter Hawkins, voicing the Daleks in their first adventure.

THE FIRST MONSTER VOICE

As heard in *The Daleks* (1963–1964)

A few minutes into *The Survivors*, the sixth ever episode of *Doctor Who*, the First Doctor, Susan Foreman and Ian Chesterton discover a Geiger counter measuring the radiation levels on the alien world they're exploring. The needle is past the danger point. The Doctor is keen to get back to the TARDIS and leave the planet at once, though Ian reminds him that first they must find their missing friend, Barbara Wright.

Suddenly they are surrounded by four alien machine-like creatures – beings we'll soon learn are called **Daleks**.

'You will move ahead of us and follow my directions,' orders one Dalek in a distinctive, grating tone – the first ever time we hear an alien creature speak in *Doctor Who*.

This Dalek was voiced by **Peter Hawkins**. He and another actor, **David Graham**, created the harsh, staccato delivery, which was then electronically modified using a device called a **ring modulator** by the BBC's **Radiophonic Workshop**.

Peter and David continued to voice Daleks in their next few appearances in *Doctor Who*. In fact, Hawkins also holds the record for **providing Dalek voices in the most number of episodes** – between this first encounter and episode 7 of *The Evil of the Daleks* (1967), he provided Dalek voices for **41 episodes**, as well as in the two movies adapted from the first two Dalek stories on TV.

THE MOST SPECIES VOICED BY ONE ACTOR

Since *Dalek* (2005), almost all the Daleks seen in *Doctor Who* have been voiced by one actor – **Nicholas Briggs**. But Nicholas has also played more individual species than anyone else:

- The Nestene Consciousness – in *Rose* (2005)
- Daleks – in *Dalek* and since
- Cybermen – in *Rise of the Cybermen* (2006) and since
- Judoon – in *Smith and Jones* (2007) and since
- A human – in the *Doctor Who* spin-off *Torchwood: Children of Earth* (2009)
- Ice Warriors – in *Cold War* (2013)
- Zygons in *The Day of the Doctor* (2013) and since

Nicholas also recorded a voice for the Mighty Jagrafess of the Holy Hadrojassic Maxarodenfoe in *The Long Game* (2005).

THE HARDEST MONSTER VOICE TO PERFORM

'Technically and vocally,' says Nicholas, 'the voices of the Judoon are probably the hardest creature to perform. But I find the Cybermen the biggest challenge because they're so blank – and *must* sound blank – but at the same time have to sort of convey some kind of meaning and be interesting to listen to.'

ALIENS WALK AMONG US, SHAPING OUR EXISTENCE

THE FIRST MONSTERS TO CONQUER THE EARTH

As seen in *Day of the Moon* (2010)

The ***Dalek Invasion of Earth*** (1964) is the first successful conquest of our planet seen in ***Doctor Who***. According to the First Doctor in ***The Daleks' Master Plan*** (1965–1966), that invasion begins in **2157**, and he arrived some 10 years later to help end the occupation.

But that invasion doesn't take place for another 130 years – long after others we've since seen in the series.

The Invasion (1968) and ***Invasion of the Dinosaurs*** (1974) are both about short-lived attacks that the Doctor helps repel. In ***The Zygon Invasion*** (2015) the Zygons are already here, and have been living peaceably if secretly among us since the events of ***The Day of the Doctor*** (2013) – in fact, they've been on Earth since at least **1562**. We might argue that since the Zygons have made a success of living among us, this is a successful invasion.

But the Silents have been around far longer than the Zygons – they tell the Eleventh Doctor in ***Day of the Moon*** that they have ruled the Earth 'since the wheel and the fire'. Wheels were being used for pottery in Mesopotamia (modern-day Iraq) by 3500 BC, and revolving tablets called 'tournettes' – sort of 'proto-wheels' – perhaps a thousand years before that.

The first wheeled vehicles seem to have appeared soon after 3500 BC, at roughly the same time in Mesopotamia (modern-day Iraq), the Caucasus and central Europe. That suggests that whoever had the initial idea, it spread far and wide quickly. Or perhaps the fact the wheel is suddenly being used over such a wide area is evidence of the Silents manipulating humanity.

In that case, we can date the period of the Silent occupation from **c.**3500 BC to 20 July AD 1969.

Many Silurians might argue that the Earth was successfully invaded long before the Silents, by a race of intelligent apes called humans.

THE ALIENS WHO MOST INFLUENCED HUMANITY

As seen in *City of Death* (1979)

In *The Dæmons* (1971) an archaeological dig being broadcast live on BBC3 unearths a huge and powerful creature called **Azal**, who resembles figures seen in ancient human myths. Undertaking research, the Third Doctor surmises that Azal's people first visited Earth 100,000 years ago. UNIT's **Sergeant Benton** can't imagine why.

'To help Homo sapiens kick out Neanderthal man,' says the Third Doctor. 'They've been coming and going ever since. The Greek civilisation, the Renaissance, the Industrial Revolution – they were all inspired by the Dæmons.'

We don't know on what sources the Doctor bases this claim, and he might just be making an educated guess. While Azal later says that his people gave knowledge to man, the suggestion is that happened a long time ago. Professor Horner, leading the dig, dates the site to **800 BC** and there's no suggestion it's been disturbed – or that Azal has awoken – in the intervening time. Azal also tells us he's the last of his people, so it doesn't seem that any other Dæmons were around to influence the Renaissance and Industrial Revolution while he slept.

The one specific thing Azal mentions doing before his sleep is destroying **Atlantis** for not being worthy of his knowledge and power. But *The Underwater Menace* (1967) and *The Time Monster* (1972) both show us different reasons for the destruction of Atlantis, so Azal isn't necessarily a reliable source. The Dæmons might well have had an influence on human development, but we don't know when and to what extent.

In *Day of the Moon*, the **Silents** say they've influenced human behaviour for thousands of years, getting humans to produce items they want, even if that means giving us a developmental push. For example, the Apollo programme that sent the first humans to the Moon is – we learn – the result of these sinister aliens wanting a **spacesuit**, which would be developed as part of that effort. But the point is that humanity still does all the work.

So the greatest alien influence on our development is down to one person, albeit one split into 12 independent but connected individuals scattered throughout Earth history. In *City of Death* (1979), Scaroth, last of the Jagaroth, speaks of a man who 'has caused the **pyramids to be built**, the **heavens to be mapped**, invented the **first wheel**, shown the true use of **fire** [and] brought up a whole race from nothing' – the implication being that that man was him. The twelfth sliver of Scaroth living latest in Earth history – in Paris in 1979 – even pushes a human scientist to develop a working time machine.

THE MOST WATCHED FOOTAGE IN HISTORY

As seen in *Day of the Moon* (2011)

According to the Eleventh Doctor, half a billion people on Earth watch the first **Moon landing** live on TV. 'And that's nothing,' he says, 'because the human race will spread out among the stars. You just watch them fly. Billions and billions of them, for billions and billions of years, and every single one of them at some point in their lives will look back at this man taking that very first step, and they will never, ever forget it.'

Which is why it's a good clip for him to insert a subliminal message instructing humans to kill Silents on sight.

MIXED MONSTERS

LIFE IN THE UNIVERSE IN ALL ITS RICH AND STRANGENESS

THE GREATEST THREAT TO CRETACEOUS EARTH

As seen in *The Crimson Horror* (2013)

Although they're known as 'Silurians', the intelligent reptiles that flourished on Earth long before human civilisation are actually from a different geological period. In *The Sea Devils* (1972), the Third Doctor says they should be referred to as 'Eocenes' – in the Paleogene period. But if – as ***Dinosaurs on a Spaceship*** (2012) and ***Deep Breath*** (2014) suggest – they lived alongside the dinosaurs such as Tyrannosaurus rex, they're from the Cretaceous.

Fossil evidence tells us that Tyrannosaurus rex had the most powerful bite force of any land animal in the history of our planet – but there were clearly worse threats to life on Earth at the time. There were plenty of other large and powerful dinosaurs, and creatures in the sea and air that were just as dangerous.

But a worse threat faced the people we insist on calling Silurians. 'My people once ruled this world,' says Madame Vastra in *The Crimson Horror*, 'but we did not rule it alone. Just as humanity fights a daily battle against nature, so did we. And our greatest plague, the most virulent enemy, was the **repulsive red leech**.'

In *The Crimson Horror*, a specimen of that leech which survives in Yorkshire in 1893 has a name. 'Mr Sweet' has a symbiotic hold over the human Mrs Gillyflower, who feeds his venom to her workers and plans to use a rocket to have it rain down on all of humanity – wiping us out.

The **greatest punishment for a Sontaran** is to have to help the weak and sick – *A Good Man Goes to War* (2011)

Sil the Mentor says that his master Kiv has the '**greatest business brain**' in the part of the galaxy in which the planet Thoros Beta resides – *The Trial of a Time Lord* (1986)

The Slitheen have not just a good sense of smell but 'the best nostrils in the galaxy' – *The Sarah Jane Adventures: Revenge of the Slitheen* (2007)

THE MOST HUMAN NON-HUMANS

As seen in *The Tenth Planet* (1966)

Lots of alien species look just like Earth's human beings. There are the **Time Lords** from the planet Gallifrey, the **Thals** from the planet Skaro, the **Gonds** and **Dominators**, and the peoples of **Peladon**, **Traken**, **Karfel**, the **brood planet of the Chimeron**, and **Sarn** – to name but a few.

For all the Doctor – a Time Lord – might look like us, he's actually very different, with two hearts and the ability to regenerate. Other human-seeming aliens have their own unique characteristics, such as **Adric the Alzarian** who heals especially quickly.

So which human-seeming alien is most like us here on Earth? Surely it's got to be the people of our twin planet **Mondas**, who turned themselves into **Cybermen**. Just as we've evolved over millions of years to best fit the conditions of our planet, they must have evolved to best fit Mondas – as from what we see in *The Tenth Planet*, Mondas is identical to Earth.

According to the Tenth Doctor in animated story *The Infinite Quest* (2007), Baltazar, Corsair King of Triton in the 14th century, is the **greatest despot that ever lived**. Baltazar says that his unnamed spaceship, which he forged by hand, is 'the **greatest warship in history**.'

THE MONSTER WITH THE MOST WEAKNESSES

The **Pyroviles** in *The Fires of Pompeii* (2008) don't like being squirted with water, and Weeping Angels can't move while being watched. But surely the creatures with the most weakness are the **Cybermen**, who really don't like:

- Being shot by their own guns
- Radiation
- High explosives
- Solvents such as nail varnish remover
- Artificial gravity
- Illogical behaviour
- Emotions
- Gold
- Jazz music
- Electromagnetic pulses
- Mirrors (especially when they have their emotions returned to them)
- Daleks
- Old age (yes, even for them)

The **greatest hero of the Martian race known as Ice Warriors** is Grand Marshall Skaldak, sovereign of the Tharsisian caste and vanquisher of the Phobos heresy – *Cold War* (2013)

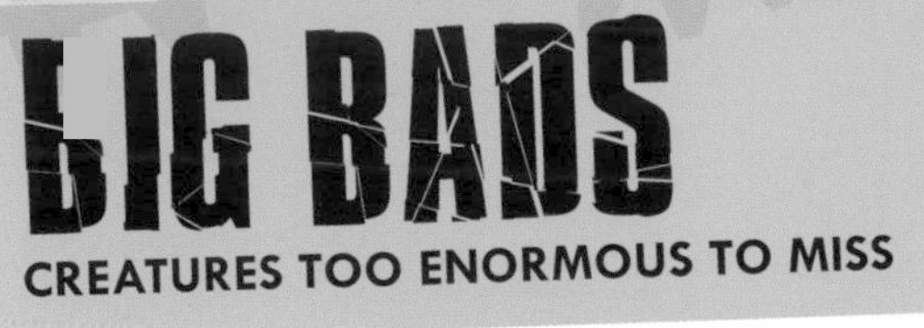

BIG BADS

CREATURES TOO ENORMOUS TO MISS

THE LARGEST CREATURE IN *DOCTOR WHO* – AS A PRACTICAL EFFECT

As seen in *The Runaway Bride* (2006)

Miniatures, CGI and other effects have often been used in ***Doctor Who*** to present enormous creatures. But the largest creature created full-size is the **Empress of the Racnoss**, the enormous spider whose babies are waiting to hatch from the centre of the Earth.

It took between three and four hours to apply actress **Sarah Parish**'s make-up on each of the three days she was on set to play the Empress. She was then fastened into an enormous rig built by **Millennium FX** for the rest of the spider's body. The rig enabled some movement on the part of the creature – the Empress could flex her legs, lift her body into the air and swivel round. Of course, that movement changes how wide or tall she is, but measured in one position the Empress was some **3 metres (10 feet) tall** and **7.5 metres (25 feet)** wide, and weighed **half a tonne**.

THE OLDEST CREATURE IN THE UNIVERSE

As seen in *The Satan Pit* (2006)

The Face of Boe is seen in the year 200,000 in *The Long Game* (2005) and doesn't die until the year 5,000,000,053 in *Gridlock* (2007).

In *Last of the Time Lords* (2007), it's suggested that the Face of Boe is the future Captain Jack Harkness. Jack is apparently in his mid-30s when he is made immortal in the year 200,100. In *Utopia* (2007) we learn Jack travelled back to 1869 where he seems to have lived through chronological time for some 140 years. In *Exit Wounds* (2008) – an episode of the spin-off series *Torchwood* – he's taken back to AD 27 and buried in the ground, where he remains until emerging in the present day.

Given this, the Face of Boe is at least 5,000,002,200 when he finally dies.

But in *The Satan Pit*, the Tenth Doctor faces the **nameless beast** which claims to be 'from before the universe' – making it more than 13,772,000,000 years old, or more than twice the age of the Face of Boe.

THE MOST POWERFUL CREATURE IN THE UNIVERSE

As seen in *Fear Her* (2006)

The Time Lords have enormous powers over the time. They're pretty evenly matched by the Daleks. But there are other races that must hardly even acknowledge the bickering of these two puny species.

The **Eternals** seen in *Enlightenment* (1983) are bemused by the mention of Time Lords: 'Are there lords in such a small domain?'

The **White Guardian** – first seen in *The Ribos Operation* (1978) – is a power in the universe that even Time Lords acknowledge. Even the Fourth Doctor calls him 'sir'.

Sutekh of the Osirans in *Pyramids of Mars* (1975) and **Akhaten** in *The Rings of Akhaten* (2013) are both extremely powerful and only defeated when faced with something of near-infinite proportions – an endless corridor in time for Sutekh, and for Akhaten the untapped potential represented in a particular leaf.

But surely the most powerful being we ever see in *Doctor Who* is the **Isolus** in *Fear Her*. As the Tenth Doctor explains, the Isolus are empathic beings of intense emotions. When they're cast off from their mother, their empathic link – their need for each other – sustains them. They cannot be alone. Together, the Isolus children, each inside a pod, ride the heat and energy of solar tides for the many thousands of years it takes them to grow up.

When a **solar flare** from our Sun scatters the pods, one lands in London in 2012, just before the opening ceremony of the **Olympic Games**. Given the Isolus depends on an empathic link as an energy source, the Doctor feeds it with the goodwill and love generated by the Olympics – and that enables the Isolus to head back out into space and rejoin its siblings.

So before this it's in a weakened condition when it draws on the fear and anger inside schoolgirl **Chloe Webber**. Together, they're responsible for more than 80,000 people vanishing from the Olympic Stadium, the Doctor and others being turned into a drawing, and Rose Tyler being attacked by an angry ball of scribble. It's an amazing show of power by such a tiny creature and her friend.

CHAPTER TEN
WORDS AND PICTURES

'DO YOU MEAN AN ALIEN'S TRYING TO STEAL THE MONA LISA?'
'IT IS A VERY PRETTY PAINTING.'

ROMANA AND THE FOURTH DOCTOR, *CITY OF DEATH* (1979)

FIRST WORDS 192
MATHEMATICAL EXCELLENCE 194
THE GREATEST ARTISTS 196
KEEPING IT REAL 198
I AM YOUR CREATOR 200
THE FINAL CHAPTER 202
A LIST OF AWARDS 204
BEST OF EVERYTHING 216

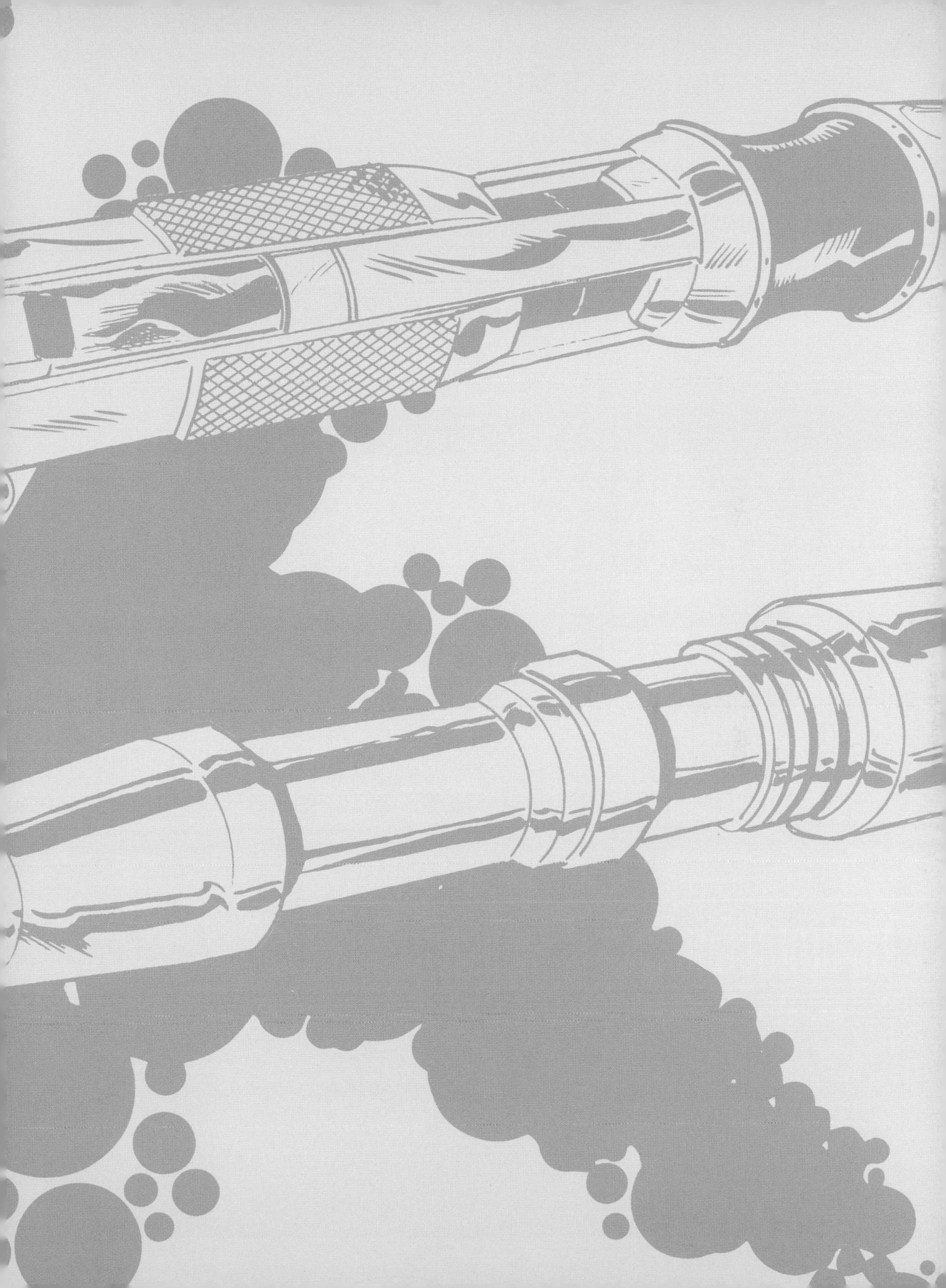

FIRST WORDS

'FIRST THINGS FIRST,' SAYS THE FOURTH DOCTOR IN *MEGLOS* (1980), 'BUT NOT NECESSARILY IN THAT ORDER.'

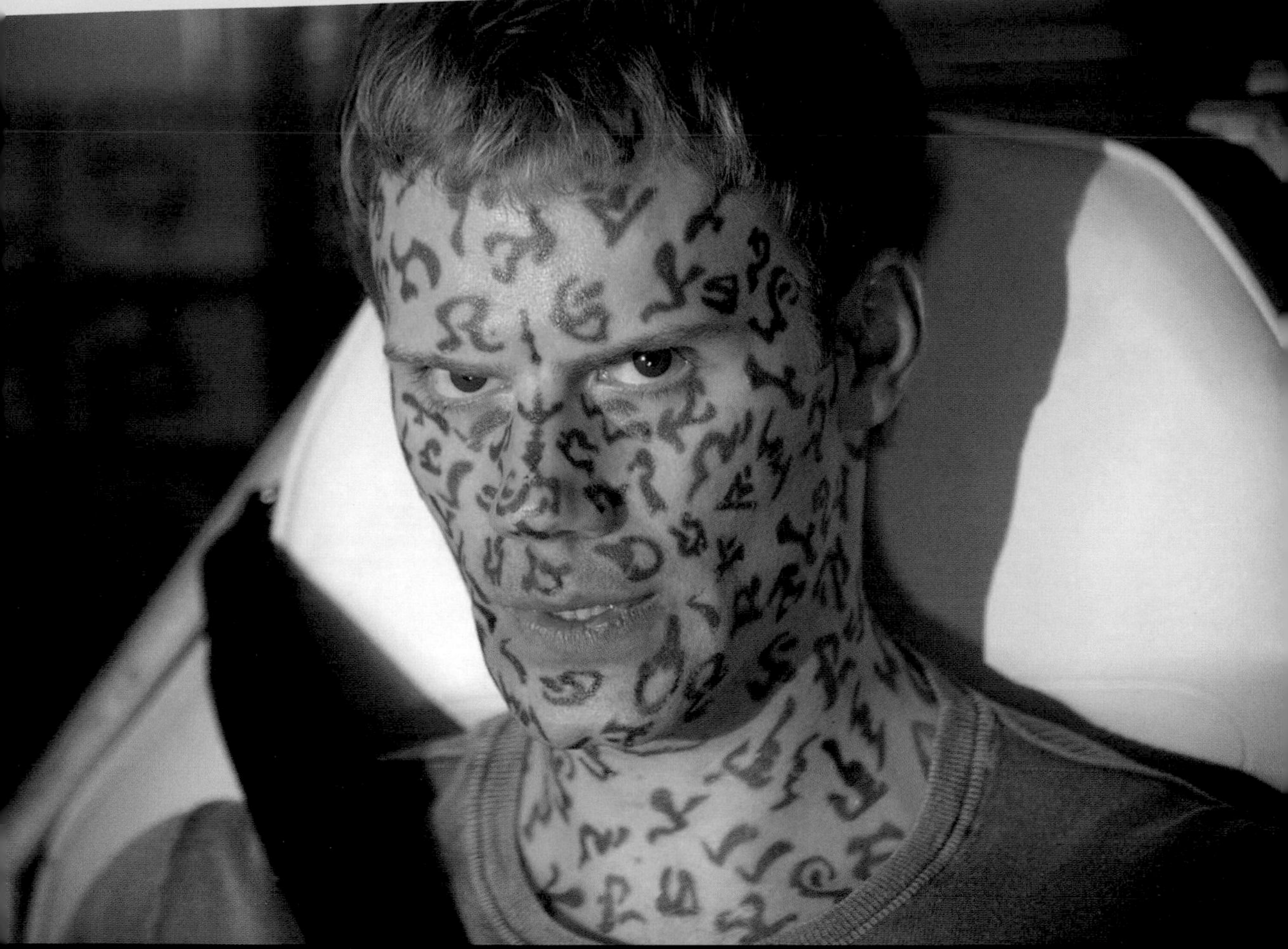

THE OLDEST LANGUAGE IN THE UNIVERSE

As seen in *The Impossible Planet* (2006)

In the 42nd century, on a sanctuary base on the planet **Krop Tor**, in orbit round a black hole, the **Tenth Doctor** and **Rose** discover handwritten **symbols**. The TARDIS seems unable to translate this strange writing into English – as it normally does.

According to the Doctor, this means the writing must be '**impossibly old**'. He later discovers that it's the writing of the unnamed **Beast**, a creature of immense power imprisoned at the heart of Krop Tor.

The Doctor isn't sure if the Beast is from **before the start** of the universe, or after it. But the Beast has certainly been imprisoned for an extremely long time. Since the symbols are beyond the powers of the TARDIS to translate, it seems this must be the oldest language the Doctor has ever encountered.

But though the language they're written in is very old, the symbols have been written recently.

THE OLDEST WRITING IN THE UNIVERSE

As seen in *The Pandorica Opens* (2010)

On **Planet One**, the oldest planet in the universe, there is a cliff of pure diamond into which are carved letters some 50 feet high. This message from the **dawn of time** has never been translated...

That is, until the **Eleventh Doctor** and **Amy** arrive and the TARDIS translates the letters as a message from time-travelling archaeologist **River Song**. It says 'Hello, Sweetie', and gives some coordinates for a meeting in AD 102.

The coordinates are written in what looks a little like Greek, but might be River using a language first seen on screen in *The Five Doctors (1983)*...

THE FIRST LANGUAGE OF THE TIME LORDS

As seen in *The Five Doctors* (1983)

In the **Death Zone** on Gallifrey, in the tomb of legendary Time Lord **Rassilon**, important inscriptions are carved into plinths.

The TARDIS doesn't appear to translate these inscriptions into English – again suggesting the language is extremely old. Instead, the **First Doctor**, the **Second Doctor** and the **Third Doctor** must work it out for themselves.

'It's **Old High Gallifreyan**,' the Third Doctor eventually explains, 'the ancient language of the Time Lords. Not many people understand it these days.' Fortunately, he does. The inscriptions suggest that Rassilon is not dead but in eternal sleep – and is willing to share his secret of immortality.

It's possible these inscriptions were written especially for the Doctor. That would explain why we can see the symbols $\boxtimes^3\boxtimes x^2$ so prominently. This is the **Doctor's name** according to the 1972 book *The Making of Doctor Who*, co-written by Terrance Dicks – who also wrote *The Five Doctors*.

In *The Time of Angels* (2010), the **Eleventh Doctor** calls Old High Gallifreyan the *lost* language of the Time Lords. 'There were days, there were many days, where these words could burn stars, raise up empires and topple gods.' At the time he's looking at an example that says, 'Hello, Sweetie!'

NEW WORDS

The first use of (real) scientific and technical terms in *Doctor Who*...

- Black hole (*The Three Doctors*, 1972)
- Blogging (*Utopia*, 2007)
- Broadband (*Dalek*, 2005)
- Cyborg (*Terror of the Zygons*, 1975)
- Computers (*The Daleks*, 1963)
- Downloading (*Dalek*, 2005)
- Emails (*Rose*, 2005)
- Headphones (*The Wheel in Space*, 1968)
- Internet (*Rose*, 2005)
- Memory [in a computer] (*The Edge of Destruction*, 1964)
- Mobile [phone] (*Rose*, 2005)
- Modem (*The Trial of a Time Lord*, 1986)
- Photocopy (*The Invisible Enemy*, 1977)
- Programmed [computer] (*The Chase*, 1965)
- Pulsars (*The Ambassadors of Death*, 1970)
- Ringtones (*School Reunion*, 2006)
- Transplant (*The Evil of the Daleks*, 1967)
- Twitter (*The Power of Three*, 2012)
- Scan (*Spearhead from Space*, 1970)
- Satellites [technological] (*The Power of the Daleks*, 1966)
- Supernova (*The Tenth Planet*, 1966)

MATHEMATICAL EXCELLENCE

THE DOCTOR HASN'T HALF GOT SOME CLEVER FRIENDS... AND ENEMIES

THE MOST QUALIFIED COMPANION

As seen from *Spearhead from Space* to *Inferno* (1970)

Most of the Doctor's companions are intelligent, practical people who can help him on his adventures. Some, such as **Josephine Grant** and **Ace**, failed their school examinations but proved their value in different ways.

Others come with formal qualifications, which we usually learn about in that companion's first story. **Adric**, companion of the Fourth Doctor and Fifth Doctor, wears a badge awarded to him for mathematical excellence. The Second Doctor's companion **Zoe Heriot** graduated in pure mathematics – and with honours. The Fourth Doctor's companion **Romanadvoratrelundar** (Romana for short) graduated from the Time Lord Academy with a triple first (the Doctor scraped through with 51% on the second attempt).

The Eighth Doctor's companion **Grace Holloway** is a qualified and practising medical doctor, which is what **Martha Jones** becomes in the time she knows the Tenth Doctor. **River Song** is a doctor and then professor of archaeology.

But the most qualified of the Doctor's companions must surely be **Dr Elizabeth Shaw** who, works alongside the Third Doctor at **UNIT** when he is exiled to Earth without the use of his TARDIS. We're told in Liz's first story that – as well as whatever she is a doctor of – she has 'degrees in medicine, physics and a dozen other subjects'.

This might be an exaggeration, but she's the only companion to leave the Doctor *because* she's **too qualified**. In *Terror of the Autons* (1971), we're told Liz returned to her work in Cambridge having remarked, all too often, that the Doctor merely needs an assistant 'to pass you your test tubes and to tell you how brilliant you are'.

We learn in *Death of the Doctor* (2010) – a story from the spin-off series *The Sarah Jane Adventures* – that Liz is on the **Moonbase**. Presumably that means she's undergone astronaut training, itself a qualification. That's ironic because, apart from a journey of a few seconds into the future, Liz never travelled in the TARDIS. The only companion to be qualified for travel in space, the Doctor never takes her there.

THE MOST POWERFUL COMPUTER

As seen in *The Face of Evil* (1977)

The Doctor has had machine companions in K-9 and Kamelion. He's battled robots and computers from WOTAN and BOSS to the CyberKing. But according to the Fourth Doctor, the most powerful computer ever built is **Xoanan**, the mission computer of the **Mordee planetary survey team**.

At some point before the events of ***The Face of Evil***, the Doctor helped program this computer for the Mordee but forgot to wipe his own personality print from the data core. This meant the computer was left with two personalities and developed schizophrenia, becoming, in the Doctor's words, a 'living creature'.

In the TV story, the Doctor returns to the planetary survey to find that the human surveyors, under Xoanan's confused influence, have regressed into two distinct groups. A tribe of warriors, the **Sevateem**, are descendants of the original survey team. Their enemies are the **Tesh**, descendants of the technicians. With the help a Sevateem warrior – the brave **Leela** – the Doctor is able to correct his mistake.

Removing the Doctor's personality print doesn't 'kill' Xoanon. Now much more agreeable, he puts his great power and knowledge at the disposal of the humans.

THE CLEVEREST MONSTER

As seen in *Time and the Rani* (1987)

The Daleks are brilliant technicians and the Master has a brilliant mind. All sorts of monsters and villains hatch ingenious schemes to conquer the universe and/or to trick the Doctor. Some of those schemes even work. But they're nothing to the awesome intelligence of the huge **gestalt brain** seen in *Time and the Rani*.

On the planet **Lakertya**, the wicked Time Lady the **Rani** collects the most creative minds in the universe – including human geniuses Hypatia, Louis Pasteur and Albert Einstein – at the height of their powers. These geniuses are wired up to the great, throbbing brain which becomes more than the sum of its parts – a truly fearsome intelligence.

The Rani constructed the huge brain to calculate a lightweight substitute for the dense but mysterious '**strange matter**', which she needs to detonate an asteroid made of genuine strange matter. This will produce **Helium II**, which will in turn fuse with the upper zones of the Lakertyan atmosphere to form a shell of temporal particles called chronons, while the gamma rays from the explosion will massively enlarge the brain. The brain and planet will together make up a **time manipulator**, enabling the Rani to rewrite history.

Unfortunately, the geniuses the Rani kidnapped have only a primitive understanding of time, so she forces the Doctor's TARDIS to crash land on Lakertya – the impact causing the Sixth Doctor to regenerate into the Seventh Doctor. The Doctor resists becoming part of the huge brain, but can't help but correct its error, thus completing its extraordinary calculation...

THE GREATEST ARTISTS

THE BEST WRITING IN THE UNIVERSE IS TO BE FOUND IN *DOCTOR WHO*

THE GREATEST WRITER IN HUMAN HISTORY

As seen in *The Shakespeare Code* (2007)

The Tenth Doctor calls **William Shakespeare** 'a genius' then corrects that to '***the*** genius. The most human human there's ever been ... Always he chooses the best words. New, beautiful, brilliant words.'

The Doctor has a point. The witchy **Carrionites** conjure magic with their well-chosen words, and Shakespeare – with a little help from **JK Rowling** – is the only one able to stop them.

The Doctor has met other writers – such as HG Wells and Charles Dickens – but their brilliance as writers didn't help save the world. Well, maybe Agatha Christie...

THE BEST WRITER OF DETECTIVE STORIES

As seen in *The Unicorn and the Wasp* (2008)

'Plenty of people write detective stories,' the Tenth Doctor tells **Agatha Christie** in 1926. 'But yours are the best – and why?' He already knows the answer. 'Because you understand. You've lived, you've fought, you've had your heart broken. You know about people, their passions, their hope and despair and anger. All of those tiny, huge things that can turn the most ordinary person into a killer.'

And that means she can solve the mystery of the giant, killer wasp.

THE WORLD'S GREATEST ARTIST

As seen in *Vincent and the Doctor* (2010)

How do you judge the contribution made by an individual artist? The Eleventh Doctor asks art expert Dr Black to rate the work of Vincent van Gogh. Black offers the following answer:

'To me, **Van Gogh** is the **finest painter of them all**. Certainly, the **most popular great painter of all time**. The **most beloved**. His command of colour the most magnificent. He transformed the pain of his tormented life into ecstatic beauty. Pain is easy to portray, but to use your passion and pain to portray the ecstasy and joy and magnificence of our world... No one had ever done it before. Perhaps no one ever will again. To my mind, that strange, wild man who roamed the fields of Provence was not only the **world's greatest artist**, but also **one of the greatest men who ever lived**.'

HUMANITY'S GREATEST COMPOSERS

As seen in *The End of the World* (2005)

Five billion years in the future, on the day the Earth is destroyed, the Lady Cassandra – last pure human alive – has an 'iPod' of 'classical music from **humanity's greatest composers**'. The music that outlives the Earth includes 'Tainted Love' by Soft Cell and 'Toxic' by Britney Spears.

Both **Russell T Davies** and **Steven Moffat** are **Officers of the Most Excellent Order of the British Empire** – they've received the OBE – 'for services to drama', which includes their work at the helm of *Doctor Who*.

THE BEST WRITER OF *DOCTOR WHO*

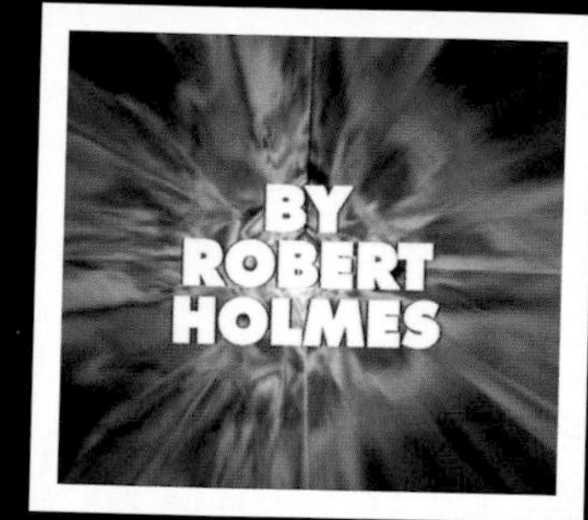

When put on the spot to name the best ever writer on ***Doctor Who***, Russell T Davies – head writer and executive producer on the series from 2005 to 2010 – chose **Robert Holmes**.

Holmes wrote for five incarnations of the Doctor between 1968 and 1986, and was script editor in charge of Tom Baker's first three years as the Doctor – generally regarded as one of the high points of the series.

'Take ***The Talons of Weng-Chiang*** (1977), for example,' argued Russell in 2007, citing one of Holmes's most popular stories. 'It's the best dialogue ever written. It's up there with Dennis Potter. [But] when the history of television drama comes to be written, Robert Holmes won't be remembered at all because he only wrote genre stuff. And that, I reckon, is a real tragedy.'

Steven Moffat, who replaced Russell as head writer and executive producer in 2010, agreed about Robert Holmes when asked the same question in 2015, and cited two other editors on the series – **David Whitaker** and **Terrance Dicks**.

But for Steven one writer stands above these worthy figures. 'It's habitual among fans to dismiss **Terry Nation**,' he said, 'but he's amazing. In the first year [of *Doctor Who*, 1963–1964], he invents how to do an alien planet story [in ***The Daleks***], an alien invasion story [in ***The Dalek Invasion of Earth***] and a quest story [***The Keys of Marinus***]. He invents the all-time best sci-fi monster in the Daleks and, a short time later, the best villain, with Davros [in ***Genesis of the Daleks*** (1975)].'

The Daleks are often credited with much of the early success of ***Doctor Who***, but Steven's right – it's as much the style and tone of story Nation provided that established the series we know.

KEEPING IT REAL

TRUTH MAKES FICTION STRANGER

THE FIRST REAL PERSON TO APPEAR IN *DOCTOR WHO* PLAYED BY AN ACTOR

As seen in *Marco Polo* (1964)

In the 14th episode of ***Doctor Who*, *The Roof of the World*** first broadcast on 22 February 1964, the TARDIS lands the First Doctor and his companions in 1289 in the Himalayas, on the 'Plain of Pamir' near the edge of the Gobi Desert.

It's a desolate, cold place – but they can't leave. A circuit in the TARDIS has burned out, the lights aren't working and they don't have any water.

Just as things are looking very bleak, they meet a caravan of travellers led by the Venetian **Marco Polo** (1254–1324) – the first real, historical figure to feature in a ***Doctor Who*** story. Later we also meet **Kublai Khan** (1215–1294).

Writer John Lucarotti based his scripts on the real Marco's own memoir, ***The Book of the Marvels of the World*** (c.1300) but made a number of changes. For example, in the story Marco is escorting 16-year-old **Ping-Cho** from Samarkand to Peking so that she can marry a 75-year-old man who is someone important in court at Peking. This seems to derive from the real Marco escorting Mongol Princess Kököchin ***from*** Peking to Persia to marry Kublai's grand-nephew. Setting off in 1291, the journey took some two years – and Marco and Kököchin arrived to find the grand-nephew had died.

THE FIRST REAL PERSON TO APPEAR IN *DOCTOR WHO* AS THEMSELVES

As seen in *The War Machines* (1966)

Kenneth Kendall (1924–2012) began his career at the BBC in 1948 as a newsreader on radio. He started reading the news on television in 1954, and the following year became the first ever newsreader to appear on camera while reading the news (before that, viewers only heard the newsreader's voice).

In 1961, Kendall left the BBC but continued to read the news on a freelance basis. He also made appearances in other programmes. On 1 July 1966, he was a Riverside Studios to record an appearance as a newsreader in Episode 4 of ***The War Machines***, adding a touch of realism to the first ***Doctor Who*** story to see an invasion of present-day London.

Ten days after recording his cameo in ***Doctor Who***, on 11 July Kendall recorded a more prominent role as a newsreader who is kidnapped and then returns to declare the impending end of the world in ***The Doomsday Plan***, an episode of adventure series ***Adam Adamant Lives!*** broadcast on 1 September the same year. He was also a newsreader in the science fiction film ***2001: A Space Odyssey*** (1968).

THE FIRST REAL PERSON TO BE NAMED IN THE SERIES AND THEN APPEAR IN IT – AS SOMEONE ELSE

As seen in *Voyage of the Damned* (2007)
In north London in 1953, it looks as if the Tenth Doctor might be too late to prevent the wicked **Wire** from gorging on the millions of TV viewers watching the coronation of Queen Elizabeth II. 'It's never too late, as a wise woman once said,' insists the Doctor '**Kylie**, I think.'

This line in *The Idiot's Lantern* (2006) – recorded in February 2006 – is surely referring to '**Never Too Late**', a 1989 song performed by Australian actress and pop singer **Kylie Minogue**. The writer of the episode, Mark Gatiss, was a friend of Kylie's creative director, Will Baker – to whom the production team of *Doctor Who* broached the idea of Kylie appearing in the series.

Kylie met with *Doctor Who*'s then executive producer Russell T Davies on 26 March 2007, and the press published the first rumours that she might be involved in the series on 22 April. It was finally announced on 3 July that she was about to begin three weeks recording the forthcoming Christmas special, *Voyage of the Damned*.

Kylie plays **Astrid Peth** – a human-looking alien on a pleasure cruise to Earth. The Tenth Doctor, the same incarnation who quoted a song by Kylie, doesn't mention her resemblance to the singer.

THE FIRST REAL PERSON TO BE NAMED IN THE SERIES AND THEN APPEAR IN IT

As seen in *The Eleventh Hour* (2010)
Sir Patrick Moore (1923–2012) was, from 1957 until his death, the presenter of the BBC's astronomy programme, *The Sky at Night*, and wrote more than 70 books on aspects of space exploration. His first brush with *Doctor Who* came in 1966, when script editor **Gerry Davis** met him to discuss the possibility of Moore becoming scientific adviser to the programme. In the end, that role went to ophthalmologist **Dr Kit Pedler** – with whom Davis devised the plot of *The War Machines* and created the Cybermen.

In *Aliens of London* (2005), the Ninth Doctor tells Rose that, after **a pig in a spacesuit** crashes in the River Thames, the Government are 'gathering experts in alien knowledge – and who's the best expert of the lot?'

'Patrick Moore?' asks Rose Tyler, teasing him.

Having been named in the series, Moore then made a brief appearance in *The Eleventh Hour* as one of the world experts taking part in a video conference call to discuss the impending incineration of Earth by the **Atraxi**.

I AM YOUR CREATOR

THE PEOPLE WHO'VE MADE THE MOST *DOCTOR WHO*

Robert Holmes appears briefly in ***The Brain of Morbius*** as one of the faces the production team at the time intended to be incarnations prior to the 'First' Doctor (see pp. 106–7).

THE MOST PROLIFIC WRITER OF *DOCTOR WHO*

Robert Holmes (1926-1986) is credited on screen as the writer in the opening titles on **64 episodes** of *Doctor Who*, from Episode 1 of *The Krotons* (1968) to Part 13 of *The Trial of a Time Lord* (1986). Holmes was also **script editor** on the programme from *Robot* (1974 to 1975) to *Image of the Fendahl* (1977), with a screen credit on all the episodes he oversaw except those where he already had a credit as writer.

In addition, we know that Holmes extensively rewrote the scripts of ***Pyramids of Mars*** (1975) and ***The Brain of Morbius*** (1976), but doesn't receive an on-screen credit as writer. Before becoming script editor, Holmes also shadowed his predecessor, Terrance Dicks, and worked on ***Invasion of the Dinosaurs*** and ***Death to the Daleks*** (both 1974).

THE MOST PROLIFIC DIRECTOR OF *DOCTOR WHO*

Douglas Camfield (1931–1984) is credited on screen as the director of **52 episodes** of *Doctor Who*, from the third episode of *Planet of Giants* (1964) to Part 6 of *The Seeds of Doom* (1976). That includes directing all 12 episodes of the epic *The Daleks' Master Plan* (1965–1966).

(Camfield was taken ill during production of *Inferno* (1970), having completed location filming and the first block of studio recording. Producer Barry Letts stepped in to direct the remaining five days in studio, working from Camfield's careful plans – and insisted that Camfield should keep his screen credit.)

THE MOST PROLIFIC *DOCTOR WHO* COMICS ARTIST

Me and My Shadow is a seven-page comic strip featuring the Eighth Doctor, first published in *Doctor Who Magazine* issue 318 in 2002. It was drawn and inked by comics artist **John Ross** – his first work on *Doctor Who*.

John provided the art for the comic strip in the next four issues of *Doctor Who Magazine*, and on-and-off since. He also drew comic strips for the first six issues of *Doctor Who – Battles in Time*, and for each of the *Doctor Who* annuals published every year since 2005. But most impressively, he was the artist on the comic strip on 363 issues of *Doctor Who Adventures* between 2006 and 2015.

Up to and including his work on *Doctor Who – The Official Annual 2017*, John has produced a staggering **1,883½ pages** of *Doctor Who* comic strip.

'Wow!' says John on hearing this. 'I'm really proud of that total. And thankful people kept sending me scripts.'

See pages 22–23 for the actor in most *Doctor Who* episodes

See page 166 for the person with the most on-screen credits

See over the page for the most prolific writer of *Doctor Who* books...

THE FINAL CHAPTER

HOW THE DOCTOR'S BEEN BROUGHT TO BOOK – IN A SERIES OF NOVELISATIONS

A SHORT HISTORY OF NOVELISATIONS

Long before iPlayer, downloads and DVDs – and even before domestic video machines – books were the only way you could enjoy a *Doctor Who* story a second time or catch up on episodes you might have missed. In those days, there weren't even many repeats.

David Whitaker was story editor of the first year of *Doctor Who* on television (1963–1964), and also wrote the very first novelisation of a TV story. He adapted the adventure that introduced the Daleks in a novelisation called, rather snappily, *Doctor Who in an Exciting Adventure with the Daleks*, published on 12 November 1964.

A hugely successful range of novelisations followed this, reaching its peak in the 1970s and 1980s. After more than 150 individual titles, the regular range came to an end in the early 1990s, when there were also no new *Doctor Who* stories to novelise. But many of the books have been republished in recent years – and there are even new novelisations of old stories.

The word 'novelisation' appears in a single TV *Doctor Who* story – *The Shakespeare Code* (2007)

In David Whitaker's second novelisation, *Doctor Who and the Crusaders* (1965, adapted from his own 1965 story, *The Crusade*), he changes the name of the man the Doctor's granddaughter Susan falls in love with. On TV that's David Campbell, in the book David's surname is Cameron.

MOST PROLIFIC AUTHOR OF BOOKS

As well as being a writer and script editor on the TV series, Terrance Dicks has written 64 novelisations of TV *Doctor Who* stories, 12 original *Doctor Who* novels, two books based on *Doctor Who* spin-offs, and four non-fiction *Doctor Who* books on which he receives a credit (plus several more on which he doesn't).

THE LONGEST NOVELISATION

The Pirate Planet (1978) is a four-episode story written by Douglas Adams. The novelisation by James Goss runs to 100,756 words – or 109,210 including appendices. That's more than double most novelisations.

THE WORDIEST NOVELISATION

Published in January 1990, Terence Dudley novelised his own two-episode story *The King's Demons* (1983) in **45,467** words – or slightly more than **15 words per second broadcast**. That makes it easily the wordiest *Doctor Who* novelisation, but Dudley had already done better. His novelisation of his script for *Doctor Who* spin-off *K-9 & Company* (1981) was published in October 1987 and comprised **49,041** words – more than **16 words per second**.

THE FASTEST NOVELISATION RELEASE

The novelisation of ***The Five Doctors***, adapted by Terrance Dicks from his own TV script, was accidentally released **two weeks** *before* the story was first broadcast in the UK on 25 November 1983.

The novelisation of the 1996 TV movie ***Doctor Who***, adapted by Gary Russell from the script by Matthew Jacobs, was published in the UK, US and Canada on 16 May 1996. That was **four days** after the first broadcast of the film – by a single station in Canada – on 12 May, and two days after its premier on US network Fox. But it was six days ahead of the TV movie being available to buy on video in the UK, and **11 days before** the first UK broadcast.

THE SLOWEST NOVELISATION RELEASE

The novelisation of *The Pirate Planet* was first published on 5 January 2017 – **39 years, two months and 15 days** after the final episode was broadcast in October 1978.

All the TV stories since *Rose* (2005) and two stories from before that remain to be novelised. To beat *The Pirate Planet*'s record, *Resurrection of the Daleks* (1984) would have to be novelised no earlier than 1 May 2023, *Revelation of the Daleks* (1985) no earlier than 14 June 2024, and *Rose* no earlier than 11 July 2044.

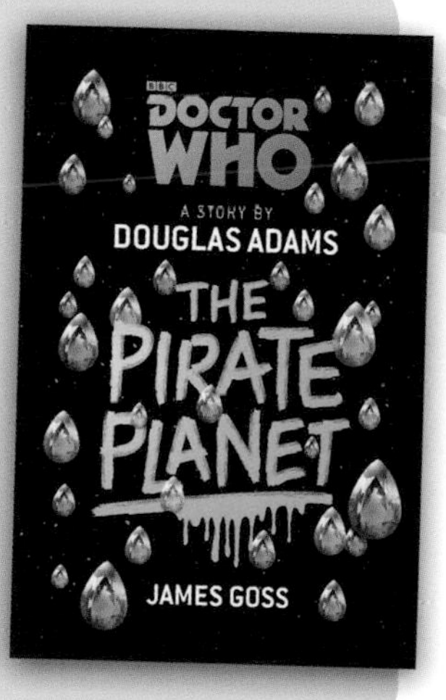

THE LEAST WORDY NOVELISATION

The War Games (1969) is a pivotal adventure in the history of *Doctor Who* and, at **10 episodes**, the third-longest single story in the series. It's about armies from all through Earth history being forced to fight at the behest of an alien power. As a result, the Second Doctor and his friends escape what they think are the trenches of the First World War only to find themselves pursued by ancient Romans.

Later in the story, and for the first time in the series, we meet the Doctor's own people – the Time Lords – and visit their planet (though it's not named until a later adventure). At the end of the story, the Time Lords exile the Second Doctor to Earth in the 20th century and force him to regenerate (again, a word coined later).

But when Malcolm Hulke came to novelise this epic tale that he'd originally co-written with Terrance Dicks, he cut anything that wasn't essential. Published in September 1979, *Doctor Who and the War Games* comprises **40,736** words – or just more than **16 words per minute broadcast**, 60 times less than the ratio of *K-9 & Company*.

A LIST OF AWARDS

'WHAT DO YOU DO FOR AN ENCORE?' HARRISON CHASE ASKS THE FOURTH DOCTOR AFTER HE MAKES A PARTICULARLY DRAMATIC ENTRANCE IN *THE SEEDS OF DOOM* (1976). THE DOCTOR BEAMS: 'I WIN.'

NOTE We've not included awards:

- won by cast and crew members but not for their work on *Doctor Who*.
- won for anything other than the 827 episodes (such as books, audios and websites).
- offered for out-takes from the recording of episodes.

AWARDS WON BY THE 827 EPISODES OF *DOCTOR WHO*

BAFTA Cymru awards

Year/Category	Nominee(s)	Episode	Result
2006 Best Drama Series/Serial	Phil Collinson		Won
2006 Best Actor	Christopher Eccleston		Nominated
2006 Best Actress	Billie Piper		Nominated
2006 Best Director – Drama	James Hawes	*The Christmas Invasion*	Won
2006 Best Screenwriter	Russell T Davies		Nominated
2006 Best Original Music Soundtrack	Murray Gold	*The Christmas Invasion*	Nominated
2006 Best Sound	Ian Richardson		Nominated
2006 Best DOP – Drama	Ernest Vincze		Won
2006 Best Costume	Lucinda Wright		Won
2006 Best Make-Up	Davie Jones and Neill Gorton		Won
2006 Best Design	Edward Thomas	*The Christmas Invasion*	Nominated
2006 Siân Phillips Award for Outstanding Contribution to Network Television	Russell T Davies		Won
2007 Best Actor	David Tennant	*Doomsday*	Won
2007 Best Actress	Billie Piper		Nominated
2007 Best Screenplay	Russel T Davies		Won
2007 Best Costume	Louise Page		Won
2007 Best Make-Up	Neill Gorton and Sheelagh Wells	*The Girl in the Fireplace*	Won
2007 Best Editor	Cripspin Green	*Tooth and Claw*	Won
2008 Best Drama Series/Serial	Phil Collinson	*Voyage of the Damned*	Won
2008 Best Director	James Strong		Won
2008 Best Screenwriter	Steven Moffat	*Blink*	Won
2008 Best Sound	BBC Wales sound team	*Voyage of the Damned*	Won
2008 Best DOP – Drama	Ernest Vincze		Won
2008 Best Costume	Louise Page	*The Shakespeare Code*	Nominated
2008 Best Make-Up	Neill Gorton and Barbara Southcott		Won
2009 Best Drama Series/Serial	Phil Collinson		Nominated
2009 Best Director – Drama	Euros Lyn	*Silence in the Library*	Won
2009 Best Screenwriter	Russel T Davies	*Midnight*	Won

Year/Category	Nominee(s)	Episode	Result
2009 Best Original Music Soundtrack	Murray Gold	*Midnight*	Nominated
2009 Best Sound	Julian Howarth, Tim Ricketts, Paul McFadden and Paul Jefferies	*Midnight*	Won
2009 Best DOP – Drama	Rory Taylor	*Silence in the Library*	Nominated
2009 Best Make-Up	Barbara Southcott	*The Next Doctor*	Nominated
2009 Best Editor	Philip Kloss	*Midnight*	Won
2010 Best Drama Series/Serial	Tracie Simpson	*The End of Time: Part One*	Nominated
2010 Best Make-Up	Barbara Southcott		Won
2010 Best Design	Edward Thomas	*The Waters of Mars*	Won
2011 Best Sound	Tim Ricketts	*A Christmas Carol*	Won
2011 Best Make-Up & Hair	Barbara Southcott	*The Vampires of Venice*	Nominated
2011 Best Editing: Fiction	William Oswald	*The Time of Angels*	Nominated
2011 Best Lighting	Mark Hutchings	*The Eleventh Hour*	Won
2012 Best Television Drama	Marcus Wilson	*The Impossible Astronaut*	Nominated
2012 Best Sound	*Doctor Who* sound team	*The Wedding of River Song*	Nominated
2012 Best Digital Creativity & Games	BBC Wales interactive team, Sumo Digital & Revolution Software *Doctor Who: The Adventure Games – The Gunpowder Plot*		Won
2013 Best Sound	The *Doctor Who* sound team		Nominated
2013 Best Editing	William Oswald	*The Snowmen*	Nominated
2014 Best Sound	The *Doctor Who* sound team		Nominated
2014 Best Special Effects	The *Doctor Who* Effects team		Won
2014 Best Music and Entertainment	*Doctor Who* at the Proms		Nominated
2015 Best Actor	Peter Capaldi	*Dark Water*	Nominated
2015 Best Actress	Jenna Coleman	*Kill the Moon*	Nominated
2015 Best Editing	Will Oswald	*Dark Water*	Nominated
2015 Best Special and Visual Effects	*Doctor Who* Production Team	*Last Christmas*	Nominated
2015 Best Titles and Graphic Identity	*Doctor Who* Production Team	*Deep Breath*	Nominated
2016 Technical Achievement Commendation	BBC Cymru, BBC Digital Creativity, Aardman Animations	*Doctor Who Game Maker*	Nominated
2016 Sound & Music Commendation	The *Doctor Who* sound team		Nominated
2016 Best Editing	Will Oswald	*Heaven Sent*	Nominated
2016 Best Special and Visual Effects, Titles and Graphic Identity	*Doctor Who* Production Team	*The Magician's Apprentice*	Won

People's Choice Awards

Year/Category	Nominee(s)	Result
2008 Favorite Sci Fi/Fantasy Show	*Doctor Who*	Nominated
2012 Favorite Sci Fi/Fantasy Show	*Doctor Who*	Nominated
2014 Favorite Sci Fi/Fantasy Show	*Doctor Who*	Nominated

A LIST OF AWARDS

BAFTA TV awards

Year/Category	Nominee(s)	Episode	Result
1977 'Harlequin' (Drama/ Light Entertainment)	Philip Hinchcliffe		Nominated
1978 'Harlequin' (Drama/ Light Entertainment)	Graham Williams		Nominated
2006 Best Drama Series	Phil Collinson, Russell T Davies and Julie Gardner		Won
2006 Best Director	Joe Ahearne		Nominated
2006 Best Writer	Russell T Davies		Nominated
2006 Audience Award (TV)			Won
2006 Break-Through Talent	Edward Thomas		Nominated
2006 New Media Developer	Jo Pearce and Andrew Whitehouse	*Attack of the Graske*	Nominated
2006 Dennis Potter Award	Russell T Davies		Won
2007 Best Editing Fiction/Entertainment	Crispin Green		Nominated
2007 Best Visual Effects	The Mill		Nominated
2008 Best Writer	Steven Moffat	*Blink*	Won
2008 Best Original Television Music	Murray Gold		Nominated
2008 Best Sound Fiction/Entertainment	BBC Wales sound team		Nominated
2009 Best Drama Series	Phil Collinson, Russell T Davies, Julie Gardner and Susie Liggat		Nominated
2009 Best Writer	Russell T Davies	*Midnight*	Nominated
2009 Best Editing Fiction/Entertainment	Philip Kloss		Won
2010 Best Visual Effects	The Mill		Nominated
2011 Best Actor	Matt Smith		Nominated
2011 Best Visual Effects	The Mill		Nominated
2012 Best Visual Effects	The Mill		Nominated
2013 Best Visual Effects and Graphic Design	The Mill		Nominated
2013 Best Original Television Music	Murray Gold	*Asylum of the Daleks*	Nominated
2014 Radio Times Audience Award		*The Day of the Doctor*	Won
2014 Best Special Effects	Milk VFX, Real SFX, The Model Unit	*The Day of the Doctor*	Won
2014 Best Entertainment Craft Team	Alex Hartman, Saul Gittens, Dan Evans, Amer Iqbal	*Doctor Who at the Proms*	Nominated
2015 Best Visual Effects	Milk VFX, Real SFX, BBC Wales VFX		Won
2016 Best Supporting Actress	Michelle Gomez		Nominated
2016 Best Visual Effects	Milk VFX, Millennium FX, Real SFX, Molinare		Nominated

BBC Best of Drama (online poll) and BBC Radio 1 Teen awards

Year/Category	Nominee(s)	Episode	Result
2005 Best Drama			Won
2005 Best Actor	Christopher Eccleston		Won
2005 Best Actor	David Tennant		Nominated
2005 Best Actress	Billie Piper		Won
2005 Favourite Moment	"The return of the Daleks"		Won
2005 Favourite Moment	"The Doctor regenerates"		Nominated
2005 Favourite Moment	"The Daleks"		Won
2005 Favourite Moment	"The Emperor Dalek"		Nominated
2005 Most Desirable Star	Christopher Eccleston		Nominated
2005 Most Desirable Star	David Tennant		Nominated
2005 Most Desirable Star	Billie Piper		Won
2005 Most Desirable Star	John Barrowman		Nominated
2005 Best Drama Website	*Doctor Who*		Won
2006 Best Drama	*Doctor Who*		Won
2006 Best Actor	David Tennant		Won
2006 Best Actress	Billie Piper		Won
2006 Favourite Moment	"Daleks vs Cybermen"		Nominated
2006 Favourite Moment	"Rose's exit"		Won
2006 Best Drama Website	*Doctor Who*		Won
2010 BBC Radio 1 Teen awards – Best TV Show	*Doctor Who*		Nominated
2013 BBC Radio 1 Teen awards – Best TV Show	*Doctor Who*		Won

BAFTA Scotland awards

Year/Category	Nominee(s)	Episode	Result
2008 Best Writer	Steven Moffat		Nominated
2009 Best Actor	David Tennant		Nominated
2015 Best Actress	Michelle Gomez		Nominated
2015 Best Writer	Steven Moffat		Nominated
2016 Best Actor	Peter Capaldi		Nominated

Television and Radio Industries Club (TRIC) awards

Year/Category	Nominee(s)	Result
2006 New TV Talent	Billie Piper (also for *ShakespeaRe-Told*)	Won
2007 TV Drama Programme	Russell T Davies, Phil Collinson and Julie Gardner	Nominated
2008 TV Drama Programme	Russell T Davies	Nominated
2010 TV Drama Programme	Russell T Davies	Won
2014 HD Drama Programme of the Year		Won

A LIST OF AWARDS

Broadcasting Press Guild Awards

Year/Category	Nominee(s)	Result
2006 Best Drama Series	Phil Collinson, Russell T Davies and Julie Gardner	Nominated
2006 Best Actor	Christopher Eccleston	Nominated
2006 Best Actor	David Tennant (also for *Casanova* and *Secret Smile*)	Nominated
2006 Best Actress	Billie Piper (also for *ShakespeaRe-Told*)	Nominated
2006 Writer's Award	Russell T Davies	Nominated
2009 Best Actor	David Tennant (also for *Einstein* and *Eddington*)	Nominated
2010 Best Actor	David Tennant (also for *Hamlet*)	Nominated
2012 Best International Programme Sales		Nominated

Other Awards

Year/Category	Nominee(s)	Episode	Result
Anglophone awards			
2016 Best Actor in a Television Series	Peter Capaldi		Nominated
Auntie awards			
1996 Best Popular Drama Series	*Doctor Who*		Won
Edinburgh International TV Festival			
2007 Best Programme of the Year	*Doctor Who*		Won
2008 Best Programme of the Year	*Doctor Who*		Won
Glenfiddich Spirit of Scotland Awards			
2007 Screen Award	David Tennant		Won
Golden Nymphs			
2007 Outstanding Actor - Drama Series	David Tennant		Nominated
2007 Outstanding Actress - Drama Series	Freema Agyeman		Nominated
Multi-Coloured Swap Shop			
1982 Top Man	Peter Davison		Won
Nickelodeon Kids' Choice Awards			
2012 Best UK TV Show	*Doctor Who*		Nominated
2013 Best UK TV Show	*Doctor Who*		Nominated
Peabody awards			
2013 Excellence in its own terms	*Doctor Who*		Won
Satellite Awards			
2008 Best Actor – Television Series Drama	David Tennant		Nominated
Seoul International Drama Awards			
2009 Most Popular Foreign Drama of the Year	*Doctor Who*		Won
TV Moments award			
2005 May/June Top Moment	"The Doctor, Rose and Jack hear a deadly voice"	*The Doctor Dances*	Won

Constellation awards

Year/Category	Nominee(s)	Episode	Result
Best Male Performance in a 2006 Science Fiction Television Episode	David Tennant	*The Girl in the Fireplace*	Won
Best Science Fiction Television Series of 2006			Won
Outstanding Canadian Contribution to Science Fiction Film or Television in 2006	Canadian Broadcasting Corporation – as co-producer of *Doctor Who*		Won
Best Male Performance in a 2007 Science Fiction Television Episode	David Tennant	*The Family of Blood*	Won
Best Female Performance in a 2007 Science Fiction Television Episode	Carey Mulligan	*Blink*	Won
Best Science Fiction Television Series of 2007			Won
Best Male Performance in a 2008 Science Fiction Television Episode	David Tennant	*Midnight*	Nominated
Best Female Performance in a 2008 Science Fiction Television Episode	Catherine Tate	*Turn Left*	Won
Best Science Fiction Television Series of 2008			Won
Best Technical Accomplishment in a 2010 Science Fiction Film or Television Series	Murray Gold (for music)		Nominated
Best Overall 2008 Science Fiction Film or Television Script	Steven Moffat	*Silence in the Library*	Won
Best Male Performance in a 2009 Science Fiction Television Episode	David Tennant	*The Waters of Mars*	Won
Best Female Performance in a 2009 Science Fiction Television Episode	Michelle Ryan	*Planet of the Dead*	Nominated
Best Science Fiction Television Series of 2009			Nominated
Best Male Performance in a 2010 Science Fiction Television Episode	David Tennant	*The End of Time: Part Two*	Nominated
Best Male Performance in a 2010 Science Fiction Television Episode	Matt Smith	*A Christmas Carol*	Nominated
Best Female Performance in a 2010 Science Fiction Television Episode	Karen Gillan	*Amy's Choice*	Nominated
Best Science Fiction Television Series of 2010			Nominated
Best Technical Accomplishment in a 2010 Science Fiction Film or Television Series	Murray Gold (for music)		Won
Best Science Fiction Television Series of 2011	Steven Moffat		Nominated
Best Science Fiction Television Series of 2012	Steven Moffat		Nominated
Best Male Performance in a 2013 Science Fiction Television Episode	Matt Smith	*The Day of the Doctor*	Nominated
Best Male Performance in a 2013 Science Fiction Television Episode	John Hurt	*The Day of the Doctor*	Nominated
Best Female Performance in a 2013 Science Fiction Television Episode	Billie Piper	*The Day of the Doctor*	Nominated
Best Overall 2013 Science Fiction Film or Television Script	Steven Moffat	*The Day of the Doctor*	Won

A LIST OF AWARDS

Hugo awards (all within the 'Short Form' category)

Year/Category	Nominee(s)	Episode	Result
2006 Best Dramatic Presentation	Robert Shearman and Joe Ahearne	*Dalek*	Nominated
2006 Best Dramatic Presentation	Paul Cornell and Joe Ahearne	*Father's Day*	Nominated
2006 Best Dramatic Presentation	Steven Moffat and James Hawes	*The Empty Child / The Doctor Dances*	Won
2007 Best Dramatic Presentation	Toby Whithouse and James Hawes	*School Reunion*	Nominated
2007 Best Dramatic Presentation	Steven Moffat and Euros Lyn	*The Girl in the Fireplace*	Won
2007 Best Dramatic Presentation	Russell T Davies and Graeme Harper	*Army of Ghosts / Doomsday*	Nominated
2008 Best Dramatic Presentation	Paul Cornell and Charles Palmer	*Human Nature / The Family of Blood*	Nominated
2008 Best Dramatic Presentation	Steven Moffat and Hettie MacDonald	*Blink*	Won
2009 Best Dramatic Presentation	Steven Moffat and Euros Lyn	*Silence in the Library / Forest of the Dead*	Nominated
2009 Best Dramatic Presentation	Russell T Davies and Graeme Harper	*Turn Left*	Nominated
2010 Best Dramatic Presentation	Russell T Davies and Andy Goddard	*The Next Doctor*	Nominated
2010 Best Dramatic Presentation	Russell T Davies, Gareth Roberts and James Strong	*Planet of the Dead*	Nominated
2010 Best Dramatic Presentation	Russell T Davies, Phil Ford and Graeme Harper	*The Waters of Mars*	Won
2011 Best Dramatic Presentation	Richard Curtis and Jonny Campbell	*Vincent and the Doctor*	Nominated
2011 Best Dramatic Presentation	Steven Moffat and Toby Haynes	*The Pandorica Opens / The Big Bang*	Won
2011 Best Dramatic Presentation	Steven Moffat and Toby Haynes	*A Christmas Carol*	Nominated
2012 Best Dramatic Presentation	Neil Gaiman and Richard Clark	*The Doctor's Wife*	Won
2012 Best Dramatic Presentation	Tom McRae and Nick Hurran	*The Girl Who Waited*	Nominated
2012 Best Dramatic Presentation	Steven Moffat and Peter Hoar	*A Good Man Goes to War*	Nominated
2013 Best Dramatic Presentation	Steven Moffat and Nick Hurran	*Asylum of the Daleks*	Nominated
2013 Best Dramatic Presentation	Steven Moffat and Nick Hurran	*The Angels Take Manhattan*	Nominated
2013 Best Dramatic Presentation	Steven Moffat and Saul Metzstein	*The Snowmen*	Nominated
2014 Best Dramatic Presentation	Steven Moffat and Saul Metzstein	*The Name of the Doctor*	Nominated
2014 Best Dramatic Presentation	Steven Moffat and Nick Hurran	*The Day of the Doctor*	Nominated
2015 Best Dramatic Presentation	Steven Moffat and Douglas Mackinnon	*Listen*	Nominated
2016 Best Dramatic Presentation	Steven Moffat and Rachel Talalay	*Heaven Sent*	Nominated

IGN Best of Television Awards

Year/Category	Nominee(s)	Episode	Result
2011 Best Sci-Fi/Horror Series			Nominated
2012 Best Sci-Fi/Horror Series			Nominated
2013 Best Sci-Fi/Horror Series			Nominated
2013 Best Sci-Fi/Horror Series – People's Choice			Won
2014 Best Sci-Fi/Horror Series			Nominated
2014 Best Sci-Fi/Horror Series – People's Choice			Won
2015 Best Sci-Fi/Horror Series			Nominated
2015 Best Sci-Fi/Horror Series – People's Choice			Nominated

National TV Awards

Year/Category	Nominee(s)	Episode	Result
2005 Most Popular Drama			Won
2005 Most Popular Actor	Christopher Eccleston		Won
2005 Most Popular Actress	Billie Piper		Won
2006 Most Popular Drama			Won
2006 Most Popular Actor	David Tennant		Won
2006 Most Popular Actress	Billie Piper		Won
2007 Most Popular Drama			Won
2007 Most Popular Actor	David Tennant		Won
2007 Most Popular Actress	Freema Agyeman		Nominated
2008 Most Popular Drama			Won
2008 Outstanding Drama Performance	David Tennant		Won
2008 Outstanding Drama Performance	Catherine Tate		Nominated
2010 Most Popular Drama			Won
2010 Most Popular Drama Performance	David Tennant		Won
2011 Most Popular Drama			Nominated
2011 Most Popular Drama Performance	Matt Smith		Nominated
2012 Most Popular Drama			Nominated
2012 Most Popular Drama – Male	Matt Smith		Won
2012 Most Popular Drama – Female	Karen Gillan		Won
2013 Most Popular Drama			Nominated
2013 Outstanding Drama – Male	Matt Smith		Nominated
2013 Outstanding Drama – Female	Karen Gillan		Nominated
2014 Most Popular Drama			Won
2014 Outstanding Drama Performance	Matt Smith		Won
2015 Most Popular Drama			Nominated
2016 Most Popular Drama			Nominated

A LIST OF AWARDS

RTS Television Awards

Year/Category	Nominee(s)	Episode	Result
1974 Best Graphics	Bernard Lodge		Won
2005 Best Costume Design – Drama	Lucinda Wright		Nominated
2005 Best Make Up Design – Drama	Davy Jones and Neill Gorton		Nominated
2006 Best Drama Series			Nominated
2006 Best Production Design	Edward Thomas		Nominated
2006 Best Costume Design – Drama	Louise Page		Nominated
2006 Best Make Up Design – Drama	Sheelagh Wells and Neill Gorton		Nominated
2006 Best Visual Effects – Digital Effects	The Mill		Nominated
2008 Best Drama Series			Nominated
2008 Best Actor – Male	David Tennant (also for *Recovery*)		Nominated
2008 Best Sound – Drama	Julian Howarth, Tim Ricketts, Paul McFadden and Paul Jefferies	*Midnight*	Won
2010 Best Production Design – Drama	Edward Thomas	*The Pandorica Opens*	Nominated
2011 Best Writer – Drama	Steven Moffat	Series 6	Nominated
20101Lifetime Achievement Award	Beryl Vertue		Won
2016 Best Effects – Special	Real SFX & Millennium FX	Series 9	Nominated

VES Awards

Year/Category	Nominee(s)	Episode	Result
2007 Outstanding Animated Character in a Live Action Broadcast Program, Commercial or Music Video	Nicolas Hernandez, Jean-Claude Deguara, Neil Roche and Jean-Yves Audouard	*Tooth and Claw* (for the werewolf)	Nominated
2008 Outstanding Visual Effects in a Broadcast, Miniseries,Movie or Special	David Houghton, Will Cohen, Nicolas Hernandez, and Sara Bennett	*Voyage of the Damned*	Nominated
2008 Outstanding Visual Effects in a Broadcast Series	David Houghton, Will Cohen, Jean-Claude Deguara and Nicolas Hernandez	*Last of the Time Lords*	Nominated
2008 Outstanding Animated Character in a Live Action Broadcast Program or Commercial	Nicolas Hernandez, Adam Burnett, Neil Roche and Jean-Claude Deguara	*Last of the Time Lords* (for the 900-year-old Doctor)	Nominated
2009 Outstanding Visual Effects in a Broadcast Miniseries, Movie or Special	Dave Houghton, Marie Jones, Matthew McKinney, Murray Barber	*The Next Doctor*	Nominated
2009 Outstanding Matte Paintings in a Broadcast Program or Commercial	Simon Wicker, Charlie Bennett, Tim Barter, Arianna Lago	*Silence in the Library*	Won

Saturn Awards

Year/Category	Nominee(s)	Episode	Result
1996 Best Single Genre Television Presentation		*Doctor Who* (1996 film)	Won
1996 Best Actor on Television	Paul McGann		Nominated
2006 Best TV Show			Nominated
2007 Best TV Show			Nominated
2007 Best Syndicated/Cable Television Series			Nominated
2007 Best Television DVD Release	*Doctor Who*: The Complete Second Series		Nominated
2008 Best Science Fiction Actor	David Tennant		Nominated
2008 Best International Series			Won
2010 Best Television Presentation		*The End of Time*	Nominated
2010 Best Actor on Television	David Tennant		Nominated
2010 Best Guest Starring Role in Television	Bernard Cribbins		Nominated
2010 Best TV Show			Nominated
2011 Best TV Show			Nominated
2011 Best Science Fiction Actress	Karen Gillan		Nominated
2011 Best Science Fiction Actor	Matt Smith		Won
2011 Best Television Presentation			Nominated
2012 Best Youth-Oriented Television Series			Nominated
2013 Best Youth-Oriented Television Series			Nominated
2015 Best Youth-Oriented Television Series			Nominated
2015 Best Supporting Actress	Jenna Coleman		Nominated
2016 Best Science Fiction Television Series			Nominated
2016 Best Television Presentation		*The Husbands of River Song*	Won
2016 Best Guest Starring Role on Television	Alex Kingston	*The Husbands of River Song*	Nominated

Nebula/Ray Bradbury Awards

Year/Category	Nominee(s)	Episode	Result
2006 Best Script	Steven Moffat	*The Girl in the Fireplace*	Nominated
2007 Best Script	Steven Moffat	*Blink*	Nominated
2011 Outstanding Dramatic Presentation	Richard Curtis and Jonny Campbell	*Vincent and the Doctor*	Nominated
2012 Outstanding Dramatic Presentation	Neil Gaiman and Richard Clark	*The Doctor's Wife*	Won
2014 Outstanding Dramatic Presentation	Steven Moffat and Nick Hurran	*The Day of the Doctor*	Nominated

A LIST OF AWARDS

SFX Awards

Year/Category	Nominee(s)	Episode	Result
2005 Best TV Show			Won
2005 Best TV Episode	Joe Ahearne and Russell T Davies	*The Parting of the Ways*	Won
2005 Best TV Actor	Christopher Eccleston		Won
2005 Best TV Actress	Billie Piper		Won
2007 Best TV Show			Won
2007 Best TV Episode	Euros Lyn and Steven Moffat	*The Girl in the Fireplace*	Won
2007 Best TV Episode	James Strong and Matt Jones	*The Impossible Planet* *The Satan Pit*	Nominated
2007 Best TV Episode	Graeme Harper and Russell T Davies	*Army of Ghosts* *Doomsday*	Nominated
2007 Best TV Actor	David Tennant		Won
2007 Best TV Actress	Billie Piper		Won
2008 Best TV Show			Won
2008 Best TV Episode	Graeme Harper and Russell T Davies	*The Stolen Earth* *Journey's End*	Won
2008 Best TV Actor	David Tennant		Won
2008 Best TV Actress	Catherine Tate		Won
2010 Best TV Show			Nominated
2010 Best TV Episode	Russell T Davies and Andy Goddard	*The Next Doctor*	Nominated
2010 Best TV Episode	Russell T Davies, James Strong and Gareth Roberts	*Planet of the Dead*	Nominated
2010 Best TV Actor	David Tennant		Won
2011 Best TV Show	Steven Moffat		Won
2011 Best TV Episode	Jonny Campbell and Richard Curtis	*Vincent and the Doctor*	Nominated
2011 Best TV Actor	David Tennant		Nominated
2011 Best TV Actor	Matt Smith		Won
2011 Best TV Actress	Karen Gillan		Won
2012 Best Actor	Matt Smith		Won
2012 Best Actress	Karen Gillan		Nominated
2012 Best Actress	Alex Kingston		Won
2012 Screenwriting Excellence	Neil Gaiman	*The Doctor's Wife*	Won

British Fantasy awards

Year/Category	Nominee(s)	Episode	Result
2009 Best Television	Russell T Davies	*Doctor Who*	Won
2010 Best Television	Russell T Davies	*Doctor Who*	Won
2014 Best Film/Television Episode	Steven Moffat	*The Day of the Doctor*	Nominated

Writers' Guild of Great Britain

Year/Category	Nominee(s)	Result
1975 Best Children's Drama Script	Robert Holmes, Malcolm Hulke, Terry Nation, Brian Hayles and Robert Sloman	Won
2007 Best Soap/Series	Chris Chibnall, Paul Cornell, Russell T Davies, Stephen Greenhorn, Steven Moffat, Helen Raynor and Gareth Roberts	Won
2009 Best TV Drama Series	Gareth Roberts, Russell T Davies and Phil Ford	Nominated
2010 Best TV Drama Series	Simon Nye, Chris Chibnall, Mark Gatiss, Toby Whithouse and Steven Moffat	Nominated
2011 Best TV Drama Series	Stephen Thompson, Steven Moffat, Gareth Roberts and Richard Curtis	Nominated

TV Quick / TV Choice Awards

Year/Category	Nominee(s)	Result
2005 Best Actor	Christopher Eccleston	Won
2006 Best Loved Drama	Russell T Davies, Phil Collinson and Julie Gardner	Won
2006 Best Actor	David Tennant	Won
2006 Best Actress	Billie Piper	Won
2007 Best Loved Drama		Won
2007 Best Actor	David Tennant	Won
2007 Best Actress	Freema Agyeman	Nominated
2008 Best Loved Drama		Won
2008 Best Actor	David Tennant	Won
2008 Best Actress	Catherine Tate	Won
2010 Best Family Drama	Steven Moffat	Won
2010 Best Actor	Matt Smith	Nominated
2010 Best Actress	Karen Gillan	Nominated
2011 Best Family Drama	Steven Moffat	Won
2011 Best Actor	Matt Smith	Nominated
2011 Best Actress	Karen Gillan	Won
2012 Best Family Drama		Won
2012 Best Actor	Matt Smith	Nominated
2012 Best Actress	Karen Gillan	Nominated
2013 Best Drama Series		Won
2013 Best Actor	Matt Smith	Nominated
2013 Best Actress	Jenna Coleman	Nominated
2013 Outstanding Contribution Award		Won
2015 Best Family Drama		Nominated
2015 Best Actor	Peter Capaldi	Nominated
2015 Best Actress	Jenna Coleman	Nominated
2016 Best Family Drama		Nominated
2016 Best Actor	Peter Capaldi	Nominated

BEST OF EVERYTHING

HIGHEST VIEWING FIGURES	*The Web Planet* (episode 1 = 13.5 million viewers)	*The Krotons* (episode 1 = 9 million)	*The Three Doctors* (episode 4 = 11.9 million)	*City of Death* (part 4 = 16.1 million)	*Castrovalva* (episode 4 = 10.4 million)	*Attack of the Cybermen* (part 1 = 8.9 million)
HIGHEST AUDIENCE APPRECIATION INDEX (WHERE GIVEN)	*The Daleks* (episode 7 = 65%)	*The Wheel in Space* (episode 6 = 62%)	*The Monster of Peladon* (part 3 = 64%)	*Image of the Fendahl* (part 2 = 75%)	*The Five Doctors* (75%)	*The Trial of a Time Lord* (part 1 = 72%)
DWM READERS' POLL 1998	*The Daleks* (voted 22nd best of a total of 159 *Doctor Who* stories)	*The Tomb of the Cybermen* (8th)	*Inferno* (14th)	*Genesis of the Daleks* (1st)	*The Caves of Androzani* (3rd)	*Revelation of the Daleks* (34th)
DWM POLL 2009	*The Daleks* (voted 37th of 200)	*The Power of the Daleks* (21st)	*Inferno* (32nd)	*Genesis of the Daleks* (3rd)	*The Caves of Androzani* (1st)	*Revelation of the Daleks* (46th)
DWM POLL 2014 (ISSUE 474)	*The Daleks* (voted 46th of 241)	*The War Games* (12th)	*Inferno* (18th)	*Genesis of the Daleks* (3rd)	*The Caves of Androzani* (4th)	*Revelation of the Daleks* (70th)

EACH DOCTOR'S GREATEST ADVENTURES – DEPENDING HOW YOU MEASURE THEM

The Greatest Show in the Galaxy (part 4 = 6.6 million)	*Doctor Who* (9.1 million)	*Rose* (10.8 million)	*Voyage of the Damned* (13.3 million)	*The Day of the Doctor* (12.8 million)	*Last Christmas* (8.3 million)
Remembrance of the Daleks (part 4 = 72%)	N/A	*The Parting of the Ways* (89%)	*Journey's End* (91%)	*The Big Bang* (89%)	*Dark Water* (85%)
Remembrance of the Daleks (6th)	*Doctor Who* (89th)	N/A	N/A	N/A	N/A
Remembrance of the Daleks (14th)	*Doctor Who* (134th)	*The Empty Child / The Doctor Dances* (5th)	*Blink* (2nd)	N/A	N/A
Remembrance of the Daleks (10th)	*Doctor Who* (152nd)	*The Empty Child / The Doctor Dances* (7th)	*Blink* (2nd)	*The Day of the Doctor* (1st)	N/A

INDEX

Abigail 35
Abzorbaloff 123
Ace 7, 25, 34, 36, 40, 65, 85, 98–9, 131, 150–1, 194
Achilles 125, 148
Adams, Douglas 202
Adjudicators 72
Adric the Alzarian 71, 95, 149, 187, 194
Aggedor 30
Akhaten 176, 189
Aldred, Sophie 98–9
Alfava Metraxis 35
Alydon 136
Alzarius 149
Ancelyn 41, 124
Andersen, Hans Christian 38
Andred 54
Androgum 123
Andromeda galaxy 55
Androzani Major 46, 58
Antiman 61
antimatter 61, 95
Apalapucia 49
Arcadia 76, 90, 140
Argolis 65
Aridius 64
Ark 126, 128
Arthur, King 31, 41, 150
Arwell, Madge 16, 44, 125
Arwell, Reg 125
Ashildr 53, 64, 82, 120–1
Asylum 142–3
Atlantis 185
Atraxi 88–9, 199
Avery, Captain Henry 91
Avery, Toby 91
Azal 185

Bad Wolf 78, 147, 150
Baker, Colin 13, 17, 43
Baker, Tom 12, 22, 77, 197
Baker, Will 199
Balcombe, Chris 135
Baltazar 187
Bandraginus 5 58
Bane 157
Barrio de Santa Cruz 123
Beast 50, 188, 192
Bede, Saint 35
Benton, Sergeant 185
Big Bang 74
Black, Dr 197
black holes 162–3
Bligh, Jack Hodges 118
Blowfish 88–9
Boneless 113, 175
Borusa, President 10, 11, 26, 53, 93, 173
BOSS 195
Bowships 92
Boyce, Dr Niall 21
Briggs, Nicholas 182–3, 183
Brillat-Savarin, Jean Anthelme 123
Briscoe, Desmond 166
Brotherhood of Logicians 124
Brown, Derren 40
Brown, Peri 48, 51

Calufrax 65
Camfield, Douglas 201
Camilla 80
Campbell, David 202
Capaldi, Peter 13, 25
Capricorn, Max 163
Carême, Marie Antoine 123
Carrionites 38, 41, 196
Cartmel, Andrew 65, 119
Catrigan Nova 58
Chameleons 130
Chapman, Dave 76
Chase, Gabriel 151
Cheetah people 34
Chelonians 88–9
Chen, Mavic 80
Chesterton, Ian 68–9, 104, 112, 117, 131, 155, 182
Chibnall, Chris 119
Chimeron 187
Christie, Agatha 38, 196
Churchill, Winston 38, 90, 91
Clarke, Arthur C 41
Cleopatra 84
clockwork robots 122, 130
Coal Hill School 121
Coleman, David 96
Conway, Richard 76
Cook, Aidan 178
Coroebus of Elis 32
Cory, Marc 69
Courtney, Nicholas 83
Crab Nebula 72, 73
Cranfield, Reg 118
Cranleigh, Lord 29
Craze, Mike 153
Crichton, John 32
Crooked Man 178
Crucible 79
Curator 12, 22
Curran, Charles 97
Curtis, Gerald 69
Cusick, Raymond 134
CyberKing 195
Cyberleader 18–19
Cybermen 7, 11, 18–19, 49, 51, 88–9, 95–6, 105, 127, 129–30, 150, 157, 177, 180–1, 183, 187, 199
Cyberplanner 84

Dæmons 185
Dalek Prime Minister 142
Dalek Supreme 139
Dalekanium 137
Daleks 11, 13, 18–19, 21, 24, 33, 36, 50, 53, 63, 69, 71, 73, 75–9, 85–91, 105, 110, 117, 130, 134–5, 138–43, 146–7, 149–50, 157, 163, 165, 168–9, 172–3, 182–3, 189, 195, 197, 202, Special Weapons Dalek 149
Dalton, Peter 157
Darrius 13
Davies, Russell T 95, 119, 143, 156, 197, 199
Davis, Gerry 152, 199
Davison, Peter 13, 29, 43
Davros 11, 18, 19, 33, 53, 73, 78, 79, 137, 139, 143, 197
de Souza, Lady Christine 19, 71, 151
Dee, Christel 77
Delirium Archive 56
Delta Magna, Third Moon of 62

Demat Gun 93
dematerialisation 93
Demon's Run, Battle of 149
depolarisers 127
Derbyshire, Delia 167, 168
Destroyer 83, 122
Dickens, Charles 38, 196
Dicks, Terrance 193, 197, 200, 202, 203
dinosaurs 37, 95, 105, 122, 128, 186
Doctor's name 193
Dominators 187
Don Salava, Karass 62
`Doomsday Weapon' 72
Dor'een 176
Draconia 110
Draconians 88–9, 180
Drahvins 47, 88–9
Drashigs 37, 62, 173
Drax 26, 27
Dudley, Terence 203

Earth Empire 47
Earth President 11
Eccleston, Christopher 43
Eighth Doctor 13, 19, 23, 27, 90, 107, 116, 169, 194, 201
Einarr 120
Einstein, Albert 61, 164, 195
Elders 11
Eldrad 70
Eleventh Doctor 13–14, 16, 19–20, 22–5, 30–1, 35, 43, 46, 48–9, 56–7, 64, 71, 75, 78, 81, 84, 88–9, 91, 107, 109, 112, 113, 118, 127, 142–3, 146, 149, 155, 162–3, 172–3, 176, 181, 184–5, 193, 197
Elixir of Life 90
Elizabeth I 19, 39, 95
Elizabeth II 95, 199
Elmes, Oliver 169
Elyon 69
Empress of the Racnoss 188
entropy 71
Erickson, Paul 148
Escoffier, George Auguste 123
Eternals 189
Eustace, Alan 14
event horizon 162–3
Event One 74, 108
Exxilon 48, 58, 111
Eye of Harmony 54, 93, 162
Eye of Orion 48

Face of Boe 147, 188
see also Harkness, Captain Jack
Faraday, Michael 165
Federico, Count 84
Fendahl 92
Fenric 85
Ferguson, Michael 136
Fifth Doctor 11, 13, 15, 18–19, 22–3, 26–9, 39, 43, 48, 74, 95, 108, 139, 146, 149, 172, 181, 194
First Doctor 11, 13–14, 20–1, 35, 38–9, 43, 47, 55, 68, 75, 79, 100–1, 107, 117–18, 136, 141, 143, 146, 148–50, 155, 182, 184, 193, 198
First Law of Time 109
First World War 147, 203
Flemming 25
Fleshkind 157
Fletcher, Jennifer 118
Fletcher, Lucy 118
Flint, Jenny 19, 91
Florana 48, 111
`fluid link' 69
flying fish 35
Foamasi 65
Ford, Carole Ann 155
Foreman, Susan (the Doctor's granddaughter) 68, 104, 112, 117, 136, 137, 155, 182, 202
Fourth Doctor 7, 10, 12, 15, 18–23, 25–7, 31, 35, 39–40, 46, 52–3, 55, 57, 60–1, 70, 82, 84–7, 92–4, 97, 108, 111, 118, 126–30, 137, 146, 149, 154, 165, 172, 189, 192, 194–5
Franklin, Paul 77
Frost, General Muriel 131

Galactic Federation 30
Gallifrey 10–11, 13, 24–7, 36, 52–5, 75, 77–8, 90, 93, 104, 140, 163, 187, 193
Galloway 91, 138
Gaptooth 118
Gardner, Dr Andrew 89
Garm 74
Gaskin, Emily 118
Gatiss, Mark 25, 199
Gejelh, Merry 176
Gelth 130, 175
gestalt brain 195
Gillyflower, Ada 19
Gillyflower, Mrs Winifred 178, 186
Giuliano, Duke 84
Glasmir Peaks 49
Gold, Murray 167
Gonds 46, 187
Gordon, Grant 118
Goss, James 202
Goth, Chancellor 10, 53, 97
Graham, David 168, 182
Grainer, Ronald Eric `Ron' 166–7, 168
Grant, Abi 156
Grant, Jo 7, 30, 37, 40, 47, 72, 91, 110, 131, 155, 194
Great Intelligence 83
Grendel, Count 84
Grun 30
Grundle 62
Guardian 72

Haemogoths 88–9
Hand of Omega 73
Hargreaves, Danny 75, 181
Harkness, Captain Jack 19, 111, 131, 147, 149, 151, 188
see also Face of Boe
Hartnell, William 12, 13, 43
Hawkins, Peter 168, 182
Headless Monks 56
Heaton, Daniel 118
Hedgewick's World 49
Hedin, Councillor 53
Helium II 195
Henry V 82
Heriot, Zoe 46, 107, 194
Hill, Adrienne 148
Hines, Frazer 152, 153
Hoix 88–9, 176
Holloway, Grace 19, 194
Holmes, Robert 197, 200
Holy Hadrojassic Maxarodenfoe 183
Home Box 56
Horner, Professor 185
Hossick, Katie 118
Houdini, Harry 41
Howitt, Rebecca 118
Hubble, Edwin 73
Hulke, Malcolm 203
Hur 68
Hurran, Nick 75
Hurt, John 13
Hussein, Waris 119
Hybrid 53
Hypatia 164, 195
Hywel 151

Ice Warriors 30, 124, 180, 183, 187
Idris 19, 108
Inter Minor 33
International Electronics 127
International Space Command 51
Interplanetary Mining Corporation 72
Irongron, Captain 87
Isolus 33, 175, 189
Ital, Dr Tarak 33

Jackson, Ben 32, 41, 131, 152, 153
Jacobs, Matthews 203
Jagaroth 164, 185
Jano 11
Jansky, Karl Guthe 165
Jones, Martha 15, 19, 38–9, 64, 78, 111, 117, 131, 151, 174, 194
Jovanka, Tegan 18–19, 108, 131, 139
Judoon 88–9, 183

K-9 93, 156, 165, 195
Kal 68, 69
Kaleds 137, 138, 143
Kamelion 195
Kandyman 181
K'Anpo Rinpoche 105
Karabraxos, Bank of 56
Karfel 15, 38, 187
Karn 59
Karra 34
Kastria 70
Kastrians 70
Katarina 148
Keller Machine 172
Kelner, Castellan 53
Kembel 87
Kendall, Kenneth 198
Kerensky, Fyodor Nikolai 105, 164
Kingdom, Sara 79, 149
Kiv 186
Klieg, Eric 124
Kököchin, Princess 198
Kovarian Chapter of the Church of the Papal Mainframe 75
Kovarian, Madame 91, 149
Kroll 62
Krop Tor 50, 192
Krotons 46
Kublai Khan 198
Kukula, Marek 14, 60, 175
Ky 47

Lakertya 195
Lambert, Verity 119, 166
Langer, Clyde 157
Las Cadenas 123
Latimer, Tim 8
Lavers, Colin 29
Laws of Time 53
Layfield, Crispin 16–17
Leandro 121
Lee, John 136
Leela 7, 21, 25, 40, 46, 82, 92, 149, 195
Lethbridge-Stewart, Colonel (later Brigadier) Alistair 11, 83, 131
Letts, Barry 85, 201
Levine, Ian 101
Library 57
Lilith 38
Linx, Commander 87
Lister, Joseph 26
Lloyd, Innes 152
Lodge, Bernard 77, 168
logic codes 95
Logopolis 57, 71
Lowery, Gordon 69
Lucarotti, John 198
Ludens Nimrod Kendrick Cord
Longstaff XLI, Emperor 49
Luna University 57, 149
Lundvik 128
Lyle beach 48
Lynda 138
Lytton 96

M1 73
Maaga 47
McCrimmon, Jamie 25, 32, 107, 117, 123, 148, 152
Macmillan, Detective Inspector 151
Magnotron 55
Maitland children 49
Malcassairo 109, 111
Malden, Sue 101
Malpha 86–7
Manning, Katy 155
Manussa 62
Mapson, Colin 76
Mara 62
Mark III travel machine 137
Mars 63
Marsh, Jean 149
Marynarde, Richard 105
Master 10, 15, 26–7, 34, 51, 53, 57, 71–2, 80, 83–4, 94, 108–9, 147, 151, 172–3, 195

Matrix 53, 55, 92, 93
matter transmitter 111
Maxtible, Theodore 165
Maxwell, James Clerk 165
McCoy, Sylvester 43, 98–9, 181
McGann, Paul 13
Me 121
Medusa Cascade 79, 163
Megron, High Lord of Chaos 23
Mentors 63
Merlin 41
Messier, Charles 73
Metebelis 3 59, 63, 105
Metulla Orionsis 71
micro-monolithic circuits 127
Midge 34
Midnight 59
Mighty Jagrafess 183
Mill 77
Millennium FX 176, 188
Miniscope 37
Minogue, Kylie 199
Minyos 55
Mire, The 120, 173
Missy 11, 19, 50, 53, 122, 173
Moffat, Steven 25, 119, 197
Mogar 63
Moment (Galaxy Eater) 24, 78, 173
Mondas 51, 187
Monitor 57
Monk 104, 137
Monroe, Marilyn 19
Moon 128, 185
Moonbase 194
Moore, Sir Patrick 199
Morbius 84
Mordee planetary survey team 195
Morgaine 40, 41
Mortimer, Harrison 149
Mortimer, Melody 149
Mott, Wilf 95
Movellans 85
Murphy, Paul 179
Mutts 47

Naismith 15
Napoleon Bonaparte 91, 117
Nathan-Turner, John 29
Nation, Terry 197
nebulae 73
Nefertiti 105
Nero 32
Nestene 88–9

Nestene Consciousness 183
Newton, Isaac 37, 41
Ninth Doctor 6–7, 19, 20, 39, 43, 65, 86, 94, 106, 116, 131, 138, 141, 149, 151, 163, 199
Nitro 9 150
Noble, Donna 19, 76
nuclear fusion 60
numismaton gas 59
Nyder 143
Nyssa 71, 108

O'Brien, Lady Cassandra 15, 19, 197
Octavian, Father 35
Ogrons 35, 77, 91, 110, 180
Old Mother 68, 69
Omega 27, 53, 54, 84, 104, 172
Ood 77
oolion 58
Osterhagen Key 78
Oswald, Clara 7, 13, 15–16, 19, 21, 24, 27, 49–50, 53, 64, 76, 78, 82, 105, 109, 112, 121–2, 128, 146–7, 176
Oswald, Clara Oswin 146
Oswald, Oswin 143, 146
Overlords 47
Owens, Craig 30

Pallushi civilisation 50
Pandorica 88, 129
Parish, Sarah 188
Parsons, William 73
Pasteur, Louis 164, 195
Pedler, Dr Kit 96, 199
Peinforte, Lady 40–1, 105
Peladon, King 30, 187
Pentallian (spaceship) 174
Pertwee, Jon 13, 90, 180
Peth, Astrid 19, 199
Pike, Captain 118
Pinfield, Mervyn 168
Ping-Cho, Lady 119, 198
Pink, Danny 109
Pink, Colonel Orson 64, 105, 109
Planet One 193
plesiosaurs 37
Poisson, Jeanne Antoinette 19, 31
Polly 32, 131, 152, 153
Polo, Marco 198
Pond, Amy 19, 25, 33, 35, 48–9, 56, 64, 71, 88–9, 91, 107, 127, 143, 149, 151, 155, 193
Pond, Melody 149
see also Song, River
Pratt, Libby 118
'psychic pollen' 62, 175
Pyroviles 187

Rani 27, 164, 195
Rassilon 10, 11, 15, 53, 54, 92, 104, 193
Rassilon, Great Key of 93
Rassilon, Rod of 93
Rassilon, Sash of 93
Raston warrior robots 173
Ravalox 51
Rawlinson, Pat 124
Reality Bomb 78, 79
red dwarves 175
red giants 175
Redfern, Joan 19
Rigg, Diana 178
Rings of Akhaten 176
Robin Hood 82, 85
Rodan 93
Rogin 126
Rokon 70
Romanadvoratrelundar (Romana) 11, 20, 26, 85, 94, 165, 194
Romans 89, 203
Ross, John 201
Rowling, JK 38, 196
Royal Navy 90
Russell, Gary 203
Russell, William 155
Rutans 87
Rymill, Gavin 135

Salamander, Ramón 15
San Helios 71
sandminers 46
Sardick, Kazran 35
Sarn 59, 187
Saxon, Harold 151
Scarlet System 50
Scarman, Laurence 165
Scaroth 164, 185
Second Doctor 13, 20, 25, 26, 32, 39, 41, 46, 51–2, 54–5, 81, 86, 96–7, 100–1, 107, 117–18, 123–4, 146, 152, 172, 193–4, 203
Second World War 7, 90, 91, 147
Seed, Gordon 17
Segal, Zohra 119
Sen, Chun 165
sentient trees 58
sentient viruses 21
Sevateem 195
Seventh Doctor 7, 20, 23, 25, 31, 34, 36, 39–41, 43, 50, 65, 73, 85–6, 91, 98–9, 104, 119, 129, 131, 146, 150, 169, 173, 195
Shadow Proclamation 57
Shakespeare, William 38–9, 82, 196
Shaw, Liz 41, 106, 131, 194
Shawcraft Models 134–5
Shephard, Adam 118
Sheyrah 119
Shockeye 96, 123
Shou Yuing 40
Sil the Mentor 63, 186
Silence 151, 184, 185
Silurians 77, 91, 128, 184, 186
Simeon, Dr 15, 146
Simpson, Dudley 167
singularities 162–3
Sisterhood of Karn 90, 157
Sisters of the Infinite Schism 57
Sixth Doctor 13, 17, 20, 23, 38–9, 43, 48, 51, 55, 74, 92, 96, 146, 195
Skaldak, Grand Marshall 187
Skaro 11, 19, 50, 63, 69, 71, 73, 75, 86, 91, 134, 136–8, 141, 143, 150, 165, 187
Skinner, Caroline 143
Skovox Blitzer 173, 179
Sladen, Elizabeth 154–5, 156
Slipher, Vesto 73
Slitheen 88–9, 130, 131, 186
Smith, Andrew 118
Smith, John 81
Smith, Luke 157
Smith, Matt 13, 16, 30, 33, 43, 181
Smith, Mickey 31, 131
Smith, Sarah Jane 18, 23, 32, 48, 52, 60, 70, 111, 126, 129, 131, 154–7, 164–5, 173
Smith, Sky 157
Solonians 47
Solos 47, 59
Song, River 15, 19, 24, 25, 26, 35, 57, 88, 112, 149, 151, 193, 194
see also Pond, Melody
sonic screwdrivers 35, 81, 84
Sontarans 10, 40, 53, 74, 87–9, 91, 93, 105, 131, 186
Sophie 30
Sorenson, Professor 60–1
Space Station Nerva 126
space-time visualiser 39
Spectrox 58
spiders 63, 105
Spillane, Luke 76
Spilsbury, Tom 25

Spiridon 86
Stahlman, Professor 129
Stewart, Kate 11, 19, 83
Stor, Commander 93
strange matter 195
Strax 91
Styre, Field Major 87
Sullivan, Harry 18, 26, 126, 131
supernovas 73, 104, 113, 162
Supreme Council 11, 54
Susan (horse) 31
Sutekh of the Osirans 129, 189
Sutton, Shaun 152
Swarm 71, 175
Sweet, Mr 178, 186
Swift, Sam 121
Sycorax 38, 84, 88, 89, 95, 131

Taltalian 41
taranium 59, 79
TARDIS 7, 11, 13–17, 19, 21, 24, 27, 29, 33, 43, 46, 48, 52, 57, 64, 68–72, 75–6, 83, 90, 94, 96, 106, 108–13, 117, 126–7, 129, 131, 134, 136–7, 139, 143, 146–53, 155, 162–3, 168–9, 182, 192–5, 198
  chameleon circuit 112
  siege mode 113
telepathic field 39
Tardises (generic) 36, 109, 111, 121, 147
  death 112–13
Taylor, Steven 47, 148, 149
Television Archive Selector 101
Teller 56
Tennant, David 77
Tenth Doctor 15, 19–20, 27, 31–3, 38–9, 41, 50, 64, 71, 74, 76, 78, 80–1, 84, 87, 95, 106, 111, 117, 123, 140, 143, 149, 151, 157, 162, 174, 187–9, 192, 194, 196, 199
Terileptils 88–9
Terminus 74, 105
Teselecta 151
Tesh 195
thaesium 47, 59
Thals 69, 71, 136–8, 143, 187
Third Doctor 7, 11, 13, 15, 20–1, 23, 26–7, 37, 39–40, 47, 52, 54, 72, 83–5, 87, 90–1, 94, 101, 106, 110–11, 117–18, 128–9, 139, 141, 146, 154, 165, 172–3, 180, 185–6, 193–4
Thoros Beta 63, 186
Time Destructor 79, 149
time loops 94
Time Lords 10, 18–19, 24, 27, 36, 51–5, 72, 73, 78, 84, 86, 90, 92–3, 97, 104–5, 109, 118, 121, 137–8, 147, 162, 173, 178, 187, 189, 193, 203
  High Council of the 11, 37, 53, 54, 55
time manipulators 195
Time Ring 111
time vortex 15, 150
Time War 24, 36, 53, 54, 75, 78, 86, 90–1, 109, 138, 140–1, 175
time warp field 106
Titanic (starship) 95, 163
Tivoli 64
Torajii system 174–5
Torchwood 131, 164
Tosh, Donald 148
total event collapse 113
Traken 71, 187
transmat engines 163
Trenzalore 15, 109, 112
Trickster 157
Troughton, Patrick 13, 43, 152, 153
Troy 148
Trumbull, Douglas 77
Tucker, Mike 76
Turlough 48, 139
Turner, Captain Jimmy 127
Twelfth Doctor 11, 13–14, 19–21, 24–5, 31, 39, 50, 53–4, 56, 64, 82, 85, 91, 105, 109, 111, 113, 118, 120, 122, 128, 146, 173
Tyler, Jackie 19
Tyler, Pete 94
Tyler, Rose 6–7, 15, 19, 31, 33, 50, 78, 94, 131, 150, 189, 192, 199

Underhenge 88
UNIT 11, 26, 40, 83, 91, 127, 131, 165, 185, 194
Uranus 59
Uvodini 88, 89
Uxarieus 72

Valeyard 55, 92
validium 129
vampires 92
van Gogh, Vincent 197
van Statten, Henry 141, 164
Vardans 10, 25, 53
Varga plants 63, 69
Vashta Nerada 57
Vastra, Madame 24, 91, 186
Vaughn, Tobias 127
Veil 14
Venusian aikido 85
Vervoids 63, 180
Vesta 95 48
Vicki 148
Victoria 131
Vigils 176
Villar, Arturo 125
Vipod Mor (spaceship) 74
Volag-Noc 64
Vorg 173

Walsh, Colonel 11
Walsh, Terry 139
Walshe, Kate 176–80
War Doctor 13, 78, 90–1, 107, 140, 146, 173
War Lord 93
Warden, May 149
Warwick, Edmund 13
Watcher 108
Waterfield, Edward 165
Waterfield, Victoria 81, 117
Way, Eileen 68
Webber, Chloe 189
Webley's World of Wonders 49
Weeping Angels 33, 35, 105, 173, 181, 187
Wells, HG 38, 196
Weston, Ben 118
Wheatley, Ben 76
Whispermen 179
Whitaker, David 197, 202
Whitaker, Professor 105, 164–5
White Guardian 189
Williams, General 110
Williams, Rory 19, 35, 127, 143, 151, 155
Wills, Anneke 153
Wire 199
Wirrn 126
WOTAN 195
Wright, Barbara 68–9, 104, 112, 131, 182

Xoanan 195

Yates, Mike 11
Yeti 83, 97, 131
Young, Jeremy 69

Za 68, 69
Zanak 65, 163
Zeta Minor 60–1
Zygons 19, 31, 88, 89, 173, 183, 184

ACKNOWLEDGEMENTS

This book was all the idea of Kate Fox, who then promptly scarpered before I realised what I'd agreed to. *Thanks*, Kate.

Mark Ayres, Nicholas Briggs, Andrew Cartmel, Frazer Hines, Crispin Layfield, Edward Russell, Richard Senior, Mike Tucker and Kate Walshe all generously gave their time to talk me through the minutiae of making *Doctor Who*. Danny Hargreaves and Paul Franklin gave gracious permission to quote from interviews I conducted with them in the past for *Doctor Who Magazine* – including material published here for the first time.

I'm grateful for the expert contributions of Dr Niall Boyce, editor of the *Lancet Psychiatry*; Dr Andrew Gardner, Senior Lecturer in the Archaeology of the Roman Empire at the Institute of Archaeology, UCL; Dr Marek Kukula, Public Astronomer at the Royal Observatory Greenwich, who checked over my astronomy; Chris Allen, Christel Dee and Luke Spillane of *Doctor Who: The Fan Show*; Chris Balcombe for his Dalek One photo, and Gavin Rymill, whose exhaustive research into Dalek history (undertaken with Jon Green) can be found at http://www.dalek6388.co.uk/

I also checked details and tried out ideas on Andrew Beech, Simon Belcher, Deborah Challis, Matt Evenden, Toby Hadoke, Dave Houghton, Paul Lang, Jonathan Morris, Steve O'Brien, Chris Petts and John Ross.

Thanks to Tom Spilsbury and Peter Ware for letting me raid the archives of *Doctor Who Magazine*. Marcus Hearn provided expert assistance with picture research. The Doctor Who Appreciation Society's fascinating 2011 interview with *Doctor Who* story editor Donald Tosh (see p.148) can be read at http://www.kaldorcity.com/people/dtinterview.html. I also made use of Richard Molesworth's book *Wiped! – Doctor Who's Missing Episodes* (Telos Publishing, second edition 2013), Paul Smith's *Based on a Popular BBC Television Serial* (2016 – and available to download for free at http://www.wonderfulbook.co.uk/basedon/) and Sophie Aldred and Mike Tucker's *Ace! The Inside Story of the End of an Era* (Virgin Books, 1996), plus the entire *Doctor Who* range on DVD – especially the production subtitles.

Thanks also to the internet – at least when it was right and even better when backed up by checkable sources.

Of course, the final responsibility for any errors (or lapses of judgement) is mine and mine alone.

Lastly, thanks to Beth, Justin, Steve, Albert and everyone at BBC Books for their patience, and to Martin and Mike for working wonders in the design.

Simon

Picture Credits

All images copyright © BBC except: p23 *Order of the Daleks* courtesy of Big Finish Productions, artwork by Simon Holub, stained-glass Dalek by Chris Thompson; p73 Photograph of Crab Nebula by Simon Guerrier; p77 Photograph of Christel Dee by MattEleven, photograph of Paul Franklin care of Paul Franklin; p87 top image courtesy of *Doctor Who Magazine*; p98 Newspaper clipping from CuttingsArchive.org; p135 Photo of Chris Balcombe © Balcombe; p179 Scovox Blitzer test image © Millennium FX; p201 John Ross artwork for *Moving In* care of *Doctor Who Magazine*

This book is published to accompany the television series *Doctor Who*, first broadcast on BBC One. *Doctor Who* is a BBC Wales production.

Executive producers: Steven Moffat and Brian Minchin

Published in 2018 by
Harper Design
An Imprint of HarperCollins*Publishers*
195 Broadway
New York, NY 10007
Tel: (212) 207-7000
Fax: (855) 746-6023
harperdesign@harpercollins.com
www.hc.com

Distributed throughout the world by
HarperCollins*Publishers*
195 Broadway
New York, NY 10007

ISBN 978-0-06-268115-7

Library of Congress Control Number: 2017936292

Printed and bound in Italy by L.E.G.O. S.p.A

First Printing, 2018

Commissioning Editor: Albert DePetrillo
Project Editor: Bethany Wright
Series Consultant: Justin Richards
Editor: Steve Tribe
Design: Martin Stiff, Amazing15, and Mike Jones
Production: Phil Spencer and Alex Merrett